Le silence des hommes

DU MÊME AUTEUR

Aux Éditions Albin Michel

LE COLLECTIONNEUR, 1993.

L'ÂME SŒUR, 1998.

L'ATTENTE, 1999.

J'ÉTAIS L'ORIGINE DU MONDE, 2000.

FRINGUES, 2002.

Chez d'autres éditeurs

LES PETITES FILLES NE MEURENT JAMAIS (sous le nom de Christine Rheims), éd. Jean-Claude Lattès, 1986.

LE FIL DE SOI, éd. Olivier Orban, 1988.

UNE ANNÉE AMOUREUSE DE VIRGINIA WOOLF (sous le nom de Christine Duhon), éd. Olivier Orban, 1990.

LA FEMME ADULTÈRE, éd. Flammarion, 1991.

UNE FOLIE AMOUREUSE (en collaboration avec Olivier Orban), éd. Grasset, 1997.

UNGARO, éd. Assouline, 1999.

Christine Orban

Le silence
des hommes

ROMAN

Albin Michel

© Éditions Albin Michel S.A., 2003
22, rue Huyghens, 75014 Paris
www.albin-michel.fr
ISBN 2-226-13698-3

« J'écrivais des silences, des nuits, je notais l'inexprimable, je fixais les vertiges. »

ARTHUR RIMBAUD

« C'est le vase qui donne une forme au vide et la musique au silence. »

RENÉ CHAR

de C. à O.

Vision

Cette nuit, j'ai rêvé, je l'ai vu comme on ne voit jamais dans les rêves. Une vision inquiétante.

Il avait ses yeux sombres, à la pupille si mobile ; son nez busqué lui donnait cette force qui m'attire ; ses cheveux châtains, mal coupés dont la mèche lui barrait le front.

Il me regardait sans parler. Pas un mot.

Le silence était son langage. La parole ne lui venait que dans de courtes phrases aussi désincarnées qu'un bulletin météo.

Le silence porte au doute. Cette falsification du sens, cette défroque sans visage nous met dans l'embarras. Et si toute la famille ordinaire de nos mots était d'un vain usage ?

On se défend mal contre le silence. Toute parole finit par s'anémier devant lui.

Seulement, tout ce que cet homme ne me disait pas avait fini par emplir ma vie.

Il était comme un jeu d'enfant, une énigme, un

canevas, un dessin à colorier ; il manquait toujours quelque chose. Il gardait la place du vide, la place de l'imagination. Et moi, je devais broder, dessiner, réfléchir. Il ne m'a donné que le contour, le pourtour, le récipient, le problème à résoudre. Il ne m'a donné ni le contenu ni la solution.

L'absence de sens m'a éclairée sur la multitude des sens.

Du vide a surgi la fascination.

Sa manière bien à lui, c'était de dire sans les mots.

Bien sûr, j'aurais préféré qu'il me parle, j'aurais préféré des mots à ce disque sans musique, à ces pages sans une ligne, à ces caresses qui m'effleuraient parfois, à ces tonnes de silence qu'il déversait sur moi et que je devais décrypter.

Avais-je le choix ? Je l'ai rejoint là où il était, dans ce monde étrange, sans un bruit, ce monde mystérieux rien qu'à lui où il m'a entraînée. J'ai pris ce qu'il m'a donné, j'ai pris ce qui est invisible, inaudible pour les autres.

Aujourd'hui, je sais que le chemin du silence m'a construite, m'a forcée à bâtir autre chose ailleurs, avec mes forces à moi. Je me suis perdue et trouvée dans le silence.

Rencontre

Tout commença dans le jardin Marcel-Proust. De façon anodine, quoique inhabituelle et peut-être illusoire. Un type assis sur un banc, tout bas, avec douceur, improvisait un air rien que pour moi, j'en étais sûre. Enfin, presque.

Je me suis arrêtée, l'homme fredonnait entre ses lèvres des sons d'un autre monde, comme arrachés au silence. Nous nous sommes regardés, moi pour m'assurer que cette mélodie m'était bien adressée, mais aussi pour vérifier que l'on ne se connaissait pas. On aurait pu se connaître. D'un seul regard cet inconnu m'était devenu familier. C'est étrange, un inconnu familier : une sorte d'évidence absurde, confuse, surgie d'on ne sait quelle mémoire.

Debout, je n'étais qu'une proie. Alors, assise sur le banc d'en face, j'ai écouté. Nous nous sommes épiés quelques instants. Quelques regards, c'est tout. Il ne s'est rien passé d'autre. Il ne s'est peut-être rien passé du tout. Il est même probable que l'homme devant

13

moi, à cet instant, ne transportait avec lui aucune promesse, aucune brûlure, aucun rêve, sinon celles et ceux de mon imagination. Je me suis mise à rougir et j'ai fixé mes sandales plates de cuir tressé, comme si j'attendais la fin d'un supplice. Quand j'ai relevé la tête, le banc, en face, était vide.

Il était parti.

Et moi j'étais différente.

Longtemps je me suis demandé si j'avais été victime d'un songe.

Le songe est réapparu trois ans plus tard, dans une galerie d'art contemporain, à l'occasion d'un vernissage : un visage, parmi d'autres visages. Comment ne pas le reconnaître ? C'était lui, bien lui, j'en étais certaine, certaine comme de l'alternance du jour et de la nuit. Il avait tout mieux que les autres, me suis-je dit. Pas vraiment beau, il était lui, cela me suffisait. Je portais une robe légère, décolletée, sans préméditation aucune. Au milieu de cette foule bavarde et piétinante, à ce moment de ma vie, je n'étais pas loin de penser que l'existence consiste à attendre quelque chose qui n'arrive jamais.

J'avais tort. L'homme devant moi, à quelques mètres seulement, ressemblait, trait pour trait, à l'image de l'inconnu assis sur un banc. Les deux images se superposaient et par chance se correspondaient.

Je le retrouvai enfin.

Lui qui, m'apercevant à son tour, d'un seul regard sut remonter le temps aussi vite que moi.

Nous avons marché l'un vers l'autre, tant bien que mal, à travers la foule.

J'allais vers lui, il allait vers moi, nous allions vers une personne que nous ne connaissions pas.

Face à face, il me regarde, l'air de dire :
« Est-ce bien la fille du jardin Marcel-Proust ? »
Je le regarde, l'air de me dire :
« Pas de doute. »
Léger décalage.
Lui : mince sourire frontal.
Moi : plein sourire de biais.
Lui : il relève la tête.
Moi : signe de défi ? Mon front se plisse, inquiétude lisible.
Lui : regard appuyé.
Moi : éblouie, je ne vois plus rien, je souris dans le vide.
Silence plein de sous-entendus.
Il a gagné, je vais fléchir, me rendre, rompre le silence.
Moi, je tente :
– Bonjour...
À vrai dire, l'inconnu s'était effacé de ma mémoire, où je l'avais maintenu pour je ne sais quelle raison, le réchauffant à petit feu, comme un plat cuisiné, le

ravivant d'une sensation, le rallongeant d'une rêverie. Puis Laurent, Lionel, la vie avec son insistance m'avait entraînée, mais je restais persuadée qu'un jour cet homme reviendrait. J'avais gardé une place pour lui.

Moi (toujours en moi-même) : je parle trop, quand je suis intimidée, je dois apprendre à me taire, mais je ne sais pas faire avec le silence. Le silence m'embarrasse.

Je recule d'un pas.

Il avance.

Drôle de duo.

J'ai l'air d'une proie et lui d'un prédateur. Il attrape mon poignet et m'entraîne vers la sortie. Sûr de lui.

Et dans ma tête : « Il m'emmène ? où ? Peu importe : il m'emmène. »

Oui, je pense une chose aussi puérile au moment où il m'étreint le poignet. Les vrais adultes n'ont pas de joie similaire, me semble-t-il ; les adultes ont un travail, des enfants, des responsabilités, des impôts, une voiture, des choses qui les ramènent sur terre et les y attachent. Moi, je décolle, je m'emballe comme une gamine.

Nous sortons de la cohue et nous marchons sans direction définie. À mesure que nous nous éloignons du vernissage, l'espace qui nous sépare se réduit.

Sa main chaude et ferme me serre et je ne tente pas de m'échapper. J'aime l'arrogance de ce geste.

Il le sait. Et je sens, à la moiteur soudaine de sa

peau, qu'il est troublé lui aussi par ce premier contact charnel. Ma résistance n'est que coquetterie.

Je tourne la tête vers lui, je balance mes cheveux mi-longs près de son visage, tandis qu'il me respire, qu'il inhale mon eau florale.

Nous marchons dans la rue côte à côte et sans rien savoir l'un de l'autre. Je ne connais ni sa voix, ni son nom, je devine juste ses intentions.

Personne ne nous a présentés.

Il doit avoir quarante-cinq ans, les cheveux encore noirs et drus, les traits forts et les rides marquées ; il est vêtu sans audace particulière, une chemise bleue, une cravate sans fantaisie, un costume clair et froissé qui laisse supposer qu'il n'est pas repassé chez lui se changer et qu'il le regrette à en juger ce geste de la main pour lisser un revers. Il ressemble juste à un homme, un garçon, tout carré tout simple. Petit, il devait porter des shorts trop courts, grimper aux arbres, jouer avec des voitures de course, au foot dans la cour de récré et plaire aux filles.

Je ne connais toujours pas le son de sa voix.

Quand se décidera-t-il à parler ? Nous ne nous sommes pas salués, ni même embrassés ; normal, nous ne nous connaissons pas.

Moi :

— Je m'appelle Idylle.

Faux, bien sûr ; mais Idylle me va comme un gant.

Il regarde mes épaules bronzées, sans savoir quel soleil les a caressées ; il regarde mes yeux et au-delà.

Remarque-t-il mon évolution depuis trois ans ? Quelques lignes verticales strient mon front et je ne peux plus rire sans que des plis au coin de mes yeux accompagnent l'éclat de ma voix. Je m'en accommode. Il ne connaît pas ce visage, notre brève rencontre ne m'avait pas laissé le temps d'exploser de joie. Il scrute mon nez, ma bouche, surtout ma bouche et, plus il me regarde – me détaille –, plus, rendue inquiète par le désir de lui plaire, je doute de moi.

– Comment vous appelez-vous ?

Pas de réponse.

Étrange.

Nous marchons. Il tire toujours mon poignet, mon bras est tendu ; rien à voir avec un couple de futurs amants qui se promènerait en minaudant sur un trottoir. Il m'enlève. Sûr de moi. Voilà la vérité.

Son alliance me taillade l'avant-bras ; il est donc marié ?

Soudain, il s'arrête, lâche mon poignet, j'ai mal, je le frotte, il sourit.

Maintenant que nos corps se sont touchés, loin de la foule, sous un de ces arbres qui, par miracle, s'épanouissent dans le béton, nos mots vont peut-être se mêler ?

Je réitère ma question : « Comment vous appelez-vous ? »

Il n'entend pas. Il dit :

– Ce n'est pas parce qu'un homme ne voit pas une femme pendant longtemps qu'il ne pense pas à elle...

Ce sont les premières paroles qu'il a prononcées.

– Vous avez pensé à moi ?

Il ne me répond pas.

Il m'envisage. Les hommes peuvent bien se taire, ils ne peuvent empêcher leurs yeux de parler. Ses yeux me forcent plus que n'importe quel mot.

Alors je lui dis ce qu'il a envie d'entendre ; que j'habite près d'ici, et des choses bien plus compromettantes encore. Je donne le nom et le numéro de ma rue et même ceux de mes téléphones fixe et portable. Je lui donne tout. Tous les moyens de me retrouver.

Il n'est pas surpris, je ne fais que répondre à son interrogation muette ; il allonge le bras d'un coup sec, sa main frôle presque mon visage, il lance un regard rapide sur sa montre.

Va-t-il proposer de me suivre ?

Pas de mots. Juste son visage qui se déplace à peine de la gauche vers la droite, en signe de négation. Il refuse l'invitation qu'il a sollicitée.

Il aurait pu mettre les formes, m'avouer, par exemple, qu'il regrettait de devoir partir, après tout ce temps, qu'il avait pensé à moi, souvent, beaucoup, tous les jours, qu'il m'avait cherchée dans tous les jardins, dans toutes les rues, qu'il aurait hurlé mon nom du haut de la tour Eiffel, si seulement il l'avait connu. Il aurait pu me dire qu'il m'avait perdue une fois dans cette ville et qu'il ne me perdrait plus. Mais pour cela, il fallait articuler des mots, bâtir une phrase ou deux. Parler !

Il dit simplement :
– Demain.
– Demain ?
Je ne suis même pas sûre d'avoir entendu, tant sa voix est basse.
Je suis sur le point d'ajouter : « C'est loin demain », mais il m'en empêche en posant son index sur ma bouche :
– Chut...
– Chut ?
– Oui, chut...
– Pourquoi chut... ?
J'insiste, encore une fois :
– Juste, dites-moi si vous aimez le chocolat ?
Pourquoi est-ce que je lui pose une question aussi absurde ? Parce qu'il va partir et que je veux le retenir.
Il sourit.
– Chut...
Chut ? Cela signifiait silence, non ?
Voilà, le mot d'ordre était lancé.

E-MAIL D'IDYLLE À CLÉMENTINE

J'ai retrouvé le type du jardin Marcel-Proust, et devine
ce qu'il m'a dit ? Il m'a dit « chut » !
Il est mystérieux, son silence m'intrigue. Crois-tu qu'il
existe un silence des amoureux ?

E-MAIL DE CLÉMENTINE À IDYLLE

Mais c'est une épidémie, ce n'est pas possible ! Mon
mari a été contaminé. Cela me rend folle, les mots se
font de plus en plus rares dans sa bouche : je crois que
le silence est un virus plutôt répandu chez les hommes
qui ont cessé d'aimer ! Ce qui me désole, tu imagines.

Visite numéro 1

– C'est moi..., murmure une voix d'homme dans l'interphone.

C'est qui, lui ?

– Qui ? dis-je, pour le plaisir d'en savoir plus.

– Moi, répond l'homme, imperturbable.

Le ton est juste, il s'agit bien de la voix qui, en sortant du vernissage, la veille, m'a soufflé : « Ce n'est pas parce qu'un homme ne voit pas une femme pendant longtemps qu'il ne pense pas à elle. »

Cette voix n'est ni faible, ni cassée, ni chevrotante, ni sourde, ni étouffée, ni aigre, ni criarde, ni perçante, ni flûtée, elle n'a rien d'un babil ou d'un gazouillement, c'est une voix d'homme, profonde, vibrante, puissante, chaude, sépulcrale que me renvoie l'interphone. Une voix qui ne se galvaude pas, qui ne s'adresse pas à n'importe qui, allait s'exprimer et se réjouir de nos retrouvailles.

Aucun bruit d'ascenseur, il grimpe les cinq étages à pied. L'oreille collée contre la porte, j'ai guetté ses pas.

23

Quelques instants d'immobilité sur le paillasson avant de sonner. Il hésite ? Il reprend son souffle ? Il sonne.

La poignée de la porte est en cuivre doré, pour ouvrir il faut tirer la targette et tourner la poignée : deux gestes. Toute mon attention, toutes mes sensations, toute mon intensité concentrées dans l'ouverture de la porte d'entrée.

L'homme que j'ai perdu depuis trois ans s'approche, comme au cinéma... Prudence...

Perturbation en vue.

Réminiscence d'année de licence...

Il est impensable que Schopenhauer ait refusé d'ouvrir à Flora Weiss ou Nietzsche à Lou Andreas Salomé quand elles venaient carillonner à leurs portes. Le tintement d'une clochette peut bouleverser toute une philosophie. La mienne, si j'en ai une, est sens dessus dessous.

La sonnette tinte ; il est trop tard pour s'interroger. Le risque fait partie de la vie... Ma main tourne le loquet. J'ai le souffle coupé, mais j'ouvre : et il est là, dans l'encadrement de la porte, debout, brun, compact, costume sombre, cravate, je ne sais plus, et silencieux, j'en suis sûre.

– Bonjour..., dis-je.

Réponse : sourire en coin, regard lourd de malice et de sous-entendus.

Il me suit dans le salon, regarde autour de lui pour

24

savoir où il a atterri : un univers blanc, ensoleillé, des livres et du désordre assez bien ordonné. Rien d'extraordinaire, OK, mais pas mal de prétextes pour entamer une conversation.

Ouf, son regard s'arrête sur une collection de coquillages.

La parole va peut-être jaillir du fond des océans, des choses, du confort, de l'encombrement, du superflu. Non.

– J'aime entendre la mer, dis-je, juste pour parler.

Lui : une espèce de « hum », comme les psys.

Il rôde dans la pièce, rien ne sort de sa bouche à part ce borborygme digne d'un primate. Il ne me complimente pas sur le raffinement du bouquet de pensées bleues, composé évidemment pour lui. Le silence nous cerne.

Il pourrait me demander un truc banal, n'importe quoi.

Exemple : « Comment allez-vous ? »

Exemple : « Qu'est-ce qui vous amenait dans cette galerie ? »

Exemple : « Il fait beau. »

Exemple : « Je suis heureux de vous revoir. »

Exemple : « J'aime l'odeur de cette bougie. Quel est ce parfum ? »

Exemple : « Je m'appelle Machin... »

Exemple : « Idylle, ce n'est pas banal comme prénom. »

Presque tous commencent ainsi.

Avec lui, aucun point de repère possible.

Retour à la case départ.

Je navigue à vue.

Je débute.

Je balbutie.

Je suis confrontée à un truc nouveau, un homme fort comme un mur.

Personne n'est aussi fort qu'un mur.

Rien, il ne dit rien, il ignore toutes les formules de politesse et se fiche de mon parfum, de mes fleurs, de ma santé, de mes mobiles, des présentations. Il est ailleurs, il est je ne sais pas où.

Il vient. Il va.

Va brûler les étapes, forcément.

Il rôde.

Je suis plus mal à l'aise avec ce silence qu'avec lui. Je connais les hommes, enfin un peu, je ne connais pas le silence. Je connais le silence des vieux couples attablés dans les restaurants, le silence des médecins confrontés à une maladie, je connais le silence de la nuit, le silence de la neige, je ne connais pas le silence des hommes.

Les mots se bousculent dans ma gorge, n'importe quels mots, pour combler, pour remplir, pour débloquer, pour dire.

Acculée, je lui propose de s'asseoir :

– Nous avons tellement de choses à nous raconter.

D'un signe de tête, il refuse mon invitation. Ma mère, il y a quelques années, lui aurait demandé : « Tu as avalé ta langue ? » Je ne suis pas ma mère, ni la sienne, et il n'est pas un petit garçon.

Il ne s'assoit pas.

Je lui propose une orangeade, j'ai pressé moi-même les oranges, je lui tends une assiette en porcelaine sur laquelle j'ai disposé avec soin quelques petits gâteaux parsemés de violettes cristallisées. Il regarde les corolles avec étonnement, je suppose qu'il n'en a jamais vu. Il ne sait pas que les fleurs se cuisinent.

Il refuse les sablés et les périanthes. Méfiant. Classique, je lui demande ce qu'il a fait pendant tout ce temps, quelle a été sa vie, etc., rien d'original, soit. Il ne répond pas à mes questions.

Il s'approche de moi, déplace une chaise et vient me chercher dans le recoin où je me suis réfugiée.

Il me regarde, menton relevé, air dominateur.

Je le regarde, tête baissée, air dominé.

Il pose ses mains autour de ma taille et s'empare de moi. Je tremble, c'est trop tôt, trop vite, j'ai besoin d'un peu de mots, d'un peu d'égards.

Je tourne la tête deux ou trois fois pour esquiver ses baisers ; j'ai besoin de savoir pourquoi il ne m'a pas parlé dans le jardin, pourquoi il est parti ; si je suis restée dans ses pensées, je veux connaître ses sentiments, ses impressions.

Il m'attire contre lui avec une certaine violence. Il méprise ma résistance, impose sa manière.

– Dis-moi... qui es-tu ?

Il ne répond pas.

– Dis-moi...

Il se tait.

Je me soumets.

Son désir se passe de mots.

Son corps s'empresse, sa bouche se colle contre la mienne.

Ses caresses gagnent du terrain. Les mains descendent, frôlent le ventre et plus bas, elles osent. Il écarte la chemise, il baisse ma culotte sans la regarder, sa bouche quitte mes lèvres pour se poser sur mes seins, sa bouche s'entrouvre sur mes seins pour les boire, j'ouvre sa braguette, je le caresse. Alors, je me passe des mots qu'il ne donne pas.

Son corps me rassure. Il m'embrasse.

Le corps ne ment pas.

– La passion, c'est le baiser, lui dis-je.

Il dit :

– Tu vois.

Ses démonstrations sont une preuve suffisante. Un discours serait superflu. Je parle trop.

Il m'embrasse à nouveau, sans doute pour me faire taire.

Nos bouches ne se décollent pas, il m'embrasse les yeux fermés, il m'embrasse en état d'hypnose, il ressemble à un bébé, pas à cause de la succion, à cause de l'urgente nécessité : embrasser. Une fonction vitale. Le temps semble suspendu à nos langues qui se promènent, à nos salives qui se mélangent.

Rien de plus intime que le baiser.

Je suis les mouvements de cette langue qui entre et sort de ma bouche, qui frôle mes dents, mon palais, mes gencives. Sa langue est une virtuose, elle vient se réfugier à l'intérieur de ma bouche, elle reste là un moment inerte pour se reposer et repartir et virevolter de plus belle. Puis il m'aspire, il attire ma langue, tout occupée à le recevoir, il l'attire au fond de sa bouche, il veut qu'à mon tour je lui rende visite, il veut que je l'investisse, que je le goûte, que je l'habite, que je le pénètre. Il m'inhale, il m'absorbe, il me pompe pour que je reste, il garde ma langue prisonnière de sa bouche, de son étreinte. J'ai mal, je gémis, alors il me lâche, et je sens ses lèvres s'entrouvrir en un sourire. Non, je ne sais pas faire l'homme, alors il a pitié, il revient en moi, et le baiser reprend son cours normal. Le baiser dure longtemps, longtemps, jamais assez longtemps. Je suis bien dans ses bras, j'aime ses épaules confortables, j'aime la chair qui l'enveloppe, j'aime sa peau qui se fond avec la mienne, nous avons la même couleur de peau.

Soudain, il me repousse un peu, ses deux mains posées sur mes côtes ne m'attirent plus vers lui, mais me plaquent contre le mur, je m'éloigne de son enveloppe brûlante pour me coller contre la froideur du béton. Que se passe-t-il ? Il n'explique rien. J'ai peur.

Pourquoi m'a-t-il repoussée ? Je dis : « Pourquoi », tout en cherchant ses lèvres, je les embrasse, je m'approvisionne. Je veux comprendre malgré les mots qu'il ne me donne pas.

Je puise dans ce baiser la force et l'assurance que son attitude pourrait m'ôter. Je n'en profite pas entièrement, je fais juste mon plein, j'ai peur de l'hiver, de la séparation, de l'abandon.

Il décolle sa bouche :

– Il faut adopter une ligne...

Je pense qu'il veut installer à son bureau une ligne de téléphone rien que pour moi... alors, je dis :

– Une ligne de téléphone rien que pour nous ?

– Non, une ligne de conduite...

– Ah ?

Il s'affaire, il va partir.

Partir ? là, maintenant ? Qu'est-ce qu'il raconte ?

Je ne pleure jamais devant un homme, j'aurais voulu éviter de pleurer devant celui-là que je ne connais pas et voilà que mes larmes coulent sur mes joues sans que je parvienne à les retenir.

Moi : je m'essuie avec le revers de ma manche.

Lui : il regarde mes larmes couler avec un drôle de sourire, pas sûr que ce soit de l'émotion.

Il m'embrasse à nouveau, mes larmes donnent un goût salé à notre baiser. Peut-être l'ultime ? Il n'était donc qu'un étranger de passage, un homme pour un baiser.

Il n'ajoute rien, il boit, il aime les larmes mélangées à la salive. Il boit ce qu'il a déclenché avec avidité. Il aime l'eau des yeux, il remonte avec sa langue la chercher à sa source, il lèche mes paupières, mes cils, je suis aveuglée, je ne vois que ce morceau de chair qui me dévore.

Il m'aime ? Il me déteste ?

Il est trop tôt pour parler d'amour ? Pas en ce qui me concerne : cette chose-là existe tout de suite ou pas. Et puis, j'ai l'impression que cette histoire dure depuis trois ans.

En attendant, il remonte sa braguette.

Il va partir, pour être bien sûr de garder le contrôle. Quel prétentieux ! Quel pouvoir s'arroge-t-il sur moi ? Pourquoi m'abandonne-t-il, le corps réchauffé par ses caresses ? Je cherche un sens à son attitude, je ne le trouve pas.

Pas de sens.

Pourquoi faudrait-il une logique à cela ? Qui est anormal ? Lui ? Moi ?

Lui : il remue la tête de gauche à droite.

Signe de négation. Il ne veut plus de mes larmes. Il est repu des larmes qu'il a provoquées. Pauvre amour ! Excuse-moi ! Quelle inconvenance, une femme qui pleure ! Mais tu sais, les filles ne pleurent pas forcément parce qu'elles sont tristes, les filles pleurent aussi quand elles sont déçues, contrariées, énervées, et même quand elles sont heureuses. Bonheur ou malheur, les larmes restent la façon la plus efficace d'exprimer nos émotions.

Il paraît même que nous avons de grandes blessures qui cicatrisent vite et que vous, les hommes, en avez de très légères qui ne cicatrisent jamais. Ceci explique cela. Tu vois, il vaut peut-être mieux pleurer.

Ce genre de discours lui est étranger.

Lui : il balance la tête en signe de négation : non, non... assez de baisers aux larmes, je veux de la résistance, je veux de la difficulté.

Moi : je ne pourrai donc pas lui offrir ce que je suis, il faudra composer, enjoliver, se durcir, le cirque habituel. Offrir ce que je ne suis pas, offrir ce que je n'ai pas pour le séduire.

Résumé : l'authenticité mise en échec.

Un classique.

Peu d'hommes vous offrent ce luxe : vous aimer telle que vous êtes. Tous veulent des femmes fortes pour ne pas avoir à les consoler même si, parfois, ils déplorent leur solidité. Parce que c'est encombrant une femme qui vous aime trop.

Voilà mon prix à payer pour rester libre, sans attaches, le prix à payer quand être une maîtresse devient l'ambition suprême.

Une maîtresse existe pour le meilleur, pas pour le pire.

Le pire, je le garde pour moi, je ne le partage pas avec les hommes, ils sont démunis devant les larmes, les hommes. Petits, on leur a appris qu'il fallait retenir les larmes de la douleur et celles de la tristesse, alors quand ils rencontrent une femme qui s'arroge le droit de pleurer, ils se vengent. Je ne dois pas le perturber.

Les larmes des maîtresses ressemblent à celles des hommes.

Elles s'avalent, elles ne se sèchent pas.

J'ai transgressé. Pardon.

Je ne recommencerai plus, je ne t'embarrasserai plus, promis.

Trop tard.

Il est parti.

Tant pis.

L'ère des gentlemen est révolue.

Tant mieux.

Ils sont compliqués les hommes du vingt et unième siècle. Ils ont leurs petites peurs, leurs petites névroses. La fragilité n'est plus l'apanage des femmes. Depuis longtemps les courants tendent à s'inverser : les femmes prennent la force des hommes et les hommes la faiblesse des femmes. Mais pour les larmes, ils résistent encore.

Résultat : un désastre.

Pauvre Idylle qui s'apprêtait à vivre un beau mélo !

Y aura-t-il une suite après ce baiser ?

E-MAIL D'IDYLLE À CLÉMENTINE

Mes deux ex (Laurent + Lionel) réunis ne m'ont jamais donné le quart de l'émotion que l'homme du jardin Marcel-Proust me procure.

E-MAIL DE CLÉMENTINE À IDYLLE

Ce mec ressemble à un abîme, et tu vas t'y engouffrer... Bye-bye, Idylle...

Après

Mon analyse :

Je suis trop confiante, je ne cultive pas assez le mystère. Lui, il a de la retenue. Et s'il était dans le vrai ? On peut toujours dire ce que l'on n'a pas osé dire, alors que l'on ne peut pas effacer ce qui a été énoncé.

Que s'est-il passé ?

Mes mots et mes larmes l'ont apeuré ; je suis fautive. Il est venu pour l'amour, le bavardage ne l'intéresse pas. Voilà et, après tout, la manifestation physique n'est-elle pas essentielle en amour ?

Clémentine et moi, quand nous étions à la fac, nous avions mis au point « la règle des six non » :

Une série de six « non » devait précéder un « oui ».

1. Décommander systématiquement le premier rendez-vous (un truc de chipie, qui fonctionne assez bien).

Le reste devait s'enchaîner, naturellement :

2. Avancer à pas mesurés.

3. Ne s'exprimer qu'avec les yeux, avant de savoir à qui l'on a affaire.

4. Ne pas se livrer.

5. Ne pas appeler, répondre à peine.

6. Utiliser la même méthode que pour le dressage des chevaux et des chiens : jouer de la carotte et du bâton, en alternance.

Enfin, accorder un baiser s'il le mérite.

Facile comme une théorie.

Abstrait comme une doctrine.

À croire qu'en ce qui concerne l'amour, théorie et réalité ne peuvent faire bon ménage. Dans le second cas, les principes paraissent faits pour être transgressés et les désirs satisfaits.

Il est erroné de croire que les fous se repèrent à vue de nez et de sous-estimer la part de masochisme existant en chacun de nous. Les fous courent la ville et les masos aussi ; il leur arrive même de se rencontrer.

Alors les mots doux rebutent et les mufleries séduisent.

Illogisme.

Bouleversement intérieur.

Inversement des valeurs.

Révocation de la règle des six « non », inutile face à un homme qui se défile.

Humanisation au programme.

Le vide s'érige en nouvelle norme.

Je suis attirée par quelque chose que je ne connais pas. Quoi ? La difficulté ?

Je ne suis ni raisonnable ni logique, je ne me comprends pas.

Je dois être amoureuse. Sinon je l'aurais poussé dehors. La vie serait si simple si elle consistait à ne pas aimer ce qui est mauvais.

Mais ce qui est mauvais est bon.

Par définition.

Derrière tout être humain se cache une énigme que l'on a envie ou pas de découvrir. L'amour pourrait peut-être même naître de cette curiosité que suscite le mystère de l'autre. Je veux savoir pourquoi cet homme est silencieux. Savoir si l'origine de ce silence était machiavélique ou romantique.

Il s'appelle « moi »

Quelques minutes à peine après son départ, le téléphone retentit, c'était lui :

– C'est « moi ».

Il s'appelle « moi », il suffit de le savoir.

Je me dis qu'il regrettait, qu'il allait revenir pour s'excuser d'être parti si vite et, bien sûr, je lui pardonnais déjà.

– J'ai une de tes boucles d'oreilles dans ma poche..., dit-il, factuel. Je ne sais pas comment elle a atterri là... Je te la rendrai demain. Je passerai vers quatorze heures.

Et mes cours ? Et le lycée, cet homme pensait que j'étais à sa disposition ?

J'étais à sa disposition.

Moi qui m'étais battue pour l'égalité des salaires entre hommes et femmes, je me soumettais à la volonté d'un homme, bouleversais mon emploi du temps, m'inventais des maladies pour annuler mes cours, décommandais des déjeuners.

Rien n'arrête une femme amoureuse, aucun principe, aucun fondement, aucune hypothèse, aucun postulat, aucune obligation, aucune logique.

Il aurait fallu m'attacher au fond d'un placard pour me retenir.

Une femme amoureuse n'a pas d'orgueil, pas de suffisance.

Mais elle peut avoir de l'insolence, de l'arrogance.

Peine perdue : une femme amoureuse n'a pas d'avenir.

Visite numéro 2

Les oranges sont pressées, les jambes sont épilées, l'aspirateur passé, les draps changés, les aisselles talquées, la bouche brillante, pas colorée ni collante cependant, la peau gommée, la pression au maximum, l'ego au minimum, la musique en sourdine. Je ne suis ni fière ni pas fière ; je suis juste une femme qui va ouvrir sa porte à un homme parce qu'elle ne peut pas résister.

Mes élèves se remettront d'un cours raté sur Lautréamont, alors que je ne me pardonnerais pas un rendez-vous manqué.

Il sonne à l'interphone, pour la seconde fois, il sonne et j'ai aussi peur que la première.

Je connais juste sa bouche, son haleine, sa manière empressée d'embrasser, son entêtement à ne rien dire. Son odeur.

J'adore ses baisers. Ça, je le sais.

Il me suit dans le salon, je lui offre un jus d'oranges pressées, qu'il éloigne d'un signe de tête.

— Qu'est-ce que tu aimes ?

— Le café, dit-il.

— Je vais t'en faire.

Sa langue claque dans sa bouche en signe de négation.

Langage universel ?

— Tu veux des chocolats au café, à la liqueur, des After Eight ou des Kinder Surprise ? Mon frigo en est plein.

Reclaquement de langue.

Relangage universel ?

Il n'aime pas le chocolat ? Mauvais signe.

Après une certaine contorsion qui l'entraîne vers la droite, il sort une petite perle de culture du fond d'une poche de sa veste.

— Tiens, dit-il en se tenant éloigné de moi.

J'attrape la boucle d'oreille du bout des doigts, je la visse dans mon lobe sans précaution tant ce geste m'est devenu familier, et je le remercie, adossée contre le mur de béton. Il marche le long de mon salon, il tourne plus qu'il n'effectue de lignes droites. Forcément, le salon est petit. Soudain, il pile devant moi :

— Je n'ai plus rien de toi ! dit-il.

Stupéfaction... Veut-il que je lui rende ma boucle d'oreille ? Pourquoi ? Pour penser à moi quand nous serons éloignés l'un de l'autre ? Donc, il envisage de s'en aller, mais en pensant à moi ?

Il s'approche, m'embrasse les yeux fermés, m'embrasse comme s'il partait à la guerre dans un sous-marin ou un bombardier, comme s'il n'allait plus jamais me revoir.

Je dis :

– Pourquoi es-tu comme ça ?

Il secoue la tête, ses cheveux raides se décollent, une vraie publicité pour l'Oréal ; ça lui va, de secouer la tête. Puis il m'attire vers la sortie en m'embrassant.

Il est sur le point de partir. Il vient pour partir. Il adore partir.

Il pense que l'amour meurt d'exister et que seuls les hommes lointains échappent à ce maléfice.

Il ne se trouve pas digne du rêve qu'il suscite. Je le rassure :

– Tu m'appelleras ?

Hochement de tête, de haut en bas.

– Quand ?

– Demain.

Je pose les questions qu'il ne faut pas. Je suis devenue un manuel de « ce qu'il ne faut pas faire ».

Mais comment se taire devant un homme qui ne parle pas ?

Et quand bien même je ne lui aurais posé aucune question, son comportement en aurait-il été modifié ? Serait-il venu si je ne le lui avais pas demandé ?

Il est impossible d'évaluer l'effet d'un mot et sa capacité de nuisance.

E-MAIL DE CLÉMENTINE À IDYLLE

Je cherche un homme qui me préfère à la lecture, à la chasse, à la finance, au bridge, au golf, aux copains, à la télé, aux journaux.

E-MAIL D'IDYLLE À CLÉMENTINE

Ça n'existe pas.
Le mien serait parfait s'il n'était pas bloqué sur « off ».
Je cherche la touche « on ».

E-MAIL DE CLÉMENTINE À IDYLLE

Même si tu trouves la touche « on », tôt ou tard, tu seras déçue. Il n'y a pas une seule note dans ton bastringue. Tu n'y entendras que l'écho de ta propre voix.

Visite numéro 3

Il a appelé, il est venu sans justifier son attitude d'hier. Il a traversé le salon sans s'arrêter et s'est dirigé vers la petite alcôve qui abrite mon lit, un matelas à même le sol.

Il s'est déshabillé tout seul, très vite, puis il a désigné d'un doigt pointé ma petite robe à fleurs et j'ai obéi à son geste, je l'ai enlevée, sans protester, sans m'insurger.

Ma première erreur fut peut-être celle-là.

Me soumettre à son doigt, à son œil, lui permettre de ne pas se donner la peine de parler.

Céder.

Il est entré dans les draps et les a relevés sur nos têtes jusqu'à former une tente. Il s'est étendu sur le dos, je me suis allongée à côté de lui et j'ai posé ma tête au creux de son épaule, comme une épouse fatiguée après l'amour, qui s'apprête à dormir.

Dormir ensemble n'était pas au programme.

J'ai caressé sa poitrine, et parfois mes doigts restaient prisonniers de ses poils.

– Comment dors-tu ? lui ai-je demandé.

Pour toute réponse, j'ai entendu un petit rire triste et étouffé dans le noir. Dommage, cela me semblait important de savoir comment il dormait.

Alors il a commencé à m'aimer en prenant son temps.

Je devance ses moindres gestes. Veut-il me retourner comme une poupée, la poupée se retourne d'elle-même, aussi légère qu'une danseuse qui s'entraîne depuis des années avec le même partenaire. Il fait l'amour dans mon dos, sur mon ventre ; il veut voir les seins, voir les fesses, il ne veut rien perdre, il veut tout connaître en une seule fois, prend tout, donne tout avec délicatesse, sans acrobaties excessives. Il est un virtuose, il montre la chorégraphie que je lui inspire. Il est beau son ballet, je crois même que je n'ai jamais rien connu de plus beau ; je ne savais pas qu'un tel duo improvisé pouvait exister. Il tient ma tête entre ses mains, me couvre de son souffle, je voudrais lui dire quelque chose, je ne sais pas trop quoi, quelque chose comme : « C'est donc cette attirance-là qui te fait peur ? » Mais il ne m'en laisse pas la possibilité ; il me tient trop fort. Je voudrais respirer hors de lui, je ne le peux pas. Il m'entoure avec ses bras, je le serre dans mon ventre.

Et moi, je me dis qu'une femme qui a connu ça a vécu.

Puis il s'est effondré, son corps allégé est devenu

plus lourd ; j'adore ce poids d'homme qui pèse sur mes seins, mon nombril, mes cuisses, mes pieds. Il ne reste pas longtemps dans cette posture, qu'il doit juger inférieure, il se ramasse, je sens que ses muscles dans un effort ultime se contractent et il s'élève au-dessus de moi, nos peaux moites se séparent comme deux feuilles fraîchement collées.

En équilibre sur les avant-bras, il se penche et embrasse mon bas-ventre encore couvert de notre transpiration, une manière de me remercier, et me demande la permission de prendre une douche.

Sa première douche chez moi.

Je n'envisage même pas de lui demander de rester. Il ne fait pas partie de ces hommes qui grillent une clope dans votre lit en racontant leur vie ou qui s'endorment le sourire au coin des lèvres.

Nous ne ressemblons pas à un vieux couple, même pas pour cinq minutes.

Un jeune couple non plus, d'ailleurs ; il ne recommence pas.

J'aurais bien aimé encore un peu de caresses, de brutalité. Juste un peu de quelque chose. Mais il a fini de donner.

L'eau coule, je l'entends se frictionner. Il ne chantonne pas, n'exagérons rien.

Alors, je ne résiste pas à sa peau nue et mouillée, je sors du lit.

Il est un peu surpris de me voir entrer sous la douche. Quelle familiarité, n'est-ce pas ? Il m'ouvre quand même les bras et me serre contre lui, puis il s'active, me savonne le dos et glisse sa main entre mes fesses.

Je le savonne à mon tour, mes mains s'amusent autour de son sexe que je couvre et que je découvre. Et nous restons ainsi, heureux, enlacés, pleins de mousse parfumée sous le pommeau d'eau tiède.

Quelques frémissements m'indiquent que l'épisode tendresse touche à sa fin. Il faut se ressaisir, le fauve rugit un peu, il enlève sa main d'entre mes fesses et me repousse avec ses bras : je ne dois ni faiblir ni oublier sa vraie nature.

Il s'est essuyé avec énergie, il a enfilé son caleçon, le même geste depuis les culottes courtes, puis son pantalon, bouclé sa ceinture, enfilé ses chaussettes en forçant sur sa peau encore humide, il a repris sa montre et quelques billets qui étaient tombés de sa poche.

— Comment tu t'appelles ? dis-je.

Il sourit sans répondre.

Je m'approche de lui, si près que nos corps se touchent, je lui chuchote à l'oreille :

— Dis-moi...

Mutisme.

Je m'éloigne, suffisamment pour me rendre compte de son sourire : alors je tambourine avec mes deux poings fermés contre ses épaules en répétant :

— Dis-moi, dis-moi, parle !

Je force la voix :

– Tu connais mon nom, mon adresse, mon numéro de téléphone et moi, qu'est-ce que je sais de toi ?

Je tambourine encore, le pouce sous les quatre doigts, comme les boxeurs.

– Pourquoi tu veux savoir ?

Il me désarme.

Je ne faiblis pas, je persiste à frapper, jusqu'à ce que douleur s'ensuive.

Contraint par mon assaut, il dit :

– Jean.

– Jean ? C'est tout ?

Lui, si magnifique, si mystérieux, les yeux si noirs, porte ce tout petit prénom pas très original ?

– Jean, comment ?

– Jean tout court.

Il soupire, accablé.

Je répète :

– Jean comment ?

Alors je laisse tomber :

– Tu te fiches de moi ?

Il sourit. Il se fiche de moi. J'aurais mieux fait de me taire.

Cet homme est si énigmatique que je m'attendais à un nom qui porte au rêve.

Je me suis trompée.

– Dis-moi quelque chose... J'ai besoin de savoir ce que tu penses, là, maintenant !

J'évite de le nommer, je n'ai pas l'habitude de prononcer ce prénom. À part Jean de La Fontaine, Jean

Racine et Jean d'Ormesson, je ne connais pas de Jean. Personne autour de moi ne se prénomme ainsi.

Jean ne bouge pas d'un poil, alors je recommence : je frappe.

Je frappe avec mes poings fermés.

Jean méprise l'impact de mes coups. C'est un roc, un bloc, une masse de béton, forcément muette.

Pourquoi est-il silencieux ? Parce qu'il n'a rien à dire ? Ses mots sont-ils aussi banals que son nom ?

À trop l'acculer, je risque d'être déçue. Autant laisser flotter le mystère.

Il attrape mes poignets avec une facilité déconcertante.

Je prononce une phrase, perdue depuis l'école mixte :

— Tu abuses de ta force...

Ses lèvres s'ouvrent, comme si elles ne pouvaient s'empêcher de rire, mais il se rétracte aussitôt et, sans lâcher prise, dépose un baiser sur mon front et se tire vite fait.

Dans ma tête :

« Salaud ! »

À haute voix :

— Un jour, tu me parleras et je ne voudrai plus t'entendre !

La porte claque.

Après l'amour

Pas de murmures, de chuchotements, de susurrements, pas de tendresse, pas de sommeil partagé, pas de cigarettes, un peu de chocolat parce qu'il lui était destiné, du vague à l'âme, plein, un déferlement, une sorte de roulis qui m'entraîne d'un côté plus que de l'autre, pas forcément du bon.

Je retourne dans mon lit, étourdie, je relève le drap sur ma tête, je recommence son geste ; je retourne sous la tente.

Il habite l'air, il est dans l'air des draps et dans celui que je respire. Il est particule, il est oxygène et gaz carbonique, il allume la vie et l'éteint, il donne l'espoir et le retire au rythme de chaque respiration, au rythme de ses inspirations.

Il suffirait de croire en lui, en sa bienveillance, pour me laisser bercer. Mais il ne me donne rien, aucun élément rassurant. Il serait prétentieux, optimiste et sûrement dangereux de croire en ce qu'il ne promet

pas. La passion n'est ni stable ni gentille et le silence
est plein de pièges dans lesquels je tombe sans cesse.

Il m'a offert ce champ libre, je le remplis de mots.

S'il m'avait parlé, je ne l'aurais pas traduit.

Il m'a offert le silence,

je suis la traductrice,

la locataire,

la visiteuse,

la maîtresse du silence.

J'habite le silence, autant que le silence m'habite.

À demain, si tu le veux, mon amour.

E-MAIL DE CLÉMENTINE À IDYLLE

Idylle, et si tu étais amoureuse du silence ?
Ça t'irait bien un truc tordu comme ça !
Moi, j'aime être aimée pour de vrai.
Mon mari était bavard et amoureux, autrefois.

E-MAIL D'IDYLLE À CLÉMENTINE

Avec un peu de chance, je finirai par le début.

Le chemin du lycée

À part quelques borborygmes, quelques onomato-
pées lancées au hasard d'une tasse de café, il n'a toujours rien dit d'important, aucun des mots qui touchent l'âme et la dévoilent. Non, jamais une suite de
phrases qui se succéderaient comme des virages dans
la montagne.

Et pourtant il laisse derrière lui un curieux silence,
un silence que je ne connaissais pas, un silence turbu-
lent, habité. Il fait vibrer la vie.

Les autres bruits, ceux de la ville, des bavardages,
des conférences, du théâtre, du cinéma, remplissent
l'atmosphère, mais ne la transcendent pas. Tout ce
tintamarre transporte moins de sens que le silence de
Jean.

À croire que l'homme se dilue dans la parole. Jean
est concentré sur lui-même, il garde ses pensées et
cultive son mystère.

Nous ne faisons pas ce que nous voulons de nos
vies : on ne se débarrasse pas d'un homme comme

d'un adjectif superflu parce qu'il n'a pas d'équivalent, parce qu'il ne rentre dans aucune définition, parce qu'il change le sens. C'est l'inverse qui se produisait avec Jean, je l'aimais parce qu'il ne convenait pas, il appelait une certaine fantaisie, un zeste de créativité. Jean était un souffle ; et moi je me disais que le jour où un tel homme se livrerait, ses mots comme autant de lucioles éclaireraient ma route, répondraient à toutes les questions restées sans réponse depuis la nuit des temps, il dirait le mystère des hommes, de l'amour, le secret du désir, de la vie et de la création.

Il se taisait comme quelqu'un qui savait.

Je me livrais moins à Clémentine parce qu'elle ne le comprenait pas ; on ne pouvait comprendre Jean si on ne le connaissait pas. Ses conseils étaient comme un costume mal taillé, ils ne lui allaient pas. Elle confondait le silence de l'ennui et le silence de l'amour. Il est possible que je ne sache pas traduire l'ampleur de ce silence, ni la trace qu'il laissait en s'éloignant. C'était un silence comme on en trouve dans une église quand on a la foi et que les mots sont impuissants à traduire ce que l'on ressent.

Jean m'éclairait sur le silence des hommes. Je voulais retracer le chemin pervers qui m'avait menée jusque-là sans parvenir à trouver l'origine de cet illogisme. La foudre ?

Encore un coup de cette maudite foudre ?

Une épreuve de force s'était engagée :

Je voulais apprivoiser le silence de Jean.

Je voulais le débloquer, le réconcilier avec les mots.

Je voulais des mots plutôt que des soupirs.

Je voulais des mots et des soupirs.

Je voulais qu'il oublie ses peurs, ses névroses, les raisons de son mutisme.

Je voulais qu'il prenne goût au batifolage, au bavardage, au savonnage, aux massages, à l'eau tiède, aux corps mouillés et collés, aux confidences sur l'oreiller, aux mots d'amour petits et grands.

Je voulais qu'il cède.

Je voulais l'entendre m'appeler Chérie, Darling, Amour, Bibiche, Bichette, Idylle, Didylle ; n'importe quel surnom, aussi ridicule fût-il, aurait fait l'affaire.

Je voulais qu'il griffonne, qu'il téléphone, qu'il poste, qu'il envoie des fleurs, des cœurs, des baisers.

Je voulais qu'il parle.

Oui, parle-moi.

Donne des mots.

Je voulais le contaminer, l'emmener de mon côté ; côté bruit, côté vie. Côté effusions, profusion et fusion.

Parfois, de mauvaises pensées s'installaient comme des parasites dans la pureté du silence. Et si Jean continuait à faire l'amour sans passion parce qu'il est un homme comme tous les autres ?

Frisson.

La vie, si c'en était une, ne se déroulait plus qu'à l'intérieur de moi. Une sorte d'autarcie. Même le goût de la musique, des lieder de Mahler et des mazurkas de Chopin, m'avait désertée pour me laisser seule avec son silence. Avec ce fatras d'ondes sans harmonie, d'émotions sans mélodie, de musique pourtant. Musique sacrée, musique spirituelle, légère, classique, moderne, folklorique, musique de danse, musique de scène, musique de chambre. Composition, arrangement, harmonisation, improvisation, transcription, transposition. Mon récital à moi n'a pas besoin de notes pour être transposé. Un homme silencieux c'est comme un livre à écrire.

C'est courir derrière quelque chose qui se dérobe tout le temps.

C'est une spécialité pour rêveur.

J'étais une rêveuse, je venais de le découvrir.

Et, secrètement, je prenais goût à ce voyage, cette intensité, cette fixation sur un seul point qui annihilait tous les autres, cette immatérialité qui me protégeait des atteintes du temps.

J'étais bloquée.

Plus qu'un amour, il était devenu une obsession, une interrogation, peut-être une solution métaphysique contre le vide.

La confusion résidait là. Mais quel amour pouvait se vanter de puiser sa source dans cette absence de signes qui le révèlent ?

Qu'importait l'origine ? L'ivresse était.

Pour rejoindre Jean, j'entrai en silence. Mais qu'est-ce que je savais de ses silences excessifs ? Rien.

Au fond, je ne sais pas pourquoi un homme ne dit

rien. J'avais cherché des explications dans des livres, du côté de Duras dans *Lol V. Stein* quand Tatiana tout à coup s'écrie : « Ah ces mots, tu devrais te taire, ces mots quel danger ! », de Peter Handke pour qui seul le marcheur silencieux « se rattrape et s'atteint lui-même », La Rochefoucauld pour qui le « silence est le parti le plus sûr de celui qui se défie de soi-même », chez les analystes dont une méthode consiste à se servir du silence. Tous les silences appartiennent à Jean. Les silences refuges, les silences de fuite. Le silence des séducteurs, des lâches, des peureux, des timides, des complexés, des paresseux, des mufles, des incultes, des cons. Le silence des savants, des puissants, des initiés, des dirigeants ne lui était pas étranger. Mais Jean connaissait aussi les silences prioritaires : le silence des philosophes, le silence contre les artifices et la dissi-mulation que sont la parole, le chant et même la musique, destinés à nous guérir de l'angoisse d'être.

Toutes les zones où le silence s'installe étaient à lui.

Je comprenais Jean par bribes, par à-coups, par com-paraison, je ne le comprenais pas tout entier. Il est impossible de comprendre une personne parfaitement.

Jean était le show-room du silence des hommes, une palette, un éventail. Tous les silences étaient en lui. Il était le plus grand collectionneur de silences. D'ail-leurs, je ne pouvais plus lire une phrase qui contenait le mot silence sans la lui attribuer. Jamais auparavant je n'avais remarqué combien le silence pouvait être présent, pervers, bruyant, utile, éloquent dans nos vies.

Comprendre ne guérit pas. Les psys le savent, ils en conviennent, même s'ils ne le disent pas toujours.

Son silence, je ne le comprenais pas toujours, mais je le lisais ainsi :

Les mots formulés te trahissent-ils ? Redoutes-tu les mots impuissants à combler la distance entre ta pensée et sa manifestation ? Tu ne sais pas articuler ? Les mots, un jour, t'ont blessé, tes propres mots se sont retournés contre toi, tu as été piégé, tes mots gentils ont été utilisés à ton insu, ils ont été galvaudés, trahis, récupérés, dévoilés, publiés, répétés, utilisés. Ton secret un jour a été mis à nu, négocié, partagé avec d'autres, amis ou ennemis.

On s'est moqué de toi, de ta tendresse. Tu es fâché avec les mots, ils sont tes adversaires ? Alors tu n'es pas en guerre contre l'amour, mais contre les mots de l'amour. Extérieurement cela revient au même, le sais-tu ? Si, à force de contradiction entre ton corps et tes silences, je ne parviens pas mieux à te lire, je m'en irai, un jour.

Mais il appelait et j'oubliais mes interrogations, mes revendications ; je cédais.

Sa voix me transformait, ses mots, même factuels, m'éclairaient, l'amertume disparaissait. La vie devenait simple.

Le silence est pervers. Le silence m'avait embarquée.

Je me suis juré qu'un jour je parviendrai à faire parler ce mec ! J'en ferai une pie, une pipelette même, une commère, une mauvaise langue ! Il ne pourra plus s'arrêter de bavasser. Trêve de plaisanterie, je suis parfois si frustrée que j'imagine ma psy me demandant « dans quel schéma antérieur la difficulté me replonge ». Tu sais, le genre de question qui occupe quatre années de ta vie et dont la résolution ne te guérit même pas.

E-MAIL DE CLÉMENTINE À IDYLLE

Je vais te faire économiser quarante-deux séances de psy : tu n'as jamais eu de peine de cœur ; depuis l'école secondaire, tu as du succès avec les hommes, alors tu profites du premier beau ténébreux pour aller voir à quoi ressemblent les tourments de l'amour ! Mais c'est embêtant, tu es un peu vieille pour un chagrin ; comme pour les oreillons, la scarlatine et la varicelle, ces saloperies-là, il vaut mieux les attraper enfant et devant le poster de Harrison Ford.

Toi qui adores parler au lit jusqu'à trois heures du matin, je te pronostique déjà une frustration assurée ! Idylle, crois-moi, zappe tant qu'il en est encore temps. Le chagrin d'amour, ne t'y aventure pas, je te le raconterai en Technicolor !!!

Révolte sur la ligne 63

Paul, mon jeune collègue, est venu m'apporter sa thèse que j'ai aussitôt égarée. Puis le directeur de l'établissement m'a fait part de sa retraite prochaine et de sa tristesse d'arrêter « en pleine force de l'âge ». Peu m'importe, je suis restée muette, incapable de compatir, pressée seulement de monter dans le bus et de retrouver Jean dans le silence où je l'avais laissé.

J'évite tout ce qui contrarie la musique du silence. J'aime ce silence où Jean s'étire à son aise. J'aime qu'il prenne toute la place. Le silence, c'est lui.

Je glisse, je sombre, la tête me tourne un peu, j'ai l'impression d'avoir fumé de bon matin. Le silence m'enivre, il m'ensorcelle, me hante, me féconde, m'isole, m'éclaire. Les choses de la terre existent bien peu et pourtant je sais qu'un jour, je ne pourrai m'empêcher de lui demander :

« Qu'est-ce qui se passe, dans ta tête ? »

Tu es bien enraciné dans cette saleté de silence, là, à repousser les mots qui te montent à la gorge, à les ravaler, à les étouffer, c'est si dur que ça de parler quand on est un homme ?

Il faut du courage pour abandonner une parcelle de soi à une femme et tu n'as pas ce courage.

Je pourrais t'appeler sur « ta ligne » puisque, malgré tes restrictions de départ, tu me l'as donnée, mais tu me contamines, tu m'intimides, tu m'étouffes et me bâillonnes et j'ai peur des mots, à présent, peur de leur imprécision, du ridicule d'être seule à me dévoiler.

Ton silence ment aussi parfois, ton silence masque, joue et dissimule parce que tu triches avec toi-même.

Arrogance du silence, avarice du silence, couardise du silence.

Tu gardes presque tout et, entre ce que tu me donnes, je dois faire le marché, choisir les fruits les moins empoisonnés, la parcelle de vérité que malgré toi tu as laissé percer.

On pourrait confondre rareté et qualité : faux.

Tes mots sont parfois piégés et contredisent tes gestes, tes mots et tes gestes sont désunis. Quand tu donnes, c'est dans le désordre de ta pensée furieuse d'être submergée par moi, je n'ai qu'à me débrouiller avec le fatras, qu'à prendre ce qui est lisible tout en sachant que si les mots m'éclairent trop, tu me les reprendras d'une contradiction, d'un contresens quelques instants ou quelques jours plus tard.

Tu apparais partout, entre les lignes, entre les points, dans l'ordinateur, sous la table et dans l'ennui que les autres génèrent. Je pensais que les gens restaient dans nos mémoires par leurs mots, leurs écrits, leurs chansons ; tu restes par les ondes, la sensation, le sentiment, le geste, par l'air et le vent que tu déplaces. Le vent souffle. Bourrasque de silence, le vide tourbillonne et moi avec.

Je ne dis rien, tu m'obliges au silence.

Tu mènes le jeu et je te suis.

Silence de peureuse, silence de pleureuse, silence de perdante, silence de dominée, silence de vaincue, silence de copieuse, de suiveuse, silence prison, silence bâillon, silence détesté et adoré ; je ne sais pas comment me rebeller. Je ne sais pas par quel bout prendre le silence, le silence n'a ni commencement ni fin : il est infini. Il n'a ni corps ni matière. Je veux protester, mais contre quoi, en fait ?

Un jour, je parlerai à ne plus pouvoir m'arrêter, un jour je te dirai les mots tus, je les jetterai au hasard, sans savoir s'ils répondent à ton silence. Quand je parlerai, la partie sera achevée.

L'arrêt du bus 63 est face à l'épicier. Ce soir, je vais acheter des pâtes, des tomates, de la crème fraîche, du parmesan, de l'ail et une bouteille de vin rouge italien fruité et me réaccoutumer aux rires, aux confidences, aux vacheries, aux taquineries, aux facilités, à la réalité, je vais inviter Laurent ou Lionel, un homme, juste pour parler.

Répondeur : cinq messages.
Premier message : Paul :
« Est-ce que vous avez eu le temps de commencer
à lire ma thèse ? Je suis impatient de vous parler. »

Deuxième message : le secrétariat du lycée :
« Bonjour ! Mme Charras au téléphone. Est-ce que
vous voulez bien venir au pot organisé pour le directeur le jeudi 31 et participer au cadeau d'adieu ? »

Troisième message : la voisine du dessous :
« Ma chère Idylle : mon fils doit commenter la
phrase suivante de Hegel : "Le destin est la conscience
de soi-même, mais comme un ennemi." Panique à la
maison. Tout le monde sèche, vous seule pouvez nous
sauver. Je vous en supplie, venez, c'est vendredi, j'ai
acheté des soles toutes fraîches au marché, on dînera
à la cuisine. »

Quatrième message : Karl Vatteau, galeriste rue de
Seine :
« Idylle, vous ne m'avez pas répondu pour le dîner
de demain soir. Pas de réponse, bonne réponse,
n'est-ce pas ? Je compte sur vous, ce sera un buffet,
on sera une soixantaine. »

Le silence des hommes

Le message le plus important :

Bip, bip... Le silence. Jean est assurément derrière ce silence qui dure quelques secondes avant qu'il ne raccroche. Je réécoute : une respiration ? même pas. Un grésillement ? peut-être. J'en suis là. À traquer les respirations et les grésillements.

Je ramasse les miettes.

E-MAIL DE CLÉMENTINE À IDYLLE

Idylle, tu n'es pas son thérapeute, laisse tomber ! Tu y perdras ta santé, mais tu ne le feras pas parler.

E-MAIL D'IDYLLE À CLÉMENTINE

Au lieu d'être défaitiste, aide-moi à trouver les questions auxquelles il ne pourra s'empêcher de répondre !

E-MAIL DE CLÉMENTINE À IDYLLE

Dis-lui que tu as croisé sa femme chez le coiffeur et que vous avez eu une longue conversation... Et tu verras comme il va s'acharner... pour te faire parler !

E-MAIL D'IDYLLE À CLÉMENTINE

Trouve autre chose.

E-MAIL DE CLÉMENTINE À IDYLLE

– Tu as ta braguette ouverte.
– Tu as reçu une lettre ici...
– C'est toi l'« amoureux anonyme » qui m'envoie des fleurs tous les jours ?

E-MAIL D'IDYLLE À CLÉMENTINE

Tu es de la vraie graine de salope ! Mais tu n'as rien compris, je ne vis pas une blague sortie de chez Farces et Attrapes ; je vis un amour différent, mais un amour !

E-MAIL DE CLÉMENTINE À IDYLLE

Raison de plus pour qu'il te le dise !

Le dîner

Voilà que pour la seconde fois un galeriste, que la recherche d'éventuels clients entraînait à brasser large parmi sa liste de relations, favorisa notre improbable réunion publique.

Talons aiguilles, mousseline et brillant à lèvres beige rosé. T-shirt Petit Bateau et coupe trash pour le style.

Il était là, derrière moi, dans mon dos, je n'avais même pas besoin de me retourner pour le savoir. Il m'irradiait.

Je restais sans bouger, n'écoutant plus rien d'autre que le bruit de ses pas qui se rapprochaient, hésitants.

Quand il m'a contournée pour me saluer, je fus surprise. Son attitude en public m'était inconnue.

C'est toujours une sensation étrange que de rencontrer l'homme du secret en plein jour. Une femme l'accompagnait, la sienne je suppose, costume de jour pour le soir, hésitante sur ses mules, corps massif, visage marqué d'une mère de famille qui n'a pas toujours eu la vie facile. Le même âge que lui.

Il ne feignait pas de ne pas me reconnaître, au contraire, il s'avança vers moi avec plus de chaleur que dans mon studio, c'était moins dangereux et très efficace. Il s'éloigna de son épouse qui continua de me sourire avec bienveillance. Quel monstre était-il ?

Si l'inconfort de la situation ne m'avait pas procuré le désir d'expier mes péchés, j'aurais compati, j'aurais volé au secours de cette femme, mais il me rendait cruelle et égoïste à mon tour.

Jean et moi n'étions pas à la même table. Tant mieux.

Je concentrais toute mon attention à ne pas le regarder, à résister à ce courant qui m'entraînait vers lui. À retrouver mon rôle de gibier que l'on convoite et qui se dérobe.

J'essayais d'écouter mon voisin, d'avoir l'air attentive lorsqu'il évoquait ses activités. Les miennes n'avaient plus beaucoup d'importance en ce moment.

Parfois, je me souvenais que j'étais professeur de lettres, qu'il s'agissait d'un dîner, que mon assiette était pleine, que de temps en temps il fallait porter ma fourchette à ma bouche.

Les aliments n'avaient pas de saveur, j'aurais pu mastiquer du plastique plutôt que du saumon.

Il était à deux pas. Assis derrière moi. Impossible d'oublier sa présence et le souvenir de nos moments.

J'aurais laissé toute cette assemblée pour le suivre

sous les draps, pour être avec lui, n'importe où, loin du monde.

Pour me libérer de mon voisin gris et du saumon rose.

Je me serais levée, j'aurais fait virevolter les volants de ma jupe en mousseline s'il m'avait demandé de le suivre. Comme dans un film.

Je les aurais tous quittés.

Mais il ne connaît pas les mots « viens », « on part », « ça suffit », « le cirque a assez duré », « je t'emmène », « je t'ai trop attendue », « on perd notre temps, notre vie », il ne sait même pas qu'ils existent.

Il redoute le laisser-aller. Aller, aller, aller, jusqu'où peut-on se laisser aller ?

Danger.

Lionel, qui étudie la médecine, m'a assuré l'autre soir, entre deux bouchées de spaghettis, que l'homme méchant est celui qui a peur. Jean serait-il un homme méchant ? Toute cette difficulté d'être ne serait-elle que la décevante conséquence d'une mauvaise nature ?

Et moi, j'en suis arrivée à la situation absurde qui consiste à simuler l'indifférence pour ne pas l'effrayer. Parce que c'est dans mon recul qu'il trouve l'envie de s'élancer.

Pour l'apercevoir, je me rends au buffet accompagnée par le moins rébarbatif de mes voisins de table.

Je minaude, cligne de l'œil, penche la tête, souris,

faussement embarrassée, moi aussi je sais jouer. Mes roucoulements sont destinés à l'agacer.

J'ai l'air d'être au buffet, de tenir une assiette en attendant d'être servie, alors que dans ma tête je suis avec lui, soulagée que la pénurie de femmes ce soir lui impose deux hommes comme voisins.

Je ris à mauvais escient, et si autour de moi on me prend pour une idiote, je m'en fiche, du moment que Jean m'imagine gaie.

Demain, encore plus tôt que prévu, il sonnera à ma porte.

Je dois m'asseoir. Trop d'émotions. Un tambour résonne dans ma cage thoracique, frappe entre mes côtes. J'étouffe, il n'y a plus d'air dans cette salle, je tremble, « il fait chaud ? dites-vous » et moi j'ai froid, oui, je sais, je suis bizarre, j'ai froid quand tout le monde a chaud, je suis pire que ça, si vous saviez... mais je ne peux rien vous confier, d'ailleurs je ne me livre à personne, à Clémentine un peu, mais elle se moque. Je ne peux rien dire parce que l'homme que j'aime ne me dit rien.

C'est étrange, non ?

Il n'est pas très loin de moi, il est avec sa femme, mais je ne suis pas jalouse de sa vie, je la trouve très bien sa femme, je ne veux pas lui prendre ce qu'elle a, juste ce qu'elle n'a plus.

J'aimerais que le silence soit un choix, pas une ruse d'homme coupable.

Jamais il ne dit : « Nous sommes amants. »

Qu'est-ce que nous sommes ? Nous ne sommes pas.

Il s'arrange ainsi.

Il fait.

Il ne qualifie pas ses gestes.

Ce qui n'a pas de nom n'existe pas.

Ce silence magnifique, ce silence qui me porte et que j'habite ne serait-il qu'une hypocrisie d'homme marié ?

Je ne réclame pas des mots officiels, je ne veux ni enfants, ni alliance. Cette vie-là ne m'intéresse pas. Je ne veux pas terminer dans une Range Rover, assise à côté d'un conducteur qui serait *mon mari*, le mot me fait rire, à tourner le bouton de la radio, à faire taire des gosses hurlants aux doigts pleins de confiture à l'arrière, à prier pour que le labrador n'avale pas le rôti prédécoupé en fines tranches rangé dans le coffre.

Non, j'ai envie d'être une maîtresse toute ma vie, je veux avoir le cœur qui bat, je veux un homme qui me soulève en arrivant. Un homme qui me plaque contre le mur et qui m'embrasse comme jamais personne n'a été embrassé. Je veux un homme qui baise tout mon corps avec tout le sien, un homme qui renifle partout comme une bête, un homme animal. Un homme qui glisse ses mains dans ma culotte dès qu'il me voit. Un homme qui enlève ses chaussettes pour que je lui baise les pieds et que je remonte jusqu'à son sexe. Un homme qui aime les odeurs, les moiteurs, un homme qui lèche, qui avale, qui perce, mais un homme qui ne s'exprime pas qu'avec son corps.

J'aime ses dents, j'aime la pâte et le crin qui les frottent, j'aime qu'il se lave à côté de moi, j'aime qu'il soupèse son sexe et fasse mousser le savon entre ses poils, j'aime son désordre, ses bruits quand il recrache l'eau après l'avoir fait tourner dans sa bouche, j'aime ses gestes d'homme, cette façon brutale de faire coulisser la serviette dans son dos, de se baisser pour essuyer les gouttes prisonnières de ses jambes, ce qui m'effraye c'est la passion qui se détend, le quotidien qui calme et rassure. J'aime l'urgence, l'inquiétude, le commencement qui ne s'arrête pas. J'aime quand l'étreinte efface la douleur.

J'aime que l'inquiétude reprenne quand il part.

J'aime que le silence continue. Pas de transition ; qu'il soit là ou pas, toujours la même musique résonne dans mes oreilles.

Je ne suis bonne à rien ; bonne qu'à lui.

Une femme qui aime l'amour n'aime l'amour qu'avec un seul homme. Ils peuvent se succéder, jamais se cumuler.

Une femme qui aime un homme ne l'enferme pas forcément dans des définitions, des explications, des précisions. Elle accepte ses manières, ses gestes, sa loi. Je ne le veux que pour l'étreinte.

Il vient pour aimer. Il vient pour faire, pas pour dire.

Ensemble, nous faisons.

Je suis une maîtresse.

J'embrasse, je caresse, je m'enroule autour de lui, je le reçois partout où il veut venir quand il veut venir. Je ne parle pas s'il ne veut pas, je m'agenouille, je m'accroupis, je lève ou écarte mes jambes quand il le demande. Je me retourne, je donne mon corps et mon esprit, je me donne en silence, comme il me l'a appris.

Je me donne comme il le désire.

Mon voisin de table a l'air de m'écouter, je ne sais pas ce que je lui ai dit.

Depuis longtemps je ne dis plus ce qui m'habite.

Ce qui m'habite est un secret.

Un secret qui ne se verbalise pas.

Mon amant a tendu une corde entre nous et ne cesse de tirer dessus.

La corde est près de céder.

S'il avait été un chien, il aurait été un fugueur, s'il avait été une femme, il aurait été une garce, une vraie saloperie de garce, mais il est un homme, un homme qui s'économise, un trouillard, un mec peu sympathique qui exécute la danse des sept voiles, qui excelle dans l'art de se taire, de se refuser, comme une starlette capricieuse et ridicule devant le producteur stupéfait. Il m'accule dans un rôle qui incombe plutôt aux hommes. Il ne me manque plus que le cigare.

Le mien est un brave mec. Il n'a jamais joué avec le silence. Le silence lui est tombé dessus comme la foudre. Le silence l'a anéanti.
S'il avait été un chien ? Il aurait été un labrador. Oui, un beau gros golden qui ne court plus assez.

Négociations

Quand j'ai quitté le dîner, son regard m'a suivie jusqu'à la sortie. Quand un regard me suit, je le sais, il me réchauffe les mollets.

Le lendemain, ravivé par le décalage entre notre intimité secrète et la retenue à laquelle les circonstances nous avaient contraints, il a appelé tôt le matin. Trop tôt peut-être.

Classique.

Il viendrait me voir en début d'après-midi. Il ne me prévient pas à l'avance, lui non plus, il ne se prévient pas longtemps à l'avance, sinon il agirait autrement. J'ai refusé. Mais les hommes savent toujours quand on dit « non » en pensant « oui ».

Normal.

« Non », lui dis-je sur le ton de la vindicte. Une tasse de thé à la main, le combiné de l'autre, j'étais agacée qu'il ne me pose jamais une question sur ma vie, sur ma santé, et qu'il prenne rendez-vous, comme pour aller chez le dentiste ou dans un bordel chic.

– Non ?

Il n'en revient pas, il en a le souffle coupé.

– Je suis occupée.

– À deux heures !

– Oui.

– Décommande.

J'adore qu'il me donne un ordre, alors je pose ma tasse de thé, j'oublie le sort commun à toutes les rencontres, le hasard nécessaire, et je me dis, non sans grandiloquence, que seul le destin pouvait avoir instruit les conditions de ce rendez-vous mystérieux dans les jardins des Champs-Élysées, allée Marcel-Proust. Et je cédai, pas à lui, je cédai à mon envie de le voir.

E-MAIL D'IDYLLE À CLÉMENTINE

J'ai envie de lui réciter des poèmes pour le réconcilier avec les mots.

E-MAIL DE CLÉMENTINE À IDYLLE

Tu es folle !
En fait, je ne sais de quel droit je te conseille. Je suis dans le même cas que toi. À la seule différence que moi, je ne l'ai pas choisi muet.
Et si larguer le mien après huit ans serait cruel, je ne comprends pas ce qui te retient !

Visite numéro 5

Il s'est assis en face de moi, le regard abattu, le verbe pauvre et l'interrogation limitée à la forme de mes chaussures et à la manière de faire le café. Oui, c'est cela, si je me souviens bien de ce fragment de discours amoureux : il soupesait la passion comme une marchandise dont il n'avait pas encore décidé si elle était bonne ou néfaste à sa santé fragile.

Il a bien dit : « Ton café est mauvais, tu devrais acheter une machine. » Ce furent ses termes, exactement.

Le mufle.

Je ne bois que du thé, mais pour lui j'achèterai une machine. Pour lui, je courrai chez Darty à peine sera-t-il parti, donc très bientôt.

La cloche.

Il dit : « Je n'aime pas tes chaussures. »

Le mufle.

Je les enlève immédiatement et je lui promets de les jeter, d'ailleurs elles ne m'ont coûté *que* cent cinquante euros, soit quelques heures de cours particuliers patiemment dispensés à mon petit voisin du quatrième étage.

Aucune importance.

La cloche.

Elle est heureuse, la cloche, de cette intrusion dans sa vie privée, heureuse, oui, qu'il s'intéresse à la manière dont elle se chausse même pour la désapprouver, ravie qu'il émette un avis sur son café, même pour le critiquer.

Oui, oui.

Les mufles et les cloches font bon ménage, parfois.

À la manière des pigeons et des garces. Histoire de névroses qui se retrouvent, se complètent et se reconnaissent.

Nos névroses roucoulent ; comme c'est touchant ! Je suis à deux doigts de le remercier pour ces délicieuses remarques.

Il sourit, satisfait de ma soumission, satisfait de cette résistance passive à son agressivité puérile.

Il a encore remporté un round, bravo, *bravissimo* ; il est super fort et je suis super faible.

À moins que je ne sois amoureuse et pas lui ?

Trop tôt pour se miner le moral.

Car la roue tourne, en amour comme dans le reste.

Pour l'instant, je ne suis pas très loin de penser qu'il a raison. Que rien n'est assez bien pour le recevoir, surtout pas moi ni ma maison.

Il est toujours sérieux.

Mes souliers et le café doivent le contrarier. J'en suis désolée ; je cache les groles à talons compensés, un peu hautes, il est vrai, mais aucun talon n'est assez élevé pour atteindre les cimes où je l'ai placé.

Il n'a pas aimé me voir parler avec un homme l'autre soir chez le galeriste, j'en suis certaine, mais il ne le dit pas.

Macho classique.

Peut-être est-il là grâce à mon voisin de table ?

Les garces, même s'il le réfute, le font plus vibrer que les cloches.

Je vais tâcher de m'appliquer.

Il se tient la tête, il soupire, du genre « il vaudrait mieux ne plus se voir », « où tout cela va nous entraîner », « on va faire du mal », « on va se faire du mal », etc.

Bien vu.

Il dit :

– Il faudrait prendre une décision.

Laquelle ? il ne précise pas ; trop compliqué, trop long à formuler, il faut le comprendre.

Cela pourrait être : « Il faudrait rompre », à moins que ce soit : « Il faudrait vivre ensemble. »

Ni l'une ni l'autre situation ne me convient, cette phrase ne présage rien de bon. Grâce au conditionnel, rien n'est décidé, tout est hypothétique.

Sauvée par le conditionnel ? Le conditionnel peut-il dans un futur proche se transformer en une forme impérative et négative du présent immédiat ?

Exemple : il faut rompre ? Je bafouille, je ne sais

pas, la solution ne se trouve dans aucun manuel de grammaire. Et je ne possède pas la moindre jurisprudence sur l'affaire du conditionnel. Non, pas un de mes hommes ne l'a utilisé dans cette situation.

– Hum ?

Ce « Hum »-là, je ne le comprends pas bien non plus. Sinon le ton interrogatif qui l'accompagne et qui pourrait vouloir dire : « Qu'en penses-tu ? » Il serait donc du genre mufle délicat. Il veut rompre, mais avec mon assentiment, un truc rare, une espèce d'animal peureux, pas très agressif, qui se protège devant l'adversité et se contente d'attaquer les chaussures et le café plutôt que la femme qu'il aime et redoute pour cette raison-là.

Il doit être du genre à ouvrir son carnet plusieurs fois par jour, à la lettre I de mon prénom faussement prédestiné, sans m'appeler pour autant ; heureux d'avoir éprouvé sa capacité de résistance, heureux de cette petite victoire sur ses sens, sur sa vie.

À l'onomatopée succède un soupir bruyant.

Traduction évidente.

Il me prend par la main et m'attire contre lui.

Langage universel.

Contradiction avec son maigre discours.

Le pire, c'est mon aveuglement, mon enfermement, aussi confus que soient ses propos, mon esprit jadis critique et même moqueur ne réagit plus.

J'ose à peine :

– Tu n'es pas logique.

– Pourquoi faudrait-il être logique ?

– Ah ?

Bien sûr, je n'avais pas pensé à cette éventualité.

Il utilise peu de mots pour répondre, mais ils suffisent.

Rébellion maîtrisée.

Il ne me laisse aucun moment de répit. Dès que je ne comprends plus le silence, dès que le silence me décourage, il consent à laisser filer quelques paroles, il lâche du lest, soucieux de garder sa petite camarade de jeux. Des filles aussi masochistes que moi, ça s'entretient. Pourtant, je regrette de ne pouvoir lui parler de la cuisine et des massages thaïs, du dernier film aimé : *In the mood for love*, de cet engouement pour la culture asiatique, de vouloir connaître son avis sur la valeur curative de la philosophie. Le training mental ; la rencontre avec soi largement développée dans les journaux ne risquait-elle pas d'aboutir à un enfermement égoïste et appauvrissant ? Mais comment envisager le monde avec ses questions économiques et politiques, les faits divers qui nous touchent, ceux qui nous divertissent, avant de nous envisager nous-mêmes ? Comment entretenir une relation avec un homme sans connaître son métier, ses passions, ses lieux de vacances, ses opinions politiques, savoir s'il aime la marche, le ski, le tennis, la mer ou la campagne, s'il redoute la chaleur ou le froid, s'il a des frères et des sœurs. Était-il bon élève ? Dort-il nu ou en pyjama, avec ou sans le bas, est-ce qu'il regarde les infos avant de s'endormir ? Aime-t-il danser, les Marx Brothers le font-ils rire ? Ses parents sont-ils toujours vivants ?

Moi : air interrogateur de circonstance.

Lui :

— Hier soir, chez Vatteau, nous avons dîné tous les deux...

Drôle de conception du dîner d'amoureux.

— En quelque sorte...

Cela signifie-t-il qu'il a ressenti une attirance proche de la mienne ?

— Parle, formule des phrases entières, dis des choses concrètes, dis ! Non, hier soir, nous n'avons pas dîné ensemble, oui, il faut être logique, non, tu ne peux pas m'aimer et ne jamais me le dire ! Non, tu ne peux pas venir et partir, me prendre et me laisser ! Pourquoi tu es comme ça ?

Alors, il se rétracte et le silence le reprend.

Moi :

— Dis...

Lui : rien.

Moi :

— Tu ne vas pas t'arrêter là, même si tu ne dis pas les bons mots, tu es en progrès. Parole, j'allais te féliciter...

Lui : il sourit, des rides courent sur son visage. Il est irrésistible quand il sourit.

Moi :

— Tu vois que ce n'est pas si difficile de parler. Tu ouvres la bouche, tu émets des sons. Veille juste à ce que tes sons soient plus agréables. Allez, dis quelque chose...

Lui : silence.

Moi :

– La mouche tsé-tsé, c'est le silence ou le sommeil ?

Lui : un regard.

Moi : un soupir.

Moi :

– On est repartis...

Lui : un soupir profond.

Moi : j'attends... Quelque chose devrait sortir de ses profondeurs.

Enfin il ouvre la bouche, l'air convaincu.

Rien.

Moi :

– Sais-tu qu'il existe des mots aussi beaux que le silence ?

Lui :

– Hum.

Encore ce borborygme, qui a aidé des générations de psys à ponctuer leurs discours, à mettre en confiance, à encourager, comprendre, menacer même parfois. Borborygme fourre-tout, celui du grand bazar, des incompréhensions et des aveux embarrassants.

– Écoute.

Et voilà qu'à court d'arguments, je me mets à parler doucement, à citer Valéry pour le convaincre de la

beauté et de l'intérêt du verbe, puisque le mien n'y
suffit pas. J'en suis là.

— Écoute :

« Ce toit tranquille, où marchent des colombes,
Entre les pins palpite, entre les tombes ;
Midi le juste y compose de feux la mer,
La mer, toujours recommencée ! »

— Il n'y a pas de quoi te réconcilier avec les mots ?
Les mots aussi peuvent être infinis, comme l'air,
comme la mer, comme le silence. Non ?

— Hum.

« Hum » de méfiance.

— On a une symphonie tous les deux dans la tête,
mais pas la même. Quelle mélodie t'habite ? celle des
chiffres, celle des notes de musique, dis-moi quelles
sont tes notes.

« Non, tu ne veux pas le dire ? Tu gardes ta romance
rien que pour toi ? Écoute encore, juste une phrase
cette fois, mais si belle que je pourrais me la répéter
des milliards de fois.

« Je me la répète des milliards de fois, parfois :

« Le silence assourdissant d'aimer. »

« C'est simple et magnifique, n'est-ce pas ? tu es
ému ? Cela t'arrive d'être ému par des mots ? Répète,
commence doucement, insiste sur les deux *s*, tu verras,

les sons se baladent comme entre les lignes d'une partition. Tu chantes, même si tu ne sais pas chanter. Cela t'arrive de chanter ? Dans ton bain ou sous ta douche, jamais ? Tu fredonnes seulement dans les jardins publics ?

Il y a des mots de l'extérieur, des mots pour décrire, sans que le sentiment intervienne comme : le canapé blanc, la boîte en coquillages, le briquet, les plantes, l'alcool, les rideaux, le gâteau, les chaussures, le café, la télévision, le portable, l'ordinateur. Il pouvait les mixer, ces mots, à la limite, les mélanger sans prendre le risque de s'engager. Il pouvait me demander si j'étais abonnée à Canal Sat, si je travaillais sur Mac ou sur PC, si je préférais SFR ou Itinéris, le restau chinois ou italien. Des mots, juste des mots, vides de sens profond. Des mots comme des camions qui ne transportent que du matériel, rien de spirituel.

Mais de ces mots-là, il n'en abusait pas non plus. Comme si ces mots pouvaient entraîner l'ouverture des portes de l'âme et qu'une personne pouvait être dévoilée selon qu'elle aimait Liza Ekdahl ou Bartoli, le vin blanc ou le vin rouge, les thrillers ou les mélos. Il s'autorisait le « café », quoi d'autre ? Pas grand-chose.

Lui :

– Pourquoi veux-tu parler ?

Que répondre à cette interrogation ?

Après dix ans d'internat, de confidences, de papotages la nuit avec mes copines de classe, j'avais l'impression d'avoir rencontré un échantillon assez large d'êtres humains. Peut-être pas.

Celui-là était inadapté à une relation normale avec une femme normale.

Sous l'identité d'un ami changerait-il, se permettrait-il de m'appeler tout le temps, tous les jours ?

L'amitié lui était-elle permise et pas l'amour ?

J'attendais ce qu'il ne pouvait pas me donner.

Assis en face de moi, il attrape ma main, embrasse le bout de mes doigts, avec tendresse je crois. Je suis perdue, je ne sais plus ce que je veux, je n'ai plus de mots pour me repérer, notre histoire flotte comme un silence sans commencement ni fin. J'ai besoin de mots autant que d'air et d'eau, alors je lui propose :

— Veux-tu que l'on soit amis ?

Il me regarde, interrogatif.

Qui sait avec les femmes ?

Il guette mes larmes.

Je ne pleure pas.

Il est déçu.

Il est possible qu'il m'ait crue, plus que moi-même. Quel lobe occipital, pariétal, temporal, quelles cellules nerveuses mes mots vont-ils atteindre ? Il me regarde. Ma phrase fait son chemin. Quelle réaction interne déclenche-t-elle ? Quel chemin sinueux de son cerveau ma proposition emprunte-t-elle ?

Cette fois, il devrait réagir, s'insurger, protester. Retenir l'amour, chasser l'amitié.

Mais non, son amour, qui se rassasie d'une broutille, d'un babil, d'un rien, ne s'affole pas pour si peu. Tout ce que je lui ai donné jusqu'à ce jour sert à cet effet : le remplir, le rassurer, lui permettre de s'éloigner repu, heureux peut-être.

Le cortex bloque, le siège de la conscience, de la mémoire, de l'émotion, du langage, de toutes les fonctions supérieures qui tournent au ralenti.

Il résiste, la plus insidieuse des phrases ne déclenche aucune réaction. J'ai envie d'aller chercher dans ma cuisine les brochettes en ferraille rouillée achetées au Maroc, les fourchettes Puiforcat héritées de ma tante et de lui transpercer les mollets puis d'en menacer sa langue s'il ne l'utilise pas immédiatement pour parler et qu'enfin réchauffé le moteur ne s'arrête plus de tourner ! Pour qu'il se livre, se délivre, et moi avec.

Ma proposition ne l'affole pas outre mesure. Une telle décision mérite l'impératif : « Soyons amis », point final. Il le sait. Les silencieux savent beaucoup.

La lèvre supérieure de Jean remonte par légères secousses, je reprends espoir. La crainte de me perdre va-t-elle enfin déclencher un flot de paroles ? Est-il enfin décidé à s'exprimer ? J'attends, accrochée à ses lèvres.

Rien. Quelques secondes passent, je récolte un demi-sourire.

Les mots de l'amitié ne le rendent pas plus loquace.

Visite numéro 6 :
« Je passe prendre un café ? »

Il m'a laissée rompue, puis il est revenu, fidèle à son instabilité, à son angoisse, à sa peur d'aimer, d'être aimé, d'avoir mal, fidèle à ce goût de première et de dernière fois, à cette simultanéité de la naissance et de la mort qu'il insufflait à toutes nos rencontres, jour après jour.

Vers huit heures trente, le téléphone sonne à nouveau.

– Je passe prendre un café ?

Et il ajoute non sans humour : « amicalement », pour s'en convaincre, pour ne pas se dédire et satisfaire tous ses trucs compliqués, toute cette cuisine particulière avec sa conscience.

Les mots sont innocents, les apparences sauves, même si, contre ses principes, il appelle. Confrontée à un tel homme, ma grand-mère italienne aurait levé les yeux au ciel et se serait exclamée : *Mamma mia !*

Et elle aurait eu raison d'implorer sa mère et même le ciel. Que faire d'autre ?

Je ne suis pas loin d'imiter ma grand-mère.

Je meurs d'envie de le voir.

Il vient.

Je lui demande encore une fois :

– Pourquoi es-tu comme ça ?

Pour toute réponse, il me souffle d'une voix vraiment virile et faussement protectrice :

– Je suis là.

Aveu arraché.

Visite de vaincu.

Il y a de l'abandon, de la capitulation, de la faiblesse dans cet amour.

Rien de moins amical que « ce café ».

À peine arrivé, après m'avoir en partie déshabillée, il m'ordonne de me retourner, là tout de suite, sans même atteindre le lit. Ma proposition d'hier a probablement déclenché de la rage et de la révolte, de la fureur, et cela n'est pas pour me déplaire.

À ce prix-là, son esprit laisse triompher son corps.

Et cette colère donne un côté encore plus sauvage à nos ébats.

Je veux le sentir avec tout mon corps, je veux caresser son ventre avec mes seins, je veux l'embrasser dans le cou, je veux le voir, alors je résiste, rebelle à ses intentions, mais il me fait pivoter, agressif, comme tous les perdants.

Moi : « Non. »

Lui : « Si. »

Moi : « Arrête. »

Lui : « Ça va venir vite. »

Et il se répand quelques secondes plus tard.

Il s'excuse, juste un peu.

Il prend l'air désolé, mais pas vraiment.

Il a eu mal, c'était trop fort, dit-il.

Pas d'autres commentaires.

Je comprends.

Les hommes qui m'ont aimée ont été émotifs.

La précipitation est un gage d'amour. Je me méfie des acrobates des premiers jours. Mais cet homme-là ne supporte la comparaison avec aucun autre.

Je me rhabille, je le plains, puisqu'il souffre.

Je l'excuse, puisque je l'aime, je ne proteste pas. Je suis tétanisée, pas humiliée, simplement triste. Je continue de chercher dans mes souvenirs. Aucun point de repère.

À moins que sa précipitation ne traduise ma punition ? Me punir, à sa manière, avant de rompre. Est-il capable d'une chose pareille ?

Oui.

Les séparations se ressemblent toutes, sur un quai de gare ou pas. Lui doit se différencier, bien sûr.

Jean s'est rhabillé, il s'installe sur le canapé blanc en face de moi.

Après l'amour, il m'évite, ne m'approche plus.

Je lui sers une tasse de Nescafé : le temps nécessaire à l'achat d'une machine m'a manqué. Probable qu'il n'apprécie pas, non plus que ce cake au yaourt cuisiné pour lui. Pardon, je n'ai pas encore appris à faire le café autrement et le cake au yaourt est la seule recette de gâteau que je connaisse. Je l'avais apprise dans un livre de Raymond Oliver, *La cuisine est un jeu d'enfant* quand j'étais une petite fille. Mais, pour lui, je vais faire des progrès et me procurer *La pâtisserie est un jeu d'enfant*.

Je me sens gênée, le mutisme après l'amour me donne envie de pleurer. Là, plus que jamais, les mots me manquent ; ces mots qui continuent la chair et prolongent l'étreinte ; ces mots pour amortir le choc, la coupure, la séparation, la retombée. Même un geste peut pallier l'absence de parole, il ne m'offre ni l'un ni l'autre.

Quelle est la signification de ce silence-là, à ce moment précis ?

La pudeur ? le regret ? le désamour ?

Je ne sais plus.

Je regrette mes cambrures, mes assouplissements, ma prosternation, mon offrande, ma docilité, ma dévotion, ma prière.

Je laisse traîner ma main ballante à quelques centimètres de la sienne, il ne l'attrape pas. Il n'y pense pas, à moins qu'il y pense et ne le fasse pas. Possible. Je ne sais pas lire ce silence. Alors, je me fie à ses yeux.

Ses yeux cachent quelque chose de bizarre. Quoi ?

Un peu d'ironie, de prétention, de contentement, de méchanceté.

Il relève le menton, sourit en coin et libère ses pensées :

– Je l'ai fait exprès, dit-il.

Silence. Le mien cette fois.

Mon regard doit exprimer quelque chose de normal : beaucoup d'étonnement, de l'incompréhension, du découragement, de la peine.

– Tu l'as fait exprès ?

– Hum.

Je ne sais pas si j'ai envie de rire ou de pleurer, je ne sais pas ce que cela veut dire pour un homme, s'il s'agit là d'une excuse, d'une vexation, d'une muflerie, d'un trop-plein de désir, vraiment je ne sais pas. Je donne ma langue au chat, au chat qui ne sait pas non plus.

– Pourquoi ?

Impassible, il sourit.

Qu'il s'arrange tout seul pour ne plus m'aimer, je n'y peux rien. Mais je ne veux pas l'aider dans cette quête du désamour, je ne veux plus qu'il m'utilise à cet effet, plus qu'il s'essuie les pieds sur moi. Je ne me sens pas humiliée, juste salie.

Ainsi il aurait fait exprès de mal m'aimer. Aurait-il travesti une préméditation machiavélique en une banale perte de contrôle ? Une manière de prendre sans rien donner. Mais son corps est rebelle et son esprit humain ; son sexe exige et son cœur s'emballe, sa volonté est mise en échec devant cette association.

La raison freine. Elle n'empêche rien.

Et je demeurai là où toutes les femmes se seraient enfuies.

Nos failles s'étaient trouvées ; son besoin de manifester avait rencontré ma docilité. Jamais je n'avais été aussi facile.

J'étais hypnotisée, victimisée comme la dernière des tartes que je ne savais pas cuire ; la coupable, c'était moi.

– Dis-moi pourquoi.

Il a soupiré en haussant légèrement les épaules comme pour dire que la vie est difficile et que lui-même est impuissant face à ses réactions les plus pulsionnelles, puis il a remué la tête en signe de négation pour me signaler que je n'obtiendrais aucune réponse à ma question.

Illogisme

L'effet dévastateur de ses chauds et froids, de ses illogismes, de ses silences lui était indifférent. Mon inquiétude, il ne l'imaginait pas, et s'il l'imaginait, elle lui convenait.

Jean fabriquait une passion. Sans le savoir, il appliquait la recette : la négation de l'amour engendre la passion. Il croyait tuer l'amour alors qu'il l'attisait.

Qui avais-je en face de moi ? Un tortionnaire de l'esprit, un idiot, un catho, un puritain, un homme blessé par la vie, par un passé que je ne connaissais pas, par une mère trop aimante ou pas assez, un névrosé, un fou, un étrange, un résistant, un peureux, un besogneux, un bourgeois, un mari, un père, un responsable, un raisonnable, un homme qui ne savait pas qu'il allait mourir, un déraisonnable alors, un janséniste, un puceau, un naïf, un emmerdeur, un empêcheur, un muet, un homme qui jouait avec le silence, qui l'utilisait comme moyen de défense ou d'attaque, une victime lui aussi ? Je n'en savais rien.

Ce que je savais, c'est que je le voulais. Malgré toutes les embûches qu'il ne cessait de multiplier, je le voulais, plus il inventait de difficultés, plus il établissait des distances, plus je le voulais.

Plus il se taisait, plus je voulais l'entendre.

Il bafouait la vie et moi je voulais lui réapprendre à être clément avec elle. Je voulais le tirer du silence, du vide, de la négation, du néant, du noir, du blanc, du creux, de l'inconnu, de la peur d'aimer, de la tristesse après l'amour. Le sauvetage était hasardeux, je risquais de me perdre dans les méandres du silence, je ne savais pas naviguer dans la signification des choses sans les phrases, dans la musique sans les notes, dans l'amour sans les mots. L'épreuve du silence, je ne la connaissais pas. Je savais du silence qu'il « est d'or », alors que la parole « est d'argent », ma mère me le répétait quand j'étais petite fille. Elle me disait aussi qu'il fallait tourner sept fois sa langue dans sa bouche avant de parler. Le silence pouvait donc, dans bien des cas, être préférable au bavardage. Mais entre nous il ne s'agissait pas de bavardage ; je ne lui voulais pas grand-chose, me semblait-il, juste laisser aller les mots, qu'ils vivent leur vie normale, qu'ils viennent un peu pour dire, pour rassurer, pour faire de nous des humains. Le silence est anormal, terrifiant. J'en étais parfois à espérer des mots aussi agressifs que ses gestes.

Je voulais apprivoiser le silence de cet homme, l'amadouer comme un animal peureux, le sortir de sa coquille comme un bigorneau, de sa tanière comme un ours, l'attirer vers moi doucement, lui apprendre les mots comme à un petit garçon, lui apprendre à dire quand il était heureux et quand il ne l'était pas, à ne pas se mentir, à répondre quand on lui posait une question, à s'intéresser aux autres, à demander de leurs nouvelles, à dire bonjour, au revoir, à bientôt, à appeler quand il l'avait promis, à complimenter, remercier, approuver, à inviter, à offrir, à aimer.

Je serais patiente, je ne me plaindrais pas, je ne ferais pas de gestes brusques, je ne poserais plus de questions, je ne m'impatienterais pas, je l'attendrais là où il pourrait venir, quand il le pourrait.

E-MAIL DE CLÉMENTINE À IDYLLE

Que se passe-t-il ?

E-MAIL D'IDYLLE À CLÉMENTINE

Je ne sais pas.
Je ne comprends pas.

E-MAIL DE CLÉMENTINE À IDYLLE

La névrose est un leurre, cette séduction-là s'effondre la
supercherie à peine dévoilée. Ton jules s'échappe pour
éviter que tu découvres sa vacuité. Il la connaît. Tu ne
dois pas être sa première victime. Tu n'y changeras rien.
Aucun remède ni contre la vacuité ni contre la folie. Si
tu en es là et que tu ne prends pas la poudre d'escam-

111

pette, tu mérites ce qui te pend au nez ! Je te comprends, ils peuvent être séduisants, les tarés. Ils sont énigmatiques, différents, ils s'échappent tout le temps pour revenir vers leur dinguerie. Leur vraie maîtresse, c'est la folie. Je ne préconise qu'une seule solution : la chirurgie ; coupe, sectionne, ablationne, de toute façon le cordon ne transmet rien, cela ne changera pas grand-chose ! C'est étrange, moins on a à perdre et plus c'est difficile de laisser un homme, n'est-ce pas ? Les femmes sont grandioses ! La souffrance, comme le silence, est un puits sans fond, ne joue pas trop avec ce feu-là. Et ne m'abandonne pas au moment des soldes.

E-MAIL D'IDYLLE À CLÉMENTINE

Je n'ai envie de m'habiller que pour lui, si je coupe le cordon, trois pulls et un jean me suffiront.

E-MAIL DE CLÉMENTINE À IDYLLE

Tu es désolante ! Alors, reste en jean et coupe le cordon !

E-MAIL D'IDYLLE À CLÉMENTINE

Je ne sais pas comment on coupe.

Le silence des hommes

E-MAIL DE CLÉMENTINE À IDYLLE

Tu es aussi lâche qu'un homme !
Si tu n'as pas le courage, profite du moment où il va t'appeler pour lui dire que tu as une extinction de voix, que tu ne peux pas parler et que tu le rappelleras dès que ça ira mieux, OK ?
Et, évidemment, tu ne le rappelles plus jamais.

E-MAIL D'IDYLLE À CLÉMENTINE

Et s'il me rappelle ?

E-MAIL DE CLÉMENTINE À IDYLLE

Tu recommences l'opération.

J'ai dit : « Mon amour. »

Un message sur mon répondeur :
Sa voix. Pas celle qui a dit : « Je l'ai fait exprès »,
une autre, toujours rare, bien sûr, une voix qui ne
s'éternise pas non plus mais qui, de manière décidée,
fixe le rendez-vous pour l'amour :
– Je passe prendre un café.
Je pense à Clémentine... Je n'hésite même pas une
seconde, je suis incapable de suivre ses conseils. Je suis
comme une balance qui ne pencherait que d'un côté,
Clémentine est tout en haut, Jean tout en bas.
Pardon Clémentine, à plus tard. Oui je sais, il est
probable que tu me ramasseras en miettes, mais la vie
est, de toute façon, une histoire qui finit mal. Accueil-
lons les bons moments quand ils se présentent.

À treize heures cinquante, avec dix minutes
d'avance, il sonne.
A-t-il oublié ce qui a été ? Je n'ai pas envie de le

115

savoir. Il me tend les bras, je m'y réfugie. Je pose la tête au creux de son épaule, il me serre contre lui. Nous restons ainsi, immobiles, un long moment. Nos corps en éveil parlent leur langage de peau, s'expliquent, se réconcilient, nous les laissons faire.

Ce jour-là, nous entrâmes dans une confrontation étrange, à la frontière de la rupture.

Il m'aimait, fâché contre moi et contre lui, furieux de ce désir que je provoquais et qui l'amenait jusqu'à moi. Et derrière son austérité, derrière ses yeux fermés, derrière son dos, nous nous offrions tous les plaisirs.

Entre deux souffles, entre deux caresses, alors qu'il était débordé par les exigences de mon corps, je profitais de l'instant pour lui murmurer à l'oreille les mots qui l'effrayaient et que je retenais depuis trop longtemps :

« Mon amour », lui dis-je doucement, si doucement que je ne sais pas s'il entendit. Ils étaient si simples ces mots, et si compliqués pour Jean.

Alors, allongée au-dessus de lui, ma bouche posée contre la sienne, mes mains enfouies dans ses cheveux rêches, je répétai les mots interdits.

Pour la première fois, ce mot, pour lui, franchit la barrière de mes rêves : Jean se laissa appeler sans se débattre.

Il n'est pas impossible qu'un court instant il les ait acceptés et aimés, ces mots.

Je ne pourrais pas en jurer, mais je suis presque sûre

de l'avoir entendu murmurer : « chérie », juste une fois, oui : « chérie ».

Une trêve, le temps d'une étreinte.

Puis cet abandon déclencha révolte et colère, ses gestes en attestèrent, et jusque dans l'intimité la plus profonde ce choc de nos deux âmes nous rendit comme des ennemis armés l'un contre l'autre.

Quelque chose de sauvage transparaissait entre nos baisers et nos caresses.

ÇA Y EST, LE CORDON EST SECTIONNÉ ? Je suis fière de toi. Tu saignes ? C'est normal. Dis-toi que tu as échappé au pire. Retrouve Laurent, tu sauras te faire pardonner, j'en suis sûre. Et puis un grand reporter, c'est pratique, il s'éloigne, tu auras un peu peur, tu ne l'auras pas toujours sur le dos, tu seras heureuse de le revoir. Venez tous les deux passer le week-end à Londres, j'ai acheté un lit king-size pour la chambre d'amis...

Visite numéro 8

Il vient après la tragédie. Quelques jours plus tôt, le World Trade Center est parti en fumée. Cet événement qui me laissa incrédule et révoltée devant le poste de télévision il n'y fit allusion en ma présence qu'une seule fois. Aussi incontournable que fût l'actualité, ensemble, elle ne nous concernait pas. Le pas en avant qu'il exécutait, le mot qu'il s'aventurait à prononcer, l'intensité d'un baiser, ces choses-là, bien plus que les nouvelles du monde, gouvernaient notre vie. L'extérieur n'avait pas de prise sur nous, nous n'en faisions pas partie. Notre vie commune, à vrai dire « nos moments communs », se déroulait hors de la réalité, entre deux parenthèses que jamais nous n'oubliions de refermer.

Il pousse la porte et je suis transportée ailleurs ; moi qui déborde de mots sans lui, je fais le vide, je deviens aphone, muette, décervelée, lobotomisée, sans esprit de répartie, inhabitée, absente à la misère du monde, à toutes les misères, même les miennes. Je fais le vide pour lui, pour lui laisser la place, toute la place, pour être envahie, débordée, pour ne rien perdre, pas une petite parcelle de sa peau, de son souffle, de son humeur, de son temps. Pour le recevoir et qu'il n'y ait que lui en moi, sans parasite. Je chasse tout ce qui peut encombrer. Je ne suis qu'un cœur qui bat, une femme qui vibre.

Il m'embrasse à sa manière à lui, il m'embrasse comme si on allait mourir, je sens les battements de son cœur contre le mien : « C'est l'escalier », dit-il en souriant pour que je ne m'imagine pas que ce soit l'émotion. Puis il s'éloigne de moi comme s'il voulait me protéger de lui-même, comme s'il allait me faire du mal et qu'il tentait d'y remédier.

Les autres cas de figure sont banals, un homme qui m'aime et qui me désire, c'est normal, un homme qui ne m'aime pas et ne me désire pas n'a aucun intérêt.

Il m'approche.

Il recule.

Il n'a pas le temps ?

Sa femme est derrière la porte ?

La culpabilité le reprend ?

Que se passe-t-il ?

Une autre forme de punition est-elle en préparation ? Il ne me pardonnera donc plus jamais de lui avoir proposé l'amitié ?

Est-ce vraiment une chance de tomber sur un tel homme ? Jamais je ne pourrai confier ces derniers épisodes à Clémentine, elle fanfaronnerait : « Je t'avais prévenue, la névrose, le zapping comme seul recours... »

J'ai envie de pleurer, les commissures de mes lèvres s'étirent vers le bas, puis vers le haut. Les larmes risquent de triompher, je vais m'effondrer à peine il s'éloignera.

Des cernes se dessinent sous ses yeux.

— Tu as l'air fatigué, lui dis-je.

Signe de tête affirmatif. Pour qu'il pense à moi, loin de moi, j'ai envie de lui donner quelque chose qui m'appartient :

— Tiens, donne-moi ta main, ouvre-la, ferme les yeux.

Je glisse mon porte-bonheur au creux de sa main.

Ne surtout pas confier ce geste à Clémentine.

Ce n'est pas le moment ? Assurément.

Il ne le mérite pas ? Évidemment, mais on n'en est plus là.

Air interrogateur. S'il parlait, il dirait : « Qu'est-ce que c'est ? »

Mais seuls ses sourcils indiquent la surprise comme dans les dessins animés.

— C'est mon gri-gri, je te le donne.

Regard inquiet (il y a de quoi).

La parole vient, enfin :

— Un cœur ? Mais c'est un bijou ?

— Oui.

Air incrédule. Il est probable que c'est la première

fois de sa vie qu'une femme lui offre un bijou. Ai-je
eu tort ?

— Garde-le pour moi chez toi, dit-il.

Il ne veut pas s'encombrer d'un objet compromettant, à moins qu'il ne trouve mon cadeau trop féminin.
Il aurait sans doute préféré une cravate, une boîte de
cigares, des pantoufles en velours noir monogram-
mées. Personnellement, j'aime l'idée qu'un homme
dissimule un secret au fond de sa poche : un cœur
offert par une femme. Troisième possibilité : il a lu la
théorie du sociologue Marcel Mauss et s'il accepte
mon présent, il redoute de devoir m'offrir à son tour
un cadeau. Jean est-il avare ?

Mon cœur n'est à lui qu'un instant. Il me le rend.
À son insu, il vient de m'offrir un bijou.

— Merci, dit-il enfin. C'est très beau, ajoute-t-il un
peu gêné. Je vais rentrer me reposer. Je t'appelle dès
que je me sentirai mieux.

Ce langage-là, je peux le comprendre ; peut-être
a-t-il besoin d'une douche, de quelques heures de solitude après un emploi du temps trop chargé ? Moi aussi
j'aime me montrer à lui sous mon meilleur jour,
l'esprit disponible, les jambes épilées, le corps gommé,
les ongles et les cheveux brillants. Des heures à me
frotter, à me crémer, à couper tout ce qui dépasse pour
quelques minutes avec lui. Normal.

Rien n'est mieux que lui.

Peut-être bien qu'une femme parfaite pourrait apprivoiser cet homme difficile. Je n'y parviens pas ; je ne suis pas parfaite.

Je lui écris des lettres que je déchire. Tant de lettres ! J'écris comme si je brodais en silence, moi aussi.

Peut-être est-ce sa dernière visite et la machine à café ne servira-t-elle à rien ? Il n'y avait d'ailleurs pas que la machine à café, il y avait la brosse à dents électrique achetée chez Darty, le coffret de soul music, les coussins en duvet d'oie pour son confort, la crème à l'abricot de Christian Dior, la crème à l'avocat de Sisley pour la douceur, les séances supplémentaires de kick-boxing pour l'épargner, et de yoga pour me calmer, les séances de dentiste pour blanchir mes dents, les livres de psycho pour le comprendre. Et les jarretelles en dentelle pour le reste.

Silence.

Je parle le silence.

Je lui réponds en silence.

Seule ? je parle seule ?

Il m'arrive de douter de lui comme de la présence de Dieu, puisque l'un comme l'autre ne se manifestent guère. Bien sûr. Je pense qu'un jour il finira par parler, par céder à la pression de mes questions et que les mots accumulés dans sa gorge comme les eaux contre la paroi d'un barrage finiront par triompher.

Je lui lirai le questionnaire de Proust tandis qu'il dormira, j'y ajouterai d'autres interrogations de mon cru. Oui, je lui demanderai s'il a déjà eu un chagrin d'amour, s'il pense que l'échec peut être un moteur, s'il a peur dans le noir, quels sont ses rêves, ce qu'il aime chez une femme, s'il y a eu un événement qui a modifié sa vie, s'il est heureux.

Triompher, pour dire quoi ? C'est fini. Arrête, stop, je n'en peux plus.

Est-ce qu'il m'avertirait si c'était fini ?

Rien n'est moins sûr.

Pourquoi m'avertirait-il ? Et si je le lui demandais ? Je ne sais même pas si je parviendrai encore à formuler mes questions, si à force de me taire mes mots ne se sont pas enfuis à leur tour. Je ne sais pas si la vérité tant de fois écartée pour le protéger ne s'est pas dissoute à jamais. Pas l'amour, la vérité. Il est possible que je ne sache plus m'exprimer que dans ma tête. Je ne sais plus si, à trop écarter les mots, Jean et moi ne sommes pas devenus irréels, volatils, invisibles comme le silence.

Où est la vérité ? La vérité est une utopie, un point de vue.

La vérité, d'avoir été contenue, se venge. Je suis vide de toutes les joies inoffensives, vide de tant de sourires qui ne m'atteignent plus, vide des préparatifs de Noël, des feux de bois, de toutes les catastrophes climatiques, de tout le malheur du monde. Je suis un monstre sans cœur qui ne pleure que lui, vide de toutes les émotions, pour ne laisser que celles qu'il me donne, de tous les paysages pour ne laisser que son visage.

Je suis repliée sur moi, obnubilée, obsessive, déprimée, rendue égoïste, délirante, perturbée par le silence. Je suis soûle de silence.

Il me repousse d'un côté et m'appelle de l'autre. Son corps me réclame, son esprit me fuit.

« Accompagne-moi », dit-il. Il m'enlace dans l'ascenseur, au troisième étage, mais son geste ressemble plus à un réflexe qu'à une étreinte.

Je marche à ses côtés jusqu'à la porte cochère de l'immeuble. Je suis aussi grande que lui. Cela ne me dérange pas. Il entrouvre la bouche. Échange de politesses ? Même pas.

– À bientôt, dit-il.

Et il s'éloigne.

Alors, c'est le silence de la vie ordinaire.

E-MAIL DE CLÉMENTINE À IDYLLE

Pas de nouvelles : mauvaises nouvelles ?
Tu es tombée au fond du trou ?... Le grand silence t'a
happée dans son abîme et tu n'as pas la force de couper
le cordon ?
Catastrophe !
Idylle, pour le shopping, OK, tu es la plus forte, mais
pas pour les mecs. Tu es un bébé à côté de moi ! Une
femme qui n'a jamais eu de chagrin d'amour n'a pas
voix au chapitre. Dans cette affaire, tu aurais dû te laisser
guider par ta copine. Dès le début, je lui aurais fait
réciter l'alphabet à l'envers, à ton silencieux !
Coupe les ponts et dis-toi que c'est la difficulté que tu
aimais et pas lui. Il suffit de le réaliser. La difficulté est
interchangeable. Les tarés sont moins rares que tu ne le
crois. Je vais t'en trouver d'autres, tu pourras ainsi les
répertorier, mettre au point un nouveau jeu des Sept
Familles. Épatant.

129

Le silence des hommes

E-MAIL D'IDYLLE À CLÉMENTINE

Parle-moi de toi.

E-MAIL DE CLÉMENTINE À IDYLLE

RAS. Je me sens disponible pour me changer les idées, mais aucun homme n'allume l'étincelle. Rien, pas la moindre vibration à l'horizon. J'ai rencontré quelques types bien, pas libres mais presque, beaux, belles situations, belles manières, etc. Rien. Alors, je pense à toi et je préfère encore ma solitude tranquille à la solitude forcée d'un amour contrarié. Réagis !

Le silence gronde

Il est parti. Le silence gronde.

Pour que tous ces instants aient un sens, que le silence ait une patrie, une signification, pour que l'air et le vent s'engouffrent quelque part et cessent de tournoyer dans ma tête, je voudrais lui souffler tous les mots qui m'agitent. Je voudrais qu'il me délivre de cette montagne, de cette pyramide de mots que son silence et ma retenue ont échafaudées. Je voudrais lui renvoyer violemment les effets du silence. Oui, expulser cette bourrasque, cet ouragan qui l'emportera loin de moi. J'ai l'impression que si j'entrouvre la porte de mon silence, je ne pourrai plus la fermer. Le silence se révoltera, trouvera les mots ressassés et oubliera la diplomatie et la retenue de jadis.

Le silence lui sautera au visage.

Je croyais que le silence venait à la fin d'un amour, après les cris et les disputes au bord du lit ou dans la cuisine, après les phrases humiliantes pour dire que l'on ne se plaît plus, que l'on ne supporte plus ses kilos, sa coloration, sa petite médaille de première communiante, son poulet à l'estragon.

Tu as contrarié le rythme de la vie, tu l'as inversé. Le silence de la fin, tu l'as balancé au début.

L'amour ne sait pas commencer par le silence.

L'amour ne s'explique pas, mais il s'illustre. Derrière le mur du silence, il y a toi, que je connais à peine, mais que je devais connaître, c'était écrit. Tu te bats contre les Écritures, contre la peau, contre les profondeurs du derme et ses exigences.

Parfois, je me demande si ce n'est pas le voyage, juste le voyage, qui m'attire. Tu es une île, un pays inconnu, un cahier blanc à remplir. J'ai le vertige, mais je plonge.

Le silence du désespoir se tait. Alors le rien domine, aucun mot, aucun souvenir, aucune image, même pas la sienne, ne peut s'y accrocher. Tout glisse, tout s'efface. Plus rien n'a de prise sur ce silence-là.

J'ai perdu les sons, j'ai perdu son visage, son sourire. J'ai perdu les codes qui m'aidaient à voir en transparence, à entendre quand il n'y a aucun bruit, j'ai perdu le fil qui nous reliait.

L'espoir s'est effacé.

Les appels des amis, des profs, de quelques élèves, de Clémentine, de Paul, de la secrétaire du psy pour les séances manquées et de l'astrologue ressuscité n'ont plus de sens.

Je n'ai envie que d'entendre Jean répondre à mes questions.

J'ai eu trente et un ans sans même qu'il s'en doute. Le dentiste m'a arraché une dent de sagesse sans qu'il me plaigne. J'ai réussi ma première blanquette de veau sans qu'il la goûte.

Quand le mystère s'épaissit trop, je parcours les horoscopes. Je l'ai trouvé. Le signe du Scorpion lui va à la perfection. Un vrai cadeau pour les ennemis. Un cadeau tellement efficace qu'on devrait élever les natifs du Scorpion ; inciter les couples à copuler en février pour s'assurer une bonne récolte en novembre. Une armée entière d'insectes aux appendices chélicères, à la queue segmentée terminée par un aiguillon crochu et venimeux. Les Scorpions pourraient aider les pays en surpopulation. Moi qui ne croyais pas à l'astrologie, je m'y accroche comme au facteur si Jean m'écrivait. Je sais à présent que les Scorpions sont exclusifs, excessifs, difficiles, torturés, compliqués, introvertis, mais je ne sais toujours pas pourquoi le mien ne parle pas.

Quand Vénus pointe, les Scorpions traversent une période propice à l'amour et s'amadouent ; quand Jupiter approche, les soucis reprennent. Octobre saura le combler, serments romantiques jusqu'au 15. La chance approche, il va vaincre ses peurs tandis que moi, au même moment, Mercure me conférera une grande agilité mentale.

Le temps passe.

Je m'égare. Je n'aime plus sortir, la rêverie m'a prise et le goût du silence avec.

Avant de m'endormir, je serre mon coussin contre

moi, je préférerais serrer un pull ou une écharpe qui transporterait son odeur, mais il ne m'en a pas donné.

Pour fixer mes pensées, je ne possède qu'un briquet en plastique rouge qu'il a oublié et que je ne lui ai pas rendu. Un briquet tombé de sa poche. Je ne peux tout de même pas avouer à Clémentine mon envie de dormir avec un briquet.

Le temps passe.

Je reprends espoir. Le temps est fait pour ça.

L'espoir transporte le désir, le ravissement, la lumière, les mots tendres, les baisers et le silence apaisé redevient tintamarre. Il suffit de peu pour déclencher ce concert : un souvenir plus tenace que la mélancolie et l'orchestre se réanime. Jean est tellement présent que je n'ai presque plus besoin de lui.

Il y a une certaine accoutumance au vide, une certaine harmonie, une continuité, un néant apprivoisé. Le cap de la douleur dépassé, il y a un confort certain, le rêve se confond avec la réalité, le bruit avec le silence, le silence avec la perfection.

Le silence peut combler, il est un royaume, une autarcie. Rien à voir avec l'attente qui me plonge dans l'impuissance, la mienne, dans le désamour. Celui que je suscite.

Un jour, tout allait s'apaiser.

E-MAIL DE CLÉMENTINE À IDYLLE

Ma chérie, as-tu retrouvé tes esprits ?

Vingt-trois heures

« Je viendrai à vingt-trois heures. »

Les aiguilles de ma montre se sont arrêtées quand il a prononcé ces mots. Depuis, le temps est différent.

Plus de reproche, les tourments du silence, je les ai oubliés.

Pourtant un instinct de survie me pousse à le fréquenter plus dans le rêve – puisqu'à présent il fait partie intégrante de mon imagination – que dans le vrai.

– À condition que tu parles...

– Tu es très forte.

– Je fais semblant.

– Cela revient au même.

Léger rire contenu.

– Tu parleras ?

– Hum...

– Hum, pour dire oui ?

– À vingt-trois heures.

Je capitule, trop vite. Je prends ce qu'il me donne. Avec ou sans paroles, je veux voir mon amant tard dans la nuit. La nuit, les félins voient, les rapaces chassent et si les hommes se mettaient à parler ?

Dans quelques heures, il allait venir... J'ai couru acheter des roses, des chocolats, du café décaféiné, parce qu'il sera tard, des bougies parfumées. J'ai pris rendez-vous avec mon esthéticienne, regonflé les rideaux en lin blanc, repassé les rubans en satin bleu ciel de ma chemise de nuit en coton. La maison et moi avons repris vie. Dans quatre heures toutes les deux seront redevenues jolies, prêtes à l'accueillir.

Mon studio est modeste, mais la hauteur des fenêtres et l'exposition participent à sa gaieté, même en hiver.

Il m'a appelée de son portable avec trente minutes d'avance :

– Je suis sous ton balcon.

Alors je me suis élancée dans l'escalier, tenant le devant de ma chemise de nuit comme une robe de bal, pour lui ouvrir la porte de l'immeuble, verrouillée après vingt heures :

– Viens !

Et nous avons grimpé les escaliers quatre à quatre jusqu'au cinquième où j'habite.

Le silence des hommes

La porte à peine ouverte, il la referme, et sans même me dire « bonsoir », il me soulève et m'embrasse comme la première fois, longtemps. J'adore ses baisers, mais il me manque quelque chose, c'est comme un discours sans présentation, comme un devoir sans introduction, un magazine sans titre, un article sans chapeau, un festin sans entrée. Il se précipite sur le plat principal, attaque le texte dans le ventre, pas de fioritures. Moi, je veux savoir comment il va, s'il a beaucoup travaillé, à je ne sais quoi d'ailleurs, s'il part en vacances, rien de très compromettant. Je veux lui donner de mes nouvelles, lui dire que je vais être mutée, que j'écris à présent dans la *Revue des Deux Mondes*. Je veux lui dire aussi pour la blanquette, je veux qu'il me regarde, qu'il aime ma chemise de nuit en satin de soie et ma nouvelle coupe de cheveux.

Pour y parvenir, je le repousse avec mes deux mains, j'émets des petits bruits étouffés, mais ses yeux comme ses oreilles demeurent fermés.

Il ne me voit pas, il ne m'entend pas non plus. Il m'embrasse avidement, il m'embrasse tout inspiré, tout aspiré, tandis que de ses mains il retient ma tête pour que je ne m'échappe pas. Et seulement quand il est assuré de l'effet de son baiser, et qu'il sait que je préfère ses baisers à ses mots, ses mains lâchent mon crâne pour s'aventurer sur mes seins. En quelques instants elles recouvrent mon buste et finissent dans mon dos, à se débattre avec mon soutien-gorge.

Et moi je tambourine avec mes poings contre ses

épaules, et quand, d'un mouvement de la tête, je parviens à m'arracher à ses lèvres, je lui dis :

– Je veux que tu m'écoutes.

Les yeux toujours fermés, il continue de chercher ma bouche.

– Écoute-moi...

Je n'entends qu'un son, une sorte de grognement d'animal furieux auquel j'aurais enlevé sa pâtée.

– Pourquoi ? dis-je.

– Comment enlève-t-on ce soutien-gorge ?

Il n'ouvre pas les yeux.

– Pourquoi tu es comme ça, pourquoi tu ne me parles pas ?

– Le soutien-gorge...

– Réponds-moi !

– Je suis là, dit-il, le visage enfoui dans le creux de mon cou, heureux d'avoir triomphé de l'armature.

Puis il se laisse tomber sur le canapé et, en prenant soin de relever auparavant la chemise de nuit, il m'attire à califourchon sur lui, s'évertue à baisser son pantalon. Il caresse mes fesses, moi je promène mon index le long de son front, son nez, ses lèvres, son menton, comme si cette promenade sur son visage pouvait m'éclairer sur les cheminements de ses pensées.

Ses traits réguliers dissimulent bien la sinuosité de son esprit.

– Je savais qu'un jour je te verrais en chemise de nuit, dit-il.

Pourquoi ces mots-là ?

– Je voudrais te dire les mots de la nuit...

– Hum...

– J'ai peur..., dis-je...

– Chut...

Alors je me tais.

Je ne résiste plus à rien, ne pense plus à rien.

Je prends le moment qu'il me donne.

Et on fait.

Il reste un instant collé, un instant encore en moi, après avoir perdu sa vigueur, puis il se retire, me tapote la tête, content de sa performance. Il y a de quoi. Je redoute son regard, une fois la substance de l'amour sortie de son corps ; la passion a tendance à le quitter avec elle.

Je suis encore à plat ventre sur le matelas, il est déjà debout, nu devant moi, il sourit.

Sourire forcé.

Son regard ne s'aventure plus sur mon visage, son regard est déjà parti ailleurs. Il a changé.

Son corps à peine affaibli, la raison en a profité pour reprendre sa place.

Dès que le vide se fait, la raison gagne.

La raison reprend ses droits.

Un homme différent de celui qui est arrivé, plein de désir, de celui qui a aimé, est en face de moi.

Il se dirige vers la salle de bains.

Il va se doucher, se savonner, tirer sur la peau de son sexe pour bien le ranger, se laver les dents pour enlever le goût de l'amour et partir.

Il ne va pas dormir, fumer, manger, bavarder, caresser, recommencer.

Il va partir.

Il me donnera bien encore une ou deux caresses, chastes et polies, mais rien d'autre. Pas un mot.

J'aurais tellement aimé l'entendre dire « je t'aime ». Juste ce soir, pour la première et dernière fois, parce qu'il est tard et alors je me le tiendrais pour dit. J'exagère ? Oui, je suis banale, attachée à ce petit mot insignifiant ; oui, je lui accorde un pouvoir qu'il n'a peut-être pas ; oui, je suis sentimentale et romantique. Je collectionne les tares pour le plaisir, je les cumule, les additionne, les empile toutes. Dans ce registre-là, je suis imbattable.

Sensible ? hyper.

Susceptible ? très.

Réceptive ? vachement.

Intuitive ? comme une cartomancienne.

J'ai vu *Casablanca* une vingtaine de fois, j'ai pleuré dans les bras d'Humphrey Bogart, j'ai été Scarlett O'Hara dans *Autant en emporte le vent*, Mme de Winter dans *Rebecca*. Je rabâche, ressasse, me remémore, je crois en la signification des mots, aux liens qu'ils créent, je lis les silences, les non-dits, je devine les intentions, interprète les regards.

Je me trompe sûrement. Je ne réfléchis pas assez, si je réfléchissais je me passerais de lui.

Je me lève et me colle contre lui, je suis nue moi aussi.

J'attends qu'il me parle.

Il sent bien qu'il ne pourra se débarrasser de mon étreinte sans un mot.

L'air siffle entre les parois de son nez, les battements de son cœur résonnent dans sa poitrine : bruits de machine, gargouillis de tuyauterie.

Ses lèvres, pourtant pleines, faites pour embrasser, jouer de la trompette, mordre dans un éclair au chocolat, envoyer des baisers, murmurer des mots doux dans une salle de cinéma, restent collées, amincies par la volonté qu'il emploie à les maintenir serrées.

Il ressent bien quelque chose, là, maintenant, après qu'une partie de son corps s'est déployée, détendue, tendue, sous-tendue, tordue, gonflée, colorée, allongée, puis retombée ? Après toutes ces modifications corporelles, ces tensions, ces attentions, cette libération, cet apaisement, il va bien franchir le pas, passer de la vie animale à la vie humaine, il va bien employer les lettres de l'alphabet, les mots du dictionnaire, y trouver les définitions d'aimable, d'aimant, d'aimantation, d'aimanter, qui le conduiront enfin au verbe aimer. Aimer : c'est éprouver de l'affection, de la tendresse, de la sympathie, de l'amitié. L'éventail est ample, il peut choisir entre chérir, adorer, idolâtrer, affectionner, goûter, s'intéresser ; il peut distinguer entre Gide, « qui aimait la vie hasardeuse », Anatole France, « qui aimait ses semblables », la Bible, « qui aime les autres autant que son prochain », Stendhal, qui en « homme passionné voit toutes les perfections dans ce qu'il aime », Zola, « qui aime que les choses soient à leur place », et Gide, encore, qui « aimait sortir avec son père ».

Il va bien réaliser qu'ils l'ont tous prononcé, un jour ou l'autre, ce mot. Tous ont osé, tous ont pris le risque d'être déçus ou d'être heureux. Une vie sans prononcer le mot... n'est pas une vie complète, c'est un peu comme mourir sans avoir vu la mer ou la montagne, sans avoir goûté aux caramels mous, sans avoir lu Perec ou Dostoïevski, sans avoir écouté *Stormy Weather* par Sarah Vaughan, sans avoir pris un bain de mousse avec un amant, sans avoir laissé des miettes de croissant dans un lit, sans s'être allongé nu sur une plage de sable chaud, sans se réveiller avec un souvenir, sans s'endormir avec un secret.

Je me colle, je me pends à son cou, je suis indécrochable, incontournable, immobile, je bloque ses pieds, j'escalade ses tibias.

S'il s'enfuit, il m'emporte avec lui.

Je suis à sa hauteur ; il ne pourra pas me détacher tant qu'il ne m'aura pas parlé. Je pèse, je suis lourde, j'écrase le tarse, le métatarse, les phalanges. Je suis un boulet d'une trentaine de kilos sur chacun de ses orteils.

J'attends qu'il m'aime.

Alors il prend ma tête entre ses deux mains et il dit :

– Je t'aime.

Je suis en extase, je vole, je flotte, je ne le crois pas, tant pis, c'est très bon quand même.

Juste après, il ajoute : « Fort. » Et il répète d'une seule traite cette fois :

– Je t'aime fort.

Pourquoi fort ? Pourquoi « m'aime-t-il fort » et ne « m'aime-t-il pas tout court », comme tout le monde ? Pourquoi cela tombe sur moi un type pareil ?

Pourquoi ne ment-il pas un peu, comme la plupart des amoureux, sans se poser de questions ? Il m'aime tout de même puisqu'il m'aime fort ; pourquoi compliquer les choses ? Après tout, cela veut dire quoi aimer ?

Dictionnaire, s'il vous plaît.

Premier sens : Éprouver de l'affection.

Deuxième sens : Avoir le goût pour...

Je suis sûre du second sens : cet homme a le goût de moi.

No comment.

Je suis moins sûre pour l'affection.

Affectionner quelqu'un, c'est lui vouloir du bien.

Je n'avais pas pensé qu'un adjectif qui traduit la puissance, la résistance, la robustesse, la solidité, la

145

vigueur pouvait aussi affadir le verbe aimer et briser la magie.

Alors je relève la tête, nos bouches s'effleurent et je lui réponds, et tant pis pour l'ego :

– Moi, je t'aime sans adverbe.

Je descends de ses pieds tandis qu'il s'éloigne vers la douche, léger, l'amour atténué d'un adverbe.

Je dois m'estimer heureuse, j'aurais pu écoper de pire ; il aurait pu dire « je t'aime beaucoup », comme ma tante Marguerite et, dans l'échelle amoureuse, je descendais encore d'un cran. J'aurais même pu aussi récolter un adverbe de négation : je ne t'aime « pas », et tout était fini, ou un adverbe de manière : je t'aime « bien », et dans l'échelle des mots horribles j'avais gagné le gros lot.

Les adjectifs comme les adverbes associés au verbe aimer l'affaiblissent.

Ils sont un contresens, une absurdité, une cruauté.

Aimer se conjugue nu.

Il ne le sait pas. À moins qu'il le sache, et c'est pire.

Je regrette son silence.

Disons que je suis la maîtresse d'un homme qui m'aime avec un adverbe et que j'aime sans.

Voilà notre différence.

J'ai trouvé un proverbe arabe pour Jean : « Tu es maître de la parole que tu n'as pas dite et l'esclave de celle que tu as prononcée. » Il a dû l'apprendre par cœur, celui-là, non ?

La boîte en porcelaine blanche

Son sperme coule le long de mes jambes. J'attrape la boîte de Kleenex sur ma table de nuit pour m'essuyer. Sa substance adorée inonde le mouchoir ; je m'apprête à le jeter, mais je n'y parviens pas. J'ai trop attendu cette nuit pour le laisser dans une poubelle.

Je vais chercher au fond de moi tout ce que je peux lui prendre, je ne veux rien perdre, pas une goutte, puis je referme le mouchoir alourdi et je le cache dans une boîte en porcelaine sur ma table de nuit.

Il sort de la salle de bains, il est déjà rhabillé.

Il s'assoit quelques instants sur le canapé, attend son café. Je lui verse un « déca » tout chaud sorti de la belle machine chromée achetée pour lui. Il l'avale sans sucre, il croque le petit bout de chocolat que je lui tends. Il regarde sa montre, rallume son portable, même à cette heure-ci :

– Il est tard...

Je m'en fiche, il peut partir comme un goujat, il

peut me regarder à peine, atténuer ses propos d'adjectifs modérateurs, il peut freiner la vie, l'amour, les pulsions, il peut me dire qu'il me parlera demain et retenir son souffle pendant trois mois, je m'en fiche : j'ai capturé de quoi nourrir mes rêves.

– Bon...

Pourquoi dire « bon » quand il ne reste que du mauvais ?

– Tu fais quoi en ce moment ?

– J'ai beaucoup de copies à corriger...

Je ne lui dis pas que je vais changer de lycée, à quoi cela servirait-il ?

– C'est bien.

– Oui...

– Il faut travailler.

– Oui...

– C'est important.

– Oui.

Voilà pour la conversation perceptible. De quoi regretter les « hum », le souffle court, le râle, les bruits de l'intérieur.

Il y a des mots plus vides de sens que le vide.

– Bon, je t'appelle...

Encore le mauvais « bon ».

Je souris... Il comprend le reproche déguisé que cache ce sourire. Alors, comme pour se défendre, il ajoute :

– Tu ne m'appelles jamais !

Et s'en va.

Je ferme la porte derrière lui, enclenche le verrou.

À peine rendue à mon alcôve, je soulève le couvercle de la boîte en porcelaine blanche. Il est là, au creux de mes mains, tout moite, tout fragile, réduit à un petit chiffon qui transporte la vie. Je le respire, transie, débordante de sentiments, de mots, de caresses, d'histoires à lui raconter.

L'homme qui m'a le moins donné est celui qui m'a le plus appris.

Bonsoir, mon amour.

E-MAIL D'IDYLLE À CLÉMENTINE

Il a dit : « Je viendrai à vingt-trois heures. » Il a dit : « Je suis sous ton balcon. » Il a dit : « Comment on enlève ça ? », « Je savais qu'un jour je te verrais en chemise de nuit », et : « Je t'aime fort. » Il a dit : « Bon. » Il a dit : « Tu travailles en ce moment ? », et même : « Tu ne m'appelles jamais !!! » Tu te rends compte ? Et il dit toujours : « Hum. »

E-MAIL DE CLÉMENTINE À IDYLLE

« Hum » ? c'est un Indien ?
« Hum » plus huit phrases ! Quel bavard ! Il faut le féliciter ? Le pauvre chou va attraper une extinction de voix, ménage-le ! J'espère qu'il ne joue pas tous les soirs au théâtre ! Puis, excuse-moi, mais le côté « je t'aime fort », c'est super nul.
Et, au fait, qu'est-ce qu'il fabrique dans la vie ?

153

Le silence des hommes

E-MAIL D'IDYLLE À CLÉMENTINE

Je ne sais pas.

E-MAIL DE CLÉMENTINE À IDYLLE

Tu te fiches de moi ?

E-MAIL D'IDYLLE À CLÉMENTINE

Non.

E-MAIL DE CLÉMENTINE À IDYLLE

En fait, il ne t'a rien dit.

E-MAIL D'IDYLLE À CLÉMENTINE

Les mots sont limités comparés à l'immensité du silence.

E-MAIL DE CLÉMENTINE À IDYLLE

Ça y est, tu es contaminée !
Tu n'as pas trop chaud à la tête ? Tu délires, mon chou !

Trêve de plaisanterie, ne reste pas seule. Si tu le peux encore, prends l'Eurostar et viens me voir ou bien appelle les urgences psychiatriques. Je ne plaisante pas ! J'ai eu ma crise de mélancolie moi aussi l'autre soir. Et j'en suis sortie en allant en boîte de nuit. Le bruit, les autres, l'agitation, ça bouscule le silence... Toi, tu restes confinée, engluée dedans, extraies-toi, tire-toi de cette colle, de cette glu, de cette poisse !

E-MAIL D'IDYLLE À CLÉMENTINE

Facile ! Oui, je peux m'extraire... Oui, je peux décrocher mon téléphone, fermer ma porte, sauter à la corde dans un night-club, partir sur une coque de noix au milieu du Pacifique, traverser le désert à dos de chameau... Oui, je peux m'éloigner de lui physiquement. Moralement, non. Que je sois en pleine mer ou au cœur du désert, ou parmi des gens se trémoussant sous les sun-lights, je penserai toujours à lui. Ce câble-là ne se sectionne pas d'un tour de clé ou d'un pas vers un aéroport. Ce serait trop facile. Tu n'as jamais été amoureuse ?

E-MAIL DE CLÉMENTINE À IDYLLE

À t'entendre, je me le demande...
C'est quoi être amoureux ?

E-MAIL D'IDYLLE À CLÉMENTINE

Être amoureux, c'est naviguer à vue, buter sur les mots comme sur un rocher, ramer un mètre au-dessus de l'eau et se noyer dans un verre vide.

E-MAIL DE CLÉMENTINE À IDYLLE

Je ne te le fais pas dire.

E-MAIL D'IDYLLE À CLÉMENTINE

Qui a dit que « c'était un état sacré » ? Sacré état, état de siège, de guerre, d'abrutissement, cet état s'achèterait que j'en demanderais remboursement. Mais que faire ? Ne me gronde pas, je ne l'ai pas choisi.

Je voudrais être habillée de mots

J'enlève mon peignoir ; je me regarde dans la glace et j'imagine sa bouche recouvrant chaque partie de mon corps.

Je voudrais être habillée de mots.

Des mots qu'il adapterait selon que ses lèvres effleureraient mon cœur, mon front ou le bas de mon ventre.

Des mots de lui, pour moi, des mots sur mesure.

À la mesure de l'absence qu'il faut consoler.

À la mesure des larmes qu'il faut étancher.

À la mesure du manque qu'il faut combler.

Les mots de l'amour me sauvent de l'ennui.

Les mots de l'amour l'ennuient. Les pauvres mots de l'amour, ce répertoire gâté, gâché, gaspillé, dilapidé, ces paroles d'acteurs, de paroliers, de chanteurs, de chansonniers, de théâtreux, de scénaristes, de romanciers, de poètes, de menteurs, de joueurs, de tricheurs, de comédiens, d'artistes. Il pense qu'aucun d'entre eux ne peut rivaliser avec l'infini, la grandeur, la liberté, la sagesse, la perfection du silence. Et surtout pas ce

157

malheureux verbe *aimer*, universellement galvaudé, utilisé comme le bouillon Kub à toutes les sauces et même au chocolat. Est-ce que l'on peut aimer à vingt ans comme à quarante, marié comme célibataire, dans le mariage et hors du mariage, soit plus que les autres, soit moins que les autres, la mer et la montagne, la chaleur et le froid, la marche et la glisse, le tennis et le foot, le travail et les vacances ? Un seul mot, toujours le même : aimer.

Jean, conscient de cette confusion, a voulu s'en démarquer : alors il place la barre très haut. Il est bien possible que Jean, par souci de perfection, se soit condamné au silence.

J'allume une cigarette, la tête me tourne. Il suffit de peu quand on ne fume pas. Je ne sais rien de cet homme qui me prend dans ses bras. « Tu ne m'appelles jamais ! » Je ne pense pas qu'il m'invite à découvrir son mystère, mais simplement à prendre l'initiative de notre prochain rendez-vous.

Après une journée entière de cours, les trajets en bus, les sollicitations des élèves, des copies à corriger ne m'enlèveront pas de la tête cette idée émise par mégarde qui ne cesse de me harceler : et si je l'appelais ? Seuls les amoureux peuvent mesurer l'envahissement de ce type d'interrogation.

Appeler ou ne pas appeler ? Quelle question ! Je pèse le pour et le contre, évalue, balance entre le oui et le non, avant de commettre l'irréparable, comme si ma destinée, ma crédibilité, ma capacité à le conquérir dépendaient de cette misérable décision.

Je m'allonge avec mon plateau de thé sur le lit, il est dix-huit heures trente, les copies attendront et mes notations dépendront de l'issue de cette entreprise. La vie est injuste. Bien sûr.

J'ai peur. Pourquoi cette envie de vivre chevillée au corps me pousse-t-elle à de telles exagérations ?

N'étais-je pas plus heureuse quand la vie recelait moins d'interrogations, plus d'explications, lorsque l'homme qui la partageait commentait l'actualité politique, cinématographique, littéraire, lorsque les autres existaient et que le thé avait encore une saveur ?

Sûrement. Mais je n'ai rien choisi. Ce type d'amour est une drogue, on prend goût à ces accélérations, à ces vibrations, à cet univers rétréci, intensifié, au risque, au jeu, à la fascination du vide comme lorsque l'on se jette du haut d'une falaise en aile volante.

Rien ne peut rivaliser avec cette transe. Il faudrait ne jamais avoir rencontré cet homme. Mais je l'ai rencontré. Le compte à rebours a commencé, il faut que je me dépêche. Je ne sais pourquoi il faut me dépêcher, mais c'est ainsi, ma situation ressemble à un état d'urgence permanent. Il risque de partir Dieu sait où. Il part toujours : il part déjeuner, dîner, en réunion, en voyage, au tennis, chez lui, à la campagne, il part.

Il est tard, la secrétaire bien sûr répondra qu'il est parti. Il reste quelques minutes à peine pour inverser les rôles et constater le changement.

Le *Boléro* de Ravel

La gorge serrée, le combiné contre l'oreille, la respiration aussi courte que ma vision de la vie, j'appelle.

Le passé ? Pas de passé.

Le présent ? Un téléphone. Juste un téléphone.

L'avenir, je ne le vois pas.

Les chiffres défilent sous mes doigts.

Une sonnerie semblable à toutes les autres sonneries résonne, semblable et différente dans les sensations qu'elle transporte.

Une voix de femme l'interrompt. Je suis une actrice de théâtre, morte de trac, que l'on pousse sur les planches, le soir d'une première. « Ne coupez pas », dit la dame. Elle a raison de le dire, je ne pense qu'à raccrocher, à m'éloigner de la scène.

Sans même attendre ma réponse, elle m'envoie le *Boléro*. Je n'avais jamais remarqué à quel point cette musique est lancinante : un seul temps, un seul rythme, une musique comme une manie : la mienne. Pas moyen de s'en sortir, un mouvement continu, un recommencement perpétuel, un enfermement, un accaparement. Le *Boléro* de Ravel est une composition obsessionnelle.

Jeter l'obsession entre les lignes d'un cahier ou d'une partition, serait-ce la solution pour s'en débarrasser ? Utiliser, transformer, travailler l'incompréhension. Avoir le dernier mot.

Interruption : « Qui demandez-vous ? » Parce que je traîne et qu'elle est pressée, la voix devient autoritaire, elle répète : « Qui demandez-vous ? » J'ai intérêt à me dépêcher, la secrétaire a autre chose à faire que de jouer avec le silence, autre chose que m'attendre. Pardon, ce n'est pas pour vous embêter, mais les mots ont du mal à venir, vous savez ? Je ne suis plus très habituée. Non, vous ne savez pas ? Pardon, c'est idiot, vous devez traiter des affaires importantes tous les jours et moi, je n'arrive pas à parler parce qu'un homme me plonge dans la censure. Cela vous fait rire, vous pensez que j'exagère ? Non, depuis que je l'ai revu, je ne sais plus téléphoner. Je dois frôler la paranoïa des sourds. Non, non, ce type de maladie, qui s'accompagne généralement d'un délire de persécution vague, interprétatif en général et hallucinatoire quelquefois, n'est pas une blague. Je n'étais pas comme ça avant de *le* connaître ; avant de *le* connaître, je n'avais rien d'un serrurier, je ne forçais pas les portes fermées. Les hommes m'appelaient pour dîner ou pour faire l'amour, souvent les deux, et je les rappelais quand cela me plaisait. La vie était assez simple. Au bureau,

Jean est-il le même ? Manie-t-il le silence dans le but de torturer, de harceler peut-être ? À vous aussi, il vous a fait ce coup-là ?

Moi je dépense, j'entasse, j'amasse, j'accumule. Je remplis les poches de silence, de mots rêvés.

Le silence est à l'oreille ce que le mirage est à la vue.

Comment définir un mirage de l'oreille ?

Des voix ? Je finis par entendre des voix ?

Pourquoi j'appelle ?

– Parce que je prends un certain plaisir à me cogner contre un mur.

– Parce qu'il ne m'a encore jamais dit « je t'aime ».

Cela revient au même.

Je ferme les yeux, prononce son nom, frappe à sa porte, puisqu'elle m'y oblige.

Je le désigne et il surgit du brouillard.

Le pire est à venir, le pire vient :

– De la part de qui ?

Je peux encore raccrocher et je ne serai pas démasquée, il faut juste que je raccroche. Trop tard, je cède, notre amour qui est un secret n'en sera plus tout à fait un.

– À quel sujet ? demande la voix.

La réponse est : « C'est privé. »

La question reste en suspens.

Il va me falloir du cran. Je suis dans l'obligation de parler.

Alors, d'un ton assuré, je lance l'effrayante banalité :

– C'est personnel.

Bravo.

Silence dans son camp.

Je suis cernée.

La dame se demande si je suis une intrigante, à moins que mon appel soit espéré, sinon attendu ? À cette idée, elle n'en revient pas la dame. Mon intonation doit être différente de celle des autres femmes, des femmes juristes ou d'affaires, je n'ai pas de chiffres, pas de lois dans la tête. Ça s'entend.

Ma voix déraille, ma langue dérape. Je zozote.

Je devrais la rassurer : plus de graves, moins d'aigus, accélérer le débit, ne pas m'appesantir en fin de phrase, veiller à contrôler ma langue. Bon, je comprends votre méfiance, mais il n'y a pas de quoi en faire un drame ! C'est une voix de famille, ma mère avait la même, mais je vous comprends ; moi non plus je ne supporte pas de m'entendre sur un magnéto et je le sais, ma voix choque au début, mais à force, on s'habitue. Mes élèves rigolent quand ma langue fourche, cela s'appelle une coquetterie ; je ne le fais pas exprès. OK ? Mais ne vous en préoccupez pas, vous ne m'entendrez pas de sitôt. Promis. Avec un peu de chance, Jean sera « en rendez-vous » et mon audace renvoyée aux calendes grecques. À moins que, dans quelques instants, ne résonne sa voix, une voix encore inconnue, une voix de bureau, modifiée par les responsabilités, ses mots rares devenus rapides, ses phrases raccourcies, l'intonation contenant à peine le stress, pas celui que je lui procure, un autre.

Dans ce monde, on ne fait pas tout un plat pour un coup de fil. Seules les contrariétés qui en valent la peine ont la capacité de modifier l'humeur : baisse de la productivité, des ventes, des stock-options ou pas, concurrence, dépassement, dépense, objectifs 2004, rentabilité, budget, augmentation, diminution, bilan, restriction, impôt. Ces mots qui collent à la réalité comme la boue aux sabots des chevaux.

Comment aller de ce vocabulaire hostile, des mots de la matérialité, de l'extérieur, de la productivité, de l'agressivité, aux mots de la tendresse, de l'intuition, de l'illusion, de l'imagination, de l'intérieur, de la chimère, ces mots sucrés qui se chantent et se récitent même à l'école, sans un sas de décompression ? Peut-être qu'à partir d'un certain âge on a fini de les employer, on les a oubliés, on a fini d'aimer ? Il est bien possible qu'après cinquante ans les hommes préfèrent dealer plutôt que baiser ; rencontrer un *tycoon* plutôt que Julia Roberts, décrocher un contrat plutôt qu'un billet doux. Je connais mes atouts, je peux affronter la concurrence d'une femme, mais d'un marché, d'un banquier, d'un président de la République ? Comment faire ? Accepter d'être une « récré ». Et pourquoi pas ? Si cela m'arrangeait moi aussi. Mais il fallait me prévenir. Me dire.

Mes copies crissent sous ma hanche, mon thé a refroidi, la crise cardiaque menace. Si une vie réussie est une vie intense, peu de chose suffit à amplifier la mienne : le silence malveillant d'une assistante dévouée. Plutôt que de corriger paisiblement le travail de mes élèves, de me vautrer dans cette songerie, je subis, le cœur battant, mon audace. Chacun son truc.

À la paix, je préfère la guerre, à la tranquillité, l'expectative. J'aime quand ça bouge sous les pieds, quand ça vibre sur le fil, quand ça swingue sur la ligne.

Il n'est pas impossible que, planqué derrière son bureau, Jean fasse de grands signes de la main pour signifier à sa secrétaire qu'il n'est pas là pour Mlle Idylle.

Mon estime baisse à mesure que les secondes s'additionnent. Encore un peu et il ne trouvera plus au bout du fil qu'un lambeau, une serpillière, une flaque.

« Ne coupez pas », dit la dame et, simultanément, sans que je puisse émettre la moindre réticence, elle me colle le *Boléro*.

Avant, j'adorais Ravel.

Mais patience, au bout de la musique, il y aura sa voix.

Ma capacité de résistance n'a pas de limites.

Je devine la proximité de Jean, peut-être écoute-t-il, lui aussi, la même musique ?

Chaque seconde me torture, l'impression de m'être fourvoyée ne me quitte pas et il est trop tard pour rebrousser chemin.

Mes amies, Clémentine en tête, me diraient que je suis une gourde, que ma vie sentimentale est un ratage, c'est ce qui arrive souvent aux adeptes du franc-parler. En amour, comme en politique, le mensonge paie.

Le *Boléro* s'arrête, *sa* voix résonne :

« Allô »...

Je le savais déjà : il y a des têtes d'aéroport et des voix de bureau. Ce seul mot suffit à m'indiquer que Jean a une voix de bureau à couper au couteau. Il ne s'agit même pas d'une voix de composition, mais d'un automatisme, peut-être même de mimétisme, de protectionnisme ? un truc en « isme » de la pire espèce.

À moi de jouer avec ma voix de flemme, de flirt avancé, de dilettante récidiviste, d'intentions déguisées, de coin du bois, de pastille Valda, de sirop à la menthe, de décalage horaire. Je glisse :

– Je voulais te dire bonjour.

Je n'ai pas le courage d'aller droit au but comme lui et de le convoquer demain à quatorze heures pour un café.

Un « bonjour » timide, pour justifier, sans trop dévoiler, mon envie de me nicher au creux de ses bras, de me serrer contre lui, de le respirer, mais aussi de l'entendre dire : « Tu m'as manqué », « Je suis heureux que tu m'appelles. »

– C'est gentil..., dit-il de sa voix de bureau.

Puis :

– J'étais en réunion, je suis sorti pour te parler.

– Ah, c'est gentil..., dis-je, reprenant ses mots stéréotypés.

Il n'y a rien de gentil dans tout ça, il n'y a jamais rien

eu de gentil : il y a du désir, de l'abdication, de la pro-
vocation, de la perturbation, de l'envoûtement, de la
passion, du désespoir. De la déprime ? Non, pas de
déprime. La dépression cloue au sol, elle ne permet pas
d'avancer.

Silence.

Cette fois, je le reconnais. Oui, je le retrouve mieux
dans le silence que dans les phrases d'usage ; bien que
son visage me manque pour parfaire ma lecture. Un
visage même muet exprime la joie, la tristesse, la fati-
gue, la compassion, l'angoisse. Cette fois, je suis privée
de tout support.

Où est-il ? Je ne connais pas son univers, je ne sais
pas si les murs qui l'entourent sont en vitres ou en
béton, s'ils sont peints ou tapissés, s'ils sont blancs ou
gris, s'il porte une cravate ou un col ouvert, un pull
ou une veste en tweed, s'il est debout ou assis sur un
siège tournant, rasé ou pas, si son visage est marqué
ou détendu. Je sais juste qu'il tient un combiné à la
main, qu'il jette des virgules en l'air, pas mal de virgules dans la stratosphère, quelques points dans le
vent, un tourbillon, un point d'interrogation tombé
comme la foudre. Il ponctue le silence.

Ma grande sœur, qui avait peur dans le noir, me
demandait de lui parler avant qu'elle ne s'endorme.
À ma question :

« À quoi cela servirait-il de te parler, il fera toujours
noir ? » elle avait répondu : « Les mots éclaireront
notre chambre. »

Les mots du paraître assombrissent l'univers.

Les mots peuvent être les écrans de l'âme.

Les mots du bureau ne sont rien, du vent, des déguisements.

Le fil est tendu entre nos deux silences, nos vibrations résonnent. Vous ne le croyez pas ? Les soupirs plus que les syllabes meublent nos conversations amoureuses.

C'est quand je ne l'entends pas que je l'entends le plus. Il y a des silences qui n'ont pas leur équivalent dans les mots.

Lui semble heureux ; je suis venue à lui, aimante, douce, amoureuse, obéissante et hésitante pourtant. Je ne sais pas si entre deux visites il pense à moi. Si je le lui demandais, après un silence méfiant, il pourrait répondre : « Souvent », comme le prince de Ligne. Jean devait souvent penser à moi alors que je le retrouvais dans tous les silences.

Voilà notre différence.

Notre lien ne ressemble à rien d'habituel.

Il reprend le combiné, juste pour dire :

– Attends.

Depuis le début j'espère ses mots. Rassurée par le fil France Télécom comme un chien par sa laisse, j'ai l'impression illusoire de servir de haut-parleur, de récipient, d'oreille, de confesseur, de l'assister tandis que, réconforté lui aussi mais par la distance, il prend son élan.

Élan interrompu, quelqu'un est rentré dans le bureau. Jean, contraint, reprend sa voix de circonstance, la voix pour les autres, peut-être même la tête anonyme des gens dans les aéroports, bien que je ne puisse l'imaginer avec cette tête-là.

Les ondes se brouillent.

L'armure du travail refait surface. Est-ce que, sans restriction, il se permet les mots qui n'engagent pas l'âme, les mots qui ne parlent pas d'amour, les mots de la finance, du commerce, de l'économie, de la vie pratique ou professionnelle ? Le blocage serait inhérent à la signification des mots, pas à leur utilisation.

Malgré l'éloignement du combiné de téléphone, je l'entends dire ces choses anodines, sans importance ni sens profond. Il n'est pas un de ces religieux qui vivent à l'écart du monde, seul ou en communauté, dans les couvents ou dans les monastères, un de ces frères, un de ces pères, un de ces lamas engagés à suivre les règles d'un ordre qui ne leur permet pas de répondre aux questions. Sans être chanoine, il tait, il freine, il empêche, il se méfie. Depuis le début, le mot aimer, tout seul, tout nu, il ne le prononce pas.

Je l'appelle, je surmonte la montagne inconnue, mais cela ne suffit pas à le rassurer, il me confronte à un autre silence, celui du téléphone, sans visage, celui-là. Si ma voix n'est pas assez convaincante, alors une musique céleste, l'*Ave Maria*, chanté par la Callas, le cri de Don Juan, les vocalises jubilatoires de Woglinde, la fille du Rhin, sauront le tirer, l'extraire, l'entraîner vers d'autres cimes. Autant me taire et coller le combiné contre le baffle.

Je doute de sa compréhension face à ce qu'il me fait subir, je ne sais même pas si, une seule fois, il s'est posé la question de ce que devait ressentir une femme à qui un homme n'adresse pas la parole.

Et si je lui disais :

« Voilà, j'arrête, c'est fini, je n'en peux plus du silence » ?

Et, transie, le dos voûté, les épaules relevées, comme si une bombe menaçait au-dessus du toit, j'attendrais sa réponse.

De toute façon, il fallait en arriver là ; depuis le début la rupture plane, depuis le début le silence glace, fige l'atmosphère, et j'ai froid dans cette mer de néant que je ne parviens pas à réchauffer. Je suis fatiguée de nager à contre-courant. Il ne sait pas qu'avec très peu de mots les femmes sont capables de faire de grands voyages. Mais Jean ne dérange rien, ne bouscule aucune de ses habitudes. Il serait capable de refuser ma proposition d'un :

– Non, il faut que l'on arrête ensemble.

C'est possible une chose pareille ?

Claquement de porte, la secrétaire est partie.

– Ça va ? dit-il comme s'il avait lu dans mes pensées. Je ne t'ai pas fait attendre trop longtemps ?

– Non.

– On doit ressentir la même chose, dit-il soudain.

Jean est dangereux et sincère par à-coups.

Le silence des hommes

Et si c'était vrai ? Si lui et moi pensions la même chose ? S'il était seulement incapable de l'exprimer ?

— Je dois retourner en réunion, je passe prendre un café demain.

Même quand ils ne sont pas silencieux au début, les hommes ont tendance à le devenir en vieillissant. Le mien ne cause plus que pour demander le pain et le vin à table. Imagine Jean dans quinze ans ! Il ne te demandera même plus le sel. J'ai vraiment l'impression de m'être fait avoir. Michel parlait, je connais son enfance, son premier flirt, sa première fois, l'histoire de ses frères, de ses sœurs, son service militaire, il ne m'a rien épargné. Un jour, sans raison, il a tourné le bouton.
Quand je regarde les hommes qui m'entourent à l'agence de pub, je me demande comment ils sont chez eux, ces hommes charmants. Je les regarde comme si je ne les avais jamais vraiment vus auparavant. J'ai l'impression que le moment est venu pour moi d'avoir un amant. À moins que ce ne soit à cause de mes gélules de bêta-carotène et mes capsules de Magné-Ginseng ; il paraît que trop de vitamines fait naître des papillons dans la tête des femmes !

173

E-MAIL D'IDYLLE À CLÉMENTINE

Peut-être les silencieux du début deviennent-ils des bavards à la fin ? Six mois et toujours pas une phrase longue de plus de soixante-quinze signes. Il doit les calibrer. Je ne connais rien de son passé, ni de son présent, en dehors de ses visites à l'heure du café. Dommage, j'aime le passé des gens et même le mien ; mes anniversaires me réjouissent ; les années m'aident à tenir debout, à m'enraciner quelque part. J'aime me retourner et contempler le chemin parcouru, aussi modeste soit-il.

E-MAIL DE CLÉMENTINE À IDYLLE

Attends quarante ans !
Quant aux silencieux du début, je pense qu'ils le restent.
Le silence ne se décante pas.

Solution pour un chagrin

La solution est peut-être dans un Body Shop.
Enduite d'huiles essentielles, de shampooing à la menthe, de lait pour lisser les longueurs et pointes abîmées,
de rouge à lèvres à la fraise, de crème pour adoucir les
mains, pour dissoudre les taches et les peaux déjà mor-
tes, d'exfoliants désincrustants, de crème de nuit
relaxante pour le corps, de *night repair advanced* pour
le visage, de parfum à l'ambre, à la rose, au géranium,
il est possible que je parviendrai à m'aimer assez pour
me protéger des silencieux. Et si je m'aime, j'aurai plus
de place pour moi et moins pour lui. Logique. Encore
faudrait-il que la logique existe en amour.

À moins que la solution ne soit dans les librairies ;
les romans d'aujourd'hui racontent plus de chagrins
qu'ils ne livrent d'antidotes. Restent les livres des psy-
chanalystes, des sociologues, tout le marché de l'équilibre intérieur, du développement personnel, de l'auto-
nomie, de la rencontre avec soi, du training mental :

« Quatre-vingt une façons de cultiver l'estime de soi », et autres balivernes.

Devenir soi-même et suivre les conseils de Carl Gustav Jung.

Devenir taoïste, bouddhiste.

Après avoir ingurgité ce savoir-là, serai-je différente ?

La solution peut aussi se trouver dans les magazines : au travers des mots d'Une Telle qui affirme ne pouvoir aimer sans retour, d'une autre qui prétend gouverner sa vie avec sa tête ou d'une troisième qui, à peine sortie de l'enfance, mesure déjà l'amour en preuves.

La tête, pas les sens, la réalité, pas la rêverie, soi plutôt que l'autre. Ces femmes-là auraient renvoyé mon amoureux muet à la première question sans réponse.

Solution à chercher également :

– Dans les voyages. Les voyages ont hissé Naipaul « vers de nouveaux domaines d'émotion », lui ont donné « une vision du monde qu'il n'avait jamais eue et l'ont élargi techniquement ».

– Dans la sorcellerie : je me souviens de Clémentine entourant son immeuble de gros sel pour se protéger de l'emprise d'un homme et de Ghislaine qui piétinait du plomb en scandant le nom de son amant, sur les conseils d'un marabout.

– Dans la compréhension : comprendre que j'ai transposé le vide provoqué par la mort de mon chat en un chagrin d'amour.

– Il y a aussi la méthode Coué : répéter vingt fois de suite, les yeux fermés, chaque matin au réveil et chaque soir au coucher « qu'il n'est qu'un moyen ».

– Dans la vengeance : lui dire qu'il a été choisi pour remplacer le silence d'une bête.

– Le ressentiment : s'en défaire à tout prix. « La haine lie à son ennemi », et je veux me délier.

– Il y a encore les astrologues, les voyantes, tous les vendeurs d'augures payés pour annoncer une nouvelle rencontre et redonner de l'espoir.

– Il y a les cours de gymnastique intensive, de body-building, d'abdos-fessiers-jambes redoutables, de sculpture du corps, de step, de stretch, de renforcement musculaire qui, à hautes doses, empêchent la pensée de monter jusqu'au cerveau.

– Il y a la religion : aimer sans attendre de retour.

– Il y a la sublimation par l'art, mais je ne suis pas une artiste.

– Il y a les autres hommes, mais sans amour cela renvoie au paragraphe gymnastique.

– Il y a l'amour, mais je ne connais pas la recette pour le déclencher à la demande.

– Il y a les cours de chant, de tango argentin, de paso-doble pour reprendre confiance en soi.

– Il y a la thérapie de groupe, le cri primal pour libérer.

– Il y a Clémentine.

– Il y a le shopping.

– Il y a le temps qui passe.

– Il y a les tartelettes sablées aux fraises des bois et le Mont-Blanc.

– Il y a le hasard.

– Il y a plus malheureux que moi : le héros d'*Un amour* de Dino Buzzati.

La révolte stagne encore. La révolte est une flaque, une eau trouble et glauque.

Je pourrais appeler une psy, un marabout, une voyante, aller à l'église, faire une razzia au Body Shop, me lancer dans une série d'abdominaux, me souvenir de tous les mots d'amour que je connais, des plus simples aux plus compliqués, me réciter le début de *L'Étranger*, la fin de *Martin Eden*, la conversation entre le renard et le Petit Prince, les poèmes de Victor Hugo sur la tombe de Léopoldine, ceux de Mallarmé, Verlaine, Baudelaire, je ne parviendrais pas à oublier son silence. Je n'oublierais pas son silence.

Sans raison, plusieurs fois par jour, mon patron passe le nez dans mon bureau et m'adresse un petit compliment, puis il disparaît. Soudain, je me souviens d'une boîte de marrons glacés à Noël et de fleurs pour mon anniversaire et je le vois différemment. C'est étrange, non, comme on peut vivre dans la proximité d'une personne sans la voir pendant des années et, tout à coup, la lumière se fait sur elle ; je la vois. Je *le* vois. D'après mon assistante, il est amoureux : et je dois te confier que cela ne me laisse pas indifférente. A-t-il l'intention de m'emmener dans une suite royale, au Ritz ou ailleurs ?

Du coup, j'ai pris du temps pour moi et je me suis mise au régime ; coupe de cheveux, manucure, pédicure, achat de lingerie. J'ai peur qu'il s'aperçoive de ma transformation... Mais peut-être ne fait-il que parler et complimenter ?

179

E-MAIL D'IDYLLE À CLÉMENTINE

À cette idée, je suis morte de rire... je préfère encore ma brute silencieuse à ton amoureux délicat.

Les relations extraconjugales se calculent en minutes, se mesurent en mètres carrés : un lit d'un mètre vingt et un canapé profond comme une banquette de métro font l'affaire, nul besoin de baignoire en marbre, de double lavabo ou double living, de gravures, de bougeoirs, de lits king-size, de décoration raffinée, de longs discours ;

L'adultère n'est ni bavard ni matérialiste.

L'essentiel est cerné.

L'essentiel se tait.

L'essentiel se fait.

E-MAIL DE CLÉMENTINE À IDYLLE

OK ! Message reçu sept sur sept.

E-MAIL D'IDYLLE À CLÉMENTINE

Si je ne peux couper le cordon, j'aimerais au moins me désintoxiquer de mon amoureux silencieux. Est-ce que tu as une recette qui marche, si je me souviens bien le gros sel avait échoué ?

Le silence des hommes

La réflexologie ! Toute la géographie de notre corps et de notre esprit est dessinée sur la plante de nos pieds. Fais-toi masser l'orteil gauche pour le dissoudre. Il est là !

Les différentes façons
de lire la carte du Tendre

Il y a différentes façons de lire la carte du Tendre.

Il y a les jours sombres où je ne lis que le mauvais de lui, comme une pièce de monnaie, et qu'une face valait plus que l'autre. Depuis quelques jours, ses expressions me reviennent en mémoire, saletés d'expressions : « Tourne-toi », « Je l'ai fait exprès », « Chut », « Hum », « Il ne faut pas. » Puis il y a l'autre chemin, le tendre chemin du Tendre, celui qui m'a perdue dans la forêt des sentiments, le chemin du silence comme un refuge, un silence où seuls résonnent son souffle, ses caresses, ses baisers, le langage de son corps qui ne ment pas, ma docilité et mes supplications secrètes. Quelle est la bonne lecture de cet homme curieux ? M'aime-t-il, m'a-t-il aimée, a-t-il joué ? Tout dépend de l'instant, de la manière dont je vois les choses, de l'impulsion, de l'influence de sa propre appréhension des autres. Ma vision peut être tronquée. Je peux me tromper. Ma peur peut l'influencer.

Dehors, l'impénitent soleil continue de briller alors

que Jean ne me dit toujours rien. L'été indien, les dernières jupes en mousseline, les dernières sandales, les dernières jambes qui s'exhibent sans bas, bientôt les orchidées, adieu les hortensias. La roue tourne et Jean se tait toujours ; il faut que des amours meurent pour que d'autres naissent, que les fleurs se fanent et que les boutons éclosent, il faut que les hommes se déclarent ou s'en aillent.

L'automne est propice à la plantation et aux résolutions, le printemps aux amours, la vie a ses rites, personne n'y déroge.

La séparation et la fin, vers quoi tendent les êtres et les choses, m'inspirent une panique incontournable. Que serait la vie si nous ne tâchions pas d'oublier que les liens se distendent, les corps se fatiguent, s'épuisent et finissent par s'éteindre ?

Alors j'habite le silence pour le garder. Je mets dans ce silence tous mes espoirs de le revoir et je ne sais plus si c'est lui ou l'écho de ma propre voix que j'entends.

Si je crois en lui, c'est qu'il m'est impossible de justifier tout ce temps à attendre qu'il se déclare. Autrement, tout ne serait que fanfaronnades, forfanterie ou rodomontades...

Je l'ai entendu parce que je l'aimais.

Dans le doute, je le perds.

E-MAIL DE CLÉMENTINE À IDYLLE

Est-ce que tu crois qu'un homme qui me récite des vers de Mallarmé et me compare à la rousse peinte par Burne-Jones ira plus loin ?

E-MAIL D'IDYLLE À CLÉMENTINE

Non.
Mais tu es mûre, alors tu vas bien finir par lui trouver quelque chose. Ce n'est pas l'objet qui crée le désir, mais le désir qui crée ses objets.

E-MAIL DE CLÉMENTINE À IDYLLE

Encore tes réminiscences de khâgne !
Le problème est que l'on ne m'accroche ni avec de la poésie ni avec le silence, encore moins avec la philosophie.

185

E-MAIL D'IDYLLE À CLÉMENTINE

Mignonne, va donc voir si la poésie mène au lit ! Hi !
hi ! Ah, j'ai failli oublier de te raconter. Hier soir, je suis
allée dîner chez des amis. Soudain, la conversation se
porta sur ce scandale déjà démodé : l'affaire Lewinsky.
« Il fallait y penser, à une chose pareille, non ? » dit mon
voisin de gauche, évoquant la petite robe de chez Gap.
« Ça n'existe pas une fille qui fait ça, on lirait une
histoire similaire dans un roman que personne n'y croi-
rait. Vous pourriez imaginer un truc de ce genre si vous
écriviez un roman ? »
Au risque de choquer mon voisin, je l'ai contredit sèche-
ment : « Mais oui, je pourrais garder la robe salie par
mon amant en souvenir, rien ne me semblerait plus
naturel ! » L'homme me considéra avec une défiance
mêlée d'un intérêt certain.

E-MAIL DE CLÉMENTINE À IDYLLE

Tu es folle de dire des choses pareilles !

E-MAIL D'IDYLLE À CLÉMENTINE

Dire ou faire ?

Le silence des hommes

Les deux.

Je l'ai dit parce que je l'ai fait.
Je l'ai dit parce que le besoin de parler était plus fort
que la pudeur.
Je devais le raconter pour le mettre à distance, pour le
sortir de moi, pour le partager, pour m'en servir, pour
le réduire à de la conversation, à un sujet comme un
autre. Le dernier amant après le dernier film, en faire
de la matière à roman, comme je dirais de la pâte à
gâteau. Le transformer en sculpture, en marionnette, en
poupée de chiffon, en Barbie, en Ken, en musique, en
roulements de tambour, en marches militaires, en
convois funéraires, en poèmes, en charades, en devinet-
tes, en papier mâché. Dire.

Ne te fâche pas, je te comprends. Parle si ça t'arrange,
ne te prive pas !
Mon mari ne parle plus, même pas pour demander le
sel.

187

Le silence des hommes

E-MAIL D'IDYLLE À CLÉMENTINE

Il existerait un silence du désamour ?

E-MAIL DE CLÉMENTINE À IDYLLE

Je le crains. Par contre, je ne crois pas au silence amoureux, quelques secondes, le temps d'un regard, pas si
longtemps. Le silence de Jean est d'une nature inconnue. Depuis le début, je me méfie de cet homme. Moi,
quand je ne comprends pas, je me barre !

Une autre saison

Six mois se sont écoulés. Je suis, sans remède possible, murée dans son silence.

Nous avons changé de saison, chez Eres les bikinis acidulés refont surface, dans les parcs les enfants rejouent au ballon, à l'élastique, à la marelle, je me suis fait épiler six fois les jambes pour rien, mes cheveux ont poussé d'au moins huit centimètres sans qu'il ait aligné plus d'une phrase qui ait un sens. Alors, mille fois je me suis répété l'observation de Proust : « Certes, les charmes d'une personne sont une cause moins fréquente d'amour qu'une phrase comme : "Non, ce soir, je ne serai pas libre." » Cette phrase, si j'osais la mettre en pratique, provoquerait Jean. Je me suis entraînée, la langue légère, la bouche en cœur, à dire : non.

Il fallait être moderne ou suicidaire, ce qui revenait au même, pour ne pas écouter Proust et en prendre de la graine.

Mais Jean appelle et Proust ne compte plus.

Proust a un siècle de retard.

Inutile de calquer sa vie sur la littérature.

La vie n'est pas un roman.

Proust ne connaissait rien aux femmes.

Odette, Mme Verdurin ne me ressemblent pas.

Je suis unique.

Je suis moderne.

Personne ne peut décider à ma place.

Je préfère payer pour mes propres erreurs que pour celles des autres, fussent-ils Marcel Proust.

Jean appelle dès qu'il est disponible, j'ai envie de le voir, pourquoi refuser ?

La vie est courte.

Bilan 1 : Excuses – mufleries = zéro muflerie, plein d'excuses.

Bilan 2 : La durée de la vie – les heures de sommeil + les heures d'emmerdes + le dentiste + le percepteur + le fossoyeur = pourquoi se gâcher un bon moment ?

Logique d'Idylle : ses empêchements suffisent pour ne pas y ajouter les miens.

Conseil de Clémentine : la chirurgie : couper, sectionner, amputer...

Dictionnaire de la médecine : Jean pourrait souffrir d'un arrêt prolongé de la communication verbale, sans lésion, à moins qu'il ne s'agisse d'une inhibition partielle.

Affirmation rituelle : « Je passe prendre un café. »

Sans sucre, sans justification.

Réaction habituelle à cette voix de boudoir le soir

au coin du feu, cette texture feutrée, cette suavité, cette invitation : je cède.

Il s'était approché de moi, dans ce garage-galerie à grands pas d'homme, je l'avais suivi dehors avec mes petits pas de femme empêchée par sa jupe droite et ses talons trop hauts. Puis il est venu, il m'a attirée contre lui et, quand j'ai pris goût à son étreinte, il s'est enfui pour revenir par éclipses, sans un mot ou presque.

Il ne me laisse pas le temps de devenir une autre.

Il est possible que j'aie peur de perdre une chose beaucoup plus importante que lui : un sentiment.

Un sentiment qui m'a tenue en éveil, une obsession qui m'a maintenue, qui a annihilé les problèmes du monde jusqu'à me rendre sourde et aveugle, une hypnose protectrice, une songerie magnifique.

J'ai peur du retour à la vie normale, banale, sans affolement excessif. Je redoute la perte de la rêverie, la plongée dans le matérialisme et dans les contrariétés ridicules. Jean aussi redeviendrait réel s'il parlait, je le verrais tel qu'il est. Construit avec des mots. Des mots empilés comme les pierres d'une pyramide qui le définiraient. Il est probable que, le rêve éloigné, je verrais un homme, pas un surhomme. Un type banal, pas un apollon. Une intelligence moyenne, pas un génie, un coureur de plus, pas un amoureux transi. Des yeux noisette, pas noirs. Silencieux, pas mystérieux. Peut-être même découvrirais-je que Jean se tait parce qu'il n'a rien à dire. Que sa vie intérieure n'est pas celle de

Zweig et son écoute ne ressemble en rien à celle de Freud.

Il ne m'a pas dit si un amour secret pouvait être un amour.

Il ne m'a pas dit s'il croyait au secret.

Il ne m'a pas dit pourquoi il ne me parlait pas.

Il ne m'a pas dit comment nommer ce que nous vivions.

Les choses, les hommes, les relations ont un nom, tout a un nom. Les fleurs, les poissons, les papillons, les virus se désignent. L'encyclopédie déborde de définitions. Pourquoi notre relation, aussi étrange soit-elle, ne se nommerait-elle pas ? Je suis révoltée à cette idée : une révolte similaire à celle que j'aurais pu éprouver contre le père de mon enfant s'il ne l'avait pas reconnu. Quelque chose de secret, d'intense, de torturé a existé, ces moments méritent une appellation, comme un gosse un patronyme, comme les morts une sépulture. Je peux admettre la fin de notre relation, je ne peux pas admettre qu'il ne la qualifie pas. Qu'avons-nous vécu ? Comment s'appelle ce type de liaison épisodique ? Une dépendance ? Une grande tendresse ? Une gémellité ? Un attachement, une inclination, une passion ? un flirt ? Non, pas un flirt, nous avons fait l'amour ensemble. Un bon coup ?

Suis-je un bon coup ? Malgré le rire que l'idée d'être un bon coup déclenche en moi, cette hypothèse ne me va pas.

Je ressemble davantage, et plus tristement encore, à

une femme qu'un homme ne s'est pas fatigué à définir ; peut-être à chérir.

Il existe des hommes insensibles à la douleur et qui se fichent de celle qu'ils suscitent, il y a des hommes incapables du moindre effort. Il y a des hommes qui ne mesurent pas la différence entre un jour et un mois parce que leur vie va trop vite et qu'ils ne peuvent imaginer que celle de l'autre s'écoule différemment. Il y a des hommes réfractaires à toute emprise. À l'emprise des définitions, des descriptions, des précisions, parce que définir, c'est presque juger. Jean appartient à ceux-là.

Jean appelle.

Réponse rituelle à une demande rituelle :

– Oui.

Les mots soulagent, mais n'empêchent pas.

Mon corps a de la mémoire.

– Je viens entre une heure et demie et deux heures moins le quart.

Je suis rentrée du lycée vers midi, les bras chargés de copies et de livres, je n'ai acheté aucune fleur, aucun gâteau, je n'ai même pas ouvert *La pâtisserie est un jeu d'enfant* à la page « mousse au chocolat », alors que je m'entraîne depuis trois mois. À quoi cela servira-t-il ? Il repartira sans même la goûter. L'esthéticienne attendra. Je fermerai les poings, comme un chat qui se retient de griffer, pour cacher mes ongles dédoublés.

Ma tenue ne doit en aucun cas être ostentatoire.

Si mes mots ne peuvent le repousser, mes fringues vont le dissuader. Rien de ce que je vais porter ne doit trahir mon attachement. Pas de jupe fendue, pas de dessous suggestifs, rien de facile à dégrafer. Les barrières de mon corps vont modérer mon accessibilité.

Équilibrer.

Rééquilibrer.

Je l'admire aussi de se présenter à moi toujours avec le même costume ou presque, sans coquetterie particulière. Oui, je peux admirer une chose aussi folle qu'une assurance qui ne dissimule rien ; cette capacité de plaire au naturel, sans risque de se renier.

Quant à la suite des événements, je la connais. Il peut dire qu'il vient « amicalement », puis doucement le désir va chasser l'amitié, le temps d'une étreinte rapide ou pas. Le désir assouvi, la culpabilité reprendra ses droits et il n'y aura même plus de place pour l'amitié, juste pour la fureur et l'éloignement.

Les choses agréables appartiennent au silence parce que je les invente ? Elles se devinent, ne se prononcent pas.

La vie va, la vie vient. Il va et vient comme la vie.

J'assouvis ses fantasmes, il assouvit mes songeries.

Il va encore m'entourer de silence. Comme un pyromane il va craquer l'allumette.

C'est un criminel.

Il veut tuer l'amour.

Je ne sais pas l'empêcher. On peut empêcher un

étrangleur, un violeur, un voleur, un homme qui a décidé de mettre fin à ses jours, à des jours. Mais un désenchanteur ?

Je connais le déroulement des choses, je connais ses empêchements, je sais combien il peut triompher contre lui-même. Je peux faire avancer le film.

La vie se répète.

Mais pourquoi revivre l'histoire quand elle génère de la frustration ?

Il est midi et demi, je suis revenue pour lui, j'ai annulé mon cours sur Vauvenargues, tant mieux, Vauvenargues se trompait quand il soutenait que « les passions ne sauraient être néfastes puisque notre nature n'est pas mauvaise ».

Faux. Les passions et les natures mauvaises existent et sont persistantes, il en existe des catalogues entiers, comme pour les rosiers : il y a les résistants, les remontants, les grimpants, les épineux.

La passion est toujours vive quand elle est contrariée et s'étiole quand elle est partagée. Ma vie est un boogie-woogie, un rock'n'roll sans partenaire. Je tourne, mais toute seule.

Dans mon lecteur de CD résonne de la soul music, la musique de l'âme... Pourquoi n'ai-je pas prêté plus d'attention aux paroles d'Ella, de Sarah, jusqu'à ce jour ? Pourquoi me suis-je laissé murer dans le silence ? Parce qu'aucune mélodie n'est parfaite, seul le silence de Jean ne comportait aucune fausse note. « La perfection nécessite l'imperfection », tu entends, Jean ? ce

195

n'est pas de moi. J'aime les fautes de goût, les maladresses, les erreurs de ponctuation, d'accents circonflexes, de syntaxe. J'aime les gens qui parlent et qui n'ont pas peur de se tromper, tout le monde se trompe, les silencieux aussi.

Les maladroits m'attendrissent ; les verres de vin rouge renversés sur une nappe en lin blanc, les assiettes pleines retournées pour satisfaire une curiosité me font rire. J'aime les gaffes, les compliments décalés, les erreurs, les bévues, les maladresses, les impairs.

À force de se retenir de parler, la voix de Jean va changer. Jean va muer. Ses cordes vocales vont émettre un son nouveau. Un son de nouveau-né ou d'adolescent.

J'attends un son. Le monde entier attend quelque chose. À chacun il manque une sœur, un ami, une grand-mère, une mère, du fric, une maison, un pays, de la chaleur, de la reconnaissance, un chien, un fiancé, un enfant, un père, un frère, un job, de l'espace. Moi, il me manque une voix. L'homme que j'aime serait parfait, complet, s'il avait des mots. Jean manque de mots comme d'autres manquent de calcium ou de phosphore.

Jean souffre d'une déficience verbale.

À la fin du cours, alors que je m'enfuyais, Paul m'a suivie. J'ai sursauté quand, pour me retenir, il a dit des mots, des tas de mots à la suite, des mots qui s'emboîtaient, s'enchaînaient, qui avaient un but et une signification. Il a prononcé des phrases les unes à la suite des autres, des phrases complètes, bien construites, avec un verbe, un adjectif, un complément. C'était étrange, ces mots assemblés, ces phrases articulées dans le but de m'intéresser et de me séduire. Paul parlait. C'est assez incroyable, un homme qui dit.

Nu, il m'aurait moins intimidée.

Il parlait et les mots, au lieu de l'habiller, le déshabillaient.

Un homme qui parle n'a pas peur d'être jugé, c'est un homme qui s'avance sans masque, parce que même les mots du mystère sont moins mystérieux que le silence des mots.

Il est grand, Paul, je lève la tête quand il parle. Il est beau, mais cela n'a pas d'importance, l'incroyable est qu'il dise des mots et que je réponde à ses mots, comme une habitude perdue et retrouvée, comme un sport que je pensais avoir oublié et qui me revient, naturellement, comme le ski ou la bicyclette, je glisse, je pédale, je réponds.

J'avais une certaine pratique de la conversation amoureuse et elle me revenait quand j'avais oublié jusqu'à son existence :

— Les passions sont la source des plus nobles activités et souvent des plus belles vertus, il dit.

— Les passions peuvent détruire, je réponds.

— Elles enrichissent ceux qui sont capables de les vivre, il dit.

— Vous croyez ? je réponds.

— Vous n'allez pas devenir stoïcienne à cause d'un mec ? il dit encore.

J'ai ri, je n'avais pas ri depuis longtemps.

— Qu'est-ce que vous en savez ? j'interroge.

— Je vous ai observée..., il affirme.

— Et vous avez tout compris, vous êtes un devin ! je m'exclame.

— J'ai envie de vous comprendre, il murmure.

Il sait tout faire.

— Je suis votre collègue, je m'indigne.

— Vous êtes une femme.

Il sait.

Je biaise, je change de sujet. Comme une professionnelle de la parole, je dirige.

— Sur quoi écrivez-vous ? Je m'intéresse, etc.

On continue, on sait répondre, s'exclamer, s'interroger, s'indigner, demander, affirmer, on sait, on roule, on glisse, on pédale, on rit.

— J'écris sur nos passions. Sont-elles ou non distinctes de nous-mêmes ?

Nous sommes des gens normaux.

— Quelle est votre réponse ?

— Il faudrait qu'on en parle... je peux inviter ma collègue à dîner ?

Il est un homme normal.

— Je dois rentrer.

Je suis une femme normale, sans calcul.

— Vous annulez votre cours ? Pourquoi ?

— J'ai mal à la tête.

— Je ne vous crois pas, vous vous fichez de beaucoup de choses en ce moment. J'espère qu'il n'en sera pas de même pour notre dîner.

Il dit et je réponds et c'est bien.

Je pose sur ma table basse mes classeurs, l'*Introduction à la connaissance de l'esprit humain*, *Libé* pour l'interview d'une actrice qui prétend « ne jamais regretter aucune décision ». J'ai un faible pour les interviews, j'y trouve toujours des solutions, comme après un voyage ou après une conversation avec une amie. Je ne sais pas encore quelle décision je vais prendre, mais je sens poindre la fin de quelque chose d'inhérent à moi, quelque chose en moi se transforme.

N'est-ce pas plus juste de dire, se perd ? Je m'éloigne à regret d'une certaine capacité à m'émouvoir, à individualiser un homme, à l'aimer peut-être.

L'important est de ne pas regretter la décision que je prendrai, comme une actrice. Pourquoi sont-elles si fortes, ces femmes qui se confient dans les journaux ? Est-ce qu'elles cachent le fond de leur âme ? L'apparence, l'arrogance, la force toujours ? Moi, je regrette souvent. Comme autant de chemins qui se referment pour toujours.

Pas d'introspection ; l'heure est à l'action. Cette fois, je vais lui dire que je suis fatiguée de cette langue qui se lie mais ne se délie pas, de ses mots pratiques, de ses énumérations dignes des *Choses* de Perec : le café, les chaussures, sans que jamais aucun sentiment vienne éclairer ses maigres propos.

Je suis fatiguée de fréquenter un type qui ne boit que du café, pas de vin, pas de jus d'orange, ne mange jamais de gâteaux, ni de spaghettis, ni de crustacés. Aucune affinité hormis la sexualité. Pas de problèmes, pas d'états d'âme, pas d'histoires. Pas de mal de tête ou de dos, pas de pipi en arrivant. Tu es peut-être un robot, un homme programmé pour l'amour de deux à trois par semaine, avec le silence comme option. Mais tu n'es pas très original, Jean. Le silence ne remporte pas la palme. Le bon Dieu en fabrique pas mal sur ton modèle. Tu as beaucoup de clones en ce moment. Tu ne te rends même pas compte combien elles prolifèrent, les bébêtes à silence.

A priori, cela aurait pu me plaire ! Ça ne ronchonne pas, ça ne fait pas le malin, ça ne critique pas, ça ne met pas son grain de sel, ça ne parle ni de foot, ni d'impôts, ni de politique et c'est mieux qu'un chien parce que ça ne perd pas ses poils et ça n'aboie pas quand la sonnerie de la porte retentit.

Il s'en est fallu de peu que j'y prenne goût.

Sur mon répondeur : « Idylle ? C'est Paul, demain à vingt heures trente à La Coupole. Je ne vous donne pas mon numéro de téléphone pour éviter que vous me décommandiez. Vous n'allez quand même pas me poser un lapin ? J'aurai de l'Aspro, du Di-Antalvic, de la Catalgine, de l'Optalidon, du Doliprane, de l'Advil, plein les poches. Courage... la vie est belle ! »

J'ouvre la fenêtre ; depuis que je sème des miettes de pain sur mon balcon, les oiseaux chantent dès le matin. « La vie est belle ! » dit-il.

Le bonheur partirait avec les grandes choses et reviendrait avec les petites ?

Le bonheur réapparaît avec les mots, les mots qui éclosent avec les fleurs et chantent avec les oiseaux.

Cet homme-là doit murmurer les mots de la tendresse, du désir, de l'impatience, de l'excitation. Je ne savais pas que dire l'amour était aussi important que de le faire.

Mes jambes sont un désastre, entre deux repousses il n'y a qu'une solution, la crème dépilatoire. Mon esthéticienne m'assure que l'effet de la crème est aussi néfaste que celui du rasoir. Ah ! la tyrannie des poils !

E-MAIL DE CLÉMENTINE À IDYLLE

Mignonne a été voir si la poésie mène au lit.
Eh bien oui !

E-MAIL D'IDYLLE À CLÉMENTINE

C'est le Jackpot !!!

E-MAIL DE CLÉMENTINE À IDYLLE

Il s'appelle Jacques.

E-MAIL D'IDYLLE À CLÉMENTINE

Le timing est parfait. Nous approchons de la fin d'une
histoire pour en commencer une autre. Je suis heureuse
de changer de disque ; le mien était rayé.

E-MAIL DE CLÉMENTINE À IDYLLE

Tu vas opérer ? Briser le cordon du silence ?... Il faudra au moins lui reconnaître un avantage à cet homme, tu ne vas pas perdre grand-chose.
Tu ne subiras rien de plus qu'un déplacement d'air, comme dans la rue lorsque le vent souffle et nous bouscule. Le vent va souffler et tu retrouveras ton équilibre.

E-MAIL D'IDYLLE À CLÉMENTINE

J'ai mis tant de choses dans ces silences ; j'y ai mis mes rêves, mes espoirs, les mots que je voulais entendre et même s'il ne les a pas prononcés, qu'importe ! Il me les a inspirés.

E-MAIL DE CLÉMENTINE À IDYLLE

Tu confonds la vie rêvée avec la vie réelle.

E-MAIL D'IDYLLE À CLÉMENTINE

Et s'il changeait ? Je dois encore lui laisser une chance.

Le silence des hommes

Il ne changera pas.
Tourne la page avant de devenir dingue ! Tu en sortiras un peu meurtrie mais très vite soulagée.
Tu verras, la terre ferme, les mots vrais, c'est plus étroit mais finalement mieux que les nuages et les chimères. Il faut redescendre, Bibiche... Et sur la terre, au milieu de la foule, à Londres, à Paris, en province, dans un bureau, dans une école ou dans une forêt, un jour tu rencontreras un homme qui te demandera de tes nouvelles, qui te dira que tu lui as manqué, qu'il a pensé à toi et la chimère laissera place à la réalité. Laisse-lui une chance.
Tu revivras. Tu verras.
Courage Bibiche !
La libération approche. On fêtera ça.

Dernière visite

Le maître du silence arrive dans trois quarts d'heure. Son pouls commence à s'accélérer, peut-être s'est-il prêté à quelques génuflexions, son chauffeur a arrêté la Safrane devant Notre-Dame et il a prié, puis il a commandé par téléphone un petit sac de chez Vuitton ou de chez Hermès pour sa femme. C'est un peu cher. Je vaux bien un sac à beaucoup d'euros pour sa femme.

Le chauffeur le laissera à l'angle d'une rue, à deux ou trois pâtés de maisons de la mienne, il finira à pied. Il est malin mon Sherlock, un vrai pro.

Je tourne en rond. Je ne range rien ; mon appartement et moi sommes en grève. Mes roses sont fanées et l'eau doit commencer à croupir, je n'ai pas passé l'aspirateur depuis des lustres. Il vient dans une demi-heure, je suis mal habillée et je m'en fiche.

Je réécoute le message de Paul : « La vie est belle ! » Oui, si l'on veut. À condition d'éviter les maîtres du silence quand ils croisent votre chemin. Aucun désir de séduction, ma culotte de jogging grise fera l'affaire. Il arrive dans vingt minutes et tout va recommencer. Le cœur qui s'emballe, le rapprochement, l'éloignement, mes supplications, mes questions, puis la déception.

Récapitulation :

Avant : le meilleur, de toute façon.

Pendant : les choses se compliquent.

Après, il se tait.

Voilà le scénario.

Il y a des choses que l'on fait et l'on ne sait pas pourquoi on les a entreprises. Il y a aussi les montagnes que l'on ne peut pas escalader, des obstacles que le cheval refuse de franchir, des os que le chien enterre plutôt que de les ronger.

D'un coup, mes découragements, mes résolutions, mes insurrections s'additionnent. Je subis mes attentes en cascades. Je ne pourrai plus ouvrir la porte à Jean.

Trop d'indifférence, de malveillance. Il aurait dû clairsemer ses indélicatesses, pas les aligner comme les perles du collier qu'il ne m'offrira jamais.

Je ne veux plus vivre cette relation qu'il n'a jamais nommée, ce temps arraché, ces mots gardés, l'amour empêché.

Je ne veux plus du silence, du vide, du creux, du blanc, de la rêverie en guise de compagnie ; je veux des rendez-vous, des plats de spaghettis et du vin italien ; je veux que l'on me dise bonjour le matin et bonsoir le soir ; je veux des lectures, des échanges, de la complicité, de la compréhension plus que la présence.

La sonnette de la porte a retenti sans qu'il ait appelé

à l'interphone, je suppose qu'en bas un voisin lui a ouvert ; je ne pourrai plus l'affronter.

Il est derrière la porte, il croit que je vais lui ouvrir, que tout se déroulera comme d'habitude. Il n'a aucune idée de la révolution qui se prépare. J'ai toujours accepté sans broncher les règles de son jeu, pourquoi se méfierait-il aujourd'hui ?

J'ai de la peine à cause de la fin. Toutes les fins me font pleurer, même au cinéma. Les provoquer m'est intolérable : « Nous ne faisons jamais, pour la dernière fois, sans une tristesse au cœur, ce que nous avons depuis longtemps accoutumance de faire. » Chaque fois que je suis amenée à quitter un lieu ou une personne, même si elle ne m'a pas rendue heureuse, je sens profondément cette vérité tirée des *Paradis artificiels*. À la tristesse de ne plus la revoir s'ajoute la terreur de la fin.

Il est moins évident que l'on ne le croit de sacrifier un présent médiocre pour un avenir meilleur.

Ma conscience s'exprime comme un banquier : économiser aujourd'hui pour profiter demain. Me voilà contaminée par le système, moi qui ai toujours préféré le présent au futur. Deux comprimés de Stilnox m'aideront à passer ce cap. Les barbituriques agissent comme un suicide de courte durée, ils m'aideront à ne pas vivre ce que mon romantisme excessif amplifierait de manière dramatique. Un miracle de la pharmacologie. Un rêve pour les longs-courriers. Une solution à renouveler pour les chagrins d'amour.

Je me sers une tasse de thé et une tranche de mon

gâteau au yaourt avant de dormir une dizaine d'heures d'affilée, sans résistance possible.

Je me déshabille, comme Cléopâtre au moment de plonger sa main dans le panier de figues, l'apparat en moins. Je jette mes chaussures d'un côté, ma chemise de l'autre, tant pis pour le désordre, tout m'est permis parce que je vais faire quelque chose de très difficile et très douloureux aujourd'hui. Alors je ne me contrarierai pas, je jetterai mes affaires si cela me chante.

Oui, aujourd'hui, je vais subir une ablation, je vais arracher un homme de mes pensées, je ne sais même pas si j'y parviendrai, si ma volonté sera assez forte pour triompher ; si en cours d'opération, alors que je me serai déjà administré le sédatif, les regrets ne vont pas m'assaillir et m'entraîner à lui ouvrir la porte, à me prosterner, à lui demander, la bouche pâteuse, pardon de l'avoir fait attendre, pardon d'avoir voulu m'échapper, pardon pour le désordre, pardon pour le pantalon de jogging, pardon pour le Stilnox qui me rend gâteuse, pardon d'avoir douté, pardon de m'être un peu moquée, pardon de mon impatience.

Ce n'est pas facile d'extraire quelqu'un de soi, même quand il est mauvais.

Surtout quand il est mauvais.

J'avale les comprimés du sommeil garanti avec une tasse d'Earl Grey. Pas de goût. Les comprimés sont lisses comme des Smarties, ils suivent leur chemin.

Dans quinze minutes, quoi qu'il advienne, ils

m'auront envoyée dans les bras de Morphée et, quand je me réveillerai, un autre jour commencera, un jour sans Jean derrière la porte. Je ne porte plus qu'une culotte et un T-shirt de coton bleu pâle, à fines bretelles, rien de très affolant, mais agréable pour dormir, certains hommes sont assez dégénérés pour trouver la culotte Petit Bateau sexy. La tête me tourne, la position allongée à plat ventre sur mon matelas me semble la plus appropriée à mon état. J'ai peur de ne pas être assez forte pour résister, de ne pas valoir mieux qu'une heure de passion tous les deux ou trois jours.

Plus que cinq minutes. C'est incroyable, malgré l'effet apaisant du somnifère, je regrette cette heure avec lui dont je vais me priver. Mon corps se révolte contre moi. Ma souffrance devient intolérable ; je suis un ennemi de moi-même.

Il aura changé, je dois lui laisser cette chance. Inutile. Dans quelques minutes, je serai modifiée au point de préférer dormir à n'importe quoi, même faire l'amour avec lui. Dans quelques minutes, je serai différente et apaisée.

Patience.

J'aime qu'une force en moi, fût-elle chimique, m'impose un comportement, une force que je n'ai pas et qui décide à ma place. Je n'ai eu la volonté que d'avaler deux comprimés.

Comment en suis-je arrivée là ?

Il sonne.

Silence.

Je ne respire plus.

Il sonne à nouveau.

Impossible de rester couchée.

Je me lève.

Il sonne.

J'ouvre la boîte en porcelaine, j'attrape le mouchoir de papier, je le respire, même s'il ne sent plus rien, je le mouille de mes larmes

Il sonne.

Je marche dans ma minuscule alcôve, je m'agenouille, le visage plongé entre mes mains.

Il sonne.

Le tintement résonne, cruel, dans ma tête.

Il ne doit rien comprendre à ce qui se passe. Pour la première fois, il n'entend pas mes pas pressés et joyeux se précipiter vers l'entrée.

Il sonne.

J'entends sa voix adorée.

Je ne me souviens plus de lui prononçant mon nom. L'a-t-il prononcé ?

Il frappe.

Il tambourine avec ses poings.

Je me lève, évite de m'approcher de la porte, me dirige vers la salle de bains, mon Kleenex à la main, le jette dans les toilettes et tire la chasse d'eau.

Je ne possède plus rien de lui.

Je m'allonge sur mon lit. La tête me tourne, j'ai envie qu'il me serre dans ses bras même si c'est pour m'endormir. L'homme que j'adore est derrière la porte et je ne lui ouvre pas. Et je m'insurge contre moi-même. Qu'ai-je fait ! Je voudrais revenir en arrière, enfoncer une main au fond de ma gorge, me laver les dents, me repoudrer le nez, mais le temps d'organiser cette opération et il sera reparti !

Je respire doucement, le médicament commence son travail ; il m'emmène là où j'aurai moins mal, là où les désirs et les rêves s'apaisent, bientôt je ne le verrai plus les yeux fermés.

Je ne le renvoie pas pour qu'il me revienne mieux, l'époque n'est plus aux stratégies, je le renvoie pour qu'il ne revienne plus.

Il frappe de ses deux poings, les voisins vont hurler.

Je me rallonge sur le lit, à plat ventre comme pour dormir, bien que je n'aie pas encore sommeil. Quand l'envie de dormir me viendra-t-elle en aide ?

Je pose mon coussin et le sien, celui qu'il n'a jamais utilisé, sur ma tête.

Je compte à voix haute, mais je ne dors toujours pas. Je bats des pieds contre le matelas. Je voudrais m'épuiser.

Les yeux grands ouverts sous la plume, je cherche des images de Paul. Est-ce que Paul pourra me sauver ?

Est-ce que je pourrai aimer assez Paul pour oublier Jean ?

Est-ce que Paul saura m'embarquer dans une rêverie aussi folle ?

Est-ce que Paul saura dire les mots de l'amour ?

Est-ce que le bonheur sera assez grand pour prendre la place du malheur ?

Mon téléphone sonne : un numéro masqué. Le maître du silence utilise son portable, je ne réponds pas, il raccroche sans laisser de message.

Je reconnais sa facture.

Il est partout, il est derrière ma porte et dans mon répondeur ; sans donner pour autant ni explications ni excuses, toujours cette présence énigmatique. Mais, grâce au Stilnox, moi aussi je vais devenir énigmatique.

Je pleure, je sanglote, les larmes m'étouffent. Le Stilnox n'atteint que mes jambes, pas mon cerveau, mon cerveau est toujours vif, plein de lui. À croire que j'ai bu la ciguë. La fin, ce n'est pas un ou deux comprimés de somnifère, c'est de ne plus jamais le revoir. Je pleure la fin, la mort d'un amour qui aurait pu être et qui ne sera jamais. La fin d'une histoire ressemble à une affliction ; je suis en deuil de ce que je n'ai pas connu et que j'aurais pu connaître, en deuil de tout ce que je voulais lui dire et que je ne lui ai pas dit. De tout ce qu'il ne sait pas. Une sensation d'étouffement m'étreint. Pourquoi ne m'a-t-il jamais laissée lui parler ? À chaque tentative, il m'en empêchait en m'embrassant ou en me quittant. J'aurais dû tenter un coup d'État sentimental, peut-être que secrètement il espérait un coup d'État pour être délivré de

214

son mutisme ? Il y a des hommes qu'il faut violer, paraît-il.

L'ai-je tenté ?

– Il est trop tard, dis-je, la voix assourdie par mon coussin.

Et j'essaie de penser à Paul pour m'aider, à Paul les poches pleines de Di-Antalvic. Je le connais à peine, juste son air prétentieux, son air d'en savoir plus que moi et qui m'agace parfois. Juste sa façon de jeter sa veste sur une épaule, de glisser ses lunettes de soleil sur la tête, de porter son cartable comme s'il pesait trois tonnes et de se retourner pour me regarder une dernière fois avant de partir. Je me souviens d'avoir été intriguée, disons pour être honnête, un peu plus qu'intriguée. Son âge m'inquiète. Je n'ai jamais fait l'amour avec un homme plus jeune que moi.

Jean frappe.

Je me lève, je me traîne vers la porte. Je suis une maso, je suis une imbécile, une prétentieuse ; je n'admets pas qu'un homme ne m'aime pas comme je le voudrais. Je suis une capricieuse, je veux jouir, je veux du temps, des attentions, des mots, des définitions. Je veux être aimée et le savoir.

Jean frappe.

C'est difficile le premier « non », c'est une abnégation, une ablation, une opération, une violence.

Mon corps est intrépide, mon corps me désobéit tout le temps, mon corps est déraisonnable, mon corps me dirige. Quand le corps domine, le désordre s'ensuit ; nos corps s'entendent, mais nos esprits s'affrontent. Son corps m'appelle, son esprit l'en empêche. Et, au travers de la porte en bois, je devine sa peau mate et soyeuse et je tremble. Je quitte le lit, je m'approche à quatre pattes sur la moquette, je rampe presque, je touche la porte, je la caresse, je pleure, mais son corps n'est pas le maître à bord, son corps est soumis : son esprit lui interdit d'être un amant attentionné, d'être un amant tout simplement.

Je ne peux rien contre son esprit.

J'aurais aimé remplir ma boîte en porcelaine, la remplir à ras bord et plus encore, j'aurais voulu collectionner les Kleenex, en avoir dix mille pleins de lui. Un jour, peut-être, dans une autre vie, j'en aurai dix mille ; je les inhalerai, les conserverai dans un récipient étudié à cet effet, je consulterai un laboratoire, j'expliquerai sans rougir à des médecins, des psychiatres, des biologistes que je veux conserver le sperme de mon amant frais et humide, que je ne veux pas qu'il sèche ni ne s'évapore.

Je leur dirai que non, ce n'est pas pour le faire chanter ni le piéger, je ne veux pas de bébé, je veux son sperme, juste pour le respirer, le soir avant de me coucher, parce qu'on ne dort pas ensemble, vous comprenez ? Parce que l'on ne vit pas ensemble, parce que je suis une maîtresse, un secret, et que j'ai besoin d'attention pour résister.

Jean frappe.

Je me traîne jusqu'à lui, ç'aurait été trop facile de le renvoyer au silence qu'il m'a fait subir.

Le silence n'est pas ma façon.

La bouche collée contre l'interstice de la porte, je lui dis d'une voix atone :

– J'en ai assez.

Réponse de Jean :

Silence.

– J'ai sommeil.

Silence.

– J'ai sommeil mais je n'ai pas fait la fête, j'ai juste avalé deux Stilnox.

Silence.

– J'aurais aimé que tu sois jaloux, comme un Italien... Tu aurais pu être italien physiquement, moralement tu es du Nord, du pôle Nord, tu es de glace.

– Mademoiselle, ça ne va pas ?

– Jean ?

– Ce n'est pas Jean.

– Ce n'est pas Jean ?

– C'est la concierge, mademoiselle. Vous avez besoin d'aide ? Je n'ai pas compris ce que vous venez de me dire.

– Madame Griffarin ?

– J'ai tambouriné à votre porte, je vous ai appelée de mon portable et vous ne répondiez ni ne décrochiez.

Ça ne va pas ? Êtes-vous seule ? Avez-vous besoin d'aide ?

– Qu'est-ce que vous faites derrière ma porte ?

– Je venais vous remettre une lettre. Un monsieur est passé et m'a demandé de vous la monter tout de suite.

– Une lettre ? Comment il est ce monsieur ?

– Il vous appelle Idylle.

– Glissez la lettre sous ma porte.

– J'appelle le docteur... ?

– Tout va bien.

– Vous êtes sûre ?

– Oui. S'il vous plaît, glissez la lettre sous la porte, vite.

Et Mme Griffarin glissa une enveloppe bleu pâle sur laquelle, à l'encre noire, était marqué : POUR IDYLLE, PERSONNEL.

À la hâte, je décachetai l'enveloppe, en sortis deux pages écrites recto-verso, mais la tête me tournait trop et la finesse de l'écriture m'empêchait de lire. Je n'étais plus qu'une barque prise dans la tempête qui, inéluctablement, chavirait. Mes yeux se fermaient. Les mots tant souhaités étaient là, rendus, alignés, mais ils ne se laissaient pas capturer par mon regard. Ils dansaient et s'éloignaient comme un mirage. Je crus lire le verbe aimer plusieurs fois, mais je suis incapable de dire s'il était conjugué au présent ou au passé, s'il était habillé ou dénudé. Ironie du sort.

N'était-ce pas mieux ainsi ?

Je ne voulais plus découvrir le mystère de cet homme.

Le silence nous avait unis, le silence allait nous désunir. J'ai embrassé, caressé, laissé glisser mes lèvres sur le papier comme j'aimais les laisser glisser le long de son sexe. J'ai respiré Jean entre les lignes. Je l'ai aimé une dernière fois, et pour toujours peut-être, la bouche collée contre les mots qu'il ne prononçait pas, puis j'ai caché l'enveloppe dans un endroit improbable en espérant ne jamais la retrouver. J'ai rampé jusqu'à mon lit.

Voilà.

De ces mois passés à l'espérer il me reste une lettre, quelque part, une machine Magimix chromée à cinq cents euros achetée pour lui, qui fonctionnera pour un autre, un briquet en plastique rouge qui avait glissé de sa poche entre les coussins de mon canapé, ce cœur que je lui avais donné et qu'il m'a rendu.

Il me restera forcément le silence.

Je l'ai aimé en silence.

Son silence nous a soudés.

Son silence, c'est la maison qu'il m'a offerte.

Je l'ai meublée.

Je ne te lirai pas.

Bonsoir, mon amour.

E-MAIL DE CLÉMENTINE À IDYLLE

Idylle, tu es triste ?

E-MAIL D'IDYLLE À CLÉMENTINE

Je te le dirai demain.

La composition de cet ouvrage
a été réalisée par I.G.S. Charente Photogravure,
à l'Isle-d'Espagnac,
l'impression et le brochage ont été effectués
sur presse Cameron dans les ateliers
de **Bussière Camedan Imprimeries**
à Saint-Amand-Montrond (Cher),
pour le compte des Éditions Albin Michel.

Achevé d'imprimer en mars 2003.
N° d'édition : 21333. N° d'impression : 030857/4.
Dépôt légal : avril 2003.
Imprimé en France

digital design using

QuarkXPress 4

Paul Honeywill and Tony Lockhart

intellect

First Published in 1997 by
Intellect Books
EFAE, Earl Richards Road North, Exeter, EX2 6AS, UK

Consulting editor: Masoud Yazdani
Copy editor: Lucy Kind
Cover Illustration: Sam Robinson

Illustrations: Screen dumps from QuarkXPress 4 and
                       material provided by both authors.

A catalogue record for this book is available from the British
Library

ISBN 1-871516-76-5

Printed and bound in the UK by Cromwell Press, Wiltshire

Table of Contents

Preface 5

Chapter 1   **You, Intuition and the QuarkXPress Interface** 7

2   **Using QuarkXPress:**

The Document Layout 13
The Toolbox 19
Text 21
Pictures 53
Long Documents 69
Colour 95
Special Effects 99
Printing 109

3   **You, Design and Working with QuarkXPress** 117

4   **Structuring a Document** 125

5   **Using Elements (Items) within a Document** 139

6   **Using Digital Type within QuarkXPress** 159

7   **When your Document leaves the Desktop** 175

Index 187

Acknowledgments

We would like to thank Quark Inc, Colorado USA for inviting us to be Beta testers of QuarkXPress 4 and offering general assistance with the book. Also, the chair of Scitex User Group UK for allowing us to see and use research findings from many reprographic houses on file encounters between themselves and the customer: we hope that the final chapter will raise awareness. We would also like to thank the students who tested Chapter 2, 'Using QuarkXPress'. In addition we would like to thank Frank Wright for his help with printing issues, Omar Al Hasso for researching the design changes in *MacUser,* Jane Weston and Katharine Reeve for their help and advice.

Trademarks

Throughout this book trademarked names occur. Rather than put a trademark symbol in every occurrence, we state that the names are used only in an editorial fashion and to the benefit of the owner with no intention of infringement.

The Phaistos disc from Crete, forms the creative source for the cover illustration. Reproduced from Sassoon, R., Gaur, A. 1997 *Signs, symbols and icons,* Intellect

This book is dedicated to:

Glynis, Lois and William – *PH*

and

Maeve Heneke and the staff of the former Paddington College, London. Now I truly know that as B. F. Skinner said in 1964 *'Education is what survives when what has been learned has been forgotten'* – *TL*

Preface

Design before computers required a detailed understanding of the processes involved. The advent of desktop publishing has led to the removal of many aspects of these processes which retained trade and professional specialisms, such as graphic designer, typesetter and so on. Consequently, dtp became branded as a lower order of design. In many cases it was a lack of design knowledge that gave dismissive ammunition to the elite few who regarded dtp in this way. In its defence, it was not the technology that reflected the design quality, it was that it was available to anybody who wanted to 'desktop-publish'.

This book addresses the problem by looking at the fundamentals of traditional design and how it compares in the digital age. It attempts to bring these two processes together by analysing what was good practice before page make-up software and how it applies to working digitally.

Chapters 3 to 7 will equip you with a foundation of knowledge which will allow you to self-learn and develop appropriate design skills by understanding what to look for, as opposed to being shown examples of clever designs which at this stage you could reproduce only by step-by-step copying without knowing why.

Chapter 2 will teach you how to use QuarkXPress 4 as a design tool. What you create with that knowledge is entirely up to you. Once you have grasped a function of the software use your own text and image files to practice. By doing so you place learning into context, *only you know what you wish to achieve.*

The object is not just to get to the end of the book in a certain time period. Teaching QuarkXPress to a beginner on a one-to-one basis would, on average, take 3 to 4 days. However, rarely does one find two people learning at the same pace. Set your own pace, proceed to the next section only when you are comfortable with what you have learned and more importantly how it relates to what you wish to communicate in your design.

To get the most from this book, we suggest that when you are using chapter 2, the QuarkXPress tutorial section, you should refer to chapters 3 to 7 for more information i.e. why is one typeface preferable to another? The design section does not tell you what is a good typeface and what isn't; what it does tell you is what to look for in a typeface so that you can make an informed choice.

The step-by-step guides are numbered paragraphs. Read these before doing anything. In the side margins are tips, hints and other additional information.

You do not have to be a computing wizard to use this book. However, it is assumed you possess the basic skills of clicking, dragging, copying and pasting in the windows environments found on both Macintosh and PC.

Important

Throughout Chapter 2 there are keyboard shortcuts for various functions. This book was produced on an Apple Macintosh. To avoid unnecessary wording we have inserted the Macintosh keyboard commands in the text. If you are using QuarkXPress 4 on a PC, simply substitute the Control key for the Command key. Other keyboard commands should work as listed. If you have a Macintosh with an older-style keyboard, use Option when asked to use Alt.

You, Intuition and the QuarkXPress Interface

When acquiring new knowledge, such as QuarkXPress, it is always best to understand the real world metaphor that the software uses to describe the tools and techniques that a graphic designer would use.

Volume low.

Volume high.

You understand the metaphor that the volume control uses to describe the real world, when you adjust the volume control this is exactly what you expect – learning to use QuarkXPress is no different.

Before beginning any class I've always found it useful for the student to understand how QuarkXPress describes the computer interface as a working graphic studio, and then position the student in relation to the computer and design. Learning software on its own is insufficient, and QuarkXPress training tends to be confined to program learning. Program understanding comes from your knowledge of the metaphor that the computer uses to describe the real world. If you, as a student, understand the logic of the metaphor and its functions, you are then equipped to self-learn, develop and exploit the nature of digital design.

You learn to navigate through the real world by recognising representational symbols that describe objects, and the actions that you should take as a consequence. With a computer you are able to adjust the sound level with relative ease. The graphic representation of volume control is familiar; an unfamiliar image would not enable you to understand its function. Learning to use QuarkXPress is no different. By unpacking and understanding these processes you should be able to familiarise yourself each time QuarkXPress is upgraded or undergoes a major redesign of its interface and functions.

By doing so you can extend this approach and apply this method to any program, such as MacroMedia Director or Photoshop. This introductory chapter could be used for any program which has been written to operate in a windows environment for either Macintosh or PC. Therefore, what is important is your understanding of what the action words mean and how the desktop metaphor of noun and verb functions. When using Photoshop a photographer would understand the actions of a Noise Filter for Despeckling or altering the radius of the Median. A graphic designer will understand the language of typography used as the action verbs within QuarkXPress, such as track (overall space between letters and words) and kern (individual space between letters). Also, the nature of design using a computer allows you to reflect upon human perception, which tends to be altered through new possibilities that the digital capability of a computer can offer. By exploring the potential of design using computers, new opportunities can be established. There are three distinct parts to effectively using QuarkXPress as a tool:

The Computer • The QuarkXPress object/action computer interface as a metaphor for working in a graphic design studio.

You • Knowledge of design, its principles and its terminology.

• Objective reflection upon elements of design that remain constant, and what elements of design can be exploited using a computer.

It is assumed you know how to operate a Macintosh or Windows computer and are conversant with clicking and dragging, Open and Save dialogue boxes and so on. If not, you are advised to take time out to learn these basics after reading this chapter and before beginning the QuarkXPress tutorial in Chapter 2. Understanding the desktop metaphor encourages learning of these new opportunities through familiarity. Pointing and selecting becomes inseparable from the desktop assumption that people are inquisitive, they want to learn, especially if the environment appears recognisable and engaging. With QuarkXPress the design studio metaphor creates an interface that allows you to use the tools of graphic design. To operate the computer you look for objects that are familiar, these objects suggest their function – language and description of functionality needs only to be approximate and not exact.

The developers of QuarkXPress know the importance of an intuitive interface. This is reflected in any upgrades or major redesigns of the program. By understanding this, you can self-learn.

The Interface as a Metaphor for the Real World

The successful operating of a computer owes much to the rules of Isotype (International System Of TYpographic Picture Education). The important factor for computer interaction is the collaboration between Neurath and Ogden, who was the inventor of Basic English (British American Scientific International Commercial). Ogden had asked Neurath to publish an outline of his visual language; Neurath (1936) agreed if Ogden also allowed Basic to be combined with Isotype in an additional book, *Basic by Isotype*. Ogdens Basic English contained 850 core words which were mainly nouns or verbs.

These two fundamental paradigms of object and action are central to the computer desktop metaphor. The decision to publish an explanation of Isotype and a version underpinned by selective language is crucial to the systems understanding and adoption for other uses. The introduction of the 1980 facsimile *International picture language/Internationale Bildersprache*, cites instructions for telephone systems, traffic signs and so on. It was not until January 1983 that the concept of icons as a plausible interface between user and computer was made possible with the development and launch of the Apple Lisa by Steve Jobs and Steve Wozniak.

Before the development of an intuitive interface all human computer interaction was through command-line instructions. This required a high level of computer understanding – computers were for computing and not for ordinary working tasks. Many graphic communication systems have evolved from the Isotype/Basic method, and it is only natural that the Apple Lisa developed the object/action interface. Learning complex Boolean logic was no longer required to operate a computer. People with real needs could now execute complex code sequences without the need to recall correct command-lines. For the PC, the metaphor was not truly complete until the introduction of Windows 95. Both Macintosh and PC operating systems have now become indistinguishable from each other – the interface metaphor is complete. Once QuarkXPress has been launched on either platform there is little or no difference.

Neurath, O. 1936
Basic by Isotype, Psyche Miniatures General Series, Kegan Paul

Neurath, O. 1980
International picture language/Internationale Bildersprache, A facsimile reprint of the (1936) English edition, Psyche Miniatures General Series, Kegan Paul, Department of Typography & Graphic Communication, University of Reading. Forward by Robin Kinross

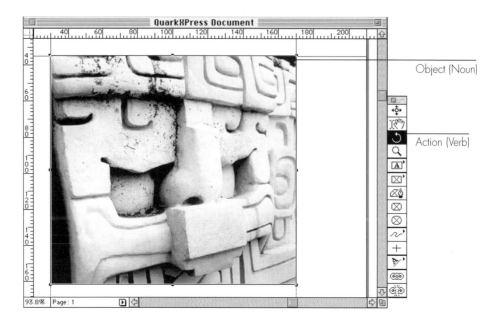

Object (Noun)

Action (Verb)

However, it was the Macintosh operating system that set the standards for computing as we now know it. Apple's (1987) *Human Interface Guidelines: The Apple Desktop Interface*, states that objects and their actions which combine representational image and language operation, allows the user to 'rely on recognition, not recall; they shouldn't have to remember anything a computer already knows'. Human computer interaction could now happen through an intuitive interface that iconically represented familiar objects found in the real world. The computer could now do real work for ordinary needs. QuarkXPress operates within this metaphor – tools such as the Bézier tool (French curves) can be found in the real world and designers use the same tools in a studio to draw uneven curves.

Neurath perceived Isotype as a helping visual language underpinned with key basic words. Visual language alone is insufficient because representational meaning can only be approximate, therefore, like Isotype/Basic, each object on the computer desktop is named. However, written words become redundant if the user is unfamiliar with the language. Yet a system where images are representational would allow the user

Object selection (the picture) and then the action (rotation, crop scale and so on).

Apple. 1987 *Human Interface Guidelines: The Apple Desktop Interface*, Addison-Wesley

Action (Verb) as Basic language.

Concrete metaphors.

Apple, 1988 *Apple Programmer's Introduction to the Apple IIGS,* Addison-Wesley

to become familiar with their own basic word usage that underpins the picture. Neurath explains that 'a man coming into a strange country without knowledge of the language is uncertain where to get his ticket at the station or the harbour, where to put his boxes, how to make use of the telephone in the telephone box, where to go in the post office. But if he sees pictures by the side of strange words, they will put him on the right way'. Therefore, for the first-time user the clue to functionality within QuarkXPress is suggested through iconic representation. Pull-down menus contain written language, as a metaphor they share no resemblance with their restaurant counterpart. They provide the choice of action after the object has been chosen. The menu as metaphor allows you to 'pull-down' menus and to browse these actions.

This consistent approach has been uniformly adopted for the development of programs for the PC, by learning one application you already know how other applications will be controlled. You are only hindered by your understanding of basic word terminology. The menu bar remains consistent between programs – File and Edit become stable actions located to the top of the bar, further actions become specific to the program. At all times you have a familiar reference point. Navigation on the desktop becomes icon selection and the available Basic word action. You are denied nonapplicable actions within QuarkXPress, the Basic text becomes 'greyed-out', you retain control guided by the computer interface. Computer navigation within QuarkXPress expands the primary desktop metaphor encouraging you to 'see-and-point' highlighting the object, and then finally action. After the noun/verb relationship has been learned, advanced interaction can be through the preprogrammed keyboard shortcut commands.

The *Apple Programmer's Introduction to the Apple IIGS* reminds the programmer of the importance of graphic images. It returns your attention to the human interface guideline and states that 'objects on screens should be simple and clear, and they should have visual fidelity (that is, they should look like what they represent). Use familiar, concrete metaphors to represent aspects of the computer and program. The desktop is the primary metaphor in the Apple Desktop interface'. Regardless of the underlying code, if any part of the two fundamental paradigms of recognition and action are not underpinned by concrete metaphors and Basic language, accessibility becomes difficult.

Central to the Isotype philosophy is the belief that images reduced to a common representation have greater effect than mere words – 'pictures make connections'. A combination of image refinement and the assumption that people are inquisitive, aids intuition and creates a human computer interface that is centred on you. However, interface designers recognise that human activity is complex and that many factors are still unknown, but the major difference is the recognition that people want to achieve tasks without the need to understand navigation through exact command-lines, 'specially at the first stage of getting new knowledge'. By doing this you are breaking free from perceived conventions and exploring the potential of QuarkXPress for yourself.

Launching QuarkXPress

From this point it is assumed that you have QuarkXPress installed on your computer. If not follow the installation guide which came with your copy of QuarkXPress. When ready, launch the application in the usual way. You will find that if you approach the use of QuarkXPress as a metaphor for the design studio, learning will become intuitive. As Apple points out, when you point, drag or click on objects within the interface you are saying to QuarkXPress, 'hey, you – do this'.

QuarkXPress 4

Using QuarkXPress:
The Document Layout

Setting Preferences

The object is not just to get to the end of the book in a certain time period. Teaching QuarkXPress to a beginner on a one a one-to-one basis would, on average, take 3 to 4 days. Set your own pace, proceed to the next section only when you are comfortable with what you have learned.

For future reference, when opening an existing QuarkXPress document, a dialog box may appear asking if you wish to change the document to the Preferences being used by the version of QuarkXPress on your computer or to Keep Document Settings. It is advisable to choose the latter to prevent the text from reflowing.

Throughout this course you will be asked to follow step-by-step instructions. Particular measurements and settings will be suggested, they are not crucial, you may insert whatever settings you wish. However, it is important you follow the steps in order to fully understand what is happening. Having completed the steps you should then experiment until you feel comfortable with what you were shown before progressing to the next section. Keyboard commands are shown in brackets.

Before creating a new document, you should set your personal Preferences. Preferences (which exist for all programs) are changes you make to the way a program operates in default mode. When you first install QuarkXPress, Preferences are set at the factory default. For example, each time you create a new document and enter text into it, the default font may be Helvetica 12 pt, but by setting personal Preferences you can change the font and size and that then becomes the default.

Preferences you set when there are no documents open become the default for all future *new* documents. Preferences set when there is an open document become the default for that document only.

Some Preferences can be quite complicated. If another user has made several changes which would take more time and effort to reset than you have to spare, it may be easier to delete the old Preferences entirely and return to the factory defaults. If you wish to do this, quit QuarkXPress, find the QuarkXPress folder and drag QuarkXPress Preferences to the wastebasket then relaunch the application. A new Preferences file is automatically created based on the factory default which contains standard settings for general typography.

Some Preference dialog boxes can be a little daunting when first encountered and the last thing we would wish to do is to put you off the tutorial by being overly technical at this stage. However, many Preferences are highly important and unavoidable. Therefore, it will be of considerable help to you if, as and when you feel more comfortable with QuarkXPress, you take some extra time to study the contents of these dialog boxes.

1. Choose Preferences from the Edit menu and pull across to Document. A dialog box appears.

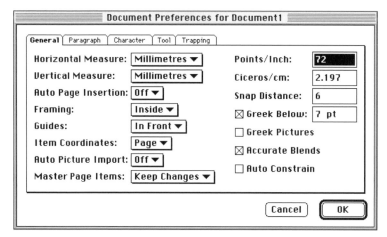

The dialog box contains a series of tab labels across the top which allow you to set Preferences for a variety of features simultaneously. Don't try to absorb all of the information in them just yet, they will make little sense. All you will change at this time is Measure, Guides and Auto Page Insertion. Check out the other settings as and when required.

2. You make settings in dialog boxes in one of two ways; either by typing or selecting from hidden menus. It will be obvious which is the correct way. Using the appropriate method (in this case menus) set the Horizontal and Vertical Measure to millimetres. Millimetres will be used throughout the tutorial, however you may use your own preferred unit if you wish, it will not adversely affect your learning.

General Preferences for Documents.

You will encounter many features which have a small box next to them (such as Greek Below etc. in this dialog). These features are activated when there is a cross (Mac) or tick (PC) in the box. One click turns the feature on/off. Don't change anything until you know what they do.

The small triangles displayed contain menus. Use these menus to make settings in dialog boxes and/or main menus. This is a common feature of most computer programs, not just QuarkXPress.

3. Turn Auto Page Insertion OFF. This will prevent pages being added to our document that you don't need just yet.

4. Set Guides to 'In Front'. This will prevent the page guides from being hidden behind text or picture boxes. There will be more details on this dialog box later. Click OK.

To Create a New Document

1. Choose New from the File menu and pull across to Document. You should now be viewing the New Document dialog box shown below, reading anti-clockwise from the top-left it contains the following sections.

The New Document
dialog box.

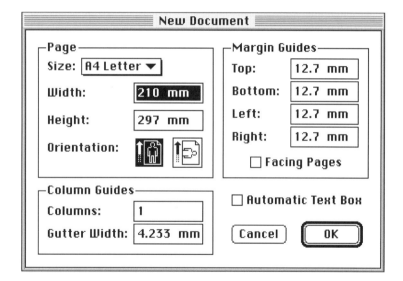

2. The Page Size. This is where you set the size of the actual trimmed page area. Set it to A4 letter. (210 x 297 mm) You also choose whether your page will be Portrait (upright) or Landscape (sideways) in shape; by clicking the appropriate icon, for the purpose of this tutorial, choose Portrait.

3. Column Guides. Set 2 columns and set the Gutter Width (the space between each column) to 6 mm.

4. Automatic Text Box. If this box is on, every new page you add to your document will automatically be ready to accept text. This is useful if you are going to import a large text file and you want the program to create as many pages as are required to accommodate it. For the moment leave this OFF.

5. Facing Pages. Here you set the type of pages your publication will have, facing or non-facing. A Facing Page would be a book or magazine, double sided. A Non-Facing Page could be a single-sided page like a poster or a booklet printed on one side only. Click the small box for Facing and Non-Facing pages on and off (a cross or tick appears when it's on) notice how the margin settings change from Left & Right (for non-facing) to Inside & Outside (for facing). Whatever type of document you are creating, it is extremely important to take into account whether you will require space for a spine or binder punchholes. For the moment turn facing pages OFF.

6. Margin Guides. This is where you decide how much space there will be between the edges of the trimmed paper and the text or images on the page. Make the margins all 10 mm. Click OK.

You should now be viewing a new page layout (*see right*) – take a moment to familiarise yourself with it. It is a two-column page with margin guides depicting the settings you made in the New Document dialog box. Along the top and left side of the page are rulers which are used to measure precise locations for text and picture boxes. Note the position of the ruler zero points

In the bottom left corner there is a percentage number. This tells you what magnification percentage you are viewing at. It has no effect on the size of the final printed page. To the right of the percentage view is the number of the page you are currently viewing. This refers to the order of the pages in the document, not the numbers which will be printed on the final pages. If you press the mouse down on the black arrow next to the page number, you can select a particular document or Master page (more on Masters later) from the list that appears. No list will show if there is only one page in the document.

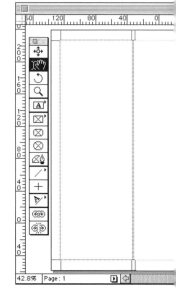

New page layout.

There may be other palettes on view besides the Toolbox, if so, choose Hide from the View menu. Leave only the toolbox on screen.

The white space surrounding the page is the Pasteboard. Use this space to place items temporarily while you work on them. On the right and bottom you have the scrolling bars. These work in the same way as all windows with one difference – there may be times when you want the page to scroll slower or faster than the default speed, and QuarkXPress allows you to control the speed of the scrolling. More on this later.

You should be viewing the toolbox also (*see note on left*) If not, go to the View menu and choose Show Tools. Those familiar with previous versions of QuarkXPress will notice changes here. A breakdown of the QuarkXPress 4 toolbox appears on page 19.

Drag ruler reset from here...to here.

Rulers and Ruler Guides

As mentioned earlier, there should be rulers across the top and left side of the page, if not choose Show Rulers from the View menu. Ruler zero points can be set to any part of the page. When using rulers to measure where items (an Item is any box or line) are on the page, the measure is taken from the top-left corner of an item in relation to the top-left corner of the page area. If the zero point of your horizontal and vertical rulers does not correspond to the top-left corner of the page you will need to reset the rulers.

Resetting ruler zero points.

1. Use the scroll bars to view the top-left corner of the page.

2. Move the pointer to the small white square in top-left corner where the rulers intersect.

3. Press the mouse button and drag to the top-left corner of the page (take care not to mistake the page area with the coloured margin guides which are inside the page area). Release the mouse when the intersection of the dotted line is directly over the intersection of the top-left corner of the page.

Around the document you can see the coloured margin guides depicting your original settings. These guides cannot be moved. However, you may add guides to help you position items. If after placing items on your page (*see next section*) your guides are not visible in front of a box, choose Preferences – Document from the Edit menu and in the General area set your Guides to In Front. Ruler guides do not print.

1. Move the pointer onto the vertical ruler.

2. Drag a guide onto the page, observing the dotted line moving along the ruler. Stop dragging when you are happy with the position Add as many guides to a page as you wish. Repeat this for horizontal guides.

3. To remove a guide drag it back to the ruler. To remove several guides at once, hold down the Alt/Opt key and click on the ruler.

Guide Colour

Occasionally you may be using colours on the page which make it difficult to see the guides clearly. To avoid this you can change the colour of guides.

1. Choose Preferences from the Edit menu and pull across to Application. A dialog box appears with the Display tab active.

2. Click on the coloured swatch for Ruler (note that you can also change the colour of Margin and Grid guides). The dialog changes. On the left, click either the HSL or RGB icon to display either the colour wheel or the RGB sliders. Don't concern yourself with the difference between these options for now, it doesn't matter which you choose, there will of course be more detail on colour systems later.

3. Depending on which system you chose, either click on the wheel or drag the small triangles along the sliders to select a new colour. A preview of the colour appears. When done click OK to return to the Application Preferences dialog box then click OK again.

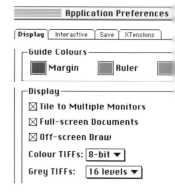

Guides are dragged from the horizontal & vertical rulers.

Preferences - Application - Display dialog box.

Using QuarkXPress:
The Toolbox

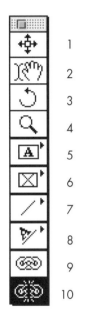

This section is for reference only. The toolbox pictured here is the standard toolbox displayed in its shortest form. If yours appears different, it is because some of the tools can be hidden when not required and when called up they may be set in a different order. The tools which have a small black triangle next to them contain a pop-out menu which is a subset of tools that appears when you press and hold the mouse button down on the tool. Each tool, and its subset, is listed below.

1. Item tool – use this tool to move any item or group of items around the page.

2. Content tool – for editing the contents of any box, not for moving the box.

3. Rotation tool – use to rotate any item.

4. Magnification tool – select and click on the part of the page you wish to magnify. Hold down the Option/Alt key and click to reduce the magnification.

5. Text Box tools – (contains a pop-out, shown below) – use to draw text boxes. Hold down the Shift key to draw a perfect square/circle.

6. Picture Box tools – (contains a pop-out, shown below) – use same as text box.

7. Line tools – (contains a pop-out, shown below) – draws lines of varying angles.

8. Line Path tools – (contains a pop-out, shown below) – use to draw text paths.

9. Linking tool – to link one text box to another. Select tool. Click the 'from' box, then click the 'to' box. When Linking tool is selected and a box is active, any existing links will be indicated by a grey arrow.

10. Unlinking tool – to break a link. Select tool and click once on the head or tail of the grey arrow – the head to break the 'to' link; the tail to break the 'from' link.

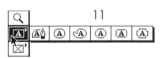

11. Pop-out text box tools – select the desired shape and draw. Hold down the Control key as you select the tool to have any subset tool become part of the main toolbox. Repeat to return the tool to the subset.

12. Pop-out picture box tools – use as pop-out text box tools.

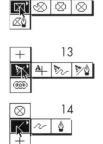

13. Pop-out text path tools – use for straight/curved paths which will contain text.

14. Pop-out line tools – use to draw straight/curved lines which will not contain text.

Preferences for Tools

Just one more short piece of technical information to see before beginning to make pages. Setting Preferences for the toolbox can be useful when creating a document which will contain multiple items with the same specifications. As you have not used any tools yet, you are not expected to make changes here. Nevertheless, do take a look at how it is done.

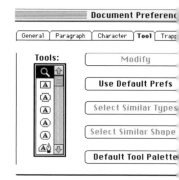

Document Preferences for Tools dialog box.

1. Choose Preferences – Document – from the Edit menu. A dialog box appears, click the Tool tab along the top.

The Select Similar Type and Shapes buttons are only available when certain tools are clicked on the left. These allow you to make simultaneous Preferences settings for several tools which have similar functions.

2. Click on the tool you wish to set Preferences for.

3. Click the appropriate Similar button if applicable.

4. Click the Modify button, another dialog box appears.

5. Click the features you wish to set, frame, background etc., make your changes then click OK in all open dialogs. More on all of these features later.

Any settings you make will remain until you either make different settings, choose one of the default options or throw away the QuarkXPress Preferences file.

In the Preferences – Application – Interactive dialog box (Edit menu) there is a box named Show Tool Tips. Click this and when you point the cursor at a tool, its name will pop-up.

Using QuarkXPress:
Text

Next you will draw and fill a variety of text boxes. If required go to the View menu and choose a view you feel comfortable with, i.e. Actual Size, Fit in Window etc.

1. Select the Rectangular Text Box tool $\boxed{\text{A}}$ Move the pointer to the left-hand column, press the mouse button and drag to draw a box which fills the column.

2. Select the Content tool (2nd down in the toolbox) click inside the text box to display the flashing text cursor and type several lines of text.

Text in boxes can be treated in the same way as a word-processing program. You highlight, cut, copy, paste, delete, and change attributes such as bold, italic, underline etc.

3. Notice the eight handles which appear around the edges of the text box. Move the pointer onto any one of these handles. The arrow changes into a pointing hand. Press the mouse button and drag to resize the box as you like. Notice what happens to the other handles when you drag any one of them, some move others don't. Play with the box size until you feel comfortable with the way it works.

Bézier Text Boxes

As you will have seen earlier, you have a choice of several shapes of text box. All are drawn as above. Bézier text box tools work differently. A Bézier box is one which is drawn point-by-point, thereby providing a much wider variety of shapes of text box. Beware! We are talking text boxes here, not paths.

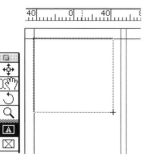

Drawing a text box. Take care not to overlap the margin guides unless specifically required. To help with the positioning check that Snap to Guides is selected in the View menu. Snap to Guides will ensure that when you draw a box its edges will sit perfectly on the margin or ruler guides. As you draw the box it will 'snap' into place. The distance a box is allowed to get before it snaps can be reset by choosing Preferences – Document – General from the Edit menu. The settings can be between 0 - 100 pixels.

1. Select the Bézier Text Box tool.

Bézier Text Box Tool.

2. Find a clear area on the page and click the mouse button once. A small square known as a 'point' appears on the page.

3. Click several more points to draw any shape you wish. Complete the shape by clicking on top of the first point you placed. Each point can be adjusted by dragging with either the Item or Content tools. When a point is dragged, notice a set of 'levers' which appears. Drag the levers to adjust the curvature of the point.

Freehand Bézier Text Box Tool.

4. Select the freehand Bézier Text Box tool. This time instead of clicking, drag the mouse around on the page creating a shape in one movement ending up at the starting point. The points are created automatically. The number of points around the box is determined by the complexity of the shape.

5. Draw several different text boxes. Adjust their shapes and type text into them. Experiment until you feel comfortable with the way it works then delete the text (Edit menu - Select All - press the Delete/Backspace key) leave the empty boxes on screen for the next exercise.

A text box which could be drawn with either the Bézier text box tool or the freehand Bézier text box tool.

Importing Text

Text can be imported into a text box. To use this feature save word-processed files in a suitable format for importing. Most of the main WP packages, MS Word, MacWrite etc. are supported by QuarkXPress. However, some are not, in which case the text should be saved in the format known as Text which converts the WP document into ASCII Text which can be imported.

When importing text, because different word processors create different styles of speech marks, the Quotes feature at the bottom of the Get Text Dialog box allows you to determine what style speech marks will adopt when text is imported.

1. Using the Content tool, click once on one of the boxes.

2. Choose Get Text from the File menu. The standard Open/Save dialog box appears. Locate a text file of your own and open it. If you have no text prepared, locate your QuarkXPress folder, inside it there is a folder named Samples, inside is another folder named Sample Text, open it, select one of the files and click Open.

Content Tool.

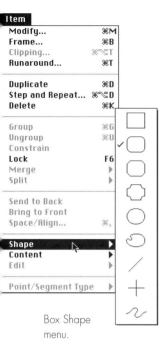

Box Shape
menu.

If you hold down the Shift
key, you can select sev-
eral Items and drag them
as a group (more on
groups later). If you press
and drag a box in one
quick movement, you will
only see the outline of the
box as you move it
around. If you press the
mouse and hold it for a
few seconds before drag-
ging you will see the box
and its contents moving
around.

The text appears in the box. If you chose a large file you may
see a small box at the bottom of the text – this is the overflow
symbol. It tells you there is more text than there is space to
accommodate it. More on this later, for now ignore it. Import
the same text into several different boxes. Note how different
box shapes hold text, it doesn't 'sit' correctly in some boxes.
There may also be excessive space around the text. Don't worry
about this for now, you'll fix it later. Leave several different
shaped boxes on the page for the next section. Save your file.

Changing a Box Shape

You can change the shape of any box using the Item menu.

1. Select the Item or Content tool (top two of toolbox) and click
   once on one of the boxes you drew.

2. Go to the Item menu and pull down to Shape. The menu
   expands to display the shapes on offer. Notice you can
   change a box into a line (more on lines later). Choose one of
   the top five shapes in the list. If you drew a normal text box
   (not Bézier) you could select the Polygon shape (4th up from
   the bottom of the list) to convert the normal box to a Bézier
   and vice-versa.

Deleting Boxes

1. To delete a box, select the Item tool, click once on the box
   and press the Delete key (backspace). To delete several boxes
   at once, click on one box, hold down the Shift key and click
   on all of the other boxes, release the Shift key and delete.

Moving a Box and its Contents

The Item tool allows you to move any item, and its contents,
around the page (see note on left).

1. Select the Item tool and position the pointer in the middle of
   one of the text boxes you drew. Don't grab the handles!

2. Press the mouse button and drag the box around the page.

Applying Attributes to Text

QuarkXPress contains many text features which can be applied in several ways. Attributes (bold, italic, underline etc.) can be applied to text using one of four methods: The Measurement Palette, the Style Menu, the Keyboard and with a Style Sheet.

You will apply various attributes to the text you created earlier using the first three of these methods. You will look at the fourth method later.

The Measurement Palette

The Measurement palette (usually visible along the bottom of the screen) is used to apply attributes and limited formatting to text and to resize and reposition items on the page. If your palette is not on view, choose Show Measurements from the View Menu (Com-Alt-M). The palette will appear and you can move it anywhere you wish. If the palette is not displaying any-thing, it will when you click on some text with the Content tool. Below is a breakdown of the Measurement palette for reference purposes. You will use all of its features throughout the tutorial.

| X: 45.257 mm | W: 10.243 mm | ⚐ 0° | ➡ X%: 23.7% | ◇◇ X+: 1.737 mm | ⚐ 0° |
| Y: 56.298 mm | H: 6.064 mm | ⚐ 0 mm | ⬆ Y%: 23.7% | ⬍ Y+: -0.353 mm | ⟋ 0° |

X and Y shows the location of the top left corner of an item in relation to the top left corner of the document, X = horizontal, Y = vertical. In the example shown right, the selected item is 44.719 mm from the left and 58.156 mm down from the top of the page. To reposition an item in this way, select the Item tool, click on the box, type in your settings and press the Return key or click on the page.

X: 44.719 mm
Y: 58.156 mm

W and H shows the Width and Height of the selected item.

W: 4.548 mm
H: 2.885 mm

Shows the current angle of the item and the number of columns (if it is a text box).

⚐ 0°
Cols: 1

The following features display when the Content tool is selected.

Use the black arrows to flip text horizontally or vertically. The upper set of white arrows are used to adjust the Leading (space between lines). The lower set are for Tracking (space between words).

Use to align text left, centre, right, justify, force justify.

Helvetica

Choose fonts from the pop-up menu behind the black triangle.

Choose font size from the pop-up menu behind the black triangle.

To use the following sections text must be highlighted first. Click once on an icon to apply an effect, a second click to remove it.

P   Plain

B   Bold

I   Italic

Ⓞ   Outline

Ⓢ   Shadow

S̶   ~~Strike through~~

U̲   <u>Underline entire line of text</u>

W̲   <u>Underline entire line of text but not the word spacing</u>

κ   SMALL CAPITALS

K   REGULAR CAPITALS

Superscript like this [2] (affects the Leading)

Subscript [2] (also affects the Leading)

Superior settings[2] (like superscript but does not affect the Leading)

1. Set your View to Actual Size. Select the Content tool and click once on a text box. Check that the text cursor is flashing inside the box.

2. Highlight all of the text either by choosing Select All from the Edit menu or press Command-A.

3. Click once on the 'B' to the right of the Measurement palette. This makes the text bold.

4. Click once on the text to remove the highlight so you can clearly see the effect. To remove the bold, highlight the text again and click once on the 'B'.

5. Try out all of the other attributes in the measurement palette (except the last three on the right. *See below*). Undo each effect by clicking on the appropriate button again before applying a different one.

6. Again with the text highlighted, press and hold the mouse button on the small black triangle next to the font name to view the available fonts. The available fonts are not unique to QuarkXPress, they are in your computer system, so the list will be the same no matter what program you are using.

7. Use the other black triangle to change the size of font. If the size you want is not in the menu list, double-click whatever number is displayed and type in your own size i.e. 11.5 pt. If you choose the keyboard method, you must press the Enter key on the keyboard to apply the change.

8. Click on the text to remove the highlight and view the changes.

9. To use the Superscript, Subscript and Superior features, type 52, highlight the 2 only and apply Superscript. Undo it then try Subscript and finally Superior. Note the difference.

Two clicks highlights one word. Three clicks highlights one line. Four clicks highlights one paragraph. Five clicks highlights all of the text in linked boxes.

To select 1 line Shift-down arrow. To select 1 paragraph Com-Shift-down arrow.

If you have applied several attributes to the same piece of text, you can remove all of them by highlighting the text and clicking the letter 'P' in the measurement palette. If you wish to remove any one attribute then click only the applicable one. You may have to click it twice.

Superscript, Subscript and Superior.

Text Alignment

The Measurement Palette Text Alignment boxes.

To increase/decrease Leading in 1 pt increments Com-Shift : "
To increase/decrease Leading in .1 pt increments Alt-Com-Shift : "

Leading Arrows.

Hold down the Alt key and click the Leading Arrows to adjust in finer increments.

If you know precisely what size Leading you want, double-click the number next to the arrows, type your setting then press the Enter key. See page 136 on the depth of a line.

The five small boxes to the left of the attributes are for aligning text left, centred, right, justified and force justified. You do not need to highlight text to align one paragraph. Simply ensure that the text cursor is flashing within it (Content Tool) then click once on the preferred alignment. You must highlight the text to align several paragraphs simultaneously.

If you choose the Force Justify option, some lines of text may be stretched out across the column. This is a result of the settings made in the Hyphenation & Justification dialog box. Do not concern yourself with this at the moment, you will be looking at that area later.

Leading

Leading is the space between lines of text. As a general guide, Leading is usually 120% larger than the type size you have used. i.e. if the type size is 10 pt the leading would be 12 pt.

1. Check the text cursor is flashing inside a paragraph of text (you do not need to highlight it).

2. Look at the section of the Measurement palette to the left of the Alignment area. There are two sets of white arrows. The upper set are for Leading. Click on one of these arrows and observe the change to the paragraph of text (*see note on left*).

3. If you are in doubt as to the correct leading to use, you can let QuarkXpress do it for you. Check the cursor is flashing, then instead of typing a number into the measurement palette, type the word 'auto'. The Leading applied when Auto is chosen is 120% of whatever the type size is. If using this method does not apply 120%, it is because your Typographic Preference setting for Leading is set to something other than 120%. You should check this before continuing.

1. Choose Preferences from the Edit menu and pull across to Document, a dialog box appears. Click the Paragraph tab.

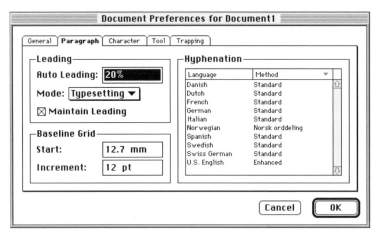

Advanced users! In the Mode pop-up menu, you can set Leading to Word Processing – which measures Leading downward from the top of the ascent on a line to the top of the ascent on the line below – or Typesetting – which measure Leading upward from the baseline of one line to the baseline of the line above it. Apply auto leading by typing 'auto' in the measurement palette. Press the Enter key (or click on the text) to apply the changes.

2. If necessary, double-click inside the Auto Leading box on the left and enter 20% (that is 20% added to the existing 100%). Obviously if you require a setting other than 20%, enter it here then Click OK.

3. Before continuing with the next section, Delete all text boxes except one rectangular box. Resize it to fit one column. Leave the text in it. Set the text to: Type Size 10 pt Leading 12 pt (or auto if you prefer).

Tracking

Tracking is the space to the right of each character in a block of text. You adjust Tracking using the east and west pointing arrows in the Measurement palette.

Tracking Arrows.

To increase/decrease Tracking in .05 em increments, highlight the text and press Com-Shift { }. To increase/decrease Tracking in .005 em increments, press Alt-Com-Shift { }.

1. Highlight a paragraph. Click a few times on the arrows pointing left and right. The text stretches or tightens. Notice the increments the text moves in. Hold down the Alt/Opt key and click the arrows for finer increments. As with Leading, you can type settings directly into the Measurement palette.

Kerning

Kerning keyboard commands are the same as tracking but you do not highlight text.

Kerning is similar to Tracking except that instead of adjusting the space between several words, it changes the space between two characters.

1. Click the cursor between any two characters so the cursor is flashing. Use the same left/right pointing arrows to tighten or loosen the Kerning (or type your desired kern amount into the Measurement palette). You will be looking at the rest of the Measurement palette later.

Tracking and Kerning can be used for practical reasons i.e. to force text to fit a set space, or design reasons, for better legibility or simple aesthetics. The Tracking and Kerning used in most publications is there for a reason. See pages 148 and 168 on the use of space in design.

The Style Menu

All of the Measurement palette features you have been introduced to so far are also available in the Style Menu with a few additions. The features Font, Size, Type Style, Alignment and Leading on offer in the Style menu work in the same way as the Measurement palette.

1. Highlight some text and try out the above mentioned commands from the Style menu. When you are comfortable with how they work, move on to the next section. You may wish to save your file before continuing.

If you require a specific shade of colour, select Other and enter the desired percentage into the dialog box which appears.

Now you will look at the features in the Style menu that are not available in the Measurement palette.

Applying Colour Using the Style Menu

The colours available in the Style menu are standard default colours which will suffice for the moment. You will be looking at colour in more detail later.

1. Select some text and choose a colour from the Colours command in the Style menu.

2. Change the shade of colour by choosing a percentage from the Shade option in the Style menu. Deselect the text to see the colour clearly.

Horizontal/Vertical Scale

You can modify text by altering its horizontal or vertical scale.

To increase/decrease Horizontal Scale Com-[ ].

1. Highlight one word and choose Horizontal/Vertical scale from the Style menu. The Character Attributes dialog box appears.

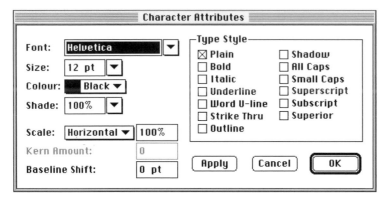

The Character Attributes dialog box appears when various selections are made from the Style Menu. It allows you to make multiple changes to text in one dialog box.

2. In the lower left section of the dialog box there is a menu offering you the option of either Horizontal or Vertical Scale, choose one of them and change the percentage to about 250-300%. Click OK and observe the change.

You can adjust the scale of text by holding down the Command key and dragging one of the corners of a text box.

3. Select a different piece of text and repeat this exercise for the other option. If the text being changed is of a larger point size it will react proportionally. You cannot apply both options to the same piece of text.

Kerning/Tracking in Style Menu

Kerning and Tracking in the Style menu work in the same way as with the Measurement palette, except you must type an amount of Track or Kern into the dialog box which appears when you select one of these options. You will notice that the menu reads Kern when the cursor is between two characters and no text is highlighted, and Track when text is highlighted. You Kern between two characters. You Track the overall space within a word, line, paragraph and so on.

Baseline Shift

To increase/decrease Baseline Shift press Alt-Com-Shift-+.

The baseline of text is, as you would expect, the bottom part. It is not the descender (the bit that sticks out at the bottom like in the letter 'p'). It is the neat line running along the bottom of each line of text. <u>This underline runs just below the baseline.</u>

When you apply Baseline Shift to all of the text, you move the text up or down its *box* without affecting the Leading. Shifting the baseline of a single line or paragraph will affect the Leading. You can shift the baseline of an entire book or just one word. A positive setting (2) will move the text up, a negative setting (-2) will move it down.

1. Select one word of your text and choose Baseline Shift from the Style menu.

2. Type – 10 in the box provided for Baseline Shift. This is a huge adjustment but serves well to demonstrate the effect. Click OK and observe the change. Try different settings. Repeat this for one line of text and an entire paragraph.

Character

As mentioned earlier, this menu command brings up the same dialog box containing all of the features offered in the right side of the Measurement palette and a few more besides.

Content Tool.

1. Highlight some text, select Character and use the dialog box to make several changes in one go.

Formats

To copy the formats from one paragraph to another, highlight the destination paragraph and Shift-Alt-click on the source paragraph.

The Formats option allows you to make several changes to the way text appears on the page as opposed to the Character dialog box which is for applying attributes. Changes made using the Formats command apply to an entire paragraph.

1. Separate your text into five paragraphs then, using the Content tool, click once inside the first paragraph and choose Formats from the Style menu. A dialog box appears.

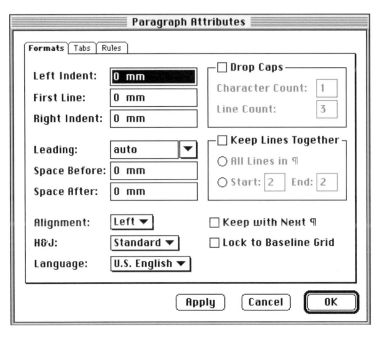

Notice the set of rulers which have appeared above the paragraph that was clicked before Formats was chosen from the Style menu (you may have to drag the window down to see them). This is to show you where any indents you are setting will appear. See page 146 on how to use text alignment.

This dialog has three labels: Formats, Tabs, and Rules. The Formats area contains several features for changing the appearance of a *paragraph* of text. Apply only these settings to each of your five paragraphs one at a time as follows:

If a dialog box has an Apply button, Alt-click the button to keep it active while you experiment with changes. You can see the effect of the change. Move the dialog box if necessary. Alt-click the Apply button again to cancel.

Left Indent: Indents text away from the left edge of the text box, not the left edge of the page. This paragraph has a 10mm left indent but no right indent.

First line: Indents only the first line of the paragraph. This paragraph has a first line indent of 10 mm. Notice a First Line indent only indents text from the left of the box.

Right Indent: Indents text away from the right edge of the text box. This paragraph has a 10 mm right indent but no left indent.

This paragraph has both **right** and **left indents** of 10 mm applied to it and it is justified. This tends to give the impression the paragraph is 'squared' off.

Hanging Indents: are created by setting a negative value in the First Line area and an equal, positive value in the Left Indent area. This will cause the first line in a paragraph not to be indented but all other lines in the paragraph will. This paragraph has a Hanging Indent of 5 mm.

Lock to Baseline Grid

We touched upon baselines earlier. This feature ensures that when two columns of text in the same box run beside each other, or even when separated by an image, the baselines of each column are aligned. In the two short columns below, the left-hand column has Lock to Baseline Grid applied, the right does not, observe the difference.

If you do not want Locking to change the document's Leading, make the increment the same as the chosen Leading.

If the Leading is higher than the baseline grid increment, the text will lock to every other line causing more space than perhaps was desired.

Both of these columns have the same font, point size (8 pt) and are set to 10 pt Leading. The text in this left hand column has Lock to Baseline Grid applied to it. The text in the right column does not. The baseline grid increment (which is set in Typographic Preferences) is 4 pt, causing this extra spacing.

This column does not have Lock to Baseline Grid applied to it. If you draw a line along the baselines you will see this text does not align correctly with the left hand column. Traditionally, this is typographically incorrect. It is not always necessary to Lock to Baseline grid to get text to align, it may look perfectly OK without locking. If it is locked however, it will always align throughout the document.

1. Completely fill your text box with. (Use the Measurement palette to set the box to 2 columns if required.) Highlight the text in one of the columns, choose Formats from the Style menu and activate Lock To Baseline Grid in the dialog box (*see note on left*).

2. Choose Preferences – Document from the Edit menu and click the Paragraph label. Change the Baseline increment to the desired amount. Click OK and see how it affects the text. Select all of the text and turn Lock To Baseline Grid off before continuing.

Dropcaps

Initial letters, known as dropcaps, are large characters used to embellish a paragraph. The first letter in this paragraph is a dropcap three lines deep. You can dropcap any number of characters in a word. The first character is always dropped.

See page 149 on using Dropcaps.

1. Check the cursor is flashing inside a paragraph, and choose Formats from the Style menu. The same dialog box you used earlier appears. Click once on the Dropcaps button.

2. Enter a Character count to set how many of the characters in the first word you want to be dropped. Enter a Line count to set the depth of the dropcap. Click OK.

When typing text into QuarkXPress and after applying a dropcap, you find that each time you press the Return key the first word of the *next* paragraph you type is also dropcapped. To stop this happening click in the new paragraph, choose Formats again and turn dropcaps off by removing the checkmark.

Rules

A Rule is a line which is anchored to a paragraph of text. It is used to enhance text or break up the page. There are several styles to choose from and a Rule can be any colour you wish. This paragraph has a Rule Above Length set to Indents but there are no indents in this paragraph, so the Rule stretches across the width of the text box. It has an offset of 12 pt so the Rule is 12 pts from the baseline of the first line of text. The width is 2 pt. The Rule Below Length is set to Text so the Rule is as wide as the last line. The offset is 6 pt so the space between the Rule Above and the ascenders of the first line is the same as the space between the Rule Below and the descenders of the last line in the paragraph. Confused? Refer back to this paragraph as you follow the steps.

The Dashes and Stripes section later in the tutorial will show you how to change Preferences for lines to create your own Rule styles.

1. Click inside a paragraph and choose Rules from the Style menu. A dialog box appears.

The Rules dialog box
when both Rule Above
and Below have been
selected.

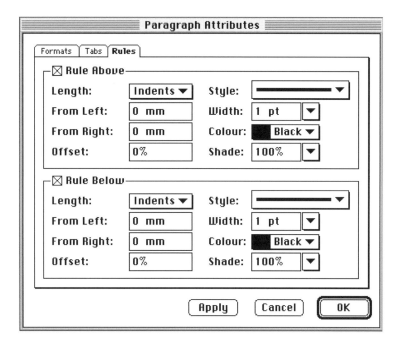

2. Try out Rule Above/Below and click the appropriate box. Experiment with a variety of Rules. See below for more information on the content of this dialog box.

Line tools.

You can draw normal
lines using the line tools in
the toolbox. The differ-
ence between a Line and
a Rule is that Rules
become part of the para-
graph, lines can be
moved in the same way
as boxes.

Length: Two options here: Indents and Text. Do you want the Rule to be as wide as the indents, or as wide as the text is?

From Left: Use to make the *left end* of the Rule longer or shorter than the setting you made in the Length pop-up menu.

From Right: As above but from the right.

Offset: Use to set amount of space between the Rule and the baselines of the first and/or last lines in the paragraph.

Styles: This is a pop-up menu offering various styles of Rule.

Width: Choose preferred Rule width or type in your own width.

Colour /Shade: Use as Colour /Shade in the Style menu.

Tabs

Tabs are used to insert specified amounts of space before text. Tables (as you would expect) usually contain tabs. Tabs can be inserted using the Tab key on the keyboard, or you can set your own Tabs so the cursor moves as far as you want it to.

If you have the text cursor flashing inside your text and you press the Tab key, the cursor will move .5in to the right. If you were creating some sort of table, i.e. three columns, each 3 cms apart, it would be much easier if every time you hit the Tab key the cursor moved 3 cms straight to the next column. This is when you would set up your own Tabs.

1. Delete all of your text and choose Tabs from the Style menu.

2. The same dialog box you use for Formats should appear, but this time with the Tabs area on view, a second set of rulers will also appear above the text box.

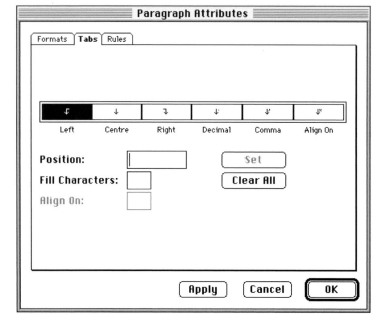

Tabs dialog box.

3. Select the type of Tab you require then click on the ruler above your text column or type the position into the Position box. A small arrow appears on the ruler.

When creating a table for real, it is advisable to set your Tabs before typing out the tables contents.

4. To apply a Fill Character like this.................between the Tabs, type a period (or whatever) into the Fill box. When done click OK. Create a small table like the one shown below. When you press the tab key the cursor will move to the position you set.

There are six types of Tab to choose from, A set of short tables with all six Tabs used is shown below. The chosen Fill Character is the period. Notice how the numbers align along the grey line according to the type of Tab used.

Once viewed, any Tabs you have set can be undone by reselecting the text, choosing Tabs again and dragging the small arrows onto the rulers.

Left: Left edges of the numbers align.
    Apples 50.755
    Pears 30.00

Right: Right edges of the numbers align.
    Apples 50.755
    Pears 30.00

Centre: Numbers align centred.
    Apples 50.755
    Pears 30.00

Decimal: Decimal points align.
    Apples 50.755
    Pears 30.00

Comma: Commas align. Commas have been inserted instead of decimal points to illustrate the point.
    Apples 50,755
    Pears 30,00

Align on: The @ is the chosen Align On character. Any other character could be used.
    Apples . . . .@50.755
    Pears . . . .@30.00

Style Sheets

You have used the Measurement palette and the Style menu to format text and apply attributes. Style Sheets allow you to apply formatting and attributes to a block of text in one step. You create and save the style, then apply it with one keypress and if you change the style, the change is automatically applied to any text that has a Style Sheet attached to it. There are two ways to create a Style Sheet:

a) Aesthetically, that is, you apply different settings to the text until you like the way it looks then you save the style or,
b) When you are instructed as to what styles to use. You create and save the Style Sheet according to the instructions, then apply it to the text.

1. Create a New document, set any page size and margins you wish. Leave Automatic Text Box and Facing Pages OFF.

You must select the
Content tool to import text.

2. Draw a rectangular text box which fills the page. For this exercise you will need a page containing several paragraphs of text. Either type it or import some by choosing Get Text from the File Menu.

3. Choose Modify from the Item menu. A dialog box appears. Click the Text label.

4. Note that among other things, you can change the number of columns in the text box here just as you can in the Measurement palette. Change Columns to 2 and Gutter Width to 6 mm then click OK.

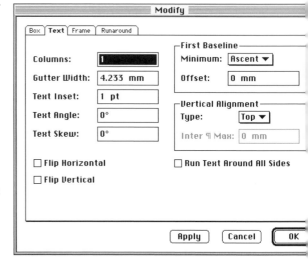

5. Select the Content tool and highlight the first paragraph of your text. Use the individual commands or the Character command from the Style menu to change the font, its size, colour and shade and apply some attributes: bold, italic etc.

Modify dialog box with
Text tab selected.

6. Use the Formats command (Style menu) change the Leading, Alignment, Left, Right and First Line Indents.

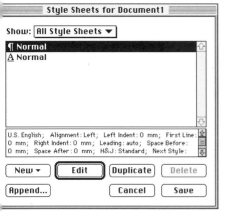

Style Sheets dialog box.

Next you will convert your settings into a Style Sheet.

1. If you deselected the paragraph, highlight it again and choose Style Sheets from the Edit menu. A dialog box appears with two Style Sheets already in it. The Normal styles for Paragraph (¶) and Character (A).

Important: You can create a *Paragraph* Style Sheet which has a *Character* Style Sheet embedded within it, or you can create an independent *Character* Style Sheet that has no *Paragraph* styles. Suppose there are several words in the text which need to have different attributes to the rest of the paragraph, like the italicized words *Character* and *Paragraph* used in this paragraph for example. By creating a separate *Character* Style Sheet, you can apply the style to a single word without affecting the rest of the paragraph. The thing to remember is that *Paragraph* Style Sheets affect how the text sits in its box i.e. Indents, Leading, Alignment, etc. whereas *Character* Style Sheets affect the text itself i.e. Font, Size, Colour and so on.

2. Press and hold down the button named New and select Paragraph. A second dialog box appears. The Description area displays any settings you made to the text.

3. In the Name area type Body Text.

4. Click inside the Keyboard Equivalent area. This is where you decide which key will be the one you use to apply the Style Sheet. You can use the numeric keypad on the right of the keyboard or the F-keys along the top. It is advisable to use the numeric keypad as some F-keys have other functions which may cause problems when you apply the Style Sheet.

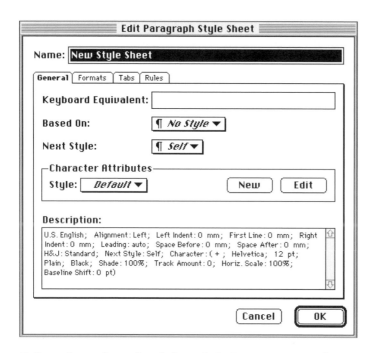

The General dialog for Paragraph Style Sheets.

Use logical numbers for each Style Sheet i.e. Keypad 1 for headings, 2 for sub headings, 3 for body text, 4 for captions. This makes sense because it is usually the order in which these items appear on a printed page.

5. Press keypad number 3 then click OK to return to the previous dialog box, then click Save to return to your document. You have just created a Paragraph Style Sheet which has a Character Style Sheet embedded within it. This is because you applied both character attributes and paragraph formatting to the highlighted text before making it into a Style Sheet.

6. Choose Show Style Sheets from the View menu.

The Style Sheet you created should be in this palette along with the styles of Normal and No Style. The keyboard equivalent number is displayed to the right of the sheet's name. Paragraph styles appear in the upper half. Character styles in the lower half. Note the symbol next to the style names; ¶ for paragraph styles and A for character styles.

Although you used the first paragraph to create your body text style, and it looks fine, it has not yet been applied to that paragraph, therefore any changes made to the style will not update the paragraph.

Style Sheet palette.

The text should change as soon as a style is applied. However, sometimes a style doesn't take hold when first applied, in which case apply No Style, then press the appropriate key to apply the proper style again. If this fails, apply the style Normal, after No Style, then continue to apply the styles to the remainder of the text. If you have imported a large amount of text, it would be a tedious task to apply styles to individual paragraphs. As there are more body-text paragraphs than headings and sub-headings, it makes sense to apply No Style, then Normal, (to eliminate the possibility of problems with styles not applying) then apply Body style to all of the text, then individually apply other styles such as sub-heads etc.

1. Using the Content tool, click once inside the first paragraph. You do not need to highlight the text to apply the style.

2. Press the key you chose to apply the style or click once on the name of the style in the Style Sheet palette. Nothing will happen to the first paragraph because it already has that style's attributes, the application of the style via the Style Sheet 'locks' the style into place.

3. Now apply the same style to the remainder of your text, click on the text and press the appropriate key (*see note on left*). When done, deselect any highlighted text.

Creating a Style Sheet from a Set of Instructions

There is a little more to this than the previous exercise. You will also be introduced to some of the features in the format dialog box which were left out earlier. First you'll create a sub-head style.

1. Choose Style Sheets from the Edit menu. The same dialog box appears.

2. Press and hold down the button named New and select Paragraph. A second dialog box appears.

3. In the Name area, type 'sub-head' (or your own preferred expression for a sub-head).

4. Press the Tab key on the keyboard or click in the Keyboard Equivalent area. Press 2 on the numeric keypad. You will set both Character Attributes and Formats for this style.

5. In the middle section of the dialog box you can see the Character Attributes area with the style named Default on view. You will edit the Default Character Attributes for the Paragraph style you are creating. Click once on the button named Edit.

6. Make the following settings: Times, 14 pt, Bold, Blue, Vertical Scale 150%, Small Caps.

41

```
┌─────────────────────────────────────────────────────────┐
│ ▒▒▒▒▒▒▒▒▒▒▒  Edit Character Style Sheet  ▒▒▒▒▒▒▒▒▒▒▒    │
│                                                         │
│  Name:              │New Style Sheet               │   │
│  Keyboard Equivalent: ┌───────────────────────────┐   │
│                       └───────────────────────────┘   │
│  Based On:          │A No Style ▼│                    │
│  ─────────────────────────────────────────────────    │
│                        ┌─Type Style──────────────┐    │
│  Font:   │Helvetica  │▼│ ⊠ Plain    □ Shadow      │   │
│  Size:   │12 pt │▼│     □ Bold     □ All Caps     │   │
│  Colour: │ Black ▼│    □ Italic    □ Small Caps   │   │
│  Shade:  │100% │▼│     □ Underline □ Superscript  │   │
│                        □ Word U-line □ Subscript  │   │
│  Scale:  │Horizontal ▼││100%│ □ Strike Thru □ Superior │
│                        □ Outline                  │   │
│  Track Amount:    │0  │                            │   │
│  Baseline Shift:  │0 pt│   ┌─Cancel─┐  ┌══ OK ══┐  │   │
│                            └────────┘  └────────┘  │   │
└─────────────────────────────────────────────────────────┘
```

The Character Style Sheets dialog.

These settings you have made are only to illustrate the point that you may be asked to create Style Sheets according to someone else's design. You may of course make you own settings if you prefer.

7. Click OK to return to the main dialog box.

8. Click once on the Formats label. The dialog box changes. Make the following changes: Left indent 3 mm. Leave the other two at 0 (because it would be very unusual to find a sub-head which was long enough to reach the right margin, therefore it does not require a right indent). Also a sub-head is usually only one line, so there is no need to set a First Line Indent. Set Leading to Auto and Alignment to Left.

Space Before and After settings can be seriously affected if the text was typed with excessive spacing i.e. Returns and Tabs. See Find/Change on page 85 for more on this subject.

Space Before and Space After

Space Before and Space After refers to the amount of space there will be before and after the paragraph. Body Text usually follows a sub-head, so when you apply the style, there will be a uniform amount of space between sub-head and body text.

1. Leave Space Before at 0. Set Space After to 4 mm.

The Formats dialog for Paragraph Style Sheets.

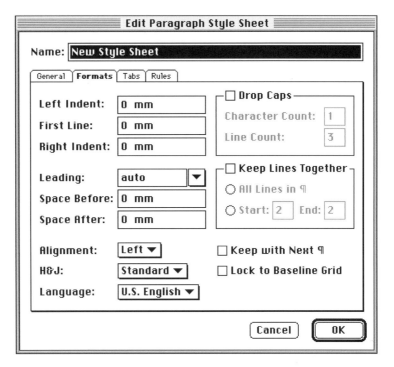

Important: If you were to set an amount of space *after* a sub-head, and *before* body text (you will be doing this shortly) you may create too much space. That is why you are not setting a space before sub-head, because in a moment you will be setting a space after the body text.

This is not to say you should *never* set space before and after a paragraph, you may of course do as you wish. When creating a new document you can never be absolutely certain as to how it will look once space has been applied. You make take a great deal of time setting up your Style Sheets but when you apply them everything may go pear-shaped. That is why Style Sheets are so useful, if things do not look as you expected, you edit the Style Sheet until the desired effect is achieved.

2. Click once in the checkbox named Keep with Next ¶ (paragraph). This setting will keep the last line of a paragraph together with the first line/s of the next paragraph. The sub-head is a paragraph in its own right. This means that when the style is applied to text, it will not separate paragraphs which fall at the bottom of a page. You are using it to ensure that the sub-head will not be orphaned (left behind on a line by itself with the text associated with it beginning on the next page or the next column).

3. You will not be setting any Rules or Tabs for the sub-head so click OK to return to the first dialog box.

4. You have just created (from a set of instructions rather than aesthetically) a Paragraph Style Sheet which has a Character Style Sheet embedded within it. Click Save to return to your document.

The next step is to apply the sub-head style to your text. If the text on you page has no sub-heads within it, create a few by typing a word or two then press the Return key to make the text into a separate paragraph.

5. Click anywhere on the sub-head and apply the style either by pressing keypad 2 or clicking once on the sub-head name in the style palette. If the style does not change apply No Style then apply the sub-head style.

Let's assume the body text Style Sheet you made does not contain all of the formatting you require so you need to edit it.

1. Choose Style Sheets from the Edit menu.

2. Click once on the Paragraph Style Sheet named Body Text (or whatever name you used) then click Edit.

3. Click the Formats label and make some changes to the Indents and Leading.

4. You have set a Space After sub-head, so do not set a Space Before body text (unless you particularly want more space).

5. You have not set a Space Before sub-head, so set a Space After body text of 6 mm.

6. Click once in the Keep Lines Together box. The dialog box expands. Read the information below before continuing.

When a paragraph falls at the bottom of a page or column, sometimes it can be broken in such a way that one line will be widowed or orphaned (widows go on ahead, orphans get left behind). If you select All Lines in ¶ the paragraph will not be broken at all, therefore the entire paragraph will not settle until it finds a space on a page large enough to accommodate it.

If it is a particularly large paragraph, it may cause peculiar things to happen to the text in the rest of your document. If you set a minimum number of lines at the Start and End of a paragraph, this should ensure there are no widows or orphans. If a paragraph has fewer lines than the sum total of the Start and End settings, the whole paragraph will be pushed onto the next page or column. Two lines at each end is the default, but some consider this not to be good practice. See page 148 for more on this subject.

7. Try setting 3 lines at the start and 3 at the end. Click OK to return to the previous dialog box, then click Save. The changes will automatically be applied to the text.

Appending Style Sheets

Style Sheets can be appended (copied) from one document to another. This is useful when you are creating a document which will have the same (or similar) styles to an existing document, so instead of having to create the styles from scratch, you append and modify them to suit your needs.

To append Style Sheets you would need to have created a document with Style Sheets and saved it, so save this document now and close it, then create a new document. The settings you make for the new document will have no bearing on the exercise. Once you have created the new document, import or type some text into it then follow the instructions below.

1. Choose Style Sheets from the Edit menu.

2. Click once on the Append button. The standard Open document dialog box appears.

3. Locate the document which contains the Style Sheets you wish to append and click the Open button. Another dialog box appears.

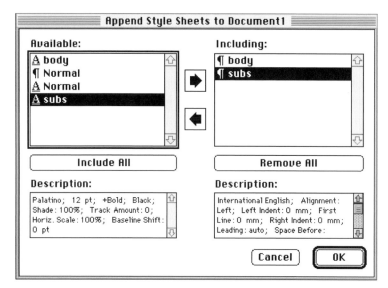

If you append several Style Sheets from different documents into the same document you may get alert messages on screen warning you that the styles being imported use the same name or keypad as styles already in your palette. You will be offered the opportunity to use the existing style and name or to use a new name.

4. The list on the left of the box contains all of the Style Sheets within the document you chose to append from. Either select some of the styles you want and click the arrow to include them or click the Include All button. The styles will move to the list on the right. If you make a mistake click the style name on the right and send it back with the Remove button. When you are happy with the list of chosen styles click OK, then click Save and the styles appear in your style palette and can be edited or used as they are.

Hyphenation & Justification

The H&Js (Hyphenation and Justification) commands control the number of hyphens in a document and the amount of space in justified and non-justified paragraphs. H&Js are linked features and as such each affects the other. H&Js can be attached to single paragraphs or embedded within a Style Sheet.

Understanding how to make the correct settings in H&Js requires a fairly solid understanding of typography and even then what is or is not correct in the present day is open to debate. If you find this section a bit too daunting at this stage of your learning, leave it for now and come back to it another time.

To use H&Js you will need several paragraphs of text. It will be easier to follow (though not essential) if the text box is in two columns. You will look at Hyphenation first.

1. Select the first paragraph of text and choose H&Js from the Edit menu. A dialog box appears displaying the standard H&J style with its settings shown in the information area.

2. Click New. A second dialog appears. This dialog is in two parts, Hyphenation on the left, Justification on the right. Enter a name for your H&J.

H&J dialog box.

3. Next you make the appropriate settings, click OK then click Save. Read through to the bottom of page 49 before making any settings. The definitions are as follows:

Auto Hyphenation: When active (cross or tick in box) inserts hyphens based on your settings. Turn this on.

Smallest Word: Minimum number of characters in a word before it is hyphenated.

Minimum Before and After: The minimum number of characters which can appear before or after a hyphen.

Break Capitalised Words: When activated will hyphenate words which begin with a capital letter.

Hyphens in a Row: How many consecutive lines can have a hyphen at the end. Zero or unlimited in this box could result in every line being hyphenated.

Hyphenation Zone: How close can a word get to the right edge of the text box or column before it is hyphenated.

Justification Method

Justification Method refers to the spacing that is applied to paragraphs which have been Justified. You can set a Space Minimum, Optimum and Maximum.

The values in the Min, Max and Opt boxes represents a percentage of the standard spacing usually applied for the font and size being used. Therefore, the settings you make for one font and size will not necessarily look the same for another font and size. Justification definitions are as follows:

Space Minimum and Maximum: The amount of space placed between words that have been justified.

Character Minimum and Maximum: The space between characters which have been justified.

Optimum for Character and Space: Affects both justified and non-justified text.

Flush Zone: The last line of text in a paragraph which comes within (n) inches of the right hand margin will be justified.

Single Word Justify: When this box is activated, a single word on a justified line will stretch across the entire column.

To apply the settings made in your H&Js, select Formats from the Style menu. In the lower left corner of the dialog box, use the pop-up menu to select your H&J. Alternatively, when creating your Style Sheets (*see previous exercise*) you can choose your H&J from the pop-up menu in the Formats dialog box.

Hyphenation Exceptions

This feature allows you to automatically prevent certain words from being hyphenated.

1. Choose Hyphenation Exceptions from the Utilities menu. A dialog box appears. Type your word/s and click the Add button. When done, click Save.

Discretionary Hyphens

If you are not satisfied with how Auto Hyphenation hyphenates, you can change it by manually inserting discretionary hyphens.

1. Click the cursor *between the letters of a word which is already hyphenated*, hold down the Command key and press the hyphen key once. You can remove a hyphen by placing a Discretionary Hyphen *in front* of the word.

Suggested Hyphenation

If you require guidance on how to correctly hyphenate a word at the end of a line, highlight the word and choose Suggested Hyphenation from the Utilities menu. A dialog box will appear displaying the word with suggested hyphens inserted.

If Justifying has made your text a bit too cramped you can insert a Soft Return to move a word onto the next line without breaking the paragraph. Place the cursor in front of the word to be moved, hold down the Shift key and press Return once. See page 146 for the use of hyphens.

Text Paths

Previously, effects like those pictured below right could not be drawn in QuarkXPress. Text on paths had to be created in other applications then imported. This new version contains a number of tools which have, for the most part, eliminated the need for those other applications. In this section you will be looking at the various text path tools. Delete all of the text on your page.

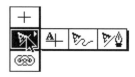

Text Path Tools.

1. Press and hold the mouse button on the tool three up from the bottom of the toolbox. The tool subset opens. Select the Orthogonal text tool for horizontal/vertical lines (the one with a cross on it). Draw a line a few centimetres long. The line is locked horizontally or vertically straight. When you release the mouse button there will be a grey line on the page, this is the text path. The two endpoints of the line can be dragged to lengthen or shorten the line.

Hold down the Control key before pressing on the subset tool to move it into the main toolbox. Control-clicking again sends it back to the subset.

2. Select the Content tool and click on the grey line. The text cursor appears. Type some text and it follows the path.

3. Repeat the above using the Orthogonal tool for angled lines.

4. Select the freehand Bézier tool. Find a clear area on your page and draw another line. With this tool you can draw any kind of line. If the start and endpoints cross over, they join up to create a text path of any shape. This is still a text path, not a text box. Add text and it will follow the outer shape.

5. Finally, select the Bézier tool. This works slightly differently. You don't draw lines, you plot them.

6. Click once on the page. A dot called a 'point' appears. Click again, and the two points join up. If you drag the mouse as you click, the new point will be curved and a set of 'levers' appears. You change the depth of the curve by dragging the levers. Click and/or drag a few more times and you will have a path made of straight and/or curved lines. Selecting any other tool completes the path. Add text as above.

Bézier points can be changed from corners to curves and vice versa using the Item Menu or the Measurement palette.

1. Using the Content or Item tools, click on any Bézier point (it changes to a small box).

2. Choose Point Segment Type from the Item menu and select the desired shape from the sub menu. You can make the same selections from the Measurement palette. When a point is active, the Bézier tools (*pictured left*) become available in the Measurement palette. Use them to change the nature of points. i.e. from a corner to a curve. Click on the point, then click on the desired point type in the palette.

Use these icons in Measurement Palette to change the nature of Bézier points. The two lower icons are only available if you have drawn a line and activated both of the end-points. You can then change a straight line into a curve and vice-versa.

Modifying text flow on a path.

Modifying Text Flow on a Path

You can modify settings for the way the text sits on the path.

1. With one of your text paths still active, choose Modify from the Item menu. A dialog box appears.

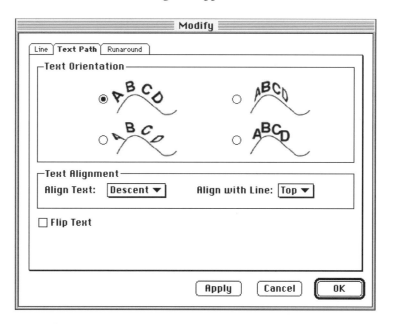

2. If necessary, click the Text Path tab.

3. Move the dialog box to see the active text path beneath then click on the four Text Orientation options one at a time. Use the Apply button to view the effect. The four options are a rainbow shape (the default setting), a 3-D ribbon effect, a skew and a staircase effect.

4. Note that by default, it is the descent of your text that sits on the line. Try selecting one of the other options in the Alignment Text and Align with Line menus hidden behind the black triangles. You can also choose to Flip the text by clicking the box to place a cross in it. Try a variety of settings until you feel comfortable with the way this feature works.

Before continuing, delete all of the paths on the page. Remember that Text Paths are items. Use the Item tool to select the paths and press the Delete/Backspace key.

Spellchecking and Dictionaries

QuarkXPress has a Spellchecker built into the program.

1. Choose Check Spelling from the Utilities menu and pull across to Document, Word or Story. A dialog box appears.

2. Wait for the word-count to finish then click OK. A second dialog box appears.

3. Suspect words appear at the top of the dialog box. Click Skip to leave the word unaltered (but not added to dictionary); click Lookup to display a list of alternative spellings, then select an alternative and click Replace; click Add to place the word to your dictionary; click Done to stop the spellchecking.

If the Add option is not available it is because you do not have a dictionary open. In this case, click Done, and do the following.

4. Choose Auxiliary Dictionary from the Utilities menu. A dialog box appears. Click New, name your dictionary and save it with your QuarkXPress documents, then start from step 1 again.

Using QuarkXPress: Pictures

There are various image file types which can be imported into QuarkXpress. Among these are TIFF, EPS, PICT, PAINT & JPEG. When you import images, what you see on the page is a PICT (low resolution) representation of the original image. However, when you print the document, QuarkXPress references the original high resolution image.

As you are aware, it is possible to create a variety of different shapes of text box, rectangular, elliptical, bézier etc. The same is true of picture boxes. Rectangular, Elliptical and Rounded Corner picture boxes are all drawn in the same way as similarly shaped text boxes. Bézier and Polygon picture boxes are drawn in the same way as Bézier text boxes.

Rectangular Picture Box Tool.

1. Select the Rectangular Picture Box tool.

2. Draw a box (any size, shape or position) in the same way you draw a text box.

3. Select the Content tool or Item tools and choose Get Picture from the File menu. A dialog box appears.

If you draw the picture box on or near text, strange things may happen to the text, this is caused by text Runaround which you will be looking at shortly.

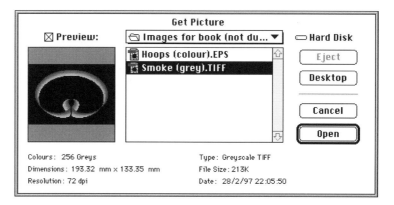

4. Locate the folder which contains your images and open it. (If you have none prepared, the Sample Pictures folder supplied by QuarkXPress contains a variety of picture types.)

5. Click once on a picture name. If required, click the box named Preview. This enables you to see what the picture is and check its file type before you import it.

6. At the bottom of the Get Picture dialog box the picture info is displayed. Check this before importing so you can be sure the image is in the correct format for printing.

7. Decide upon an image and click Open. When importing a greyscale TIFF image, if you hold down the Shift key as you click Open, the number of levels of grey is reduced to 16. This is useful when there is not much memory available and you don't need to see the image in 256 levels of grey. Hold down the Command key to reduce colour TIFFs to greyscale. Hold down the Command key to reduce greyscale TIFFs to line art.

8. With the picture box still active and the Content tool selected, take a look at the Style menu. It now displays settings for pictures. You should be able to change the colour and shade. You can also select Negative and adjust Contrast. Try some of these settings to see the effect they have. Some commands in the Style menu are not available for certain image types (try an EPS, JPEG, or PICT file for example).

Generally speaking, images are not usually adjusted once they have been imported into QuarkXPress. However, there may be occasions when you need to adjust an image size. You will be looking at this in the next section.

After inserting several pictures into a document, you may find it takes a long time to scroll through the pages. If so, choose Preferences – Document from the Edit menu and select Greek Pictures. Greeking replaces the picture with a grey box to speed up screen refresh, it does not affect printing.

Resizing, Reshaping and Positioning Pictures

You can alter the size, position and shape of a picture and/or its box in several ways. As with text features, all produce the same result, it is a matter of personal preference as to which method you use. Each method is explained below.

As mentioned earlier, picture sizing should be prepared in an image processing application before importing. However, there may be occasions when this is not possible.

1. Make a picture box larger than the image inside it by dragging the box handles out so you have plenty of white space around the image. Leave the box selected after resizing.

2. If necessary call up the Measurement palette from the View menu. Look at the settings in the palette when a picture box is active.

The palette is in sections. Reading from the left of the palette, they are as follows: *Take note of when it is the box not the picture that is referred to in these sections. Features which affect the picture can only be changed when the Content Tool is selected.*

| X: 45.257 mm | W: 10.243 mm | ⚐ 0° | → | X%: 23.7% | ⟷ X+: 1.737 mm | ⚐ 0° |
| Y: 56.298 mm | H: 6.064 mm | ⚏ 0 mm | ↑ | Y%: 23.7% | ⥮ Y+: -0.353 mm | ⟋ 0° |

1. X and Y = Origin. How far the box is from the top and left edges of the document page.

2. W and H = The Height and Width of the picture box.

3. The next two symbols are used to rotate a box and to set rounded corners if you are using a rectangular box.

4. The black arrows pointing east and north are Flip Horizontal and Vertical. Select a picture using the Content tool and click once on these arrows. Click again to undo.

5. X% and Y% = Scale. The Horizontal and Vertical scale of the image, not the box. To change the image size, type in new settings and press Enter.

6. X+ and Y+ = Offset. The location of the image in relation to the top and left edges of its box (the white arrows move the image in 1 pt increments or type in new settings and press Enter).

7. The two icons with the degree° symbol are the Picture Angle and Skew. Type in new settings and press the Enter key.

All of the above commands are available when you choose Modify from the Item menu and click the Picture tab. You can also use a series of keyboard commands to change the size of a picture.

1. To force a picture to fit its box but lose proportions, select the Content tool, click on the picture, hold down the Shift and Command keys and type the letter F.

2. To force a picture to fit the box retaining its proportions, press Shift-Alt-Command-F.

3. To centre a picture within its box, Shift-Command-M.

Picture and Font Usage

If you edit the original image (i.e. in Photoshop not in QuarkXPress) *after* it has been imported, you can update the image displayed in your QuarkXPress document using the Usage or Auto Picture Import commands.

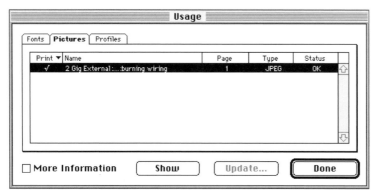

> You can fine-tune an image's position within its box using the Arrow keys on the keyboard. One press on an Arrow key will move the image in 1 point increments. Holding down the Alt key and clicking the Arrows will move the image in 0.1 point increments.

> The Picture Usage dialog box.

> If you modify a picture after importing it but do not update it, QuarkXPress will automatically print the modified picture not the one in your QuarkXPress document.

If the Picture Usage dialog box says the picture is 'missing' it will print OK on a desktop laser printer but not if you send the QuarkXPress document to a commercial printer. See Collect for Output on page 115 for more on this.

1. Choose Usage from the Utilities menu. A dialog box appears (*pictured previous page*). Click the Picture label. The box displays the names of all the pictures used in your document, plus the page the picture is on, its type, status and whether or not it will print. The word Print on the left has a hidden menu which allows you to choose whether or not to print a picture. This enables you to print a document without pictures if required. Clicking on a picture name and clicking to remove the tick in the Print column will prevent the picture from printing.

2. When the document contains images which have been altered, the word 'Modified' will appear under Status. Click on the name of the picture which has been modified and you wish to update.

3. Click the Update button. Changes you made to the picture will now show in your QuarkXPress document. Use the same procedure if you have moved the original image to a different part of your disk since importing it. The difference being that the file will be 'missing' rather than 'modified' and you will have to locate the folder the image is in, then update it.

4. You can automatically update modified pictures each time you open the document by selecting Auto Picture Import from the Document – Preferences and choosing On or On Verify. On Verify means QuarkXPress will ask you before updating, On does it without asking. However, if Auto Picture Import is set to ON, documents take much longer to open while QuarkXPress checks all the pictures in the document.

The same dialog box is used for Font Usage.

1. Click the Font tab in the usage dialog box. The box now displays the font list. The Show First button displays the first occurrence of a font in your document. The Replace button allows you to change a font like using the Find/Change command in the Edit menu.

Layering Items

QuarkXPress allows you to 'layer' or 'stack' items on a page. You would use layering when you wish to have items overlapping each other, such as text on a picture.

1. Draw three text and/or picture boxes and fill them. Delete what is currently on your page if necessary.

2. Using the Item tool, drag the boxes (by their centres) so they all overlap but you can see some part of each box.

Layered items can be of any type, text, picture or lines.

The stacking order of the boxes is the order in which they were drawn. The first box drawn is at the back, the second is in front of that box and so on. You change the order of the stack by clicking once on a box and choosing Bring to Front or Send to Back from the Item menu. If one of the above commands is not available it is because the box is already where you are attempting to send it to.

If you hold down the Alt/Option key *before* going to the Item menu, the menu changes to allow you to choose Send Backward or Bring Forward which will move the item just one layer at a time rather than bringing it all the way to the front or sending it to the back.

Text boxes can be layered on top of picture boxes. If the picture is not visible behind the text it will either be because the text box is still selected (in which case deselect it) or the text box has a background colour, probably white. You fix this by giving the box a background colour of None.

If you wish to move a group of layered items together, select them all with the Item Tool and choose Group from the Item menu.

Use the Shift key to select several items.

1. Activate the box and choose Modify from the Item menu.

2. Click the Box label if necessary. Locate the Background Colour area and choose None from the pop-up menu, then click OK.

3. Deselect the text box by clicking the white space outside of the page area and the picture should be visible. You can of course do the same for the background of picture boxes.

Frames

Any text or picture box can have a frame (border) applied to it. There are several types of frame to choose from.

1. Activate any text or picture box and choose Frame from the Item menu. A dialog box appears.

The box pictured above has a 50% grey Thick-Thin-Thick frame with a different shade for the gap.

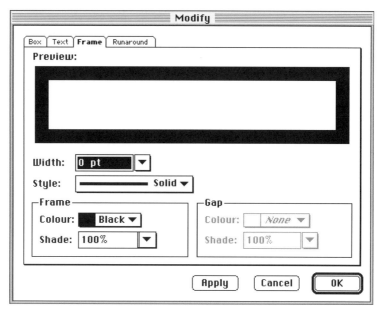

2. Use the menus to choose a frame style, width, colour and shade. On the right, choose a colour to fill in the gap between the frames lines (this is only active when certain frame styles are selected), try out a few settings and click OK.

When a frame is applied you can set a preference for whether the frame sits inside or outside the box.

1. Choose Preferences – Document from the Edit menu. A dialog box appears. In the area marked Frames, choose your preference. If a frame is set to Outside the overall height and width of the box will increase. If the frame is set to Inside there will be less space inside the box for the text or image within it.

Text Runaround

Runaround is how text wraps around boxes or lines. You can also have text wrap around the shape of an image inside a box.

1. Clear your page and draw a new text box which fills the page. Set it to 1 column using the Measurement palette or the Item – Modify – Text menu. Fill the box with text.

2. Draw a rectangular picture box in the middle of the page about a third of the width of the page and fill it.

3. Choose Runaround from the Item menu. The Modify dialog box appears with Runaround already selected.

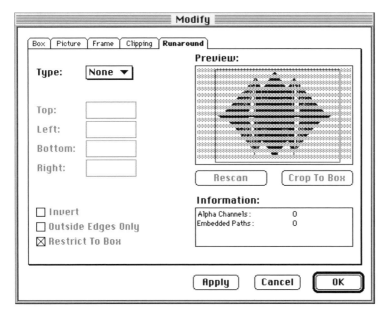

Item Modify dialog box with Runaround selected.

Try switching between the two commands Send To Back and Bring To Front (Item Menu) to see the change.

4. Choose None from the Type pop-up menu. You are given a preview of the effect but it is not all that clear. To get a better view of how this affects the page click OK.

With None selected, text runs either behind the picture, if the picture box is the front layer, or in front of the picture, if the picture has been sent to the back. The one thing the text does not do is run around the picture box.

5. Once again choose Item – Runaround, this time choose Item from the Type pop-up menu.

When Item is selected, text runs around the box edges.

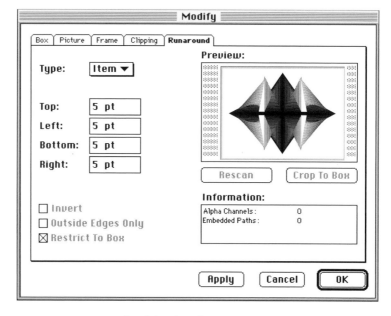

6. Enter 5 pt in each of the four boxes, top, left, bottom, right and click OK. The text should run around the picture box keeping at least 5 pts away from the edges of the box, this is known as Offset.

In the Preferences-Application-Interactive dialog box, turn on Live Refresh in the Delayed Item Dragging area to see the text runaround change as you drag the picture.

7. Drag the picture box (Item tool) closer to the edges of the page. Once you reach a certain point the text will switch to flow around the opposite side of the picture box. This is because in traditional typography it is incorrect for the flow of text to be broken by an image (more on this later).

This is a sample of a picture box with text runaround set to Item with a 5 pt Offset. Text will not cross the borders of the box. Nor will it get closer than 5 pt to the boxes borders. This is a sample of a picture box with text  runaround set to Item with a 5 pt Offset. Text will not cross the borders of the box. Nor will it get closer than 5 pt to the boxes borders.This is a sample of a picture box with text runaround set to Item with a 5 pt Offset. Text will not

This is a sample of a picture box with text runaround set to Picture Bounds. The text runs into the box's borders. This is a sample of a picture box with text runaround set to Picture Bounds. The text runs into the box's borders. This is a sample of a picture box with text runaround set to Picture Bounds. The text runs into the box's borders. This is a sample of a picture box with text runaround set to Picture Bounds. The text runs into the box's borders. This is a sample of a picture box with text runaround set to Picture Bounds. The text runs into the box's borders. This is a sample of a picture box with text runaround set to Picture Bounds. The text

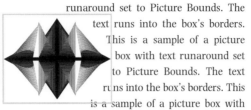

When Picture Bounds is selected, text 'hugs' the picture edges.

8. Try different offsets with different shaped boxes. Before continuing, return the picture box to the middle of the page.

9. Choose Item – Runaround again. Choose Picture Bounds from the Type pop-up menu. Enter 5 pt Offsets and click OK.

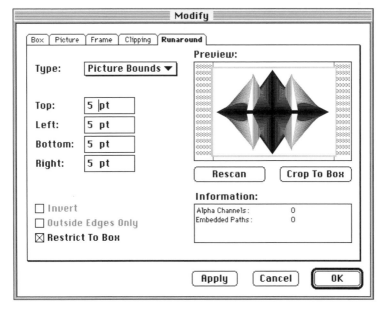

Runaround dialog box with Picture Bounds selected.

Bézier points have appeared around the picture on the page (magnify if necessary). You can adjust the points as you would a normal Bézier path but first you must choose Edit – Runaround from the Item menu.

The image on the page after applying Picture Bounds.

After selecting Edit – Runaround from the Item menu the points can be edited.

Take care not to mistake the outer *box* points for the inner *picture* points.

An image on a page after Picture Bounds has been applied and Edit-Runaround has been selected from the Item menu. The points have been edited to bring the text closer to the picture. This is similar but not the same as Clipping Paths on page 65. Always take care not to mistake the inner picture points for the outer box points. An image on a page after Picture Bounds has been applied and Edit-Runaround has been selected from the Item menu. An image on a page after Picture Bounds has been applied and Edit-Runaround has been selected from the Item menu. The

As with all Bézier curves, you can delete or add points.

To delete a point:

1. Move the pointer over one of the points, hold down the Alt/Option key (the pointer changes into a small white square with a cross in it) then click the square to delete the point.

To add a point:

1. Move the cursor to the part of the line where you wish to insert a point (not on top of an existing point), hold down the Alt/Option key (the cursor changes into a small white square) then click once to add a point.

All points can be adjusted to create the desired shape.

Run Text Around all Sides

Although it is considered by many not to be good typographic practice to run text around all sides of an image, it can be done in QuarkXPress v4.

This image had a white background, so a Clipping Path was used to remove the white (Non-white areas was selected with zero as the Outset). The text box has been set to Run Text Around All Sides. The Runaround for the picture was set to Same As Clipping. This image had a white background, so a Clipping Path was used to remove the white (Non-white areas was selected with zero as the Outset). The text box has been set to Run Text Around All Sides. The Runaround for the picture was set to Same As Clipping. This image had a white background, so a Clipping Path was used to remove the white (Non-white areas was selected with zero as the Outset). The text box has been set to Run Text Around All Sides. The Runaround for the picture was set to Same As Clipping. This image had a white background, so a Clipping Path was used to remove the white (Non-white areas was selected with zero as the Outset). The text box has been set to Run Text Around All Sides. The Runaround for the picture was set to Same As Clipping. This image had a white background, so a Clipping Path was used to remove the white (Non-white areas was selected with zero as the Outset). The text box has been set to Run Text Around All Sides. The Runaround for the picture was set to Same As Clipping. This image had a white background, so a Clipping Path was used to remove the white (Non-white areas was selected with zero as the Outset). The text box has been set to Run Text Around All Sides. The Runaround for the picture was set to Same As Clipping. This image had a white background, so a Clipping Path was used to remove the white (Non-

This image had a white background, so a Clipping Path was used to remove the white (Non-white areas was selected with zero as the Outset). The text box has been set to Run Text Around All Sides. The Runaround for the picture was set to Same As Clipping. This image had a white background, so a Clipping Path was used to remove the white (Non-white areas was selected with zero as the Outset). The text box has been set to Run Text Around All Sides. The Runaround for the picture was set to Same As Clipping. This image had a white background, so a Clipping Path was used to remove the white (Non-white areas was selected with zero as the Outset). The text box has been set to Run Text Around All Sides. The Runaround for the picture was set to Same As Clipping. This image had a white background, so a Clipping Path was used to remove the white (Non-white areas was selected with zero as the Outset). The text box has been set to Run Text Around All Sides. The Runaround for the picture was set to Same As Clipping. This image had a white background, so a Clipping Path was used to remove the white (Non-white areas was selected with zero as the Outset). The text box has been set to Run Text Around All Sides. The Runaround for the picture was set to Same As Clipping. This image had a white background, so a Clipping Path was used to remove the white (Non-white areas was selected with zero as the Outset). The text box has been

1. Clear your page or create a new document. Draw a new text box, set 1 column (Item menu – Modify) and fill it with text.

2. Draw a picture box and place a picture in it.

3. Activate the text box.

4. Choose Modify from the Item menu. A dialog box appears. Click the Text tab.

5. Click the Run Text Around All Sides checkbox to put a cross or tick in it then click OK.

Left. Text Runaround normal. *Right.* Text running around all sides. To make the text fit more 'snugly', a Clipping Path was used. *See next page.*

Clipping Paths

A Clipping Path is a Bézier path drawn around a picture to isolate it from its background. You may be familiar with drawing paths in photo-editing applications and therefore will also be aware that a path created in such an application is attached to an image then imported into other applications. That is called an Embedded Clipping Path. QuarkXPress v4 allows you to create these paths on the page as well as import them. However, paths created in QuarkXPress are not embedded in the image, they are part of the QuarkXPress document.

1. Draw a rectangular picture box and place a picture in it.

2. Check that the picture box is active and choose Clipping from the Item menu. A dialog box appears showing a preview of the image.

3. Choose Picture Bounds from the Type pop-up menu. A coloured line appears around the image in the Preview area. Click OK.

Although they are related, this is not the same as choosing Picture Bounds for text Runaround.

In the picture on the right, the black area is part of the picture therefore the clipping path will appear around the rectangle.

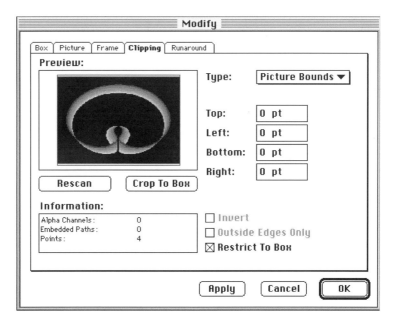

65

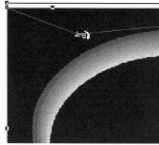

4. Go to the Item menu, pull down to Edit and across to Clipping Path. The path you saw in the Preview dialog appears around the image. Now you can edit the points in the same way as any other Bézier path.

5. If you began with a rectangular picture box, there will only be four Bézier points around the path. Add more points as described on page 63.

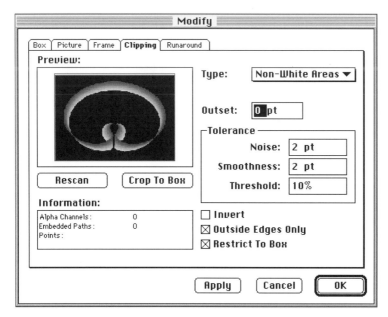

Editing a Clipping Path point.

If you set a Runaround (see page 60) for an image which has a Clipping Path, you can choose Same As Clipping so the text runs around the same shape as the path. If you make changes to the picture, the path will update automatically.

The Clipping dialog box contents (*pictured above*) are as follows:

Rescan redraws the path according to new settings made in the dialog box; also cancels Crop To Box.

Crop To Box means any part of the path that is not inside the box is cut out.

Information area shows if the selected image contains any alpha channels and/or embedded paths – you can also check the number of Bézier points in the clipping path.

The **Type** pop-up menu includes:

Item means the selected picture does not have a path.

Picture Bounds creates a path based on the rectangular shape of the picture as it was when imported. The boundary of all pictures is rectangular regardless of the content, which is why clipping paths exist, so you can remove the rectangular shape leaving only the image.

Embedded Path creates a path based on any embedded path attached to the image in other applications.

Alpha Channel creates a new path based on any alpha channel you created in a picture-editing application. Alpha channels are grey masks. Only the highlight and midtone areas of the Alpha become part of the QuarkXPress clipping path. Anything black or close to black, will not. You use the Threshold box (located in the Tolerance area) to set how close an Alpha Channel can be to black before it is excluded. Settings made in the Tolerance box determine how much of the mask will be visible inside the clipping path.

If your picture contains one or more embedded paths or alpha channels, they can be selected from the appropriate pop-up menu.

Non-White areas is used to create a new path based on the picture, not the box. If the picture has no white areas, the path will be the same as the settings for Item.

Threshold works like the Tolerance for Alpha channels, but for white areas not black. When you choose Non-White Areas for a colour image, the path is set as for a greyscale image.

Noise means any path smaller than the noise value will be deleted. Most likely to be used in embedded paths.

Smoothness affects printing. The lower the setting in here, the more points in the path. A higher number of points creates a path that is less likely to produce printing problems but is not as accurate. If you experience printing problems with paths there may have to be a trade off by increasing the smoothness to reduce the complexity of the path.

Invert will inverse the interior of the path with the exterior.

Outside Edges Only determines whether QuarkXPress will allow paths within paths. If you have created a path within a path (such as one path for a car tyre and another for the wheel hub if you wanted to keep just the tyre) and Outside Edges Only (meaning outside path) is checked, the inner path will be ignored.

Restrict to Box means parts of an image not visible inside the box will still be visible in the document and will print (see below).

If you edit a Clipping Path using Bézier points, the next time you open the Modify Clipping dialog box the Type pop-up menu displays User Edited Path allowing you to adjust the Outset etc. of your path. If you select Type when User Edited is displayed, click cancel to restore the User Edited Path. Selecting a new Type will result in your your path being deleted.

Both of the images above have a Clipping Path drawn around the subjects head and left elbow. The image was then moved within its box causing parts of the picture to be hidden. The image on the right then had Restrict to Box turned off thereby allowing the clipped areas to be visible. This will allow you to add emphasis to the picture content. See page 154 for more on using images.

Using QuarkXPress:
Long Documents

Master Pages and the Document Layout Palette

In long documents to move cursor up/down 1 paragraph: hold down the Command key and press the up/down arrows on the keyboard.

To move cursor to end of line Alt-Com-right/left arrow.

To move cursor to end of document Alt-Com-up/down arrow.

In this section you will be using the Document Layout palette and Master pages simultaneously as the two go hand-in-hand.

Just as you can create Style Sheets for text you can also create styles for the structure of document pages; these are known as Master pages. With these you create various styles then apply them to the pages in your document.

You use Master pages to automatically place running heads, page numbers or other items that will appear on several pages of the document. Look at any magazine or reference book and you will see where a page style is repeated at intervals throughout the publication.

Master pages are used so that you do not have to create the same structure several times in one publication. They can be appended (copied) or drag-copied from another QuarkXPress document (see page 87 for more on drag copying, and page 125 on how to structure a QuarkXPress document).

Setting up a Master Page

You will need a substantial text file ready to be imported later. Create and save one now or use the Sample Text supplied by QuarkXPress. It will be easier to follow this exercise if you begin with a new, blank document, so close the document you have on screen. Save the document if you wish, but you will not be needing it again.

1. Create a new document by choosing New from the File menu and make the following settings, then click OK:

Page size: A4
Facing pages: On (× in box)
Margins: 10mm Top, Bottom and Outside: 20mm Inside
Columns: 2
Gutter Width: 5mm
Automatic Text box: On (× in box)

2. Choose Preferences – Document from the Edit menu. Make sure Auto Page Insertion is set to End of Document. Click OK.

Important: There will be occasions when you will want Auto Page Insertion to be turned off. However, although it is something you have not yet been introduced to, for future reference note that if you intend to create an Index for your long documents (see page 92), both Automatic Text Box (New document dialog box) *and* Auto Page Insertion (Preferences - Document) must be ON.

3. Choose Show Document Layout from the View menu (see description of the Document Layout palette on page 73).

4. Look at the top of your Document Layout palette. There should be one Master page named A-Master-A.

5. Double-click that A-Master-A icon to view the Master page. You get confirmation that you are viewing a Master page in the bottom-left corner where the page number is usually displayed; instead of this you will see the name of the Master page you are viewing.

6. Choose Fit in Window from the View menu. You can see both the left and right side of the facing-pages Master.

7. Return to the document page by clicking on the small number beneath the A icon for page 1 in the Document Layout palette.

To Go to a specific page type Com-J and enter the page number (enter 'end' to go to last page. Alternatively, to go to first or last page use diagonal arrows on keyboard.

Next you import the text file. After doing this, you will see that the Document Layout palette has several additional pages in it. This is because Auto Page Insertion (Preferences – Document) and Automatic Text Box (New Document Dialog Box) are both set to ON. If either of these features is set to OFF, QuarkXPress will not automatically create new pages to accommodate the text being imported and you have to do it by manually linking the pages – you will be doing that later.

1. Select the Content tool, click once on the empty text box on page 1 of your document and choose Get Text from the File menu (Command-E).

2. Locate your text file and open it. In a moment the text will appear and your Document Layout palette will have several pages in it. This assumes the file contains enough words. If not, import it several times until you have at least three pages in your Document Layout palette. The cursor should be at the end of the text on the last page.

Sometimes the page number displayed in the bottom-left corner of the document page may not be the page you are actually viewing on screen. For verification, always click the icon in the Document Layout palette for the page that you wish to view.

3. Either click the number 1 beneath the page marked A1 in the Document Layout palette or double-click the A1 icon to view page 1.

4. Set the View menu to Fit in Window. Only one page is visible on the screen.

5. Click the icon for page 2. Now you are looking at two pages, page 2 on the left and page 3 on the right. Odd numbered pages always appear on the right as you would expect to find them in a book.

6. Click the icon for page 3 and only one page is visible. You can also use the horizontal and vertical scroll bars to scroll through all your document pages.

On the subject of scrolling, try dragging the small grey square which is on the scroll bars between the arrows. You may have to move palettes to see the square. Does your page scroll as you drag? Whether it does or not take a look at how to set Scrolling.

Preferences – Application – Interactive.

1. Go to the Edit menu and choose Preferences – Application. A dialog box appears (*pictured right*).

2. Click the Interactive tab. In the Scrolling area at the top of the dialog box, click once in the box 'Live Scroll' to put a cross or tick into it then drag the slider to a midpoint between Slow and Fast.

Scrolling bar.

3. Click OK, then try dragging the grey square on the scroll bars. The page should be moving as you drag.

Now that you have some pages to work with, you will go on to create new Master pages to apply to the document.

Creating New Master Pages

There are two ways to create new Master pages. The first (Method A) is for when you want a Master that is different from any you already have. The second (Method B) is when you want a new Master which is a modification of an existing Master. Try both as described below to create at least two new Masters.

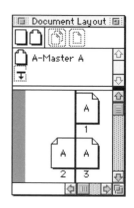

Inserting a new Master page via Method A.

Method A

1. Click on the New Page icon at the extreme top of the Document Layout palette (2nd icon in from the left) and drag it down into the Master page area until the pointer changes to a down-pointing arrow with a flat bar across the top (*see right*). When the mouse is released, the new Master page appears. It is named B-Master. If there is not enough space in the Master page area, drag the small rectangle (just above the scrolling bar) down to expand the area.

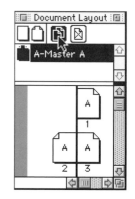

Inserting a new Master page via Method B.

Method B

1. Click an existing Master page icon and click the page duplication button to the right of the Master page icon (*see right*).

The Document Layout Palette

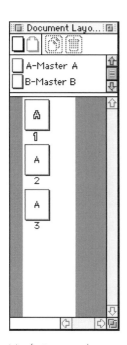

Non-facing page layout.

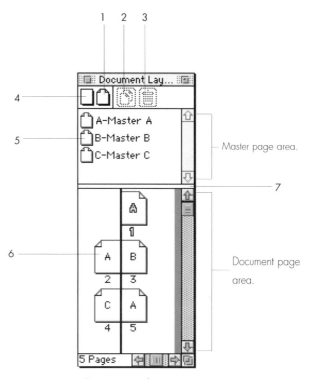

Facing pages layout.

To view a document page either double-click the icon in the palette or single-click the number beneath the icon.

1. New Page icon for a facing pages document - drag into Master page area to create a new Master page. Drag same icon into document page area to create a document page that has no Master page specifications.

2. Duplication icon – select Master page icon and click to duplicate the Master.

3. Page deletion icon – select Master or document page icon and click to delete.

4. New non-facing page icon – use as 1 above.

5. Master page icons – highlight names to change them if required.

6. Pages 1,2 & 5 have A-Master assigned to them. Page 3 has B-Master. Page 4 has C. You can create 127 Master pages.

7. Drag this small rectangle down to open out the Master page display area.

Modifying & Applying Master Pages

Typical of the items you place on a Master is a text box containing something you want to appear on many document pages i.e. a Running Head, as you can see on the pages in this book, or page numbers (more on this later).

1. Double-click one of your Master page icons to view the Master page layout and set your View to Fit in Window.

2. Draw a text box across the width of the left-hand Master page then use the Item tool to position the box in the upper-left corner of the page, staying inside the margin guides.

3. Use the Measurement palette to change the height and width of the box to a size large enough to contain a book title.

4. Type some text into the box and using either the Style menu or the Measurement palette set attributes for the text size, font, colour etc.

5. Choose Duplicate from the Item menu (Com-D) and use the Item tool to drag the duplicated box across to the right-hand Master page.

6. Click the page 1 icon in the Document Layout palette to view the actual document pages.

7. Drag the icon for the Master you have edited down over a page in your Document Layout palette until it is highlighted, then release the mouse. The items placed on the Master should now be visible on the document page. However, because you already had text boxes on your document pages, you may need to use Bring To Front/Send to Back (Item Menu) to ensure any additional boxes placed on Masters are not covered by the main text box.

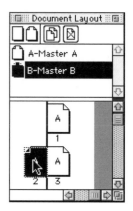

Applying Master page B to a document page.

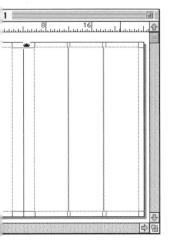

The Master pages layout.

Master Guides dialog box.

To apply a different Master page to several continuous document pages i.e. pages 1, 2, 3, 4, 5, 6:

1. Click once on the first document page icon in the Document Layout palette, hold down the Shift key and click on the last page in the sequence. This highlights all of the pages between the two clicks, then hold down the Alt key and click once on the chosen Master page icon.

To apply a new master to a discontinuous group of pages i.e. 1, 4, 5, 8, 11:

1. Click once on the first page in the sequence, hold down the Command key and click once on each of the other page icons to highlight them. Then hold down the Alt key and click once on the chosen Master page icon.

If, after applying a Master page to your document pages you then make changes to the Master page, the changes will automatically be applied to all of the document pages which have that Master assigned to them.

You will have noticed that the page layout settings you made when this document was created, (margin guides, number of columns etc) are automatically applied to the new Master page with the exception of the Automatic Text Box. You can change the page layout settings of a Master page.

1. Double-click the icon for the master page you wish to change and choose Master Guides from the Page menu. A dialog box appears.

2. Make the necessary adjustments and click OK.

3. Double-click one of the document page icons to return to the normal document view.

4. Apply the new Master page to the document page/s as before.

Master Page Items

The Master Page Items command is a preference setting which determines whether items placed on a master page are retained or deleted when a new Master is applied to a document page.

1. Choose Preferences – Document from the Edit menu. A dialog box appears which you should now be familiar with.

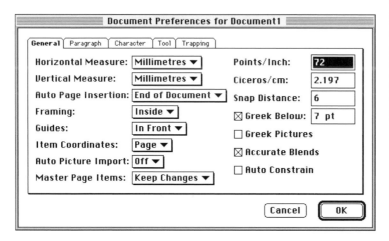

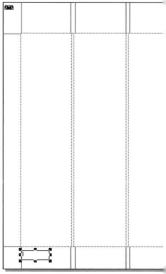

Remember to use Bring To Front (if necessary) to ensure page numbers are not obscured by other text or picture boxes. See page 132 on how to use elements that are placed outside the grid.

If you change a document page's Master, and you do not want the items associated with the previous Master to be removed from the document page when you applied the new Master, set Master Page Items to Keep Changes. If you want the items associated with the first Master to be deleted, set Master Page Items to Delete Changes.

Page Numbers

Page numbers must be placed on a Master page in order to be automatically applied to document pages.

1. Double-click the icon for A-Master-A.

2. Select the Rectangular Text Box tool and draw a small text box in the bottom-left corner of the left-side master so that it sits outside the margin guides. When you release the mouse, the text cursor should be flashing inside the box.

3. While the cursor is flashing hold down the Command key and type the number 3. If you succeeded, the page number symbol (<#>) should appear inside the text box. Treat this symbol as text. Highlight it and use your preferred method to set it to a sensible size for page numbers and Align it Left.

Above. Drawing a text box on the Master pages for page numbers.

Remember, your document has facing-pages. Therefore you must put page numbers on both the odd and even numbered masters. You have only set page numbers for the even numbered pages (left-sided pages). To set them for the odd numbered pages it makes sense to duplicate the left side page number and drag it to the right-hand Master page.

1. Check that the text box containing the page number icon is still active. Select the Item Tool and choose Duplicate from the Item menu (Command-D).

2. Drag the duplicated text box over to the bottom-right corner of the right-hand page. Take care not to drag its corners.

3. Switch to the Content Tool and select all of the text inside the box.

4. Change the Alignment to Right. This ensures that page numbers on right and left pages will be the same distance from the document margins.

5. When you have finished, go back to page 1 in the Document Layout palette. Scroll through your document and check that the page numbers are where they should be. If they are not, redo this exercise. If you insert (or delete) any pages (see exercise below) QuarkXPress will automatically reset the page numbering throughout the document.

Page Numbering using Section Start

Sometimes you may wish to create a document which contains sections. This tutorial (the whole of Chapter 2) began as a separate sectioned document. Section 1 begins on page 13 so the first page in the Document Layout palette was made into a Section Start from page 13 instead of the usual page 1. The whole chapter was then inserted into the other chapters which had also been sectioned and the numbering sequence was retained.

1. In the Document Layout palette, click once on the icon for the page which you want to begin the new section and choose Section from the Page menu. A dialog box appears.

2. Click Section Start. In the Prefix area enter whatever type of prefix you want (i.e. 'App' for an appendix).

3. In the Number area enter a number which becomes the number of that page and of course other pages follow on from there.

4. In the Format area, select the type of numbers you want to use (Roman numerals, letters and so on) then click OK.

The new Section Start will be marked by an asterix and if you gave the Section Start page an odd number, it would automatically move over to the right-hand side of the Document Layout palette.

When using more than one type of Master page in a document, you must create the page number symbol again (copying and pasting its box is the easiest way) on the left and right sides of the new Master page.

Section Start dialog box.

When you have a sectioned document you could, if required, set Auto Page Insertion to End of Section, which would simply mean any new pages created as a result of adding more text, will appear at the end of the section rather than the end of the document.

Manually Inserting New Document Pages

So far you have only inserted new document pages through Auto Page Insertion. There are two other ways to insert pages; with the Page menu and by dragging.

Page Menu Method

1. Check you are viewing a document page not a Master.

2. Choose Insert from the Page menu. A dialog box appears.

The Insert Pages dialog box.

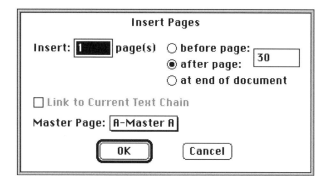

3. On the left side of the dialog box, type in how many pages you wish to insert. Insert at least five for this exercise.

4. On the right of the dialog box, choose where you want the new blank pages to appear i.e. before a certain page? after it? Choose End of Document.

If you have a linked Text Chain (this is when you import text when Automatic Text Box and Auto Page Insertion are On) the text boxes on your existing pages are linked. If you insert new pages and Link to Current Text Chain is set to On, the last text box in your current chain will be linked to the first of the new pages no matter where in the document you insert those new pages. Be careful with this. If you had ten document pages full of text and all linked and you then manually inserted five new pages after page 7 and chose Link to Current Text Chain, the story which was flowing from page 10 would flow to page 8, which is the first of the five new pages inserted after page 7.

5. You can also apply a Master page style to the new pages here (instead of using the Document Layout palette) by choosing a Master from the pop-up menu at the bottom of the dialog box. Choose whichever master you wish and click OK.

Dragging Method

1. Move the cursor to the A-Master icon in the Document Layout palette (or another Master if you prefer) and drag the icon down beneath the existing page icons in the document page area of the palette, until the icon changes into a white page icon (see right). When the icon is in the desired position, release the mouse and the page appears in the palette.

Multiple Page Spreads

A 'spread' refers to pages which are arranged horizontally such as those you would find in a publication where one or more pages opens out.

1. Drag a page icon from either the Master page area (if you want the spread to have a particular Master style) or the new page area (if you want to give that page an individual style) to the left or right side of an existing page. If you are inserting the spread between an existing spread, the pointer changes into a small arrow with a flat base. If inserting before or after an existing page, the pointer becomes a small white page the same as when dragging normal pages. When the mouse is released the page will be inserted.

When you add new pages to create spreads, QuarkXPress automatically renumbers the pages (assuming you have inserted page numbers in the first place). To print Spreads you must click the Spreads button in the Print dialog box (more on printing later). After creating spreads, the horizontal ruler increments will split up so there is a zero for each page of the spread. To have the increments be continuous across the spread open the Preferences – Document – General dialog and set Item Coordinates to Spread rather than the default setting of Page.

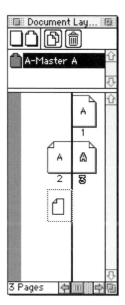

Dragging a new page into the Document Layout palette.

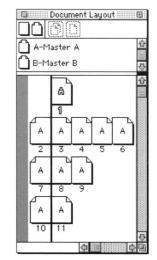

Document Layout palette with multiple spreads.

Linking and Unlinking

When text is imported with Automatic Text Box and Auto Page Insertion both set to On, the boxes containing the text are linked together and as linking is dynamic, changes made to one box affects text in the other boxes. You will on occasions wish to manually link boxes together, for example when you are using Jump Lines (page 83) i.e. when a page contains a full page advertisement or image and is therefore not part of the main story. Remember, it is the *text boxes* that are linked, not the pages. Therefore you could link text to several boxes on the same page.

1. Create a New document leaving Automatic Text Box ON (only to save you having to draw them on every page).

2. Choose Document – Preferences – General from the Edit menu and turn Auto Page Insertion OFF.

3. Import a large text file into the document (it will not flow past the first page.

4. Manually insert a new page by dragging the A-Master down and to the left of page 1 in the Document Layout palette.

5. Select the Linking tool and click once on the box the text is flowing FROM (in this case the box on page 1 (a dotted line appears around the box).

6. Scroll to bring page 2 into view and click once on the box the text is to flow TO. The text flows into the box. The first text box you click after choosing the FROM box will be the one the text links to.

7. Continue adding pages and linking them until there is no more text to flow.

8. To unlink boxes, select the Unlinking tool, click on a box containing a link (grey arrows appear showing the links).

9. Click on the head or tail of the arrow/s depending on whether you wish to stop text flowing into or out of, a box.

You can scroll through the document to bring empty pages into view even though the linking effect is active on a page.

If you decide not to make a link after clicking the FROM box, click on the Content tool to cancel the link.

Linking Icon on Master Pages

When you add new Master pages to a document and place text boxes on the Masters, there is no Automatic Text Box on them. You may have noticed an icon in the top-left corners of the Master pages which looks like the Linking Tool. This is used to make text boxes which have been placed on new Master pages become Automatic Text Boxes, just as if they had been set to automatic when the document was first created.

1. Create a new Master page, draw a text box on it.

2. Click on the Linking Tool, then click on the icon at the top of the page and the linking arrow appears. Remember to set both left and right Masters.

Text imported into document pages that have that Master assigned to them will now behave as Automatic Text Box pages.

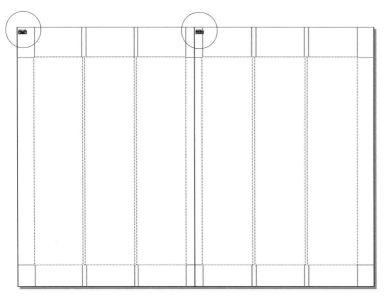

Master pages showing the linking icon in the top-left corner of each page.

Jump Lines (aka Text Continuation Notices)

At some point you will have read a magazine story and reached the end of a column and been met by the words 'continued on page #'. You go to page # and it reads 'continued from page #'. This is known as a Jump Line or Text Continuation Notice. To create Jump Lines you must first have established a link (either automatically or manually) between the two pages which the story is flowing from and to. There would also, of course, have to be pages between the To and From boxes which do not contain any part of the story, else there would be little point in having a continued from and to message.

1. Create a small text box (inside the main text box) at the bottom of the page where the story will continue FROM and type 'continued on page ' put a space after 'page', then, with the cursor flashing after the space, hold down the Command key and type the number 4.

2. Create another small text box (inside the main text box) at the top of the page where the story continues and type 'continued from page ' then with the text cursor flashing after the space, hold down the Command key but this time type the number 2. The correct page numbers will automatically appear in these boxes and if you move any pages the page numbers will automatically be updated in the Continued From and To boxes.

In the example of a text continuation notice (*bottom right corner of this page*), the text was formatted using the same Style Sheet as the main body text but with a slightly smaller point size; the horizontal alignment was set to right; the vertical alignment was set to bottom (Item – Modify menu) to make the jump line sit in the bottom-right corner of the text box.

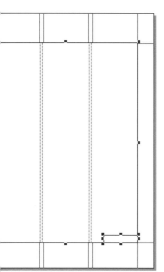

Ensure you place the small text box *inside* the main text box that contains the story.

Continued on page 84

Anchoring Boxes to Text

If you have created a document with the pictures mixed amongst the text and you then edit the text, the document will be reflowed resulting in the images which are referred to in the text no longer being in the appropriate area. This can be avoided by 'anchoring' picture boxes to text.

1. Draw a picture box on top of the text box on one of your pages *not quite as wide as the text box* and place an image in it.

2. Select the Item tool and click once on the picture box.

3. Choose Cut from the Edit menu (Command-X).

4. Select the Content tool and click once in the part of the text where you want the picture to be anchored. Make sure the text cursor is flashing inside the box.

5. Choose Paste from the Edit menu (Command-V). If the anchored picture box disappears, it is because it is too wide for the text box it is being anchored to, choose Undo from the Edit menu (Command-Z), resize the picture box and begin again from step 2.

Removing Anchored Pictures

1. Select the Content tool, click once in the space immediately after the picture to display the text cursor (which should be larger than usual) then press the delete key.

You can anchor a text box to another text box and the text in both boxes can still be edited as normal using the Content tool.

Anchored boxes cannot be dragged but they can be resized.

You can adjust the indent of the anchored box by selecting the anchored box with the either the Item or Content tools, then clicking on the two options which appear on the left of the Measurement palette.

Options for indenting anchored picture box.

Invisibles

Invisibles are hidden characters which all computers use when you press keys which do not print a character on the page, such as Return, Tab or the Spacebar. If your text is not behaving as you would expect it to, particularly when you have made settings in the Paragraph Formats dialog box such as Space Before or After, then it may be that the document contains extra tabs, returns, or spaces and this is interfering with the text flow.

1. With some text on your page, choose Show Invisibles from the View menu. A series of symbols will appear throughout the text.

2. Press the Tab, Return and Space keys and notice the symbols which appear. If there are excessive returns for example the paragraph symbol ¶ will appear more than once at the end of a paragraph. Use the Find/Change command (below) to remove any unwanted spacing.

3. Choose Hide Invisibles to return to normal view.

Find/Change

The Find/Change feature is as it sounds, used to find text and replace it with other text. If you have a wordprocessed document which you are going to import into QuarkXPress, often it will contain excessive spaces, tabs and/or returns. Some people place two returns between paragraphs (sometimes even more) or two spaces after a full-stop, or use the space bar when they should use the Tab key and so on which can create problems inside dtp applications.

As you know, Style Sheets allow you to place a precise amount of space between all paragraphs which ensures your document spacing looks uniform. However, if the imported text was typed as mentioned above, the spacing feature will never produce the desired results. You use the Find/Change feature to remove all unnecessary spacing.

1. Check the cursor is flashing inside any text box and choose Find/Change from the Edit menu. A dialog box appears.

The left side of the dialog is where you type what it is you want found, the right side is where you type in what you want the found thing changed to. When found, you use the buttons to find and change the text. To search for Tabs, Returns etc. see notes on right.

To find particular styles of text i.e. fonts, sizes, attributes etc, or even text that has a particular Style Sheet:

2. Click the Ignore Attributes box and the dialog extends as below.

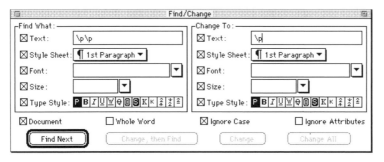

At this point you activate the appropriate features for the search you require by clicking to put a cross in them and deactivate features which you do not want to search for. For example, to find 'car' but not 'carrier' you activate Whole Word. To search for bold text regardless of size you activate Bold but deactivate Size and so on.

To find double spacing press the spacebar twice (or more if required) in the Find area.

To find double returns hold down the Command key and press the Return key twice. This will put /p/p in the Find area.

To find excessive Tabs again use the Command key but this time with the Tab key to place /t/t (or more if required) into the Find area.

More often than not you will want to replace a Tab with a space so you would simply enter a space in the Change To area.

Drag Copying

Top. Two documents in Thumbnails view sat alongside each other.

Below. Page being dragged from document on right to one on left.

You cannot drag pages from a facing-pages document into a non-facing pages document.

Any Style Sheets attached to the document you copy from, are automatically inserted into the document you copy to.

If the page structure of the two documents is different, the document you copy to will automatically have a new Master page added to the Document Layout palette.

Occasionally you may need to copy complete pages from one QuarkXPress document to another. You could do this using a Library (see next section) or by drag copying. To drag copy:

1. Create two documents each with at least two pages and set your View for both documents to Thumbnails.

2. Resize and position both documents so they each take up half of the screen.

3. Click once on one of the pages in the document you wish to copy from and drag it to the other document.

4. When the page is in position the cursor changes to a page icon. Release the mouse and the page is copied.

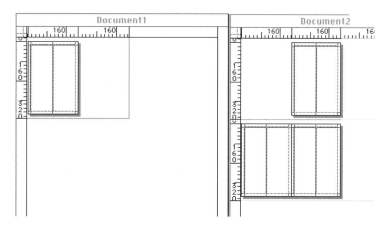

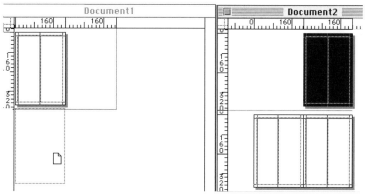

Libraries

QuarkXPress contains a library feature which allows you to store items which can then be dragged into any document. Any item or group of items can be stored in a library. A library can hold 2000 items. First you must create a library.

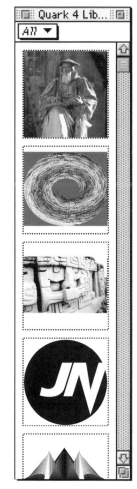

1. Set your view to something other than Thumbnails. Choose New from the File menu and pull across to Library. The standard Save As dialog box appears.

2. Name the library.

3. Locate a suitable place for the library to be stored (the same place you would save a document makes sense).

4. Click the Create button. After a few seconds an empty library will appear on screen.

5. Items can be copied to the library by dragging with the Item tool. The size reduces to a thumbnail going in, but will be normal size when dragged out.

6. Double-click an item in the library to apply or change a label.

7. In large libraries, choose a particular item from the library by selecting its name from the pop-up menu at the top.

You can drag a box containing text into the library and its Style Sheets will go with it. When you drag the text box from the library into another document, delete the text and you are left with just the Style Sheets.

You can have as many libraries as you computers' storage space will allow.

The contents of a library are not saved until you either close the library or quit QuarkXPress. However, if you choose Edit – Preferences – Application, you can turn on the Auto Library Save feature. This will save a library as soon as you put something in it.

Several libraries can be opened at the same time and items can be dragged from one library to another. You can expand a library to view more by clicking once in its top-right corner.

Lists

A List is used to automatically build a TOC (Table Of Contents). You search your document for words which have a particular Style Sheet, and when the style is found QuarkXPress takes the text that uses that style and puts it into a List with the page number that it appears on next to it. You then save the List and it becomes your contents page.

To make a List you will need a document that contains a substantial amount of text and of course Style Sheets must have been applied to the text.

1. Choose Lists from the Edit menu. A dialog box appears.

Edit Lists dialog. Empty because no List exists yet for this document.

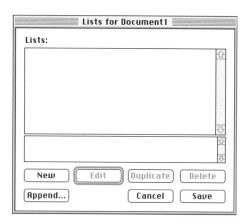

2. Click the New button. The dialog box changes to:

The Available Styles area displays all Paragraph styles for the active document.

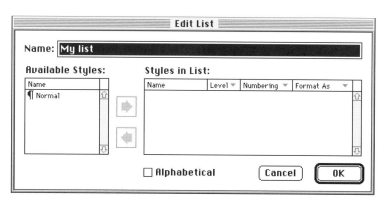

3. Name the List. Your Style Sheets will appear in the Available Styles area on the left. Click the style name you want to search for (sub-head styles are a logical choice) then click the arrow to send that style into the List area.

4. Choose a number from the Level menu. Level is for choosing the hierarchical viewing order of the Lists the next time you open this dialog. Lower numbers appear at the top.

5. Numbering is where you choose how each item in the finished List will appear in relation to the page number on which it was found. The numbering style determines where page numbers will appear in relation to the pieces of text that are copied into your finished List. You can choose to have the page number before or after the item in the List or not to have the number printed at all – choose Text Only for a text to appear without a page number – choose Text Page for text to appear followed by a page number – choose Page Text Only for text to appear after a page number.

6. Format As is where you choose a Style Sheet to define how the text in the final List will look. Choose one of the Style Sheets already in your document.

7. Alphabetical is used when you want your List to be generated in alphabetical rather than reading order. Make your settings then click OK to return to the List dialog, then click Save.

8. Choose Show Lists from the View pop-up menu. The palette appears. Select Current Document from the Show List menu.

9. Choose the List name from the pop-up menu. The scrolling area of the palette now displays the keywords which have the appropriate style.

Building the Table of Contents

1. To create the TOC, draw a text box, click inside it with the Content tool, then click Build in the Lists palette. The text box containing the List can now be inserted anywhere in your document and edited as usual.

Lists palette.

When no documents are open the List dialog displays all default lists.

When a document is open Lists for that document are visible.

You can create 1000 lists per document.

Making Books

The Add Chapter icon.

This feature allows you to take several separate QuarkXPress documents, and compile them into a book. You will need two or more documents.

1. Choose New from the File menu and pull across to Book.

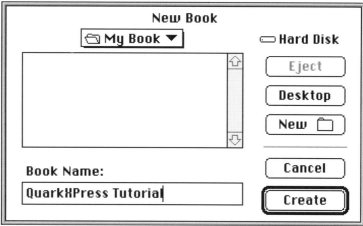

Added to palette.

2. Name the Book in the New Book dialog box and click Create. The book palette appears.

3. Click the Add Chapter icon on the left (looks like an open book). Find the folder which contains your documents. Click the Add button and the document appears in the book palette. Repeat this until all documents are added.

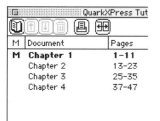

The first chapter you add becomes the Master, so choose the one which has the styles you want to use throughout the book.

4. When all chapters are in the palette, the two arrows next to the book icon let you organise the chapters into the correct order if required. The wastebin removes chapters from the palette. The printing icon prints the book. The arrows on the right are used to synchronise the documents, so the next time you open them all of the Style Sheets, Colours palettes and many other features will have changed to those used by the Master Chapter. The Status list tells you if the document that makes that chapter is still where it was when placed into the book palette.

Indexing

Selecting words to add to an index cannot be automated; you have to go through the document selecting them yourself. Once that is done, the building of the index is automatic. First take a look at the Preferences:

1. Choose Edit – Preferences – Index. A dialog box appears. Note you can choose a new colour for index markers and insert punctuation marks. In the box marked Before 'X-ref' (cross-reference), type \p\t (new line and Tab) to put X-ref entries on a new line, and indented with a tab.

Inserting Index Markers

An index marker is a set of brackets that appear around a word that is indexed.

1. Choose Show Index from the View menu. The Index palette appears. Starting from page 1, highlight a word and choose First Level from the Levels pop-up menu, then click the Add button once (the word appears in the Entries area and brackets appear around the highlighted word in your text – the brackets do not print). Repeat until all the words you wish to index have been inserted.

X-refs (Cross-References)

Do not break the following sequence; click only when asked.

1. Using the Content tool, click anywhere in the main text. Click once on an entry in the Index palette, then choose X-ref from the Scope menu. A menu appears next to X-ref. Choose See, See Also or See Herein.

2. Click once on the entry you wish to cross-reference, then click once on the Add button. Repeat steps 1 to 2 until all X-refs have been added.

X-refs can have a different Style Sheet to the main index if required. To do this you need to prepare a Character Style Sheet.

Requirements:

To create an index you need a document containing a substantial amount of text. Either, set Automatic Text Box and Automatic Page Insertion to ON or, create a new Master page specifically for the index and use the Master page linking tool to give that Master an Automatic Text Box. Also, create Style Sheets specifically for the index.

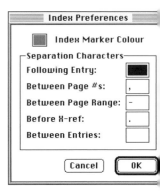

To view the X-ref, click the small triangle next to the entry you applied the X-ref to.

1. Click the triangle next to an entry which has an X-ref. Double-click the X-ref and choose a Style Sheet from the Entry Style pop-up menu in the index palette. Click anywhere in your main text when this is done.

Building the Index

You can replace an existing index and add letter headings if required.

1. Choose Build Index from the Utilities menu. A dialog box appears. Click the Nested button. The X-refs in this book are on a separate line and indented, because we inserted the \p\t in the Index Preferences.

2. Choose the Master-page style. Click OK. The index is created and can be edited as any other text.

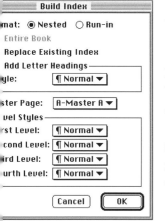

Remaining commands in the Index and Build dialogs are listed below. Many of these features are only applicable if you have created an index by highlighting text over a number of pages.

Sort As – Apply when you have a number like 2001 in your index but you want it to be listed as if it is spelt with a T but without actually changing the spelling.

1. In this case double-click the 2001 in the entries area and type 'two thousand & one' into the Sort As area. Click anywhere in the main text when done.

Provided you insert the appropriate commands in the Preferences or use a suitable Style Sheet, a Nested Index appears like this:

entry

    entry

        entry

A Run-in index appears like this:

entry, entry, entry

Levels

A Level is used to add subsets to an index that will not be indexed alphabetically, as you wish them to become second, third or fourth levels for another entry. Suppose your index is:

Apples 1-3
Farms 4
Trees 2

With a second level it could be:

Apples
    Granny Smiths 3, Golden Delicious 1
Farms 4
Trees 2

To create a 2nd Level entry:

1. Highlight a word in the text then click on the left of the triangle beside the entry you wish the 2nd level to appear. A curved arrow appears next to the entry. Apply the desired Style, Scope etc. then choose the required Level and click the Add button once.

3. Choose Build Index from the Utilities menu and apply your chosen Styles Sheets in the dialog box which appears.

Important! The Level entry will appear slightly indented in the Index palette, but will not be indented in the actual index unless you apply a paragraph Style Sheet which contains indents.

Scope – You have seen how the Scope pop-up menu can be used to create an X-ref. The other commands in this menu are:

Selection Start and Selection Text – When you highlight a word and add it to the index, brackets appear either side of the highlighted word. You can select a block of text (a range) and add it to the index. If the text covers more than one page, and you apply Selection Text, the index will contain a range of page numbers i.e. 1–3. By applying Selection Start, only the page number containing the opening bracket appears in the index.

To Style indexes the page numbers of a range of text until a different style is encountered to the one that the first word has. Highlight an entry and select a style from the pop-up menu.

Specified # of ¶s indexes page numbers from opening bracket to a specified number of paragraphs after the closing bracket.

To End Of allows you to choose End of Story or End of Document for the index page numbers.

Suppress Page # – Omits the page number from the index. Use this when you do not want a main index entry to have page a number because it contains levels or X-refs that do have numbers.

The Pencil tool is used to edit the entry in the Text area. Click the entry, then click the Pencil, then make your changes in the text area. Same as double-clicking an entry.

The Wastebin deletes selected entries. Click on the entry, then click the bin.

Using QuarkXPress: Colour

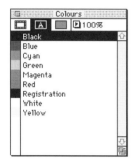

Colours palette displaying
standard default colours.

If your palette is different,
it simply means new
colours have already
been added.

The colours on display in
the dialog box (*pictured
right*) are the same as
those in the colours
palette.

If you intend using colour for commercial output and are not
familiar with the various types available, see page 151 and/or
speak to your commercial printer for advice on which colour
type to use for your publication. The following section explains
how to create and apply new colours using the colour palette.

Creating New Colours

1. Choose Show Colours from the View menu. The colours
palette appears. The colours on display should resemble the
standard, default colours (*pictured left*). More on this palette
shortly.

2. Choose Colours from the Edit menu. A dialog box appears.

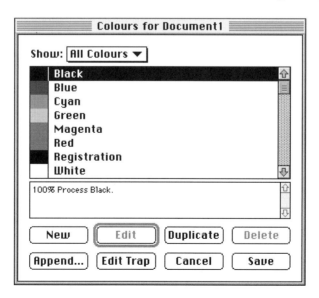

3. Click New to display the Apple Colour Wheel dialog. Note the Area named Model, it contains a menu.

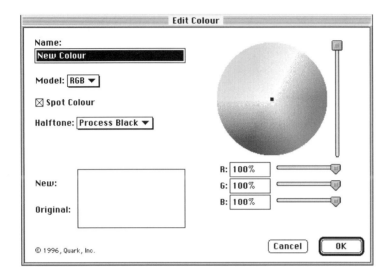

The Model menu is where you select a colour type i.e. RGB, CMYK, HSB, PANTONE etc.

4. Leave Model on RGB. Click on the wheel to place a colour into the New area on the left. Alternatively, drag the sliders until the desired colour is achieved. You can also type in specific percentages. You must name the colour by typing into the Name area. Practice these features before proceeding.

5. Select Pantone from the Model menu. The dialog changes to:

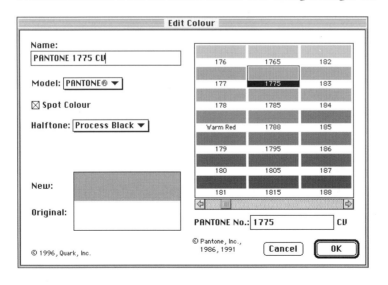

When editing an existing colour rather than creating a new one, the original colour would be displayed beneath the new one to give you a comparison. This applies to all colour dialogs.

Spot colour; Model: PANTONE®; Colour: 1775

Remember! You can save yourself a lot of work by importing colours (just as with Style Sheets) from other QuarkXPress documents using the Append button.

6. Use the scroll bar (below the colour swatches on the right of the dialog box) to view the colours. Locate the desired colour and click on it. The colour name automatically appears in the name area and the Pantone number appears beneath the colour swatches. When done, click OK to return to the first dialog. Your chosen colour/s appear in the list (*see left*).

7. Click Save to accept just one new colour or choose New the same way as you did from step 3, then click Save. The new colours appears in your colour palette.

Applying Colour using the Colour Palette

You have already seen how colour can be applied to text and images using the Style menu. With the colour palette you can apply colour to text, the background of any box and the frame of any box. From left the icons at the top of the palette are:

Frame Colour

The palette is for changing the colour of the frame not creating the frame. That must be done through the Item menu.

1. Click the box containing the frame. Click once on the frame icon in the top-left corner of the Frame palette. Click once on a colour name.

Text or Picture Colour

1. Highlight text or click on a picture using the Content tool (only applies to certain types of picture i.e. TIFF).

2. Click once on the icon in the upper-middle area of the colour palette which looks like the rectangular text box tool.

3. Click once on the name of your chosen colour. If nothing happens check that the Shade area is not set to 0%.

Background Colour

Colour can be applied to backgrounds in two ways. Incidentally, when you select the Background colour icon the palette changes slightly to allow colour blends to be created, ignore that for the moment.

Chapter **2**

1. Activate a box and click once on the icon for the Background Colour. Notice the change in the palette. The pop-up menu should read Solid, if not fix it then do 2a) or 2b) below.

2. Click once on a colour name. The colour is applied to the box but not the content. Deselect the box to see the effect.

   or

3. Drag the colour swatch that is next to the colour name and hold it over the top of the box without releasing the mouse. The colour appears but is not applied until the mouse is released. The colour will be removed if you drag the mouse back to the palette.

If the active box was a picture which completely filled the box, you would not be able to see a background colour. You can also apply colour by choosing Modify from the Item menu, click the Box tab and change the background colour of the box.

The area on the right of the palette is for the Shade of colour.

Colour Blends

Colour Blends can be applied to the background of any box using the colour palette.

1. Click once on the Background colour icon, the palette changes.

2. Choose the desired style of Blend from the pop-up menu (anything other than Solid). This activates the Blend buttons.

3. Click the #1 button then click the first colour in the Blend.

4. Click #2 button and choose the second colour.

5. Make sure the shading box is not set to zero.

6. Set an angle for the Blend by typing into the box on the right of the # buttons.

7. Deselect the box to see the effect.

The colour palette when Blend is selected.

Using QuarkXPress:
Special Effects

Text to Box

Before Text to Box.

After Text to Box but before
picture inserted.

After Text to Box with
picture inserted.

After Text to Box with
blend inserted.

One of the most interesting features in QuarkXPress is the Text to Box feature. This allows you to transform text into a Bézier outline box which you can then put pictures into. This feature has been around in various painting and drawing packages for some years, but that meant you had to purchase additional programs to create certain types of graphics which would then be imported into QuarkXPress. Now it is possible to create the graphics in the QuarkXPress document. To use Text to Box you must use either a PostScript font (with Adobe Type Manager active) or a TrueType font of 36 pts or larger. If in doubt, use the Usage dialog for font and click the More Information box to see the font characteristics. For the next exercise clear a page but keep a text box on it.

1. Type qx4, (as in the examples shown left) highlight it and select a suitable font (sans serif with a bold weight) and size (72 pt). To increase/decrease Font size using presets as available in the Font Size menu 7,9,10,12,14 etc. Com-Shift < >.

2. Choose Text to Box from the Style menu, the text is duplicated and can now be treated as a Bézier picture box.

3. Try dragging the handles around to reshape the box. Obviously if you reshape too much the qx4 will no longer look like qx4. It will be a new letterform.

4. Place a picture into the box in the usual way using Get Picture from the File menu. Remember to use the Content tool (see pages 169 and 171).

Splitting Items

The Split command enables you to create two or more text boxes from one original. It is not exactly the opposite of the Merge command (next page), but it's close.

Type unaltered.

1. Draw a rectangular text box and type BOOK, use a point size over 36 pt and a TrueType or PostScript font.

2. Highlight the text and choose Text to Box from the Style menu, the text is duplicated.

After Text to Box and then a picture has been placed within.

3. Use the colour palette to fill the duplicated section with a colour to distinguish it from the original. At this point you could put a picture into one of the boxes and it will appear spread across all of them. You can still use the keyboard commands or use the Measurement palette to adjust the picture size (page 56).

After Split all Paths.

4. Go to the Item menu and choose Split – Outside Paths. The letters look the same but they are now separate boxes and can therefore be edited individually. Try giving each letter a different colour.

5. Click on the letter B, this time choose Split All Paths from the Item menu. The B has now split into three parts. The main B shape and the two 'holes' in the curved areas. You can repeat this for the letter O.

After separating letters B and OO.

6. Drag the upper main shape away and you can see the two curved sections underneath. All are now individually editable.

After regrouping the separate sections.

7. Do the same to the other letters. Notice how the letter K has split into two. Obviously this command will affect characters differently according to their shape. You cannot put one picture across all of the letters at this stage, but you could put a picture or colour into each section, then join them together again by Shift-clicking to select all the sections and choosing Group from the Item menu (see page 104).

Merging Items

This feature is used to create various Bézier shapes by merging two or more shapes together.

Three shapes overlapped before Merge command.

1. Draw three picture boxes, any shapes you wish.

2. Using the Item tool, drag all three boxes so they overlap.

3. Using the Colours palette (View menu-Show colours), give the three boxes different colour backgrounds.

After Intersection.

4. Still with the Item tool, click on one box, hold down the Shift key and click the other items to activate all three.

5. Choose Merge from the Item menu and Intersection from the sub-menu. Observe, then choose Undo from the Edit menu.

After Union.

6. Go through all six commands undoing each one then try various shapes and positions until you are comfortable with the way Merging works. The order in which the shapes are layered affects the end result. The six commands in the Merge sub-menu are explained below.

After Difference.

Intersection: Cuts out any areas that do not overlap the item.

Union: Makes one shape from all the selected shapes, even if the shapes do not overlap. Non overlapping shapes are separated in space but act as one item.

After Reverse Difference.

Difference: Deletes the overlapping items that were at the front, making a hole in the item at the back where the shapes overlapped. Great for punching holes in the back item.

Reverse Difference: Cuts out the back item but retains the others. If back item is overlapped, its shape is cut out of others.

After Exclusive Or.

Exclusive Or: Cuts out only overlapping parts. If you edit the points surrounding the cut-out area, you can see there are two corner points where two lines originally crossed.

After Combine.

Combine: Similar to Exclusive Or except that no points were added where two lines crossed.

Step and Repeat

This feature allows you to duplicate multiple items (boxes or lines) in one move while maintaining a specific space between each item. Pictured *bottom right* is an example of a block of boxes created with Step and Repeat. One box was drawn, a frame applied to it, then it was repeated horizontally, the line of boxes was then grouped together and finally repeated vertically.

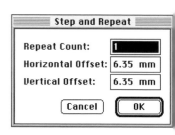

Step and Repeat dialog.

1. Locate a clear area on the page, draw a small text or picture box and position it on the left of the page leaving room for the other boxes.

2. Use the Measurement palette to accurately set the box size (ours is 9 mm square).

3. Apply a frame and or colour (if desired) using the Item menu.

4. Choose Step and Repeat from the Item menu. A dialog box appears (*top right*).

5. Set the desired number of repeats (in our case we wanted 3 boxes across, so the repeat number was 2).

6. Set a Horizontal Offset. (This must be at least the width of one box plus your preferred amount of space between the boxes.

7. Set the Vertical Offset to 0 then click OK.

8. Using the Item tool, select all of the boxes and group them together (Item Menu – Group or Command-G).

9. Choose Step and Repeat again from the Item menu, set a Vertical offset but no Horizontal Offset, then click OK.

After applying Step and Repeat.

If you set both Vertical and Horizontal Offsets, the boxes will be drawn diagonally across the page. Also, the settings you make in this dialog box become the default for the Duplicate command in the Item menu.

Space Align

This is another way of spacing out multiple items, the difference being all the items would have already been drawn. Space Align does not duplicate items.

1. Draw several items (they can be any type, shape or size).

2. Use the Item tool to select all the items (Shift-click).

3. Choose Space Align from the Item menu. A dialog box appears.

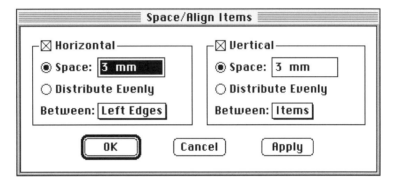

4. Click the Horizontal and/or Vertical checkboxes and make settings in the Space areas.

5. Choose a method of spacing from the Between pop-up menus. Try centres to begin with, then experiment with the other settings. There are no hard and fast rules here, what you set is totally dependent upon the items selected, their location on the page and what you want to achieve. The best way to find out what will happen is to try all of the options with the same set of items, undoing between applications.

The settings displayed in the dialog above were the settings used for the three shapes (*pictured left*), causing a 3 mm horizontal stagger between the left edges of the items and a 3 mm vertical space between them.

Grouping Items

When you want to move several items simultaneously, you can group them.

Grouped items can still be individually edited using the Content tool.

1. Draw several text and/or picture boxes on the page, they do not have to be filled.

2. Select the Item tool and click once on one of the items.

3. Hold down the Shift key and click on each of the other items.

4. Release the Shift key and choose Group from the Item menu (Command-G).

When you click on the items in the group, a dotted line appears around the entire group. When you drag with the Item tool, the group moves as one. To ungroup:

1. Select the Item tool and click once on any one of the items. Choose Ungroup from the Item menu (Command-U).

Constraining Items

You can constrain the movement of items within groups using the Constrain command.

1. Choose Preferences – Document from the Edit menu and click the Auto Constrain box to activate it. Click OK.

2. Find an empty page in your document. Draw any box (this becomes the constraining item because it was drawn first).

3. Draw a smaller box on top of it. The two items are automatically a group so you cannot move either of them separately as you normally could with the Item tool.

4. Select the Content tool, hold down the Command key and try moving the smaller item. It will not move outside the boundaries of the background item. To cancel Constrain choose Unconstrain from the Item menu and turn off Auto Constrain in the Document Preferences.

Locking Items

When you have several items on a page, to prevent accidental moving, you can Lock them into place. (You could group them first as described previously if required).

1. Create several items on a page.

2. Select the Item tool and click once on one of the items. Choose Lock from the Item menu.

3. To Lock several items simultaneously, click on one item, hold down the Shift key and click on all of the other items, then choose Lock from the Item menu. To unlock an item or group of items, select with the Item tool and choose Unlock from the Item menu.

An EPS (Encapsulated PostScript) file is an image which has its printing information (images and fonts) embedded within the file. Thereby enabling a file to be printed by another application as it originally appeared on screen.

When the pointer is over locked items a small padlock appears. You cannot move locked items. However, you can edit the contents.

Save Page as EPS

This feature allows you to create an EPS picture file out of any document page.

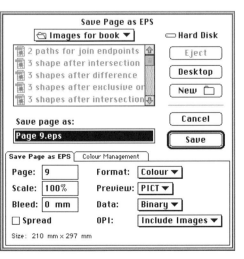

1. Choose Save Page as EPS from the File menu.

2. Make the desired settings then click Save. The file can now be treated as any other EPS picture file, even brought back into the QuarkXPress document using Get Picture.

Scale: Enter your preferred percentage.

Bleed: Enter whatever bleed you require (bleed is when an image flows off the edge of the page).

Colour or greyscale: As it sounds.

Preview: Allows you to decide the on-screen image quality of the document.

Save Text

As well as saving a page as EPS, you can save the text in a
QuarkXPress document as a word processing file. Use the Save
Text command in the File menu. Highlight the text before
choosing Save Text if you want to save only a portion of it.

Append

The Append feature in the File menu, allows you to append
Style Sheets, Colours, H&Js, Lists and Dashes & Stripes from
other documents. You can append into an open document or
when there are no documents open, the latter would result
in the appended items becoming the defaults for any new
documents created after appending.

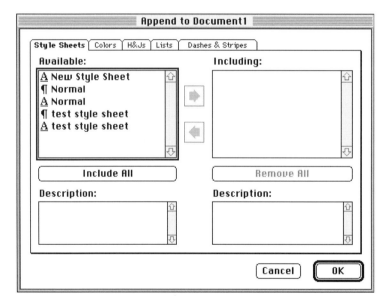

1. Choose Append from the File menu. The Save dialog appears.

2. Locate and open the document you wish to append from, a
   second dialog box appears.

3. Select the appropriate label for the feature you wish to
   append and use the arrows to add the items available on the
   left to the list on the right. When done, click OK.

Dashes & Stripes

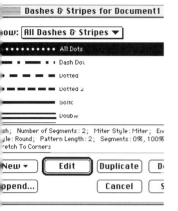

As you are aware, after drawing a Line or applying a Rule to a paragraph, you can choose from a variety of styles using the Measurement palette or the Modify and Rules dialog boxes. Dashes and Stripes allows you to edit the style of lines on offer in these areas.

1. Choose Dashes & Stripes from the Edit menu. A dialog box appears which contains buttons you should now be familiar with (New, Edit, Append etc. *see left*).

2. Click the style you wish to Edit or press and hold down on New to select a new Dash or Stripe (to avoid changing the default settings, click New until you understand how it works). The dialog changes to:

Try dragging across or clicking on the % area (shown by small arrows) then check the Preview area to view the effect.

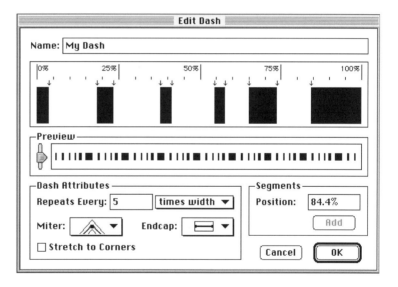

3. Name the style then try clicking or dragging on the percentage markers. Experiment by entering various settings in the Dash Attributes and Segments areas (click the Add button after typing into the Segment box). When done, click OK, then click Save. Your style will now be available in above mentioned dialogs. The Stripe dialog is more or less the same except the percentage bar runs down the left side.

Preview

Occasionally you will need to view your work in progress at 100% without the guidelines and palettes on screen.

Preview is not available on the PC for the first release of QuarkXPress 4.

1. Choose Preview from the View menu.

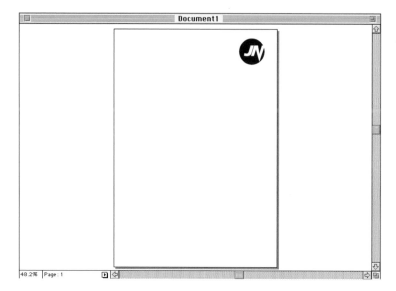

Preview allows you to see only the elements that you place on your page.

2. When complete, choose Exit Preview from the View menu.

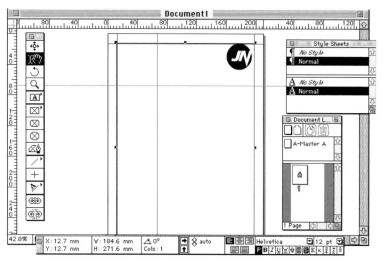

Exit Preview.

Using QuarkXPress: Printing

Before printing your QuarkXPress document on a desktop printer, there are several stages and dialog boxes to go through. What these dialogs display will vary according to the printer you have attached to your computer or what has been selected in the Chooser, and it would require another book to list all of the possibilities. Most dtp users have a laser printer so we will take you through the process for standard laser printing. It is assumed you have a document on screen ready to be printed.

1. If required, check Picture Usage as described on page 56.

2. Choose Print from the File menu. A dialog box appears.

Print dialogue box with Document selected.

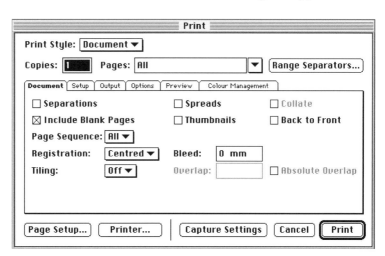

3. Check that the Document tab is selected so the box you are viewing is the same as the one above.

As you can see there are a variety of functions performed in this dialog box:

Copies: Enter the number of copies you want printed.

Pages: Leave this set to All or enter a selection of pages to print. To print a continuous group of pages, (say, pages 1 through 5) delete the word All and enter 1-5. The hyphen is essential, that is your Range Separator. To print a group of non-continuous pages, (say pages 1,3,6, and 22) type in 1,3,6,22 using a comma instead of a hyphen as the Range Separator (*see right*).

If you have not printed a range of pages, the menu hidden behind the small black triangle in the Pages area is not available. Once you have printed a range, then that range is stored in this menu and can be selected to be printed again.

Separations: Not to be confused with Separators. When you print in more than one colour, the printing press will print each colour separately. Process colours print in various dot combinations to give an illusion of many colours. Spot colours are single colours that also require a separate printing (see page 151 and page 185).

Spreads: Allows you to print double page spreads together as a visual aid for you, or as a client mock-up of the final publication.

Collate: Activate this box when printing several copies of a document consisting of more than one page. The printer will output them as blocks of complete documents instead of blocks of page 1 then 2 etc. which you would then have to sort out.

Include Blank Pages: Outputs pages even if they are blank.

Thumbnails: Allows you to print your complete document as small pages on a sheet to give you an overview of the design.

Back to Front: Use to print page 1 last instead of the usual first. Important in long document printing using one of the many printers which deliver pages face up rather than face down.

If you have used hyphens or commas as part of your page numbers, (unlikely but possible) then you cannot use hyphens as Range Separators, in this case click the Range Separators button and enter your own preferred separator character.

Page Sequence: Choose to print All, Odd or Even pages.

Registration: Places a trim and target mark outside of the printing area, so that the printer can bring your separations together and trim the page to size.

Bleed: Use to allow items to be printed off the edge of the paper.

Tiling: If the page dimensions of your document are larger than the paper your printer can output, you can use Tiling to print the document on separate sheets of paper which you then glue together. Be sure to set an overlap measure (3-6 mm) so the separate sheets can be put together as one.

Now click the Setup label. The content of the box changes to:

Print dialogue box with Setup selected.

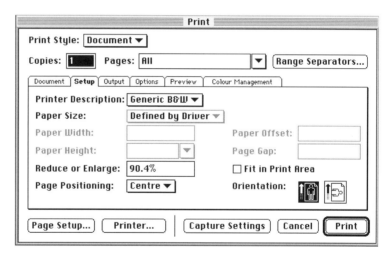

Printer Description: Make sure the name of your target printer is visible here. If not available choose Generic B&W or Colour.

Paper Size: If US Letter is selected here and your document setup is A4 Letter, you will experience printing problems. Many software programs default to US letter. Check this setting for every document you print.

Paper Width and Height: Confirms the size of Laserwriter paper used in your printer, or other media (film).

Paper Offset and Page Gap: Active if an Imagesetter is selected in the Printer Description area. 'Gap' means the space between pages printed on roll-fed imagesetters. Paper Offset is used to maximise space when the document is smaller than the film size.

Reduce or Enlarge: Use this command to output the document onto one piece of paper instead of using Tiles, or to print an enlarged copy of a document without actually changing the size of the document on screen.

Page Positioning: Determines where on the paper or film the document appears. A bit like using align left, right, justify etc.

Fit in Print Area: Use to force the contents of a page to print on one piece of paper. i.e. an A3 document on A4 paper.

Orientation: Click the appropriate icon to have pages printed in Portrait or Landscape format.

Click the Output label. The box changes to:

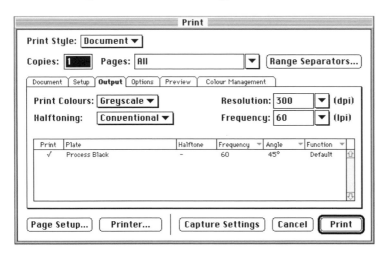

Print dialogue box with Output selected.

Print Colours: Choose whether you wish to print in colour greyscale or black and white.

Resolution: Set the resolution of the printer here. Do not set a higher resolution than the device can output at.

Frequency: Set the lpi for printing halftones here. What you set is determined by the output resolution of your printer and the type of paper being used.

The bottom of this dialog displays information about settings made in dialogs above. If, for example, colour printing had been selected, CMYK plates would be visible instead of process black.

Click the Options label. The box changes to:

Print dialogue box with Options selected.

PostScript Error Handler: Prints information about any PostScript errors which may have occurred during printing.

Prepress File: Use this to output to a PostScript file instead of a printer. Used in prepress systems for colour correction, separations or impositions. It produces a file that does not include the printer driver, PostScript code or embedded fonts.

Page Flip: Use for printing pages upside down, back to front etc.

Negative Print: Prints negative images when outputting to film.

Pictures Output: High uses data from the original picture; Low uses the screen picture; Rough will not print the picture.

Data: Binary prints faster. ASCII is more portable.

113

OPI: Choose Include Image when not using an OPI (Open Prepress Interface) server. OPIs thumbnails are low resolution images that can be replaces by high resolution images during final output.

Overprint EPS Black: When on, black elements in EPS pictures will overprint, overriding settings made in Trapping dialog box.

Full Resolution TIFF: Use to print TIFFS based on resolution of your printer. If off, a TIFF image will print at reduced resolution, based on any Frequency settings you made in the Output dialog box.

Click the Preview label. The box changes to:

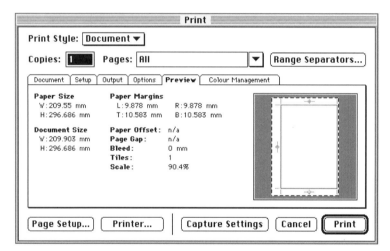

Print dialogue box with Preview selected.

This box displays information based on settings made in all of the previous dialogs. As you can see, the registrations marks are also displayed on the right. Page Setup, Printer, Capture Settings and Print are available in all of the dialogs mentioned above.

Page Setup: This takes you to the usual dialog box you get when choosing Page Setup from the File menu.

Printer: As above for when you choose File – Print.

Capture Settings: Click this button to save the print settings you have made within the QuarkXPress document.

Print Styles

You can set a style for printing much as you would set up Style Sheets for text.

1. Choose Print Styles from the Edit menu. A dialog box appears.

2. Click New to create a print style using all of the dialog boxes shown above or...

3. Click Append to copy a print style from another QuarkXPress document or...

4. Click Export to open the standard Save As dialog box. Name and save the style, it then becomes a document which can be imported by another QuarkXPress user.

Collect for Output

To send a QuarkXPress document for commercial printing you must include the original scanned images *and* the fonts used in the document. *The printing house will not be able to output your document without these items.* QuarkXPress will carry out part of this process for you. You will need a saved document on screen for this procedure.

1. Save your document. Choose Collect for Output from the File menu, the Standard Save As dialog box appears. Locate the disk you are going to use to send to the printing house.

2. Click New Folder, name the folder, decide on a place to save it and click Create.

3. Click Collect. QuarkXPress will duplicate the document and all of the images used in it, place them in the folder you created along with a report containing technical data for the printing house. PICT files are not collected and neither are fonts, technically, it is illegal to give copies of your fonts to other people. For more details of this see page 186.

4. To make copies of fonts, locate your System Folder, find the Fonts folder, choose the appropriate fonts and drag them to the output folder. Ensure you copy all of the fonts used in the document. Use Font Usage (Utilities menu) to check what fonts have been used. If you are in doubt as to whether you should send fonts, consult your printing house.

PostScript Files

As an alternative to Collect for Output you could create a PostScript file. The benefit of this is that you do not need to send any fonts, they are embedded within the document, also, the printer does not need to own QuarkXPress to output the document. The downside is, whoever you send the file to must have a PostScript printing device in order to output PostScript files, and, if there are any errors in the document, they cannot be corrected.

To make a PostScript file you simply click the PostScript button in the Print dialog box. The Print button changes to Save, which you then click. This will create a document which is the PostScript version of your QuarkXPress document. Send that to your printing house.

This concludes the QuarkXPress tutorial.

You, Design and Working with QuarkXPress

Knowledge gives you choice. By knowing the basic rules you can exploit the nature of digital design using QuarkXPress.

The proceeding chapters explore the key factors that you should consider. They have been written to help you decide where the rules still apply and what you can now do. Further indepth reading is referenced in the margins.

As discussed at the beginning of this book there are three distinctive parts to effectively using QuarkXPress as a design tool. You have already used QuarkXPress and have worked with its design studio metaphor. This part of the book is about you and your understanding of design and its language. Designers and printers use QuarkXPress because of its design capability and its terminology. They are familiar with how all functions are named. The following chapters describe good practice when handling digital files, the basics of design and the terminology which QuarkXPress uses.

The language of design, and design itself, has always been influenced by the technology that allows you to communicate your ideas. The methods used to chisel letters in stone and cast individual letters from lead have altered the perception of what design should or can be through the available technology of that time. Using a computer is no different, it creates new opportunities of how you can express your communication, and in doing so alter the perception of what design now is. Before you begin to exploit the nature of digital design you will need to analyse the conventions which have been established. Some of these conventions continue to be adopted and reapplied to meet the needs of new technologies. So before you can make the most of QuarkXPress you will need to know the basic rules.

There is nothing to say what you should or you should not do, this is not engineering, where the design has structural implications. With page design there is no 'bridge' to fall down. However, other people's perception will determine whether or not you are successful.

You, Design and Working with a Computer

Design tasks for print happen because of an intended purpose. The person that you undertake a design task for will want to disseminate material for an audience, there is a purpose to the publication. People who want your knowledge may vary from those who need the occasional leaflet to the professional publisher who will not continue before certain conditions have been satisfied. Publishing has developed sophisticated methods of production from the initial idea to the point-of-sale. It is important for you to know how a professional publisher is thinking, and then change that model for other design tasks such as newsletters, leaflets and so on. Therefore, not only will you need to master technology and an understanding of design, but also its appropriateness to the audience.

Task originator	• Do people want or need this publication.
	• Who are these people, can they be defined.
You	• Have they got access to all the material such as text and images.
	• Has all the material been received as promised.
Task originator	• How many people would actually have the publication.
	• Can enough be sold to ensure the publishing cycle.
Both of you	• Is the publication designed and ready for reproducing.
You	• Have all the computer files been gathered for output.
Task originator	• Is everybody who needs to know aware of the publication.

The second, third and fourth points above are crucial for you, they define the intended readership and the availability of the material, and neither should be in doubt before the design process begins. You will also need to establish the media format of the material such as transparencies (slide film), computer text files and so on. The seventh point highlights the freedom or limitations of your design by letting you know what the production restraints are.

You will also need to establish points of agreement for the work flow. This will help to eliminate problems at a later stage, for example, if the text has been agreed and then changes are made, errors can occur. The diagram opposite indicates the main points of contact and agreement. Again, this will vary according to your task, such as the print production route, and delivery of the work for distribution, but the overall model holds true and should be adapted by you. Begin the work when agreement has been reached. Also, a tight brief (job description) will restrict creative input, while a brief that indicates an unsure outcome could result with you starting from the beginning again. To avoid this Dorothy Goslett (1984) in *The Professional Practice of Design* suggests that the ideal person for you to undertake work for knows what they want, and will allow creative freedom to enhance your outcome.

Goslett, D. 1984 *The Professional Practice of Design*, 3rd Edition, B T Batsford

The Design Task Originator

		You as Design Implementer	
Idea	• Simply have one		
Viability	• What is there to gain from this		
Gather	• All text and illustration		
Design	• Explaining the task and its audience to you, and provide the materials	**Thumbnails**	• Try out various quick ideas • Eliminate and refine
		Consider	• Does this reflect the original idea
		Visualise	• For all to consider and agree
Schedule	• Production cost, time, quality		
Audience	• Can they be reached and how	**Support material**	• To produce design within cost, time, quality and return all proofs for final agreement
Commit	• To produce		
Produce	• Print and distribute		

By understanding an overview of the relationship between you and the design task originator, and especially their reason to proceed you can direct your knowledge of design and technology at the audience. At this stage thought must be given to the personality of the publication, and your thinking must be shared with the task originator. This allows your design to evolve out of the subject through their perception of the intended audience. The focused aim of the design is to stimulate the reader, be applicable to the audience, retain legibility and work within output limitations – this requires self-criticism and a disciplined approach to working methods.

The problem with design tends to be a holistic approach, you need to have gone through this exercise several times to know that many decisions are grouped together and experiential. Most designers spend hours sketching out possible solutions that might work. Each series of quick sketches build on the strength of the previous sketch, eliminating the weak points until a solution has been achieved that satisfy all the questions of audience and production constraint.

Analysis, synthesis and decision completes the first cycle of thought, each cycle adds another level of design understanding through reflection. The philosopher Ryle (1949) in *The Concept of the Mind* considered the cycle of thought as 'very much a matter of drills and skills'. Successive cycles build knowledge, and without critical reflection, the danger becomes the formulaic solution. To avoid this you need to:

Ryle, G. 1949
The Concept of Mind, Hutchinson

Analyse	• Who are the intended readership and what are the constraints.
Synthese	• Integrate the needs and constraints.
Decide	• Implement the design.

Edward de Bono (1968) in *The Five Day Course in Thinking*, warned against formulas and suggested that it is 'more important to be skillful in thinking than to be stuffed with facts'. In short, when considering the nature of digital design, like design methodologies before computers, each solution can be different. Digital technology has created the immediate availability of thousands of typefaces allowing expressive freedom for some and confusion for others. Expressive freedom can only be obtained by knowing which factors influence the design, instead of merely knowing what to apply.

de Bono, E. 1968
The Five Day Course in Thinking, Allen Lane

The same task can have multiple solutions, there is no 'right way', and to apply a formula that has worked before would deny any of your understanding and self-learning of the design process. To help you with this in the proceeding chapters you must consider what was good design practice before computers, and what computers can offer to enrich design.

Hand, Eye, Pen, Paper and Good Design Practice

Keep your ideas achievable, one idea for one design. Keep other ideas for potential future solutions. The accessibility of this technology can allow for an unchecked riot of ideas which will confuse and not clarify the idea that you are trying to convey.

The nature of digital design means that you are both the artist of the page and the user of QuarkXPress, and knowing when to apply which in the design process is important. The thinking process of design should have been completed before launching QuarkXPress, as the computer is best suited for refining the design. By starting the work directly on a computer you are limited to your understanding of the technology, therefore restricting your creative ability. Once on the screen the first solution becomes precious – change becomes uncomfortable and undesirable.

When you look at good design, it has been developed through a series of reworkings, each layer refining the design until the desired outcome has been reached. Even the design process for the interface of a computer program involves paper, card, pen and glue at the initial stages, while the actual program requires functionality to be explained in plain language before complex command-lines are written.

Design your publication with set standards. This will allow your reader to recognise parts of the page for what they are, sub-headings, captions, quotes and so on. At the computing stage this information can be applied to the Style Sheets.

After the design task has been discussed, and the material has been received, examine all the work to be done. Hand and eye are not impeded by the potential limitations of technological knowledge. At the initial stage simple tools such as pen and paper are still the best method of expressing creative ideas. Work with thumbnails (small sketches), remembering that the aim is to make it easy for the reader to understand the points being made; thumbnails will allow you to add emphasis to these points. Thumbnails can be erased and replaced, building the design to gain the required emphasis.

When progress needs to go beyond small sketches, build a kit by outputting images, headings in various sizes, and some text. Make sure that your layout area has a border so that you know the relationship between the paper edges and your elements. This kit will allow you to keep the design fluid and also aid in the thinking process. By physically cutting and pasting you have full control of the publication's appearance, and working with paper allows a visualisation stage that should be experimental while retaining a clear focus on your readership.

To make effective thumbnails you will need to have read Chapters 4 and 5.

Hand, Eye, Pen, Paper and the Computer

Proper design planning on paper should also include the role of the computer. When the design has been worked to a satisfactory level on paper, include notes for image sizes, the use of typography, and any other design elements that you plan to use. More detail now will require less memory recall at a later stage, also this information will be required when establishing page formats and Style Sheets.

It is at this point that decisions can be taken regarding the digitisation of any images. How you acquire and use images will depend on the specification of your computer. Insufficient processing power or RAM (Random Access Memory) for large amounts of high-resolution images in a working document can be equivalent to using the exhaust pipe to turn your car around, instead of using the steering wheel.

You must consider sending your images to a reprographic bureau or scanning them yourself, depending on your design. If the approximate size of each image is known, sending them to a bureau will allow you to manipulate the low-resolution thumbnail OPI (Open Prepress Images) returned by them. Another alternative is to scan the images yourself as FPO (For Position Only) images. If, however, you intend to manipulate these illustrations within an image-processing program you will require the bureau to scan the images and return the LIVE image (files containing the data for the final printing resolution) for manipulation (see page 178). The advantage of using a bureau is that they can digitise a range of differing media formats at your required resolution. PhotoCD can be an alternative method of acquiring images: for this, you will need to receive the material in a transparency format (see page 156).

When in a digital format, place all files in a folder that clearly describes your work. Create additional folders for images, text and the QuarkXPress documents. Place these folders into the first folder. A well-organised hierarchy of folders will ensure that files are not forgotten at a later stage when they leave your desktop for output by another computer. This organisation of work also helps locate files when you Get Text or Get Picture.

Print

All ▼

tions ⎸ Preview

☐ Spreads
☒ Thumbnails

Bleed: ⎸0 mm⎸
Overlap: ⎸   ⎸

r... ⎸ ⎸ Capture Settings ⎸

QuarkXPress will also
allow you to output
thumbnails to give a clear
overview of your design.

If you are planning
different file destinations
see the diagram on
page 156.

The next task is to establish the format of your document and
the required amount of pages. Adding or deleting pages at a
later stage can disrupt page linking. After establishing the
format you can set your Style Sheets so that all imported text
can be readily converted into headings, sub-headings, body text
and so on. Working with thumbnails does not end at the paper
stage of the design process. On a large document you cannot
see all aspects of the design; as with paper sketches it is important to output computer thumbnails to give you this overview.

Not only has desktop technology combined many skills, it
has also added different media outcomes. This might need to be
included in your design plan. Dissemination of knowledge is no
longer only about paper, other digital formats might be required
for CD-ROM or the WWW (World Wide Web). This is where
digital technologies really extend the possibilities; the original
content can be used as the base material for many solutions.

Allowing for this at the planning stage will determine
different file destinations and kinds of document if unnecessary
reworkings are to be avoided later. Your small thumbnail
sketches then become supplemented and overlaid with 'Web
maps and multimedia storyboards'. However, each media is
different and should not be confused with simply viewing
the publication through a screen. It is not just a matter of
changeover; nobody makes videos of still text and pictures.

Who should be Responsible

Originally simpler tasks such as page layout were taken over
by the person with multiple skills to exploit the multi-task functional nature of the technology. This is merely the reorientation
of historical roles, as compositors would hand-set type for pages
using a set of rules for typography. Without this understanding
the nature of digital design cannot progress as a true demo-
cratic process.

As you are now aware, desktop technology has combined
many tasks – the designer can edit the text, and the editor can
now design the page – one person can make many mistakes.
There is greater opportunity for skills to be diluted and there

are many skills within the process. A publication is physical, being produced by many people. Each will view the publication differently – the words, the design, printing, binding, and so on. The technology allows the temptation to make the maintenance of any ongoing publication the domain of the computer user who understands QuarkXPress. Yet the instigation of any design or modification undertaken in QuarkXPress should be the jurisdiction of the person who understands design and its terminology. They can reflect objectively, and make informed decisions applying knowledge of the nature of design before computers.

People who require printing regularly, such as a publisher, will have agreements with paper suppliers, reprographic houses and book printers. They will work within set specifications making each supplier compatible with the other. This in turn affects how many pages can be printed together (imposition) before folding into a section, and so on. Paper, film, plate and press allow for final checks on the end product. Technology streamlines these processes as the computer can output directly to plate, or digital press, shifting further responsibility to the desktop.

Structuring a Document

Work flow should be organised so that the route of each file is easily managed.

QuarkXPress documents, text files, LIVE Images, FPO Images and OPI Images should all have a separate folder within your digital 'job bag'.

Human perception tends to change gradually through exposure to new ideas, especially how we perceive the layout of the page within advanced consumer cultures. Before computers were in regular use, the different parts of the publishing route tended to be defined by what people did. The work flow would involve the design including the copy-fit/cast-off (calculating how many pages ordinary text would cover when changed into a typeface) to be correct before any marked-up copy (the ordinary text with typographic style instructions) was sent for typesetting. The returned galley (continuous typeset text) would be physically cut and pasted as artwork.

As both typesetter and designer were separate people, terminology had to be exact. Columns were mostly drawn-up with regular measurements because of the problems of knowing where the text would finish. Artwork surfaces would be hand drawn to include all non-printing grid structures (guidelines) reproduced in blue. Type was then cut and pasted into position. The final artwork would allow for a further detailing which separated out dtp from traditional working methods. All elements (text and image) of the design were stored in a 'job bag'. You should create the digital equivalent for all your working files.

The QuarkXPress interface owes much to this working method. The desktop becomes a metaphor for the drawing board complete with a full set of tools. Text is edited within a word processing program and images are manipulated and sized within an imaging program. The format of the publication and the page extent will have been decided before these elements are imported into QuarkXPress. Now the on-screen design becomes artwork and remains fluid. Instead of a collection of physical items, all the design elements are in a digital format, such as LIVE images pictures scanned at the final printing resolution. FPO images scanned by you on a low-resolution desktop scanner, and will be rescanned at high-resolution for the final output. OPI thumbnails which are small file size images of the final scan. These thumbnail images allow you to handle the image file with ease and will be replaced by the LIVE high-resolution file for final output (see page 176). Your working folder should contain folders for these items and your QuarkXPress documents and text files.

After your design has been resolved on paper and before you place any elements within QuarkXPress, the page format and your personal preferences should be your first task, followed by the page furniture (page numbers and running heads). Unlike traditional methods, digital design allows you to manipulate the entire page and any design that is not planned first can and probably will suffer. In this respect the grid structure (format) is one of the most important design features at your disposal. It defines the selective positions for the four basic elements of design, which are the headings, body text, images and white space on the page (see page 139).

The grid also provides a consistent framework for manipulating these differing graphic elements, and therefore maintaining page-to-page cohesion. Grids vary according to the kind of publication, books normally have one grid throughout, whereas a magazine will often have five or as many as twelve differing grid structures. In a more complex publication multiple grids allow the reader to distinguish between the various sections. Whether the publication is single column or a mix of multiple columns, they all have one common aim, and that is to avoid static balance in relation to the page edges.

Pages of a publication are normally viewed as pairs, if you consider that the grid is the framework in which the elements of your design are located, then the back margin (the folding middle of a publication) should be closest to the inside fold. This is because space in the middle increases when the pages are viewed together. Also, any element placed on the page at the

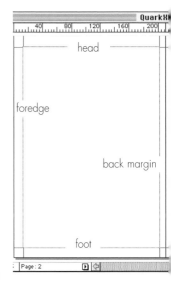

Parts of the left hand (verso) page.

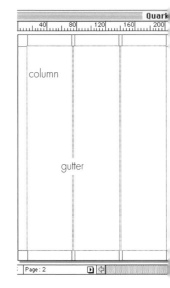

Page grid structure (Format).

The optical centre of the page is higher than the mathematical. Choose Preview from the View menu to judge by eye.

A descending order of asymmetrical elements beginning with the grid and ending with the body text is desirable.

Mathematical centre and the different size of serifs.

mathematical centre, optically appears to be below the centre, being pulled downwards. If the element is adjusted by the eye to appear central (optical centre), mathematically the element will be above the central position. This is why the judgement of your eye should be relied upon and not the mathematical decisions of a computer. This also applies to the smallest elements of any page design, the crossbars (horizontal strokes) of uppercase (E) and lowercase (e) characters (letters) are always above the mathematical centre. If you look closely at the serif characters (bottom left) static balance has been avoided. The serifs on opposite sides of a letter are often not exact mirror images. Your mind demands variation in what the eye perceives to remain alert. Most publications use a serif typeface for the main body text (words that make-up the main story – this is body text) for this reason. Applying these fundamentals to the grid will help to keep your reader stimulated.

The largest margin should always be at the foot (bottom) of the page, and the smallest margin should normally always be the back margin (between pages). Visually both back margins should be equal to the foredge margin (outside). Publications where the foot is not the widest margin tend to give a visual appearance of the text falling off the page. The head margin (top) should be proportionately bigger than the back margin followed by the foredge margin. This gives you a sequence to follow which will avoid static balance and stimulate the readers eye when your elements are imported into the page. Simply put:

At 3 o' clock is the smallest margin and then growing larger in an anti-clockwise direction; 12 o' clock, 9 o' clock and finally at 6 o' clock is the largest margin.

The formula above describes the left hand (verso) page. The right hand (recto) page starts again from the centre and is followed around clockwise. These rules are an indication of page edge to text relationship for a single text column. At this point it is worth mentioning the classic proportions described by Jan Tschichold for the margins as 2:3:4:6 and the page width and height proportion as 2:3. It avoids static balance, and interrupts eye movement to stimulate the reader. This stimulation is what you need to achieve. The QuarkXPress margin guides default to a uniform border for all margins. Today most designs have many demands and differing purposes, and cannot afford the luxury of classical proportions. The illustration below demonstrates Tschicold's formula extended closer to the page edges.

It is however, important to give this kind of consideration to the main working area of the page, but it is also important to consider the internal structure of the grid in relation to the elements of your design. A well considered grid will assist in the placing of your text and images. Your page format needs only millimetres difference to avoid static balance.

Columns within the Grid

The next important addition to the grid are the columns contained within. Obviously this depends on the type of publication and the final page size. Single column grids work well on smaller page sizes, 186 x 123 mm (Metric Crown 8vo) which can normally be found in use for fiction publications or 198 x 129 mm (Metric Large Crown 8vo) which tends also to be used for fiction and other types of trade paperbacks. On larger page formats the single column becomes very difficult to read. If the line of text is overly long your reader will have difficulty moving from line-to-line (more on this later).

More than one Column within the Grid

A well considered grid will allow you to place the elements of the design effectively. Therefore, the elements within the design which are the most dependent on the grid and column structure is the type, and normally the least dependent are the images used in support of your text. In most cases you should design the column width for use with the text. One of the most useful formats is the three column grid. This structure provides an orderly arrangement of elements, while maintaining their flexibility. It does however, create a strong flow line (top grid line) of elements, which alters page balance.

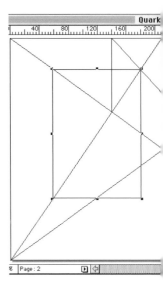

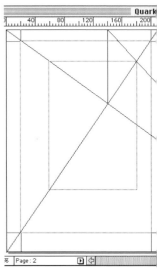

Top. Jan Tschichold's (1953) classical proportions are overgenerous. It does demonstrate the relationship between text and page edges. *Below.* A more acceptable format.

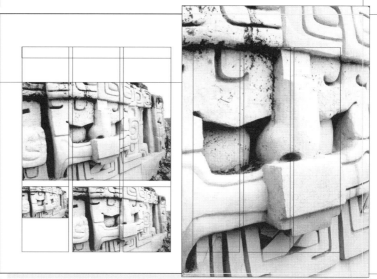

Top right. When using images the three column grid allows for greater flexibility and dramatic use of scale. Large images can be balanced against small images. This will give you the freedom to enliven the page and retain new interest for your reader each time they turn the page. *Top left.* Two columns have less combinations of image use.

At 3 o' clock the two smallest inside margins face each other, viewed together they should appear visually equal with the outside margin opposite at 9 o' clock, the margin at the bottom should be the next biggest margin at 6 o' clock and have sufficient space so that the type does not appear to fall off the page, the margin at the top then becomes the biggest at 12 o' clock.

Magazines tend to have multiple columns normally of equal width, and foredge margins become narrower. Both back margins still equal the foredge margin, and white space gravitates upwards towards the head of the page. The sequence and proportion of the spacing of the grid change. The head has more space than the foot. The relationship between the head and foot are dictated by the elements of the design, such as the visual greyness of the body type, position of the page furniture outside the grid and so on. The advantage over the two column structure is that images that fit within and adhere to the grid structure have more combinations of use (illustrations above).

Both serif type and grid should have an asymmetrical quality, and accordingly columns don't necessarily have to be identical measurements. The measure of any column can be unequal. The three column can be two larger columns and one smaller

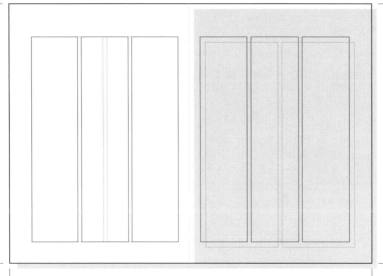

Magazine design tends to require a higher level of sophistication, the designer can achieve this by developing a complex grid system:

1) By creating an unequal column measure.
2) By reflecting these unequal measures from the right hand page (recto) to the left hand page (verso).
3) By using more than one grid.
4) By allowing elements to begin on one grid and finish on another.

column. Increasing the size of one column against another which gives the columns of type an imbalanced axis which causes visual disruption is desirable. These complex relationships allow for even greater flexibility, you can place an element that begins within one structure and finishes within another (*bottom right illustration*).

Once you have established a grid for your publication, don't feel bound by its constraints, as text tends to conform to the grid, especially the body text. Images tend to anchor to the grid and then break through the grid. Large images at the bottom make the text at the top of the page visually fall forward unless they have been balanced with other images across your spread (double page layout). Pages tend to balance well with contrast, large images and small images, this again confirms a hierarchical order of how the page is read. Be dramatic with images, decide which one is important and in what order, give your spread a focal point. This adds visual interest to your page yet still links it to the format.

The format should also allow ease of transition from one section to another, ensuring that your reader does not get lost. By being consistent with key elements you have taught your reader your rules of navigation.

Elements beginning in the two column and finishing in the third column.

More than One Grid on the Same Page

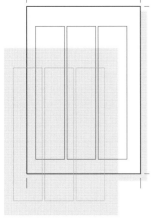

Complex designs not only overlay one grid architecture over another, but can rotate the grid and reposition it within the same margins, or mirror the grid from left to right, especially if the column structure is asymmetrical. Different kinds of grid structures also help the reader to identify different parts of the publication. Closer investigation of many high-street magazines are clear examples. Grids are non-printing guidelines to help you position elements. Once they have been removed by choosing View – Preview during work in progress or when printed, the publication takes on a visual coherence.

When you have identified more than one you can:

1) Identify where sections of a magazine begin, and therefore understand why the structure has changed.
2) Join and overlay the tracing paper sheets when you suspect more than one grid on a page.
3) Reflect/rotate the tracing paper from one page to the next.

To understand these grids, take some tracing paper (*top left illustration*) and position this upon a magazine page that has a clear structure. Ignore images, headings and so on, look for the strong visual lines created by the body type. Draw all the outer grid margins of the page, and the columns within from the top of the grid to the bottom. Place the grid template on other pages, this will determine if there is a new architecture. If a new structure is encountered rotate and mirror your template to see if it has been used in a different way. If not add this to your collection and start afresh. This very simple exercise will help to explain how the structure of the design has been used and how they change between sections.

Once you know that this is what you are trying to achieve, you can then challenge the traditional use of grids. If you analyse the structure of the magazine *Raygun* you cannot fail to notice that the publication appears to break every known rule. It contradicts these rules with a consistency of opposites. The designer knows the rules and has decided to develop a set unique to *Raygun* as part of the magazine's graphic personality. Each page is designed to illustrate the content, and pages become art within their own right.

You also need to consider the elements which exist outside of the grid. Technically the furniture is part of the margin, these elements also establish a relationship with the grid and should be thought about at the same time.

Other Parts of the Page Outside the Grid

Both running heads (as Chapter 4, *left*, and Chapter title *above right*) and folios (page numbers) aid navigation, both should be unobtrusive, yet easily identifiable for what they are. Other text (furniture) can establish the name of the publication, date, volume number, extent of the pages in the article and so on, this kind of additional information is useful in academic publishing, other publications might have different requirements. Together with other page furniture, neither the running head or the folio should interfere with the reading of the main text, or be large enough to be confused with headings or sub-headings. Space should be used in proportion to size, position and size depend on the publication. It is not necessary to use furniture on all pages, for instance, books do not require furniture on prelims (title page and so on) or at the beginning of chapters. New chapters do however require folios for page reference.

How will the Pages be Viewed?

Viewing elements in print and on-screen is different, what you see is not necessarily what you get. Screen resolutions are lower than print resolutions, type can appear too small to read at actual size on-screen. A comfortable viewing size is 12 pt (point, explained opposite), yet when output (printed) the same type will appear too large. Using type management which has been set to preserve best character shape will make the font appear smoother by anti-aliasing the pixels (adding grey or intermediate coloured pixels around the letter edge) but does not resolve on-screen legibility of size.

When designing the grid the computer screen can also give a false impression of the proportions of the page. Computer screens are flat, printed pages are not. Perfect bound publications will require more back margin space than their saddle stitched (stapled) counterpart. Perfect bound publications require more space, and making a dummy (mock-up) will help to decide the width of margins. Manipulating the grid structure through a computer does give you the flexibility to make adjustments before you place any elements.

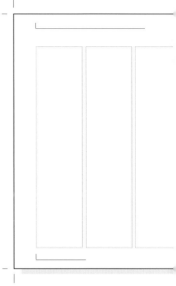

Running heads or folios should not interfere with the reading of the body text. All positions should isolate these elements from the grid.

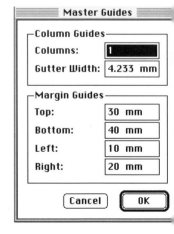

Page Proportions.

How Long is a Line of Type within the Column?

The next two pages describe measurement. The logic of printing measurement can seem confusing. It is however, the language of the industry and one of the main reasons why QuarkXPress has been widely adopted by design and print.

For PostScript 72 pt is the default value. The traditional non-digital value is slightly larger.

Before designing the page structure there are many combinations of measurement that you can set within the QuarkXPress Preferences dialog box. Most of the options that are available are based on the printers' measurement system, inches or metrification. QuarkXPress also allows you to set the measure in Agates which is generally used for measuring vertical column depth in classified advertising. In the United Kingdom, North America and elsewhere, the points system (Pierre Fournier) is used. Other parts of the world that do not use this system such as have adopted the French Didot (François Didot) as their standard. QuarkXPress therefore allows you to calibrate the measurement dialog for all these systems. Neither system is compatible with each other. The Didot point is slightly larger than the English/North American point:

> 12 points make a pica
> 12 didot points make a cicero
> 12 didot = 12.9 pica

England has adopted a metric unit of measure which is being enforced by EU regulations. Therefore paper now tends to be measured metrically, whereas America has retained inches for paper sizes. Even after metrification the printing and publishing industry still retains imperial sizes which they have to convert to metric. Inches do not readily convert, 32 x 42 inches become 812.8 x 1066.6 mm. When pages are imposed (planned into a printing order for the same sheet), sheet sizes that represent the inch measurements have been kept.

Measuring systems that have been based on the inch have traditionally used the point system because it corresponds closely to the imperial measurement. As a guide 72 pts corresponds to one inch and is the PostScript and QuarkXPress default value (the exact traditional measure is considered as 1 inch to 72.272 pts). However, this measure can be set at any value between 72 pts and 73 pts in .01 pt increments. The reduced size extends the column width and increases the line space, whereas the increased size tightens both. QuarkXPress recalibrates point-to-inch measurement values. Any measurement which has been assigned a constant value before the adjustment will remain physically unaltered, but with a new recalibrated typographic value based on the PostScript default. This is also true of the continental Didot system where the ciceros-to-centimetres conversion can also be set at any value between 2 to 3 in .001 increments.

The computer allows you to mix the measuring systems, yet it would be desirable to standardise between paper size, typeface, column measure and vertical depth. Whatever system is preferable to you will be interpreted by the computer. However, the result of changing measurement systems after beginning the layout of your design can give some rather garbled measurements.

QuarkXPress allows you to set the Document Preferences for the vertical and horizontal measure separately, this will allow you to measure the column width in 'pica-ems', and the vertical depth in millimetres, if you so desire. There are 12 pts to the pica-em, which is a fixed measurement regardless of type size, and there are approximately 6 pica-ems to the inch.

Changing the Document Preferences of the horizontal measure from millimetres to picas will allow precise control. For example, indentation of paragraphs are normally based on the pica-em space of 12 pts. If you have set up the measurements as millimetres, to indent the paragraph 1 pica-em the metric measure in the Format dialog box is 4.233 mm.

To understand how the computer is calibrating between the different measurement systems, set the Document Preferences points/inch to the default value of 72 pts. The Format dialog box would read 1p2.173 for a 5 mm indentation, just over 14 pts. The 'p' equals the amount of pica-em spaces, numbers after 'p' equal points, until 12 pt has been reached which then becomes one additional pica-em. North American and United Kingdom typefaces continue to be measured in points and are normally referred to in point size increments. The length of the line has been traditionally measured in pica-ems.

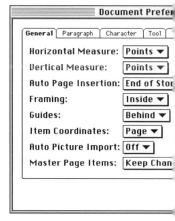

General Document Preferences.

The QuarkXPress gutter width default value is 4.233 mm, which is 1 pica-em.

For further reading on the use of typographic rules:

University of Chicago Press 1993 *The Chicago Manual of Style*, 14th Edition, UCP

Length of the Line

Deciding how many columns within the grid structure has a direct relationship between the size of the type and how many words can be used within a column. This is one aspect of the design process that has remained constant between digital design and human perception. Therefore, how many words you use in a line will influence the readability of the publication. QuarkXPress measures the 'em' space on the horizontal area taken up by two zeros '00', and half of this space, an 'en' space by one zero '0' of the type size being used. Printers have always considered the ratio between typeface size and width of column to retain legibility. An example of size and length would be:

48 zeros and 24 zeros of the size of type being used.

OOOOOOOOOOOOOOOOOOOOOOOOOOOOOOOOOOOOOOOOOOOOOOOOOO
OOOOOOOOOOOOOOOOOOOOOOOO   readability tolerance

abcdefghijklmnopqrstuvwxyzabcdefghijklmnopqrstuvwxyzabcdefghijklm
abcdefghijklmnopqrstuvwxyzabcdefghijklm

12 pt type size, and the column width should be no greater than 24 em spaces, or 48 zeros of the type size being used. 12 pt type size, and the column width should be no less than 12 em spaces, or 24 zeros of the type size being used.

Another general formula for line length would be 1.5 to 2.5 alphabets, this also takes into account the 'unit of set' size for the typeface.

A column width should be no greater than 1 pt of type size to 2 em spaces of column width, and no less than 1 pt of type size to 1 em space of column width, approximately ten to twelve words. This amount of words makes a good line measurement for single column text, however, when more columns are used together on the page this measure should be slightly reduced to eight to ten words per column, as both measures are within your guidelines ratio. Too long a column measure and the eye can find it difficult to return to the next line, too short and the eye becomes fatigued through spending time going from line-to-line. The third factor which can increase the line length is the spacing between the lines.

The Depth of the Line

The typographic elements on the page can be perceived as contrasting through colour. Columns of text are considered for their greyness and headings for their blackness, unused space is white space. Depending on the choice of typeface, and its appearing size, readability can be affected by the leading (space between the lines of text). Originally leading was inserted between the lines to increase the space. The characteristics of the typeface determined the size and variation of the body on which the characters sat. This gave the font an appearing size but not a true size. The space between lines of type could therefore vary between typefaces. Computers measure the depth of the type from baseline-to-baseline (the words of this line sit on the baseline), and do not take into account the proximity of ascenders (dlkb) or descenders (pqjg) between the lines unless optically equalised leading (auto leading) has been selected. QuarkXPress then bases the equalisation of the line space on the amount of tall and deep characters on each line. Unlike the physical inclusion of lead spacing computer software can equalise in fractions of a point measurement between the lines.

Type size, leading and the length of a line of type are inseparable. All three are highly controllable, like leading, the type size and column measure are capable of fractional point adjustments. Alter one of these three, and the possibility that the others have to be changed needs to be considered. A long line of type will need more leading so that the reader can return their eye across the page to read the next line. The leading for body type with between ten to twelve words in a line should approximately be 120% of the type size. Therefore, if the body size is 10 pt, then there should be an additional 2 pt of leading or, 10 pt body with 12 pt from baseline to the baseline of the next line of type. This ratio works well with body text, however percentage spacing will look too plentiful when applied to display sizes. The auto leading characteristics can be set by percentage or by increments of .001 pt. The typographic attributes of the type family being used should also be considered.

The space between the lines effec the overall greyness of the text it also increases or decreases the re ability according to how much s has been used. A long line of typ will need more leading so that th reader can return their eye acros the page to read the next line of

The space between the lines effec the overall greyness of the text it also increases or decreases the re ability according to how much s has been used. A long line of typ will need more leading so that th reader can return their eye acros the page to read the next line of t

Correct line spacing aids the readability of the text.

The QuarkXPress default value is 20%, this is an averaged value for body text. You should reduce this amount of space for display sizes.

The Appearing Size of the Line

Typography is an optical art and not an exact science, the relationship between font size, column width and baseline to baseline measurement can appear visually correct for some typefaces and awkward for others when a constant leading value has been assigned. It is the x height that optically determines the interlinear spacing, the greater the x height the greater the space. Although typefaces optically sit on the same baseline, the x height, ascenders and descenders can have different weights and sizes, The appearing size also impacts upon legibility, the readers eye will tire if the body size for a large amount of text appears smaller than 9 pt or larger than 14 pt. Photina has a tall x height whereas Bembo has a smaller x height making one appear larger than the other when they are both at the same point size. The only way of knowing the true size of a typeface is by using the foundry specimen sheets for different sizes, or outputting your own for comparison.

The component parts of type which make up the personality of a typeface can be diverse between typefaces of the same point size. A book published in one typeface could have a different amount of pages for the same book published in another typeface. Characters vary in width for the same type size. For example two typefaces, 11 pt Bembo regular has 51 characters and 11 pt Photina regular has 49 characters across a column measure of 20 picas, both are serif typefaces. The computer needs to know 'set-widths' (letter widths) and also their 'side-bearings' (space each side of the letter), this determines how letters 'fit' with each other. The computer does not measure the line of type in point sizes but divides the characters up into 'set' postscript fractions. By measuring the line in 'units of set' the computer can then calculate when the line is full and what adjustments need to be made for justification, hyphenation and so on. This allows the font to form other relationships with characters and spaces in the formation of words which have been predetermined by the foundry. If the column measurement is short avoid a typeface with a wide unit of set (wide letters).

Photina 12 pt
Bembo 12 pt
Photina 11 pt

The top two fonts are set in 12 pt. This is their 'appearing size'. The font below is set in 11 pt. 12 pt Bembo appears roughly the same size as 11 pt Photina. It would therefore, not be unusual to see Photina used with a smaller body size than Bembo for body text.

e set units of character width
set units of character width

The first line is set in Bembo regular, the second line is set in Photina regular. Each font has been set in 11 pt, each has a different character-set width.

Reading from Line-to-Line

Line space needs to be balanced with other visual considerations. For instance, justified type tends to create visual rivers running through the column if the number of letters and spaces in a line are less than 51 characters. If the line length is greater, then space between the lines need to be considered. The eye will take the easiest return route to read the next line by following the line of white interlinear spacing. When the line has less than 51 characters 'visual rivers' of white space flow erratically downwards through the column. Eye blinking tends to occur after reading an average line of text, these rivers encourage the eye to wander down the channel when the eye is refocusing during a line return. Ideally the line length should be ten to twelve words so that the blink occurs at the line ending for the average fluency of a reader, and the word space should be no less than the space occupied by an 'i' and no greater than 'm' of the font being used.

Digital type has no physical body for separation between the lines. Proper leading ensures that the tops and bottoms of characters do not touch. Too much space between the lines has the same effect, the lines become difficult to relate to each other. If you have a large volume of text and wish to alter the length of a publication, rather than increase the size of the type you could change the typeface, format of the grid or leading. These simple calculations should be considered at the beginning of the design process. Even after a satisfactory conclusion has been reached, no solution is perfect, and attention should be paid to the details. It is the optical balance between typeface, measure and space, and many other details that distinguishes the designed page from the desktop published page.

Counting 51 characters includes word spaces and assumes an average of 5 characters per word.

Ideally the line length should be ten to twelve words so that the blink occurs at the line ending for the average fluency of a reader, and the word space should be no less than the space occupied by an 'i' and no greater than 'm' of the font being used.

If white space is stronger on the vertical axis rather than the horizontal line of the leading, your eye will be forced down through the column.

Using Elements (Items) within a Document

At the simplest level this can be described as:

1) The relationship of items to each other in the formation of one element.
2) Elements and their relationship to each other.
3) Establishing a consistent use for these elements.
4) Using contrasting elements to direct the reader.

There are four basic elements of design – headings, body text, images and white space. Each element can contain many items within with the exception of white space. QuarkXPress allows you to modify individual items within an element, or treat a group of items as one element. Colour is important, but is not a basic element, any good design should also work well as black, grey and white. What is important to you for either print or multimedia is the ability to make the elements of your design merge or standout. This organisation of elements helps to communicate your message more effectively. The organisation of what is reproduced on a page takes place in your mind through the eye, and is referred to as Gestalt (German School of Psychology). Your perception of the world is always trying to form relationships, by understanding these relationships you can stimulate the reader, and visually control your message.

The Relationship of Items in One Element

Your mind attempts to form patterns with the ten square items.

The basic building block of your design is the single item within an element. If you consider the number ten in a pack of playing cards as a series of ten individual square items, you very quickly perceive a pattern, these ten items can appear as two groups of five, or two lines of four and so on, your mind is trying to form relationships. If you then scatter the ten items you randomise their relationships, the pattern becomes disjointed, the items lack any form. Items that are close and organised merge to form one element or two and so on. There are no distinguishing features between the squares, they are merely items. If you understand this very basic rule of Gestalt, you can begin to organise the page. The simplest example on a page would be the characters that form a word or a symbol which brings together other items to construct one overall element. The logic of the process can then be followed through to organise elements in relation to each other. When seen together with other elements you will need to re-evaluate items and their elements, such as size, position and so on.

Elements and their Relationship to Each Other

You know that your mind organises shapes into patterns, it also stabilises form and creates imaginary lines between elements by linking the line of least visual resistance. These visual connections are strongest on the horizontal and vertical axis. Your mind perceives a common line even though one does not physically exist, and therefore establishes a relationship. In the example of the number three playing card there is a strong axial line which exists down the centre. At this point there are no distinguishing features between the elements, they are simply aligned.

The simplest example of page components would be words that form a line of type or paragraph. This will also be true of multiple columns of text hanging from a strong horizontal top margin. These elements have greater values of meaning because they are now working together in sequence. These elements harmonise with each other, but lack direction, other relationships need to be established. You now need to prioritise these elements into a reading order for both text and image.

Establishing a Consistent Use for these Elements

Your design needs to establish a regular rhythm, the treatment of all the elements within your design needs to work within a set of rules to determine order. Your reader needs to be able to identify different types of information set within a hierarchy. Decisions need to be taken concerning all the elements on the page, such as the typeface for the body text, headings, sub-headings, captions and so on. This is also true of any illustrative material included within the design. In short, the establishment of a typographic Style Sheet is needed (set of rules) which is

Your mind tries to form relationships, but there is no pattern to follow.

Three elements aligned on a vertical and horizontal axis.

Your eye is drawn to the bottom element.

Establishing a reading order through the use of contrast:

1) Centre right page.
2) Top left page.
3) Bottom left page.

Elements can be pictures or text in the reading order.

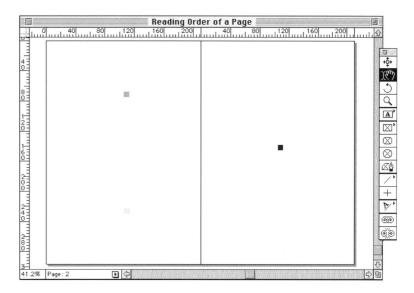

Your eye is drawn to the darker element first.

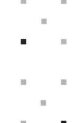

Your attention is halved.

appropriate to the design, including a policy on the use of images. If you were totally consistent in your treatment of text and images the design would lack interest, you need to alter the rhythm and retain a positive reading order.

Using Contrasting Elements to Direct your Reader

If we continue to use the playing card analogy, you can now alter the size of one element and rank the reading order. The three elements at the same size have no definite starting point, the elements are merely visually aligned. If you increase the size of the element at the bottom, your eye will prioritise that element, you are drawn by size. If you intensify the hue of one element amongst the ten you are drawn by colour. If you alter a second square element to the same hue your attention is halved and so on. At the initial stages of your design, thumbnail sketches can very quickly establish this positive order.

Magazine designers regularly use these techniques. You are subconsciously directed around the page through their understanding of these principles. Open any high-street magazine at an article, and note where your eye first falls. The established order for reading is normally accepted as top left, along, back and down one line to the next. By knowing this

141

you can alter the reading order of the page, by altering the emphasis and position of the components. You can now direct your reader to view a picture on the right hand page first, and then to the top of the left page to read the heading of the article, and then allow their eye to begin reading the article directed by some other element used at the beginning of the main body of text. It is also an aid for the reader to very quickly decide if they wish to continue to read the article, drawing them gradually into the subject, layer by layer.

Basic Elements —	**Page Colour** —	**Combinations of the 4 Elements**
Headings	Page definition	**Conflict**
Body Text	such as blackness	No visual definition between the elements
Images	or level of	**Harmony**
White Space	greyness	Little definition with a close use of elements
		Contrast
		High definition with a positive difference
		between the elements

The simple example of the playing cards can be applied to the diagram above. The four basic elements of design can be altered through how you use them as page colour to make your page conflict, contrast or become harmonious. The blackness or greyness of the page can be determined through your choice of elements and how they are used. Contrast will give your elements a positive reading order. Major elements become primary information (everything you need to know about the story before you begin), and secondary information – the story itself.

Positive primary information such as sub-headings, headings, images and so on leave you in no doubt where your eye should go. The four basic elements can also make the page conflicting or harmonious. Conflict should be avoided, however, certain publications demand a dignity that only an harmonious arrangement can provide. Legal documents should refrain from competing for your attention and a harmonious arrangement with a tight use of elements is preferable, such as the same type family throughout with a change of size and weight.

Contrast and harmony can also work together on a page. Contrast can give you a positive reading order, and harmony can allow your reader to settle upon information of equal importance.

Close together the squares form a cross. When the space has been equalised visual oscillation (balance) occurs. The shape of the space has now changed and this can alter the relationship of the elements to each other.

The colour of the page refers to the appearing blackness, greyness and whiteness of the page elements. Page colour helps to establish reading order of the page. To see the colour of a page clearly, view through your eyelashes.

The space that is not used creates shapes (white space), and should also be considered as an element of design. When four squares are placed close together a fifth white shape is created between positive and negative space. Visual oscillation occurs when both positive and negative space are balanced. Your reader is not directed or detracted from the elements. Add more space and the squares become four individual items. Space now serves to break up the relationships. These relationships apply equally to small items such as words and their letters, and also larger elements. Columns of text, headings, and the position of the images all form these relationships with each other, and amongst themselves.

Each area of design uses the relationship and organisation of elements to best suit the intended communication. Magazines allow the reader to select very quickly subjects of interest. Novels use continuous text with old style origins that are legible, allowing the reader's eye to flow from line-to-line. Directories use typographic weight difference to distinguish between the elements. All have used a relationship to achieve their primary purpose of communication. Now that you understand the basics of the psychology of how elements are used within a design, you can now consider how they inform, rather than simply being placed on a page.

Colour of the Page

Any good design should work well as black, white and grey. The colour of the page refers to the whiteness, lightness and darkness of the page elements. Body text is considered for its differing levels of greyness. Headings, sub-headings and so on are considered for their blackness, and white space provides contrast between the two. The greyness of body text depends on the family, size, weight, line length, leading, justification or non-justification. By viewing the page as different densities of whiteness, greyness and blackness you can control the rhythm of the page, create contrast between the elements, emphasis the importance of certain elements – in general direct the reader around the page.

White Space

Space can be considered at different levels, there is space between letters, words and lines. These blocks of grey text interplay with other elements of the design, space then becomes an issue between headings, sub-headings, images and so on. These relationships are not finally resolved until all the elements have been brought together. Space within a grouping of elements such as the beginning of new sections can allow the reader to rest or pause, look elsewhere and return without loss of place.

The reader should be able to identify which elements belong together. Too much white space within a group of elements appears trapped, this creates visual holes in the design, and can disturb the reading order of the page and break up the story. This is especially disturbing when the white space surrounding the elements is less than the space between the elements. More white space added to the outside of the grouping (*far right*) brings the elements together and can help your reader to focus attention. The squares on the previous page relate to each other, even after separation. When the page edges are added (*right*) these elements then form a relationship with the edges and become unrelated.

Headings and Sub-Headings

Sub-headings also break the flow of the columns, create white space, and like paragraph endings can be a resting point for the reader's eye. Depending on the nature and extent of the text there will probably be more than one hierarchical level of sub-heading importance. All categories of sub-head need to be considered in terms of how much differentiation is required. Sub-headings which overstate their importance can be distracting to the reader, normally 1 or 2 pts of larger type size with a stronger weight difference will be sufficient to draw the reader's attention without being understated. Typographically the sub-heading should be a member of the body text family or compatible with the heading. Depending on the publication, there should normally never be more than two contrasting type families within the design.

White space does not necessarily mean large blank areas of the page. Your use of white space determines how page elements relate to each other.

Unrelated elements, each square has a stronger relationship with the edge of the page rather than each other.

Related elements.

All uppercase letters can have some awkward fits, such as the letter space between LA.

The sub-head break causes a change of greyness creating contrast within the column. The reader can look away, and return with little effort. The space which surrounds the sub-head should have the least space between the proceeding text column to which it belongs. More space is desirable above, and will visually separate the sub-heading from the previous text. You can also run a sub-heading into the paragraph on the same line. It should be the same size as the body text, but distinguishable through a contrast of weight. Sub-headings also have the advantage of being potentially added, disposed, or edited, allowing the designer/editor another method of line control within the column.

A body text that reads well does so because of its blandness, these type families have normally been developed and digitised from 'old style' faces and have retained their elegance through the plainness of their form such as Garamond or Baskerville. Depending on the kind of publication, headings can reflect more of the personality of the subject. The heading should contrast with the body text size and draw the reader's immediate attention. As stated, the norm is to restrict typographic use to two contrasting families. You have full control over the direction of the reader – what matters is the blackness/greyness contrast between the elements on the page.

Headings and sub-headings should avoid all uppercase (capital letter) setting, unless you are able to make letter by letter decisions regarding the shape of certain 'character-fits' (how letters appear together). Upper and lowercase (this text) have a better fit. Their overall density throughout the word means that letter spaces will require less adjustment, rather than space that cannot be controlled. Any punctuation used on larger display type sizes (headings) look overly large and have traditionally been reduced by 1 pt. Baseline-to-baseline measurements can also be less than the body text for display type. This also adds to the blackness of the heading and increases contrast with the body text. There are many other combinations of weight and size difference that work well. Simply ensure that your reader's eye is directed on turning the page.

Text Alignment

Columns of text can either be justified, ranged left, ranged right, force justified or centred. Sliding type (arranged by your eye) is another option which needs line-by-line optical balancing. Ranged left text has a ragged right hand margin. Justified columns of text have a flush left and right margin. Range left and justified text are the most legible of formats, and are therefore probably the most common form of setting. Justified type suffers from irregular word spacing especially over a short measure. Hyphenation can in-part rectify this problem, for this reason H&Js (hyphenation and justification) are inseparable (see page 47-49).

Two consecutive hyphenated lines reduce legibility, three consecutive hyphenated lines can force the reader's eye to skip a line. As seen, QuarkXPress allows you to decide how many characters are contained within a word before it is broken, and how many characters before the break and after. Your choice of column measurement and alignment will determine the frequency of breaks.

Both ranged left and justified text are the only practical alignment solutions for a column of text. Ranged left text has even word spaces which gives a smoother greyness, and over a long column measure needs less hyphenation. The irregularity of the ragged margin also helps the column avoid static balance, appearing more dynamic than justified text. However, the ragged edge of the right hand margin should be visually averaged. Any deep indentation into the column as a result of long word length should be hyphenated. Unlike word processing software QuarkXPress uses an algorithm to hyphenate words. Again the computer is making the value judgments and some word breaks can be undesirable. QuarkXPress allows you to define hyphenation exceptions. However, sometimes it is best for you to make the decision with a discretionary hyphen break. QuarkXPress will also allow you to force the justification of a text line. This can solve problems within justified lines of type that require a manual hyphen ending. If, however, large word spaces do occur, then change the tracking (see page 148).

The text alignment you choose will decide how many words can be used on a line.

	Edit Hyphe
Name:	
Standard	

☒ Auto Hyphenation

Smallest Word:	6
Minimum Before:	3
Minimum After:	3

☐ Break Capitalised Words

Hyphens in a Row:	2
Hyphenation Zone:	0 mm

The Edit Hyphenation & Justification dialog box.

The line represents visual averaging throughout a ranged left column. Hyphens ensure that there are no deep indentations into the body text.

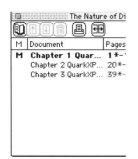

The Style Sheet from the top chapter has been assigned to all documents within the Make Book dialog box.

Range right, centred and sliding type are not a legible option for the main body of the text. They should be reserved for typographic difference on the page, allowing the reader's eye to rest, and relieving the visual monotony of continuous text. Centred or sliding type can add emphasis to a 'pulled quote' (small enlarged text which tells the flavour of the story).

On completion of the page format all these specifications should be added to the typographic Style Sheet, before the text and images of your design are imported into the QuarkXPress document. This will ensure that if work has already been undertaken in other documents which will be combined as one, then no reassignment of styles will occur. This is because in addition to creating new style palettes for the document, QuarkXPress will allow you to combine existing documents and assign one master Style Sheet for all when brought together as a book.

Paragraphs

Normally each new text will begin simply with no indentation.

The next paragraph will need some form of separation, such as a 1 pica em indent.

Certain reprographic departments will reserve QuarkXPress for high quality illustrated colour design, and use a system based on SGML (Standard Generalised Mark-up Language) for text only documents.

Even when the paragraphs have the desired endings, space and how the reader proceeds from paragraph-to-paragraph also need to be considered. New texts can begin by focusing the reader's attention to the starting point by using a graphic such as a symbol or a drop cap, raised cap (large initial letter) and so on, normally each new text will begin simply with no indentation (like this paragraph after a sub-heading).

After this initial start to the text each paragraph needs to be clearly identified. Most texts tend to have a 1 pica em indent, with little or no additional spacing between the paragraphs. Additional spacing that does not conform to the baseline-to-baseline measurement will probably require vertical justification of the lines to ensure that the page measure is equal. This has the problem of making the text appear visually non-aligned when text is set as several columns on a page. Additional space created by vertical justification and space between paragraphs that do not conform to the regular text spacing are less noticeable on single column pages. For large single column text only documents QuarkXPress is not the solution.

Widows and Orphans

The beginning and ends of paragraphs are an important detail. The typographic rules for your publication affects whether or not you increase the possibility of widows and orphans. A widow is a single word or a short line of text that falls at the end of a paragraph. An orphan is a single word or short line carried to the top of a column at the end of a paragraph. The most common way to eliminate widows and orphans is to edit the copy. However, sometimes this might be impractical.

Depending on your column structure it is possible to increase or decrease the tracking of the text. Over a certain depth of type the column will reflow, eliminating the problem. A value of 1 entered into the Tracking (overall letter space) dialog box adjusts the character spacing by 1:200 em. Clicking the tracking arrows in the Measurement palette adjusts space by 1:20 em. Adjustment need only be +/− 1 to achieve the desired effect. Tracking alters the overall character fit of the text and therefore alters the overall visual greyness of the column. For body text, any tracking after +/− 2 will make the overall greyness of the paragraph more noticeable.

A widow is all alone and goes on ahead, the orphan gets left behind.

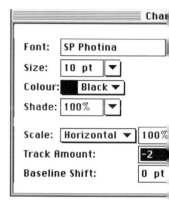

Tracking a paragraph can remove widows and orphans. It can also alter the overall greyness of the text.

Ligatures

Ligatures are linked letters either through their past association with earlier forms of script such as œ æ, or through visual considerations of how certain movable type 'character-sets' worked together, such as ffi ffl. Your eye reads the overall shape of the word, and by joining certain character-sets together the word shape suffers less disruption. Movable type created standards of character fit. Many special linked letters were cast as one with all the necessary visual alteration incorporated for that size of type. Digital type retains these special character sets, however digital type allows both pair kerned and tracked movement of characters, because of this justified lines tend not to require ligature substitution when the tracking is loose. Yet display sizes need a tighter fit and can create visually disturbing combinations if ligatures are not used.

An example of some ligature character sets.

Initial Paragraph Letters

Initial letters can fine tune the reading order of the page.

After the primary information has been absorbed, the reader's attention is then drawn to where the text begins by one drop cap.

If more than one initial paragraph letter is used with the same weight and size the reader's attention will be divided.

Individual letters have different shapes. Use Preview to decide if the position of a hanging drop caps is visually aligned.

Initial letters should be used sparingly, more than one on the same page reduces their impact, causing the readers eye to be pulled in different directions. Initial letters such as drop-caps, raised caps and hanging dropcaps on every paragraph disrupt the reading of continuous text. For dropcaps QuarkXPress allows you to specify between two and sixteen lines of type depth for the initial letter. Line depth becomes disproportionate to the line length when five lines have been exceeded and lacking in impact at two lines deep. The leading value for the lines opposite the initial letter should also have fixed values to avoid vertical justification. Again optical consid-erations affect the positioning of the letter, visual balancing might be required to adjust the appearing cap height against the top of the ascenders (the points measurement of the Measurement palette changes to percentage when the dropcap has been selected).

Raised initial caps should be at least twice the size of the body text and should sit on the baseline: using raised initials within the main body of text causes spatial problems between the paragraphs. Again, like dropcaps, they should ideally be used at the beginnings of sections to direct the reader's eye to the starting point. Outdented hanging drop caps need other spatial considerations (letters in the margin). Like dropcaps the top of the letter should visually align with the ascender line. With hanging dropcaps letter shape is important, and should appear flush right to the left hand margin. Letters with a pronounced slant, such as 'W', visually drift away from the paragraph and should be used tighter to it.

If several initial letters are used on the same page with the same size and weight, the reader's attention will be divided by these competing elements. However, this might be desirable if the information is of equal importance. Instead of using initial letters you can harmonise the page through the use of graphic elements. These can aid the reader by indicating the content of the information.

Colour

Colour effects us in different ways, your everyday association of how colour has been used determines meaning. These cultural factors influence the choice of colour, and therefore your perception of mood and meaning. For example in Belize, Central America, certain colours have stronger associations with political parties because of the general standards of literacy (election ballet papers contain colours to aid choice). Green is acceptable as a warning on hurricane posters, red is not.

Culture influences choice and can sometimes appear irrational to those who have different values. There is however, certain objective factors which should be considered. For example, colour can create page harmony or tension depending on intensity or proximity. Complimentary colours used together make each other appear more intensive. They resonate with each other.

Colour therefore affects the overall contrast of the page, and what works well as different levels of greyness can be dramatically altered through the use of colour. Elements which balance at a grey/black level can become overpowering or understated when colour has been applied. When applying colour to any design the alteration of contrast, the creation of conflict and reading order needs careful consideration. Page elements in the higher reading order such as headings, sub-headings, and so on, are your only real choice for colour applied to type, and will probably need adjusting in size and weight, in relation to the tonal value of the colour.

Body text was developed for purposes of reading, and should be considered for its greyness against white paper, as colour reduces the legibility of body text when applied over a large volume of copy. If colour is to be applied to body text it should be used economically to draw the reader's attention, much in the same way as you would use other graphic elements or an initial letter at the beginning of a text. Like initial letters, if colour is to be used to direct the reader it should also be used sparingly. Used once will get the reader's attention, heighten impact, retain contrast and reduce conflict.

Colour is mainly subjective depending on culture. However, certain factors can be objective regardless of culture.

For further reading see:

Itten, J. 1973 *The art of color: the subjective experience and objective rationale of color*, 2nd Edition, Van Nostrand Reinhold

The tonal value of colour applied to elements can alter page contrast. The elements' size will need to be adjusted to a tonal value to avoid becoming overpowering or understated.

Colour on the Screen and in Print

For further reading see:

Green, P. 1995
Understanding digital colour, Graphic Arts Technical Foundation

Colour can be applied to different materials, such as buildings, vehicles, computer multimedia and so on. When a design scheme is applied to a building, interior and exterior lighting conditions will be different. Coloured material is adjusted according to the light reflected from its surface, which helps your mind and eye to equalise colour for different lighting conditions and surfaces (metamerism). If the exterior and interior material were placed together under the same lighting conditions they would appear to be different. Paper and computer screens both deliver colour to your mind and eye, and, as with other materials, they both need equalising. This is achieved by colour matching and colour calibration through colour management. To understand this you need to know how the computer creates colour and how paper reflects colour.

True colours stored as RGB with 24 bits per pixel have 8 bits allocated to each channel. This gives 256 shades each, and therefore, 16.7 million shades combined. CMYK uses a fourth black channel creating an additional 8 bits, or 32 bits per pixel.

Addition
- The computer screen mixes the primary additives RGB (red, green and blue) light. These three channels mixed together create white light.

Subtraction
- Two additive primaries combined create a third subtractive colour. If all three channels were mixed together they would produce black.

In full colour continuous tone printing three subtractive colours, Cyan, Magenta and Yellow are mixed in various dot combinations to give the illusion of many continuous tone colours. However, unlike mixing light, printing such densities of ink to obtain black would be detrimental to some parts of the image, and so a fourth black channel is added to make a four colour printing process (CMYK). This process has a limited colour range (gamet). QuarkXPress has expanded the gamut by adding the Pantone Hexachrome six colour process model. This goes beyond the four colour process with the addition of vivid orange and green. Occasionally an additional special (spot) colour has to be included during the printing because of certain reproduction limitations.

When designing on-screen the computer is giving an interpretation of what the colour should be when printed on paper. Like any scheme which requires a mix of media, computer-generated solutions need a colour management system that ensures that the white point, and gamma response of the screen display, is adjusted to a colour reference standard for paper. Any calibration of screen colours should reflect this difference.

CMYK – Depends upon regular half-tone dots to give an illusion of multiple colours. The dots achieve this illusion by being used in different size combinations. The dots for each colour process are then set at optimised screen angles away from each other. This is because if each screen did not contain sufficient angles from each other when dots are printed they will create a moirÉ (unwanted interference pattern). Therefore, it is better if each colour has either no relationship or an irrational relationship.

Hexachrome – Creates more screen angles. With a conventional dot structure there would be a definite pattern to the image. Therefore the solution is to use a randomised microdot structure. For example, because there are no screen angles, randomisation eliminates cross-hatching in skin tones and neutral colours which contain the largest concentration of subtle colour blends, there is less detail loss and no moirÉ. A six colour process is ideally suited to a digital press, because it is a dry process and has a tighter registration than an off-set litho press, and can reproduce the process more faithfully on subsequent reprints (see page 185).

Hue, Saturation and Brightness – There are further options available to you from the Colour dialog box, such as HSB. Colour calibration becomes crucial if you want to use this model. HSB allows you to mix colour in the same way an artist mixes colour on a palette. Hue allows you to select a colour pigment, saturation adjusts the amount of pigment, and brightness controls the amount of black mixed to the hue and saturation. Spot colour models have swatches, three colour models such as HSB don't.

| Process Inks: | ✓ CMYK |
| | Hexachrome |

Cyan, Magenta, Yellow and Black can be supplemented with vivid orange and green to increase the colour range. Hexachrome is therefore a six colour process ideal for digital colour printing.

Imported colours can appear to be different in QuarkXPress. This is because different programs use their own methods of building the screen preview. Ensure that both QuarkXPress and the imported file have the same specification colour match.

Spot Colours – Process colour printing mixes the dots while being printed, to create the illusion of different colours. Spot colours are mixed before the printing process and applied to the press as a special colour. The mix of different inks depends on a reference number generated by the computer or as specified by you for that colour. For this reason QuarkXPress does not allow you to edit process colour. It does allow you to 'mix' your own spot colour. The computer screen mixes light, a printer mixes ink. Spot colour paper guides show the colour as it will print. If there is doubt between the two a colour matching paper guide such as Pantone, TruMatch or FocalTone should be used in preference to screen values. A printer will mix the ink according to the paper guide reference and not your screen.

Black and registration should also be mentioned as they both appear in the Colour dialog palette. Black is normally the only colour that overprints, other colours are made from translucent ink. However, black overprinted across certain colour combinations can still allow these background colours to blend with the black. This is when you need to use an additional rich black. This black is mixed by you with the addition of 30% Cyan, 30% Magenta and 30% Yellow. The combinations and percentages can be different.

The Colour dialog palette with Rich Black added and the colour value of Registration altered.

Registration allows you to place your own crop marks (how the paper is cut-up after printing) into your document. You can decide to change the colour of Registration from black to any colour which identifies the mark as a crop instruction, and not as part of your design. Any colour that you allocate does not matter, the final output will always be black (see page 184).

Finally the printing surface itself can be different. On coated surfaces the ink sits on the surface, on uncoated surfaces ink is absorbed into the paper. The same ink appears a different shade of that colour according to the surface. The QuarkXPress colour models can emulate these differences for the same colour on-screen. To help you distinguish between the two surfaces a suffix is added to the colour's identifying number. Coated paper has the suffix *c* and uncoated paper the suffix *u*.

Images

Much of your design will normally need images to explain the points being made. Illustration has more power to convey complex ideas by being selective of what is included within the image, and can therefore be more manageable. Photographs can be more decisive, their reality can better describe the moment. How you initially plan the design will indicate the kind of images you require. However, many images especially photographs can be predetermined – the choice is how you interpret their use. Cropping parts of images (showing a selective part of the picture) and resizing can focus an image away from visual information within the picture that is irrelevant to the story's message. A well composed image implies the mood of the text and further illustrates the story in the mind of the reader. To do this an image needs to be imaginative, clear and focused on the main point.

> **Imaginative images** avoid the obvious stereotypical solution.
> **Clear images** are achieved by eliminating any visual clutter.
> **Focused images** give the eye a positive viewing order of the elements within the picture.

Images that contain all three points and illustrate the text might not be readily obvious, yet cropping and sizing images can help to direct the eye to the main purpose of the illustration, focus on the subject, and fill the frame. Images can and should work as a composition independent of the text. All elements on the page are considered for their relationship to each other, and how an image is composed should be no different. Like other elements on the page pictures should also avoid static balance. Therefore, focusing on the main point does not mean centred. This main focus can break the confines of any border, and create additional tension to the page.

The additional focal qualities of an image can enliven a picture that could otherwise be dull. It is, however, a mistake to think that by adding tension to the image the reader can better understand the story being illustrated. The image can only aid

Publications tend to work within certain guidelines according to the intended audience. Publishers will issue guidelines to photographers and illustrators alike. For example, publications that will be distributed in North America will require a different ethnic mix than Europe.

Clipping paths allow you to make normal images focused with a clear direction.

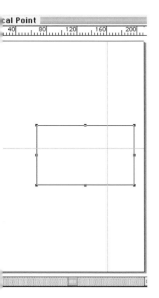

The focal point of any image does not mean the centre of the picture. Like other page elements, an asymmetrical quality is also desirable.

the reader if it is visually concise in its message content, and is aesthetically pleasing. Therefore, an image might not necessarily help if the picture you use is merely decorative, or when the text illustrates the story better than the picture. If this is the case then some other element to inform your reader, such as a pulled-quote might be better. If the image is to help the reader visualise the story it must also contain what is explicit within the text, by the text being implicit within the image. A good picture should tell the story.

An image within a complex page design does not necessarily stand alone. Any image mixed with type and white space requires other considerations. The content of the image should not distract the eye from settling away from its associated type matter. Conventionally squared up photographs should allow white space to flow around them, with balanced space against the gutters and between the columns. Parts of photographs can be removed from their background and integrated with the text. A clipping path (cut out) can dramatically lead your reader's eye. Again optical considerations are required, not only for the implication of the shape that the clipping path image makes, but also the balance between the text that runs around the image should not impede legibility, by creating visual rivers through the type.

The reading order of any double page spread does not necessarily need to begin with the heading, the inclusion of an image can be the focus of the page, and first in the viewing order. This order can be dramatically affected by placing a large image on the right hand page, especially if the other elements of the design are uncluttered. Visually heavy or large images are normally placed on this page for that reason. Publications that have complex architectures (grids) have more freedom of image use. If pages become predictable then the contrast of breaking the architecture through the use of a cut out, or bleeding off the page edges (5 mm of the image goes over the page edge, and will be trimmed off) enlivens the page and stimulates the reader. If the image fails to inspire because of the predictability of its content, then avoid its use, a bad image can destroy credibility.

The Digital Image

There are many kinds of imaging media, there are many ways to acquire an image, and there are many uses for images. Print demands a large amount of digital information if the required quality is to be attained. Images which are to be used only in conjunction with computer screens such as the Internet demand less information. Multimedia publishing opportunities allow files from the original source to be reused in different sizes and formats. The diagram below suggests possible routes depending on the source and intended use.

Digitised images create many possibilities for different publishing media. You should consider different outcomes during the planning stage.

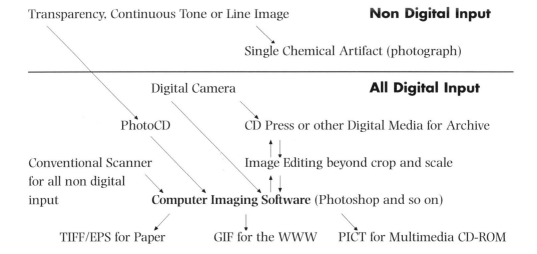

Transparency, Continuous Tone or Line Image **Non Digital Input**

Single Chemical Artifact (photograph)

Digital Camera **All Digital Input**

PhotoCD CD Press or other Digital Media for Archive

Image Editing beyond crop and scale

Conventional Scanner for all non digital input **Computer Imaging Software** (Photoshop and so on)

TIFF/EPS for Paper GIF for the WWW PICT for Multimedia CD-ROM

It is not only the appropriateness of an image that is important, there are also some technicalities which need to be considered. Images require a sound midtone range, they also require contrast with a good black and white at each end of the range. It is also important that the image is sharp because reproducing the document in print sends the completed file through many processes. Each non-digital stage reduces the quality of what is being reproduced, and images with tonal values can suffer the most. How an image has been digitised also affects the final quality of the publication. High quality print demands high quality LIVE image acquisition by a drum scanner that has a

Each final file format for your images will have a different colour gamut (colour range).

192 × 128

384 × 256

768 × 512

1536 × 1024

3072 × 2048

Five PhotoCD file sizes.

More details of using PhotoCD can be found at:

http://www.kodak.com/digitalimages/aboutPhotoCD/aboutPCD.shtml

If you manipulate your image try not to loose data. JPEG (Joint Photographic Experts Group) in its extreme is a lossy compression. LZW (Lempel-Ziv/Welch) is a data lossless compression algorithm (see page 177).

full computer CMS (Colour Management System). Drum scanners carry out a range of tasks which include colour separation, sharpening the image, under colour removal, grey component replacement and so on.

Dtp flatbed scanners import the digitised image directly into the computer, colour management is only as good as the colour management of the imaging software, which in turn is effected by the colour scanning depth of the flatbed scanner. Therefore, algorithms built into the software to digitally interpret colour and density range determine the final output. The problem with PhotoCD as a LIVE image is not in the acquisition of colour, but the limitations in the density range. This is most noticeable in the digitisation of transparencies which contain sensitive visual information in the darker areas. However, Kodak state that depending on the type of transparency film used, and if the image has been processed correctly, the final printing can be as good as any image acquired through a drum scanner. With PhotoCD no instruction is required as the SBA (Scene Balance Algorithm) automatically corrects transparencies.

Conventional high-end scanners are different, and so is the PhotoCD equipment of the supplier. The type of PhotoCD scanner dictates the kinds of transparency formats that can be handled. A high-end Kodak scanner will handle transparency formats other than 35 mm, and is capable of manually adjusting the image. However, this incurs cost and defeats the time/cost/quality equation of using PhotoCD. The finished PhotoCD will contain five file sizes for the same image. The largest file size for a 35 mm transparency is 2048 x 3072 pixels, which is adequate quality for a high-end output of a small/medium image. A Pro PhotoCD disc can contain an additional sixth file size of 4096 x 6144 pixels for a 35 mm transparency, the approximate uncompressed file size is 72 mb.

PhotoCD XTentions allow for direct importation into QuarkXPress. When you first install QuarkXPress the Kodak Precision CMS is placed directly into your system folder as a start-up item. This is not the only CMS. Macintosh uses ColorSync and Windows use ICM (Image Color Matching).

The CCD (Charged Couple Device) of low-end flatbed scanners, and digital cameras that use compression for storage should only be used for low-resolution output. Digital information brought into the computer needs to match the output. If the two are unequal either the file size is too big and space is merely wasted, or the software tries to mathematically make up the difference when the maximum optical rating has been exceeded. The latter becomes interpolated (adjacent pixels are averaged) to avoid pixelation of the final output, you are at the mercy of the software for the final result. This suggests that the best result will be obtained by the equalisation of the dpi (dots-per-line) and the lpi (lines-per-inch), yet unfortunately in practice this is untrue. There is however a simple dpi/lpi equation between input and output for images with tonal values.

Line illustration (no tonal values) should be scanned at a resolution to match the final output, there is, however, no appreciable difference after 600 dpi has been reached. If the line illustration is to be scaled after scanning then problems will occur, and pixels start to become evident. Line illustration should be drawn to size and scanned at a 1:1 ratio or larger. The only other solution is to create the line illustration within a drawing program which retains the data to reconstruct the lines. Created as a computer file the illustration can be scaled and sized accordingly and then imported into QuarkXPress.

Again designing on paper first will determine the technical size of a digital image. On knowing the final size, these images can be cropped and scaled in other imaging software. Once the file has been opened within imaging software the dpi information should not be reduced for ease of image manipulation, this causes interpolation when the dpi is recalculated against the final lpi for tonal images. When importing the image into QuarkXPress you still have a small amount of upward scaling latitude. However, any image that has been digitised should only be scaled downwards to avoid interpolation. If file size is a problem high-end scanning produces an OPI thumbnail image for ease of manipulation which will be replaced during high-end output by the scanning provider (see Chapter 7).

For tonal images the dpi should be twice the final lpi.

An example of low-resolution output would be: 144 dpi for 72 lpi

An example of high-resolution output would be: 288 dpi for 144 lpi

For line work, after 600dpi at a ratio of 1:1 no appreciable difference can be noticed for either high or low-resolution printing.

If a large line scan is to be reduced in the final document make sure that fine lines have sufficient weight so that they will not degenerate when reproduced.

Using Digital Type within QuarkXPress

Typefaces are grouped into families, and changes of weight within the family (bold, italic and so on) is known as a font. This chapter does not classify families and their fonts for use on your desktop. Instead the chapter explores what to look for, and how to differentiate between the choice and variety that is available. Indeed there are many manuals solely devoted to showing complete ranges of families. There are however, certain type families which continue to develop for each change in technology. Baruch Gorkin and Tom Carnase (1995) in *The best in digital classic text fonts*, have researched a series of families from different foundries that have made the progression from metal through to photo-typesetting and finally digitisation. Their book gives a comparative analysis of the relevant factors such as outline, side-bearings, kerning and hinting (explained later) which affect typographical authenticity. The main type foundries all carry their family collections on CD. Monotype, Linotype and Adobe all allow you to preview their typographic collections. To unlock this material codes are available through an exchange of credit card details, normally per font.

New technologies change the nature of type – Adobe's multiple master-fonts allow more control over a letters shape, while QuarkXPress allows you to split the outline path of individual letters creating new typographic forms. Typography creates personality, each typeface has its own characteristics, and it is best to remember that typefaces are not intrinsically legible, you have learned their shape and meaning, any radical alterations that do not conform to what a reader expects reduces legibility. Type families and their fonts that you select for headings, sub-headings, body text and captions influence the way a reader

Gorkin, B., Carnase, T. 1995 The best in digital classic text fonts, Graphis

reacts to your ideas. There are over ten thousand fonts which can be formed into more than two thousand type families that visually shout, whisper, demand and so on. These families can be classified into eight basic groups – Old Style, Transitional, Modern, Square Serif, Sans Serif, Decorative, Script and Gothic.

Linotype, 1989 *LinoType Collection Mergenthaler Type Library*, Linotype AG

Old Style influenced by the quill pen with lightly bracketed serifs.

Transitional represented a change from the quill pen to a more contrasting change of stroke.

Modern was the first purely typographic face with fine unbracketed serifs and a strong contrast between thick and thin strokes.

Square Serif moved typography towards heavy rectangular serifs with little difference between the overall letterform weight.

Sans Serif represented the functionality and versatility of the twentieth century, the terminal strokes had the serifs removed, again there is little difference throughout the letterform.

Decoratives tend to be 'catchy' rather than legible, and are normally used for display purposes, mimicking computers, stencils and so on.

Scripts imitate handwriting, calligraphic, brush or copperplate.

Gothic or more commonly known as black letter such as Old English.

With so many combinations and possibilities at your disposal, choice can become subjective. Understanding design fundamentals, regardless of the technology that you use, will allow you to make objective choices. It is not the quantity of typefaces that you use that designs the page, it is your ability to recognise why typography has subtle differences. By knowing this you can use typography effectively and in the right context. Adrian Frutiger (1989) explains slight typographic differences by pointing out that, 'You may ask why so many different typefaces. They all serve the same purpose but they express mans' diversity. I once saw a list of Médocs all of the same year. All of them were wines but each was different from the others. It's the nuances that are important.'

What to Look for when Choosing a Typeface

Until recently small printers carried a limited range of fonts. Digital technology has extended the available choice to thousands. However, probably only 50 families form the basis of any good design. The characters within these typefaces fit well together within any word. For example, if you look at a line of type the words of the lower case characters appear all the same size, yet physically the 'x' sits on the baseline, but the 'c' sits below the baseline and above the x height, although optically both appear on the same line (*opposite*). This is true of all well designed serif and sans serif typefaces. A typeface that has been reused over a long period tends to be a sign of a good typeface design.

The letterform of the Roman alphabet is an optical art and not an exact science based on mathematical positioning. Both the serif and sans serif can be traced back to the chiselled inscriptions found on the Roman monuments such as the Trajan column. The characteristic of the serif can be attributed to the tools which inscribed the letters onto the stone. This combination gave the final inscription the shape of letters that we recognise, that is, 'stressed' strokes of different thicknesses. Frederic Goudy (1910) was influenced by the letterform qualities of these inscriptions. By returning to base source Goudy was able to use the past to inform typography for the future. All good typeface design looks back, recognises the qualities and places this into an appropriate context for the present. Digital typography should be no different, it is merely another kind of reproduction.

Unlike the serif face, sans serif type normally has an equal monoline weight throughout with squared features. Developed to express the aspiration of the twentieth century it still converges on the past. For example, Edward Johnston's san serif used for the London underground in 1918 was based on the old style script of the Roman inscriptions, the thick and thin strokes were given an even weight and the serifs were removed. The face was an ideal adaption of the past for the London underground, where large single words needed to be clearly

The x height is always given as a size value because it is the only character with four flat terminals at the end of the main letter strokes that rest exactly on the baseline and at the upperline of the lowercase. The *c* is physically larger, yet optically equal.

McLean, R. (ed) 1995 *Typographers on Type*, Lund Humphries

Sasson, R. (ed) 1993 *Computers and Typography*, Intellect

recognised against other competing styles of typography used in advertising. The design group Banks and Miles reviewed the design for the London Underground in 1979, adding new fonts to the original. Sans serif type families can themselves be sub-divided into 'uneven-width monolines' (Futura), and 'even-monolines' (Univers). The uneven-width retains old style proportions, whereas the even-width monoline has modern style proportions.

What Influences Change in a Typeface

In order to understand these differences it is important to look closely at the optical structure of a typeface, and the decisions around its construction. Newspapers, journals, traffic sign systems and car manufacturers have produced their own versions. Monotype Times New Roman was developed for *The Times* and is probably one of the most successful typefaces of this century. If you consider the development of a typeface for a specific use then Stanley Morisons' campaign for typographic reforms for *The Times* serves as a good example. Before Morison English newspapers where mostly set in modern faces. These faces tended to be of a fine typographic construction, reflecting the style that worked for a previous technology.

Printing machine speeds and volume of print were increasingly leaving the final newspaper impressions of these modern faces grey or squashed. Morison had made the connection and understood the problem of using type in the wrong technological context. His solution was to use modern features yet retained the legibility of an old style face, and by doing so, regain the clarity of impression that had been lost. The alteration of the typographic features of many typefaces such as Baskerville, Perpetua and Plantin were tested.

It was a revised Plantin which was finally used by Morison. The redesigned family became Times New Roman restoring both the aesthetic and legible qualities suitable for machine composition. Dtp is no different, as Morison had to consider technical limitations, such as 'ink-spread'. PostScript fonts are outlines of the letterform, when printed there is hardly any

Futura is a sans serif uneven-width monoline which retains old style proportions.

Dreyfus, J. 1973 *The Evolution of Times New Roman*, The Penrose annual. *The Times* was set and published in Monotype Times New Roman on the 3rd October 1932.

distortion. However, when you use the fonts installed on the computer, and you select Times, you are not selecting Monotype Times New Roman, you are probably selecting a different version. Each type foundry has a slight variation for their style of the same type family. Digital fonts are not physical, software generates the font as either an outline for the printer or as a bitmap for the screen. The font data is stored in the system and can be outputed directly to lithographic film/plate, inkjet printer or digital press, refreshing each character as new.

Therefore, typography has always adapted when media has been changed. Digital typography has evolved to meet the demands of new technology. With movable type each size had to be physically manufactured. Optical adjustments were made for the size differences of body text and display type. Creating a digital version of a typeface is through informed interpretation and not as a faithful copy of the original.

A more recent example of using digital type either chosen or designed for an audience was when *MacUser* appeared on the shelves completely redesigned on the 22nd July 1994. Certain parts of the magazine went untouched. The *MacUser* logo was kept the same in order to retain the character and image of the magazine. It was the design of the magazine that changed and not the editorial contents, the same sections appeared in the same places throughout the magazine. Again, this would have been done so as not to totally alienate regular readers. With the change a certain amount of familiarity had to be maintained. Like other high-street magazines *MacUser* has continued to change gradually through the influence of other magazines which compete for the same readership.

Obviously during 1994 the senior art director Matt Williams and his team were aware that a large part of *MacUser's* readership were people who were involved in design themselves, and who produced magazines and other materials on computers so they were 'redesigning to a critical audience, many of whom know as much as we do'. The three major areas of the redesign were in the structure of its format, the visual elements and typography, but not the style or identity of the *MacUser* brand.

MacUser's brief for the redesign was:

'to modernise the look of MacUser, but... the constraints placed [upon us] were to do this while maintaining a similar word count in most sections, to maintain clarity... and to make the same budget do more. We also had to ensure the design would work within a fortnightly production schedule'.

MacUser vol 10 no 15

The new page structure has a header that appears at the start of articles that is directly related to the front cover: the contents page has changed quite dramatically. The new design makes it easier to locate different sections of the magazine and that is, first and foremost, the main objective of a contents page. The page structure is asymmetrical in design throughout; beginning with the page layout and finally ending with the choice of typography. There is a clear hierarchical reading order to page elements that contrast with each other, creating a definite page colour. The coded icons help to keep the relevant areas together, helping the reader to distinguish certain sections when looking through the magazine. There are no new sections and the positions of the headers have remained in the same order in relation to each other but have moved down to the lower half of the page. This again is part of the familiarity that regular readers can associate with the 'old' *MacUser*.

New icons were created to make each page look distinctively like *MacUser*. These icons, which feature throughout the magazine add identity, continuity and humour to the pages. These discrete visual units of representation help the reader to identify certain parts of the magazine more easily. These icons also serve to keep a section together that may be split by advertisements. However, the redesign retained certain characteristics of previous icons, keeping a certain amount of consistency and familiarity with previous issues, the reader was not required to relearn a system – merely adapt to the new.

Choosing and using Typefaces Together

The new fonts chosen for *MacUser* were Frutiger, Officina and Visage, before the redesign Franklin Gothic was used for headings, sub-headings and so on. Frutiger, like Franklin, has a wide range of fonts for heads, sub-headings and so on. Franklin Gothic appeared at the beginning of the century and went through a major revival in the 1950s when a wide range of weights were added to give the family versatility. Frutiger was adapted by Linotype in 1976, originally designed for Charles de Gaulle Airport, as it combines clear graphic communication

Structure Both grid and elements within are all asymmetrical giving the pages a dynamic appearance.

Page hierarchy There is a clear reading order and rhythm to the main feature pages, headings, pull-quotes and images establishing the mood of the content of each article very quickly. Hierarchical order is not confined to the main elements of the page. After ascertaining the content of the story the reader still needs direction. For articles drop caps are used sparingly.

MacUser uses different graphic devices all of the same size to attract the reader's attention. When these devices are used the first word has a heavier weight, this 'fine tunes' the hierarchical order.

Display type Frutiger is used for headings, captions and so on, where the families' function is to inform, and direct the reader's attention to the main body of text. Article sub-headings clearly contrast with the body text. They are larger, colour pushes them back into the page so that they are not overstated.

Body text Visage is a serif faced used for the bulk of the body text, however unlike a book, a magazine is not a continuous read. Officina is a sans serif used for smaller amounts of body text. It is mixed on the same page with Visage and Frutiger, there is sufficient contrast between the three to emphasis the difference.

To deconstruct the structure of a magazine see page 131.

with the aesthetics of good letterform. With their 'critical audience' in mind, *MacUser* carefully chose this font for primary use as 'Frutiger Condensed comes in a whole range of weights from light 47 to black 87, it can be used expressively creating a limitless combination of possibilities for typography... The actual shape of Frutiger Condensed also provides the designer with opportunities for creative typography.'

Visage is a new serif font brought in by *MacUser* especially for the redesign and is used for the bulk of the body text. Based on an old style the letterforms have a thick/thin transition and the contrast between both is relatively moderate. As the font is light in overall greyness, it is an ideal body text for reading. Officina, designed by Erik Spiekermann, is a sans serif monoweight with square serif overtones. A 1990s digital font, which is functional and informative, its overall greyness is darker than Visage. Officina links throughout the magazine, not only being mixed with Visage for body text contrast, but also through the pagination and running heads.

What is important in the example of *MacUser* is that the publisher knows the profile of its readership and how they can attract an audience through the application of design and editorial content. For you as a student there is an important lesson to be learned from analysing any high-street magazine. *MacUser* clearly shows that the redesign is specifically aimed at the publisher's perception of the readership. This profile is very important if they are to attract advertising revenue and, therefore, continue to publish. Since 1994, the redesigned *MacUser* has continued to evolve. Like other magazines, it is in a constant state of flux – change becomes gradual or innovative, but always constant, and not alienating to its readership.

Like *MacUser*, anything that you design has a purpose aimed at your perception of the audience. We all read magazines that interest us, and if you have back copies of any title the example of *MacUser* can be applied to it. If you can deconstruct and interpret how a magazine uses design and why, then you are best equipped to adapt what you learn and apply this to other formats such as leaflets, brochures, newsletters and so on.

Digital Type is Different

PostScript fonts comprise of the bitmapped screen information and the printer description. A font that has been digitised will draw the letter each time the character is called by the printer or by the screen preview. Each character has an optimum amount of plotting points to draw the outline of the letterform. Too many plotting points and the letterform's screen display and printing time are increased. Too few and the subtly of shape is lost. PostScript has been developed for high-resolution printing and will appear in the font menu as different weights. TrueType appears in the font menu as a family name only, and its weight is altered by the Style menu. For example, PostScript Photina has additional 'expert' fonts.

To avoid printing problems during high-resolution imagesetter output, PostScript families should be used by selecting their appropriate font. Type styles applied to PostScript fonts will print on Laser proofs, but are ignored by high-resolution printers. When you print a TrueType font on a PostScript printer substitution could occur if there is a font name conflict. The advantage of TrueType is that it has been designed for low-resolution Laser printers giving the character more form at a low-resolution. It also does not need a PostScript interpreter built into the printer.

To explain this further fonts tend to be designed for 'bottom-up' low-resolution output, or high-resolution 'top-down' output. Both give a false impression when used at the wrong resolution. The 'collateral' approach of being neither for high-resolution or low-resolution, attempts to average quality at both resolutions. Here typography subtly attempts to balance between course detail and fine detail. It is always best to know the final output resolution and choose accordingly. The Macintosh use of Postscript has mainly adopted the top-down approach for font usage. It is for this reason that PostScript top-down fonts can look badly constructed at low-resolutions. Characters can appear too tight or too loose within a word, giving a false impression of letter-fit, and of the actual thickness of the strokes.

HelveUltCompressed
Klang MT
L Futura Light
L Helvetica Light
LB Helvetica Black
LBI Helvetica Black Obliqu
LI Helvetica Light Oblique
LO Futura LightOblique
M Photina
Monaco
N Helvetica Narrow
New Berolina MT
New York
O Futura BookOblique
Old English Text MT
Palatino
Script MT Bold
✓ SP Photina
SP Photina Expert
SP Photina Expert Italic
SP Photina Expert SemiBo
SP Photina Expert SemiBo
SP Photina Italic
SP Photina SemiBold
SP Photina SemiBoldItalic

The family highlighted is a TrueType version of Photina. The font ticked is a PostScript version of Photina. To change a PostScript font you must select a different weight from this menu such as Photina Expert Italic and so on. The PostScript family can also appear as a sub-menu.

The need to develop type families that take the guessing out of typography, and for use with low-resolution printing, is a welcome development for office solutions. Indeed the intended purpose of the standard PostScript range installed on the computer was to give you a varied choice of display, body text, script, typewriter and computer style typefaces. Taking the guess work out of typography has seen the development of bottom-up fonts such as ITC Stone (International Typeface Corporation) which has a series of good weight variations and also a serif and sans serif version.

The low-resolution features ensure that the Stone family avoids fine strokes and joins associated with high-resolution printing. It has been designed for mixed use of the serif and sans serif without you having to consider how different families can contrast each other. Unfortunately, these low-resolution typefaces lack subtle differences which become apparent when output through a high-resolution printer. Therefore, to choose a family for dtp use, you will need to know what the final printing resolution will be.

In comparison ITC Eras has been designed for a complete family use with no serif version. Unlike Stone it is a top-down sans serif face that has a dramatic weight variation, from light through to ultra bold. The family also has a slight inward curving on all upright strokes. These variations are not detectable on low-resolution laser proof outputs, but are very apparent on the final high-resolution output. The family has no italic, all characters lean forward and the loops are unjoined. It has a 'wide-setting' (wide letters) making the family readable as a text face used in small quantities and pleasing in display sizes. Eras is a recent family which is an uneven-width monoline designed by Albert Boton and introduced by ITC in 1976. Other top-down digital fonts based on older families can present problems of authenticity especially when comparing the original font to the digitised version. Families that have been redesigned for use with computers have been optically compensated to incorporate new methods of reproduction. The design of digital type outlines produce what is essentially a new font.

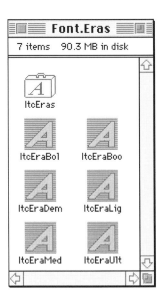

ITC Eras is a PostScript font. The top single folder contains the screen information for the six fonts. The other multiple files contain printer information for each font difference.

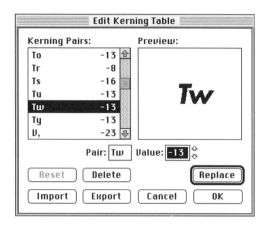

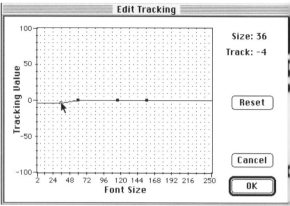

Fitting Digital Letters Together

Computer monitors and printers work with pixels. A computer monitor normally has a resolution of 72 dpi, a high-resolution printer will have 2,540 dpi. The printed size of the pixel therefore depends on the output resolution of the printer, what you see and what you get depends on the font outline plotted by the output device. Lower resolution printers become less accurate because the plotting process is mathematical, and because fewer pixels to the inch decides whether a pixel is included or excluded during output. Well designed fonts contain 'hinting' instructions to reduce the arbitrary 'in' or 'out' of pixels. Hinting attempts to retain the true typographical characteristics normally for high-resolution printers.

Hinting attempts to faithfully reproduce the letterform, whereas 'side-bearing' and 'kerning' determine how letters fit with each other inside a word. Good kerning considers the overall relationship of the possible pairs of letters. Badly spaced characters do have a tendency to disrupt the reader. Side-bearings determine the relationship of space between a letterform and its neighbour on both sides. A well designed font will set side-bearing values, which have an optical equivalent of give-and-take or 'wrenching'. However, some pairs of characters require a special relationship, these character-sets are 'pair-kerned' according to a table designed by the foundry, this table is alterable within QuarkXPress. A font which has been

Ye Yo Yp Yq
Ye Yo Yp Yq

You read the overall shape of the word, pairs of letters that have unusual fits can be pair kerned. This will reduce the space between certain letters so that the word appears together. *Top left.* Notice how the *w* fits under the cross bar of the *T*.

Top right. The Edit Tracking dialog box allows you to alter the overall spacing of the text. Larger display sizes will require greater tracking than body text sizes.

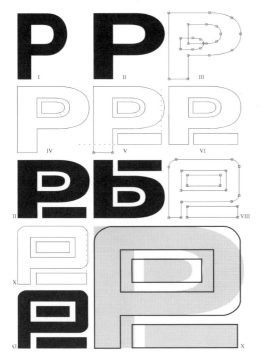

Using the past to inform the present. Corporate Identity for Print/Publish Belize. The character outline of Helvetica (*P*) was adjusted to echo Maya carvings at Xunantunich, 'The Maiden of the Rock', near the Belize boarder with Guatemala.

designed with loose tracking side-bearing characteristics will require a smaller amount of kerned pairs. Fonts which have tight tracking and large pair kerning tables contain more computer data, and will print and refresh on the screen slower.

Outline characters are mathematical. Points of letters are recorded so that the outline of the character can be rendered (drawn) by the computer. Many points are required for curves, and curves on letters are not circular, and therefore require a varying curved line. To achieve this curves pass through bézier points on the outline. QuarkXPress allows you to make shape alterations to characters. This requires a knowledge of the optical properties of letterform. The illustration for a corporate identity above needs to be placed into context against Central American culture, and only then as a logo. It has had all typographic refinement removed that would normally be associated with bézier curves, yet it has retained optical balance. Such program features should be limited to this kind of use, modification of the body text characters would make reading difficult.

The Difference of Size

Body text is normally between 8 pt and 14 pt, display type is anything above 14 pt. Loosely tracked spatial relationships that work well on small sizes normally require tighter adjustment on the larger sizes. True display type has finer strokes than body text, the optical appearance of display sizes needs to fit better because the eye is reading the overall shape of the word. All that is normally required of a body text face is a plain, italic, bold and bold italic font for family completeness. Adobe has developed multiple sizing, these fonts contain the optical refinement of predigital fonts. A multiple will carry a small and large size where the font can be interpolated by size, weight, width and style. QuarkXPress support for 'Multiple font Masters' can be accessed through the Font Creator found in the Utilities pull-down menu. It does however, require a full understanding of letterform construction.

Profile Manager...
Build Index...
Tracking Edit...
Kerning Table Edit...
Font Creator

The font creator can be found in the Utilities pull-down menu.

When you need more than the Alphabet

The computer can also give additional variations to a font through the selection of a style such as underline, outline, shadow, small caps and so on. This is an averaged solution, added to the font by the dtp software of the computer. Linotype Times Cancelled is different from Times Strike Thru. You are at the mercy of the computers software for the line width. Specially drawn expert type variations contain additional character sets for small caps, ligatures, superior characters, old style non-aligning figures, fractions and so on.

An example of ~~Strike Thru~~ can be found on legal documents.

If you are using a type family without an expert font set, QuarkXPress will allow you to alter the value for small cap font sizes, and also superscript, subscript and superior. When altering the horizontal or vertical scale of PostScript or TrueType fonts, mathematical and not optical corrections are made, and finer serif faces tend to suffer the most. Also, fonts that have been scaled will default to their original proportions if the Text to Box feature has been applied. If you are using this combination, scale after Text to Box using W and H (width and height) from the Measurements palette.

aɑa

Strike Thru from the Style menu for Photina, Futura and Bembo. Note strike thru line position in relation to each character.

Text tool

Circle tool

Picture tool

Line tool

Marine Security Limited ™

Linear blend

Using Tools, Type and Blends

Top left. Combining a freeform line tool, picture box tool with a linear blend and a typeface (Eras) strengthens the identity and sense of belonging throughout all company items. *Top right.* The applied identity.

The advent of dtp was originally associated with low-resolution 300 dpi output. Typographic democracy, but not typographic discrimination was open to all. QuarkXPress now allows you to go beyond page layout with 'pop out' text, picture and line tools. Other design features such as the Bézier Text Box allows you to alter the shape of letters and insert images as part of a letter or word's overall texture. Choice of letterform for such treatment becomes important. Characters with finer letter strokes can break-up. Good word shape matters, after learning a word your reader recognises its meaning through shape.

By recognising this, the wholeness of the word as a readable image can have the meaning strengthened through the selection of a typeface that suggests subject association. The example above mixes a standardised family of type with freeform shapes within a logo. The circle encloses the letter 'M' and freeform 'S', both elements of the design are balanced within the circle.

171

A picture box blend underlines the 'M'. Finally the logo is coloured blue so that when the logo is reproduced on the side of marine craft, the spectral sensitivity of the human eye can identify the mark in failing light conditions.

Not only was Eras chosen for its range of weights, it was also used because the visual characteristics of the font help the words to project authority. The range of weights allow you to be firm or gentle but always projecting a feeling of strength. Family completeness and extent will also aid legibility. By using the same family throughout, you can also be sure that fonts from the same family will harmonise well together. The standardised family is then used throughout all business communication and publications. The type family through the logo becomes associated with the company as part of their identity.

Harmonious and Contrasting Type

With dtp mixing and matching typefaces is very easy, and the temptation is there for all. It is best to limit any selection to two families that contrast with each other. Two families from the same group used together lack adequate visual variation and conflict because neither are sufficiently different. Using one harmonious family for all typographic elements of the design maybe desirable if the communication is intended to link throughout. However, if this is not the intention then contrasting family groups should be used – normally serif and sans serif.

There are exceptions; uneven monolines such as Optima are difficult to mix because the thick/thin transition of the strokes retain the characteristic of a serif although the serifs themselves have been removed. By knowing what to look for, and looking closely at the characteristics of the type family, choice becomes objective. The choice of family then becomes subjective, most decisions are based on common sense and a concern for a balance between legibility and personality. The simplest example is a face such as Helvetica Round, where the sans serif is rounded and not square. In a heavy weight, this would be appropriate for fast food. Letterform creates meaning through association, the elegance of a script face would be inappropriate.

Harmony creates a formal page when one type family is used with little variation between weight, size and so on.

Contrast emphasises the difference between the typographic elements on the page.

Conflict occurs when similar type families with little or no visual difference are used together.

There are many sans serif families, such as Frutiger, Futura, Gill Sans, Helvetica, and so on. These straight-forward typefaces aid the contrast of your design and are ideal for headings and sub-headings. For example, Univers is an even-width sans serif monoline designed by Adrian Frutiger for optical uniformity. Normally a family of fonts is distinguished by being bold, italic, light and so on, but because of the range of weights, Frutiger dispensed with these descriptions and adopted a numbering system to indicate precisely where the fonts fitted within the family group. Lower numbers indicate light font variation, odd numbers are for regular, and even numbers are for italic.

QuarkXPress allows you to take display typography one stage further, by allowing you to alter the font outline and its fill. This is achieved by applying special effects to type through the Text to Box and Splitting Items feature (see pages 99-100). However, because a feature is there, it does not mean that it should be applied, and to use this feature effectively your choice of font needs certain characteristics. The simple shape of the heavier weight sans serif families will survive such treatment, whereas a fine serif will not as its features will compete for attention with the applied effect.

Headings, sub-headings and so on have set the tone of the publication's content. If your reader has reached the main body of the text, it means that they intend to read the story. If you want people to read the text and your publication is large, choose a bland face. Old style serif families such as Baskerville, Caslon, Garamond, Bembo and so on look similar to each other and are all slightly irregular. This helps to stimulate eye movement. Eye stimulation through disruption helps to keep your reader alert aiding legibility and making the blandness of families based on old styles ideal for large amounts of text. If your document is small then you can still use a sans serif typeface for the body text.

Research into the legibility of typefaces has indicated that serif characteristics enable your reader to complete a text quicker. A family such as Bembo is one of the original old styles; digitisation has produced a version with a distinct family range

sans serif

Sans serif makes a better display face for headings because of font variety and single word legibility.

serif

Serif faces are better for body text because they disrupt eye movement.

and an expert character set. What makes Bembo legible is the open counters and thicker serifs; like most serif typefaces the cross-lines contribute an easy letter-by-letter transition to your reader's eye.

Finally, you must also remember that human perception changes and one clear method of dating your work is through your choice of typography. Typefaces that have been well-designed and continue to be used will ensure that your publication suffers less from ageing.

For further reading and examples of typographic trends and thinking:

Poynor, R. (ed) 1997 *Typography Now: The Next Wave*, Booth-Clibborn Editions

When your Document leaves the Desktop

Documents which leave your desktop for output at another location must contain the QuarkXPress documents, LIVE images and all PostScript screen and printer fonts. Collect for Output will gather all files and place them in one folder, except the fonts.

A beam of light moves back and forth across a photo-sensitive surface. The path of the beam is called a raster after the Latin for *snake*.

This chapter is mainly concerned with how your QuarkXPress documents behave once they have been sent for high-resolution output. There are software solutions that will automate the process of checking what you send away from your desktop to be either used by others or output at a high-resolution, for example, FlightCheck lists all problems and suggests remedies (more on this later). However, before simply installing software that takes the chance out of prepress, it is important for you to know what the potential problems are.

Most bureaus will prefer you to send your files as QuarkXPress documents, images and fonts. Others will except PostScript files but cannot be held responsible for the final output as this format has limited modification possibilities, and therefore is considered as generally uneditable – what you send is what you get back. The bureau will know the capabilities of their high-end equipment, allowing them to make alterations on your behalf that do not alter your design is preferable. Adobe Acrobat files are unlike saved PostScript files and EPS (Encapsulated PostScript) pages. Acrobat will allow the bureau to edit the document while still containing all the necessary document, font and image data. If your design has more than one final output destination it also has the advantage of making files visible within any WWW browser. However, simply collecting all files for output to a bureau is insufficient.

Desktop computing, including Laser proof output, is an inexpensive investment, high-end imagesetter output through a RIP (Raster Image Processor) is not. A reprographic bureau is a service provider for many kinds of graphic output needs such as books, magazines, posters, leaflets and so on.

There is much to be gained by using the service provider correctly, and discussion of what you should submit for production as digital files, marked-up laser proofs and labelling of transport media should form part of your planning process. As mentioned earlier the computer compiles the digital artwork, your thought processes design the publication, and planning for print, knowing final image sizes etc, is crucial for a smooth work flow.

The Scitex User Group UK has for many years being compiling reports from reprographic services that output QuarkXPress files from different sources. Digital artwork is fluid, unlike artwork that was physically cut and pasted. Problems can arise when the files are transported from a Macintosh or PC computer to a high-resolution output service provider. When you digitally design a document the computer puts you in charge of the print production process. All decisions of how your documents are outputed, what problems the service provider might encounter and what costs could be incurred are taken by you. The Scitex UK document was developed as a discussion paper between you and the reprographic house. Most of this chapter has been provided by them so that you, can best understand what you are trying to achieve. If in doubt ask 'mutual and collective ownership of the project (from design through production printing) should be agreeably established', this relationship is in the interest of both parties. Many bureaus will supply guidelines of their requirements.

LIVE Images

Laser proof and high-end imagesetter output is different, if correct digital output procedure is not followed then problems can arise. A well planned project, planned in the same way as the design of the publication will normally ensure that the QuarkXPress document will require a minimum of processing. A LIVE image is any image element in an QuarkXPress file that will be incorporated into the final output. This includes high-resolution scans and PhotoCD digitised by somebody else, and computer scans and graphics generated by you. Before using LIVE images ensure that your Macintosh or PC has

These items must be marked *LIVE* on the laser proofs.

The objective of using LIVE images is to capture enough data to achieve the desired detail and keep the file size as small as possible.

sufficient RAM to manipulate the images. If not, the reprographic service will scan images for you and retain the original for the final output. You will be provided with an OPI (Open Prepress Interface) thumbnail that you can manipulate with ease. The LIVE images will be replaced when the final document is returned for high-resolution imagesetter output.

When using OPI images, do not rename the file. The file name is the link back to the high-resolution image stored by the bureau. It is best to provide meaningful file names for your images before they are scanned. Unfortunately, OPI thumbnails have limited graphic capabilities and can only be cropped and scaled, any manipulation within an imaging software program will have no effect.

When requesting images from a service provider for manipulation it is important not to alter the resolution or CMYK colour model that has been provided. Using the algorithms to convert your file to RGB and then back to CMYK on your desktop computer can have a less predictable outcome on return for high-resolution output. Returning the file as a JPEG (Joint Photographic Experts Group) is a lossy compression, on decompression if the data is not present pixels will have been downsampled (averaged against adjacent pixels). If possible always compress with non lossy compression such as LZW (lempel-Ziv/Welch). Orientation of the original image is also important, pictures that have been rotated on your desktop computer, will not have the algorithms to reposition pixels at a high-resolution. Rotating a LIVE image with QuarkXPress could require the image to be rescanned to maintain quality.

Another option is to provide your own FPO desktop scans. These must be clearly marked on the proofs indicating the image which needs to be replaced by the high-resolution scan. The FPO must contain enough visual information to determine scaling percentage, position and crop details. When using a desktop scanner each image should be scanned separately, as opposed to ganged-up images (many images grouped together) scanned as one image file. This allows for one single image placed in each picture box in the QuarkXPress document

When you name a file, give it a name that has the same meaning for everybody i.e. PalmTree.Tif instead of PT.Tif. This will help memory recall later.

Lossy compression uses a technique that cannot expand the file back into its original data composition.

Non Lossy compression ensures that when the file is expanded it will be identical to the original.

When scaling images ensure that proportion is maintained between height and width (anamorphic scaling).

layout. Multiple images increase the file size resulting in your laser proof taking longer to output. If you do decide to use multiple scans crop each to size within an imaging program and save each one as a new file.

A problem with FPO files is that the service provider cannot reproduce accurately any graphic effects that you create with a low-resolution file. If the effects are simple or merely technical, make a note of the desired effect on the laser proof for the service provider to produce the desired results. If your desired effects cannot be achieved, an alternative would be to request the high-resolution image, and do any retouching or special effects yourself.

When working with FPOs certain characteristics must be taken into account: low-resolution PICT files usually look better on-screen than TIFFs, but worse than TIFFs when output to a laser printer. EPS files look good on-screen and default to the local printer values if the file has been preinstructed to do so. LIVE and FPO images look exactly the same on-screen this is because both appear the same at screen resolutions. Without clear communication the danger exists that FPOs that remain within the document could be mistaken for LIVE files. It is always best to remove FPOs from your document before sending for final output. Make sure that the Image has been printed on the final Laser proof which will accompany your QuarkXPress document to the bureau.

Any image created within the computer should be treated differently to those that are scanned into the computer. Computer generated images created within drawing programs call upon the necessary algorithms at the time of output. Therefore, the file should remain unaltered in the LIVE file folder and in its final printing position on-screen

Image files have the greatest tendency to crash computers and hang laser printers. If this happens then it will probably happen on an imagesetter – higher resolution output requires more complex processing. If your QuarkXPress document does print on a laser printer it still does not guarantee that it will print flawlessly on an imagesetter.

If you are using a Macintosh with QuickTime another option is to combine the screen and output qualities of TIFF and PICTS files. Save your Photoshop image as an EPS file with a JPEG preview. Unfortunately the additional data required to render the image will slow the screen refresh.

Unlike TIFF files (Tag Image File Format), PICT files are intermediate files, requiring an additional format.

Using Fonts in a QuarkXPress Document for High-Resolution Output

Fonts are probably the best example of printing problems, and are probably the most widespread reason for interruptions to workflow. One of the most common faults occur when moving QuarkXPress files from one computer to another. Fonts can be forgotten during transport, such as printer fonts which causes the output device to substitute an alternative like Courier. Another problem is TrueType styling applied to a PostScript font. Both PostScript and TrueType fonts will allow styles to be applied from the pull-down menu, it is only TrueType that functions this way. Both will show typographic styling on-screen and on laser proofs such as bold, italic and so on. PostScript will remain unchanged, and defaults to the font's original regular style when output through an imagesetter. Use the actual font variation for the PostScript family. The difference is obvious in the font menu. A TrueType font will only show the family name once in the menu, a PostScript family will show all fonts of that family that are available to you.

When a QuarkXPress document is moved to another computer, matching screen and printer fonts must be installed in the system or the document will not print properly. Version numbers and type foundry must be identical. Apple compounds the problem by installing TrueType fonts into the system folder, sometimes with the same name as the PostScript Type font. If an imagesetter has the PostScript font with the same name as the TrueType supplied by you, there is an additional problem in that the PostScript version will probably be used as the default by the output device, causing the document to reflow. If you intend to use TrueType, inform the service provider. Most bureaus will have standardised on PostScript. Mixing both types of font within a document can compound these problems and also cause longer processing times and, or sections of type output as bitmaps. QuarkXPress will allow you to check font usage by pulling-down the Utilities menu and selecting Usage. Select More Information and you will be able to see the name, type and version of the font that you are using.

Setting styles such as bold, italic and so on for a PostScript font creates a pseudo version of that families font. Imagesetter RIPs ignore pseudo commands, and will print without the instruction in the fonts original style.

Select More Information from the Usage dialog. This will allow you to check the font version.

PostScript and TrueType fonts are not equal, this is also true of different families from different foundries, as poorly written fonts could be node heavy (having been built with to many points), or have bad kerning pairs or incomplete character sets reducing printing and screen refresh time. Fortunately, these characteristics tend to be restricted to display fonts which are normally used in larger point sizes and have limited use. It is best to convert such fonts to outlines, even well considered fonts used sparingly at larger sizes should be converted to outline to reduce the printer font call. If the type has been used from within QuarkXPress the Text to Box command transforms the selected text into a Bézier-outline.

QuarkXPress will allow you to edit the shape of the characters by selection of the Bézier points. If the type has been created outside QuarkXPress, such as type integrated into a logo or illustration use 'Convert to Paths' in FreeHand, 'Convert to Outline' in Illustrator, and 'Convert to Curves' in Corel Draw before exporting to QuarkXPress. When text has been converted it can be treated as a graphic and will not look for the printer font during output. However, any image imported into the drawing program and integrated with the type will be nested a further layer away from QuarkXPress. By importing images directly into your document to combine with type any problems caused by loosing parts of images will be reduced.

Foreign Language fonts such as Hebrew or Japanese should also be mentioned because they usually require a keyboard file to operate correctly. If this file does not accompany the QuarkXPress document again characters will appear correctly on the screen of the service providers computer, yet like missing image files and printer fonts will fail to print properly. The service provider will also require a keyboard map if any changes are to be made on your behalf, as the operator is unlikely to be familiar with the positions of the characters. PI (picture) fonts should also be treated in a similar fashion, although a keyboard map is unnecessary for limited use. PI fonts are probably one of the most infrequently used fonts, but are probably the most overlooked part of any document sent to a reprographic house.

Like nesting (*opposite*) always use Get Picture to import images, never copy and paste images already placed in your document. Get Picture creates a route to the image file. This can eliminate high-resolution printing problems at a later stage.

Imported Files

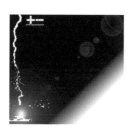

File created in an imaging program (bitmap).

Text converted to paths within a drawing program (vector).

Image and converted text combined within the drawing program. When imported the file above the image is nested three layers deep, and the text is nested two layers deep from the printer. Import the image into QuarkXPress and use special effects.

QuarkXPress treats imported image files as electronic 'pick-ups'. When called for output QuarkXPress will follow the route back to the image file. After the file has been placed within the document do not move its location or change its name. This is why during the planning stage files and folders should be created as a digital 'job bag'. QuarkXPress looks for the route, file names are a critical reference link. If you do alter the image file after placing within the document you should always update this by pulling down the Utilities widow to Usage as this will show name, type of file and status. Select More Information and you will be able to see the path route to the file, the file size, when it was last modified and its dimensions.

Elements like these that are designed in other programs for import into an QuarkXPress document can occasionally create other problems. An imported file sits outside (nested two layers deep) of the document for purposes of printing. If for example, a file has been created by imaging software and is then imported into a drawing program and then exported to QuarkXPress, the image file is now nested three layers deep. During processing the RIP will spend time trying to follow the links back, beyond two layers deep can occasionally cause problems, parts of the second layer will print, while the third could produce a bitmap or drop the image completely. The third layer element can be isolated and placed with a QuarkXPress document and integrated with type, or saved as an EPS file for export which will retain the data from the third image, nesting both at two layers.

When your document is complete unwanted digital data should be removed. It is insufficient to cover up unused elements with a white box, the RIP of a high-end imagesetter will continue to process the data regardless. Return to the imaging program (to crop any excess image area). Images which are cropped within QuarkXPress still process the data behind the unseen area of the picture box. Images should be treated in the same way as film composition. The Image should be digitised at a 1:1 ratio allowing for 3 mm for each edge so that it can be fitted behind the edges of the picture box.

Trapping

Trapping is applying the lesser of two evils to resolve a problem created when some colours are printed which overlap. There are two major reasons for Trapping – the movement of a printing press and the translucency of ink. Paper is normally white, when two translucent colours are overprinted a third colour is created. This is normally undesirable, except for black. Secondly, printing presses move quickly, and it is this movement that can create a slight nonalignment of these images. Simply put, images that are different colours are on different printing plates, and movement can cause misregistration.

Misregistration becomes apparent if one image, for example a square, had to reproduce inside another larger square. The larger square would have a knockout (hole exposing the paper background) of the shape of the smaller square. The small square will fit inside the larger square retaining its colour integrity. However, if the hole and the square were the same size the movement of the press could make one square misregister against the other. The result could be that two sides of the square could overprint onto the other square, and leave a gap on the other two sides. This would cause the white of the background to appear on the other two sides. To solve this, the smaller square is made larger, or the inner white background is made smaller.

This brings in the second factor, deciding whether the small square is made larger, or the inner white background is made smaller. Printing ink colours are normally translucent, and whichever square is the lighter of the two colours will normally be increased in size. If the larger square with the knockout is lighter the knockout is choked (the hole is reduced). If the small square that fits into the knockout is lighter the ink is spread (the small square is made larger).

The amount of trapping depends on the kind of press. The thickness of the trap value (the ink overlap) should be no greater than the press movement. You will need to know the kind of press and its amount of misregistration if you intend to set your own values.

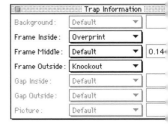

The Trap dialog.

Fitting the same size square into the same size knockout will cause misregistration.

Fitting a slightly larger square into a smaller knockout will overcome registration problems. Size differences can be as little as 0.144 pt.

Small Type and Colour

Avoid designing the page with fine serif type which is less than 8/10 pt which has been made with two or more colours. Like trapping there is movement during printing, and fine small type printed using the four colour process can misregister. For the same reasons avoid reversing out small type (the type is knocked out from the background colour to white) out of screen tints built from more than one colour.

Single solid spot colours can also create problems for small serif typefaces. Single spot colours are normally used over large areas because building a solid colour from several process colours can cause colour unevenness. Single colours mixed and then applied to the press can hold the amount of ink required to print an even colour. The amount of the ink used to create the solid can therefore fill in the serifs. Small sans serif type tends to suffer less from these problems because of the lack of fine character strokes.

Blends and Shade Stepping

QuarkXPress allows you to apply a series of colour blends such as linear, rectangular, diamond, circular and so on. These can reproduce with unpleasant bandings when tints do not smoothly blend into the next level. This can be minimised or prevented with a little more planning in the design process. There are several approaches to building a blend that will not band at a high-resolution output.

While the QuarkXPress algorithm for blends are sophisticated, if the combination of blend are apparent on a laser proof, an imagesetter will improve the outcome, but the banding could still be evident. To reduce the possibility of banding happening when your document is output at high-resolution increase the tonal percentage within the band range. A narrow range has a greater potential for banding. You can also visually disrupt banding by placing other elements, such as type across the blend. There is also a distinct relationship between the length of a blend and the number of steps in a blend. Too few steps on a long blend will show banding.

The Single QuarkXPress Document

Not all QuarkXPress files are large documents: business cards, letterheads and compliments slips are all regular work for many designers. These tend to be items that will be printed using spot colours. If smaller elements of the design do not bleed off the edges, they can all be stepped and repeated into one document page. This is an advisable method for reproducing several business cards with different names. In this case, each card can be stepped and repeated into the document with no space between the cards so that when they are cut they become individual cards according to your outer crop marks.

There should be a gap between your artwork and the Registration marks. Ensure that you select Registration from the colour menu for all crop marks, and assign a different colour so that there is no confusion between crop, registration and your artwork. These marks will then preview on-screen in your chosen colour but will print black.

Prepress Document Checks

Problems generally do not arise when you develop a document on the same workstation. Problems can arise when your document is opened on another workstation. The first part of this chapter has explained how your QuarkXPress images and fonts should be used. Proper planning of your document at the initial stage should reduce problems. Therefore, the automation of checking your document should be used as a fail safe, FlightCheck assumes knowledge. The FlightCheck manual reminds you that 'it might be just true that one should always strive towards not using FlightCheck'.

Even the best made plans are subject to human error. FilghtCheck is a utility designed to analyse your document for an extensive range of problems. For example, RGB images that have escaped the conversion process are flagged, and colours that are neither Pantone or process are brought to your attention. FlightCheck goes further and allows you to open images that have the wrong dpi output calibration and correct PostScript fonts which have pseudo style settings.

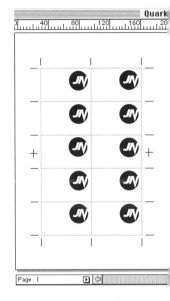

Step and repeating small items such as business cards.

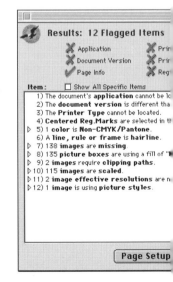

FlightCheck, Markzware.

Digital Files Printed on a Digital Press

Digital printing brings the final output and your desktop closer together. It eliminates the preparation of film, plates and ink. Proofing becomes simpler because printing and proofing become one and the same. Digital printing also has other implications for the way printed material is distributed. Printing traditionally involves producing the publication and then distributing. Digital technology changes this approach, you can distribute then print according to the actual demand. Wide band digital communication networks enable your document to be distributed to different locations for output and/or customisation to satisfy local needs.

Traditional printing works on the principle that grease and water do not mix. Full colour printing can only print on one side at a time because of the wetness of the paper. A digital press needs no water, ink for a digital press dries instantly so that two sided full colour printing is possible. Therefore, with the digital method the sheet is fed back into the impression cylinder for immediate printing on the opposite side.

Another advantage of a dry system over a wet system is that the paper does not stretch, registration becomes tighter, trapping becomes finer and more colours can be easily printed. QuarkXPress allows you to choose between CMYK four colour process and the Hexachrome colour process, so that you can send six colour process documents directly to a digital press.

Digital printing changes the nature of working, as the set-up procedure is simple compared to a conventional press. Your document is input directly to the RIP which inturn makes the press ready. In the same way as you use your LaserWriter to proof the document you can then print one or a thousand. There is also no wastage, colour registration is immediate, unlike a conventional press. Although digital technology allows you to output your document directly to film or to a lithographic plate, digital printing goes one stage further – directly to the press. Also, printing time is greatly reduced, and there is no reason why you cannot alter the document being printed so that each becomes unique.

Software that leaves your Desktop

Fonts are normally the main software copied from your computer and sent to bureaus. Fonts come from many different manufactures, each has a licensing policy on how their software can be used. However, many type foundries have adopted the licensing policy of Adobe. While Adobe's license may influence other font manufacturers, questions about individual licensing issues should be addressed to that company.

Printers, and service bureaus maintain licensed versions of all fonts used in their production process. It is your responsibility to maintain licensed versions of the fonts you use. Both you and the service provider should handle fonts in a legal manner, as licensed by each font developer. Fonts are software programs, and you accept their license agreement. The agreement usually states that the software will only be used on your computer. Illegal use of software reduces the research and development capabilities of the manufacturer, a weakened developer of software is not in you interest. However, due to your need to use bureau services to obtain high-resolution results, there has been much sharing of fonts.

Type Foundries are not inflexible or unaware of practicalities, and in recognition of this in 1994 Adobe modified their licensing agreement. Adobe fonts can only be installed simultaneously on up to five computers by the same owner. Fonts bundled with other applications can only be licensed to a single computer. The fonts remain licensed for permanent downloading to only one printer. Adobe's policy on you sending complete screen and printer fonts along with your QuarkXPress document is, that it is OK, as long as the service provider already has some licensed version of that type family. This is because different versions of the same font create different results when printing. By sending your version, the integrity of the QuarkXPress document is maintained.

Licensing agreements change. This section is for your awareness and general guidance. You are legally bound by the current software usage agreement between you and the software provider. Check their current position.

Index

All Lines in ¶ 45
Anchoring Boxes to Text 84
    Removing Anchors 84
Append (File Menu) 106
Ascenders 34, 136
Asymmetrical Layout 126, 127,
    129, 131
Auto Leading 27, 28
Auto Page Insertion 14, 15, 70
Auto Picture Import 56, 57
Automatic Text Box 16, 38, 70

Baseline Shift 31
Bézier Curves 10, 63, 169, 180
    Adding points 63
    Deleting points 63
Bézier path 65
Bézier Text Box Tool 22
Bézier Text Boxes 21, 22
Bézier Text Path Tool 50
Blends and Shade Stepping 183
Body Text 126, 129, 136, 140,
    142, 143, 145, 159, 165,
    167, 170
Box Shape 23
Bring Forward/Front 58

Character Attributes Dialog 30,
    31
Classic Page Proportions 127, 128
Clipping Paths 65. *See also*
        Runaround, 155
    Embedded 65
Coated Paper 153

Collect for Output 115. See also
    PostScript Files
Colour 95, 106, 150
    Addition/Subtraction 151
    Applying Colour using the
        Colour Palette 97
    Background Colour 97
    CMYK 151-152, 177
    Colour Blends 98, 171
    Colour Management 157
    Colour Models 96
    Colour Wheel 96
    Colours Palette 95
    Creating New Colours 95
    Frame Colour 97
    Hexachrome 151-152
    Spot Colour 152
    Text or Picture Colour 97
Column Guides 15, 128, 129, 130
Consistency 164
Constrain/Unconstrain Items 104
Copy-fit/Cast-off 125

Dashes & Stripes 106, 107
Deleting Boxes 23
Descender 31, 136
Digital Printing 185
Display Type 145, 167
Document Layout Palette 69, 73
    Duplication icon 73
    Master Page Icons 73
    New Non-facing Page Icon 73
    New Page Icon 73
    Page Deletion Icon 73

Dots-per-line 158
Drag Copying 87
Dropcaps 34, 147, 149
Drum Scanner 157
Duplicating Items 74

EPS 175

Facing Pages 16, 38
Find/Change 85
Formats 31, 126, 128-131
First line 32
    Hanging Indents 33
    Left Indent 32
    Length of the Line 135
    Line Depth 136
    Right Indent 32
Formats Dialog 32, 42
    Rules/Tabs 32
FPO Images 126, 177, 178
Frames 59
Freehand Bézier Text Box Tool 22
Freehand Bézier Text Path Tool 50

Get Picture 53, 54, 181
Get Text 22
Go to 71
Grids 126, 128, 129, 130, 131, 132
Group/Ungroup Items 104
Guide Colour 18
Guides 14, 125
Gutter Width 15

H&Js (Hyphenation & Justification) 27, 47, 106
    Auto Hyphenation 48
    Break Capitalised Words 48
    Discretionary Hyphens 49
    Hyphenation Exceptions 49
    Hyphenation Zone 48
    Hyphens in a Row 48
    Minimum Before and After 48

    Smallest Word 48
    Suggested Hyphenation 49
Half-tone Dots 152
Headings and Sub-Headings 143, 144, 145, 164
Horizontal/Vertical Measure 14
Horizontal/Vertical Scale 30
HSB 152
HSL 18

Importing Text 22
Indexing 92
    Building the Index 93
    Creating 2nd Level Entries 94
    Inserting Index Markers 92
    Levels 93
    Nested Index 93
    Run-in 93
    Scope 94
    Selection Start and Selection Text 94
    Sort As 93
    Specified # of ¶s 94
    Suppress Page # 94
    The Pencil 94
    The Wastebin 94
    To End Of 94
    To Style. *See also* Inserting New Document Pages
    X-refs (Cross-References). *See also* Inserting New Document Pages
Initial letters 34, 149 *See also* Dropcaps
Inserting New Document Pages 79
    Dragging Method 80
    Page Menu Method 79
Interface Metaphor 9
Interpolation 158
Invisibles 85
Isotype 9
Items 17

Basic Elements of Design 139
Conflict 142
Consistency 140
Contrast 141-144, 145
Harmony 140, 142

JPEG 157, 177
Jump Lines (aka Text
    Continuation Notices) 83
Justification 137, 138
Justification Method 48
    Character Minimum and
        Maximum 48
    Flush Zone 49
    Optimum Character Space 48
    Single Word Justify 49
    Space Minimum and
        Maximum 48

Keep Lines Together 45
Keep with Next ¶ 44
Kerning 29, 137, 145, 168
    Pair-kerning 168
    Side-bearing 137, 168

Landscape 15
Launching QuarkXPress 12
Layering Items 58
Leading 25, 27, 33, 117, 136,
    138, 143
Legibility 132, 135, 137, 159,
    162, 172-173
Line Length 138, 146
Letter-fit 166
Libraries 88
Ligatures 148
Line Illustration 158
Lines-per-inch 158
Linking and Unlinking 81
    Link to Current Text Chain 79
    Master Page Linking Icon 82
Lists 89, 106
LIVE Images 126, 156, 176-178

Live Refresh 61
Lock to Baseline Grid 33
Lock/Unlock Items 105
Long Documents 69
Lowercase 127, 145
LZW 157, 177

Magnification 16
Making Books 91, 147
Margin Guides 16, 18, 127
Marked-up Copy 125
Master Page Items 126, 131, 132
Master Pages 69
    A-Master-A 70
    Continuous and Discontinuous
        Document Pages 75
    Master Page Items 76
        Delete/Keep Changes 76
        Modifying & Applying Master
        Pages 74
    New Master Pages 72
    Setting-up 69
Measurement Palette 24, 149
    Align Text 25
    Angle and Skew 56
    Flip 25, 55
    Font Pop-up Menu 25
    Font Size Pop-up Menu 25
    Font Styles 25
    Item Angle 24, 55
    W and H 24, 55
    X and Y 24, 55
    X% and Y% 55
    X+ and Y+ 56
Merging Items 101
    Combine 101
    Difference 101
    Exclusive Or 101
    Intersection 101
    Reverse Difference 101
    Union 101
Modify 38, 56, 58, 60
Modify Dialog Box 38

Clipping 65
Text 38
Alpha Channel 67
Crop To Box 66
Embedded Path 67
Frame 59
Information area 66
Invert 68
Item 67
Noise 67
Non-White 67
Outside Edges Only 68
Picture Bounds 67
Rescan 66
Restrict to Box 68
Runaround 60
Smoothness 67
Threshold 67
Type 67
User Edited Path 68
MoirÉ Pattern 152
Moving Boxes 23
Multiple Page Spreads 80

New Documents 15
Non-Facing Pages 16

Object/action 9
OPI 114, 126, 158, 177
Optical/Mathematical Centre 127

Page Balance 130
Page Colour 136, 142, 143, 145,
    164, 165
Page Hierarchy 164
Page Numbers 77, 126, 132
    Section Start 78
Page Size 15, 125
Paragraphs 147
Pasteboard 17
Paths 21
PICT 156, 178
Pictures 53, 130, 154

Angle and Skew 56
Digital Image 156
PhotoCD 157, 176
Resizing, Reshaping and
    Positioning 55
Point Segment Type 51
Pop-out Line Tools 171
Pop-out Picture Box Tools 171
Pop-out Text Box Tools 171
Portrait 15
PostScript 133, 137, 162, 166,
    167, 170, 179
    Bottom-up Font 166
    Top-down Font 166
PostScript Files *See also* Collect for
    Output
Preferences 13
    Application 18
    Application-Interactive 61, 72
    Document 18
    Tools 20
    Typographic 27
Prepress 184
Preview 108
Print 109. *See also* Collect for
    Output
    Options 113
        Data 113
        Full Resolution TIFF: 114
        Negative Print 113
        OPI 114
        Overprint EPS Black 114
        Page Flip 113
        Pictures Output 113
        PostScript Error Handler
            113
        Prepress File 113
    Output 112
        Frequency 113
        Print Colours 112
        Resolution 112
    Preview 114
        Capture Settings 114

Page Setup 114
Printer 114
Print Document 109
  Back to Front 110
  Bleed 111
  Collate 110
  Copies 110
  Include Blank Pages 110
  Page Sequence 111
  Pages 110
  Registration 111
  Separations 110
  Spreads 110
  Thumbnails 110
  Tiling 111
Setup 111
  Fit in Print Area 112
  Orientation 112
  Page Positioning 112
  Paper Offset/Page Gap 112
  Paper Size 111
  Paper Width/Height 111
  Printer Description 111
  Reduce or Enlarge 112
Print Styles 115
  Appending 115
  Exporting 115
  New 115

Reading Order 141
Rectangular Text Box tool 21
Recto 127
Registration 152, 153
RGB 18, 151
Rich Black 153
RIP (Raster Image Processor) 175
Ruler Guides 21
Ruler Zero Points 16, 17
Rulers 17, 34
  Rule Above/Below 34
Rules Dialog Box 35
  Colour /Shade 35
  From Left or Right 35

Length and Width 35
Offset 35
Styles 35
Run Text Around all Sides 64. *See also* Runaround
Runaround 60
  Item 61
  Picture Bounds 62
  Text 60

Sans Serif 160, 161, 173
Save Page as EPS 105
  Bleed 105
  Colour or Greyscale 105
  Preview 105
  Scale 105
Save Text 106
Scene Balance Algorithm 157
Scrolling 17, 72
Send Back/Backward 58
Serif Faces 127, 129, 160, 161, 173, 174
Snap to Guides 21
Software Licensing 186
Space Align 103
Space Before/Space After 42, 45
Special Effects 99
Speech Marks 22
Spellchecking and Dictionaries 52
  Auxiliary Dictionary 52
Splitting Items 100
Spreads 80, 130
Static Page Balance 127, 128
Step and Repeat 102, 184
Style Menu 29
  Applying Colour 29
  Kerning and Tracking 30
  Pictures 54
  Shade 29
Style Sheets 38, 87, 90, 106, 123, 140, 147
  Appending 45
  Character 39, 41

Creating 39, 41
    Edit Character 42
    Edit Paragraph 40, 43
    No Style 41
    Normal 41
    Paragraph 39
    Style Sheet Palette 40
Subscript 25, 26
Superior 25, 26
Superscript 25, 26

Tabs 36
    Align on 37
    Centre 37
    Comma 37
    Decimal 37
    Left 37
    Right 37
Text Alignment 27
Text Attributes 24
Text Boxes 21
Text Flow on a Path 51
Text Paths 50
Text to Box 99, 171, 173, 180
Thumbnails 119, 121, 123, 141
TIFF 54, 156, 178
TOC (Table Of Contents) 89
    Building the TOC 90
Toolbox 17, 19
    Item Tool 19
    Line Path Tools 19
    Line Tools 19
    Line Tools 35
    Linking Tool 19
    Magnification Tool 19
    Picture Box Tools 19
    Rectangular Picture Box Tool
        53
    Pop-out Line Tools 19
    Pop-out Picture Box Tools 19
    Pop-out Text Box Tools 19
    Pop-out Text Path Tools 19, 50
    Rotation Tool 19

Text Box Tools 19
    Unlinking Tool 19
Tracking 28, 146, 148, 169
Trapping 182
TrueType 166, 170, 179
Type 132, 133-136, 159, 180
    Agates 133
    Body Text 165, 173
    Choosing 161, 164
    Conflict 172
    Contrast 172
    Didot 133
    Display type 165, 170, 173
    Expert Fonts 170
    Families 159, 160
    Harmony 172
    Hinting 168
    Monoline 161, 162, 167
    PI (picture) fonts 180
    Pica 134
    Point 133
    Small Type and Colour 183
    What Influences Type Change
        162
    Wide-setting 167
    x height 137, 161
Type Size 137
    Appearing Size 137
    Unit of Set 137
    x height 137

Uncoated Paper 153
Uppercase 127
Usage (Picture and Font) 56, 109.
    See also Auto Picture Import,
        179, 181

Verso 127

White Space 129, 142, 143, 144
Widows and Orphans 45, 148
Word Processing Applications 22
Word Spacing 25

TER WITH CAKE

GIN'LL FIX IT

A GUIDE BOOK FOR THE CONFUSED

SIMON DREW

GARDEN PESTS and their solutions

- snail — solution: garlic butter
- rabbit — solution: plant carrots next door
- neighbour's cat — solution: buy a tiger
- black spot — solution: tippex
- mole — solution: make a glass of mole'd wine
- pigeon — solution: dress neighbour as a scarecrow
- bindweed — solution: combine harvester
- greenfly — solution: anti-aircraft gun
- gnome — solution: no solution discovered yet
- nosey neighbour — solution: hide his binoculars
- caterpillar — solution: grenade
- slug — solution: banish to a salt mine

ANTIQUE COLLECTORS' CLUB

to
caroline

LEONARDO'S PENGUIN

ISBN: 978-1-90537-755-8

British Library Cataloguing-in-Publication Data
A catalogue record for this book is available from the British Library

Printed in China for the Antique Collectors' Club Ltd., Woodbridge, Suffolk

THAT'S LIFE
or, as the French say : SAILOR V

how to remember...
THE SIX WIVES OF HENRY VIII

Catherine of tarragon

Anne bowling

Jane see more

Anne of cheese

Catherine Howard (sister of Frankie)

Catherine par

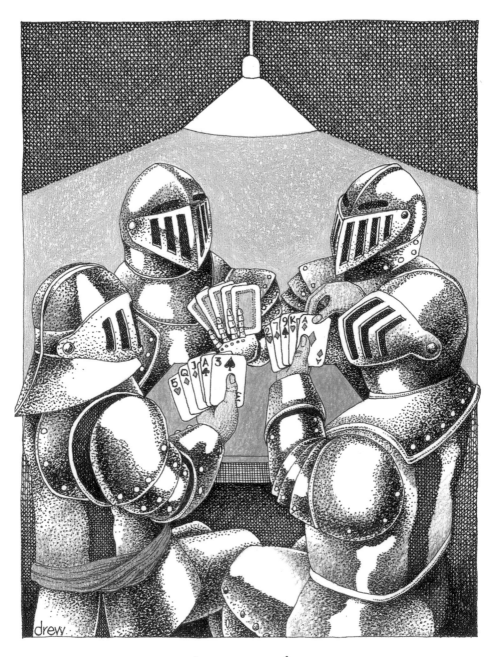

knightsbridge

OLYMPIC JAMES

100 metres

cycling

pole vaulting

rowing

marathon

gymnastics

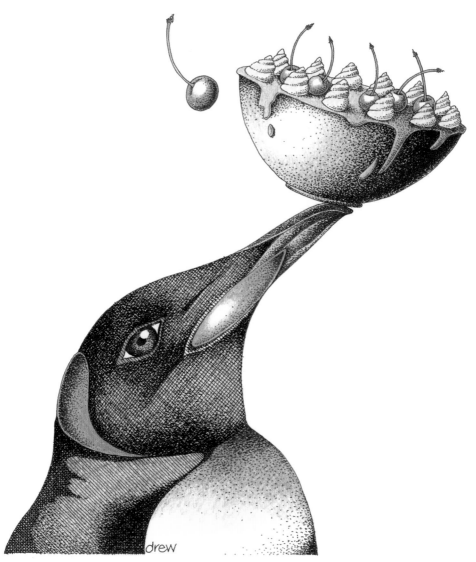

A TRIFLE UNBALANCED

SPOT THE FOOTBALL CLUB

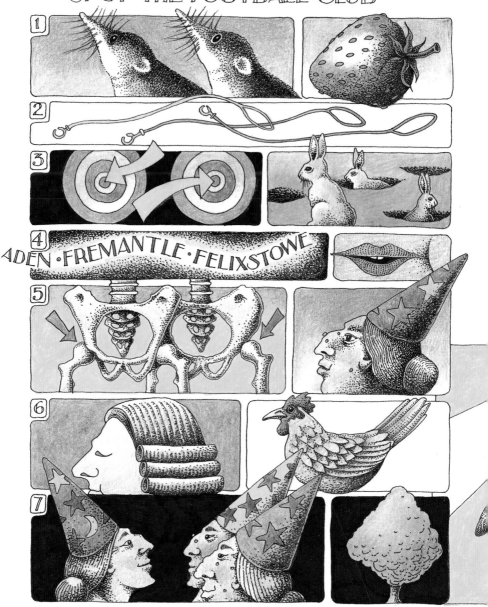

ADEN · FREMANTLE · FELIXSTOWE

8

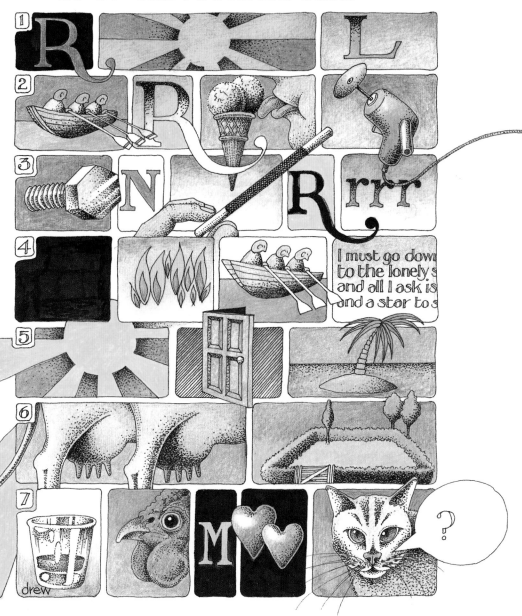

WIMBLEDON

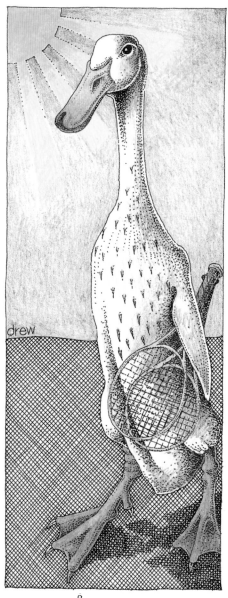

june

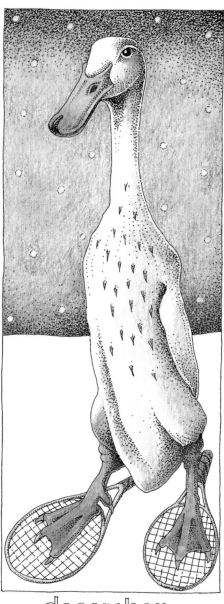

december

a fashionable pair of high-heeled shrews

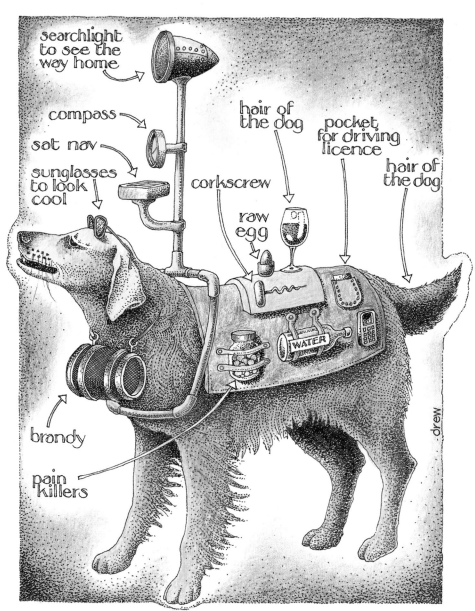

searchlight
to see the
way home

compass

sat nav

sunglasses
to look
cool

brandy

pain
killers

hair of
the dog

corkscrew

raw
egg

pocket
for driving
licence

hair of
the dog

WATER

drew

guide dog for the inebriated

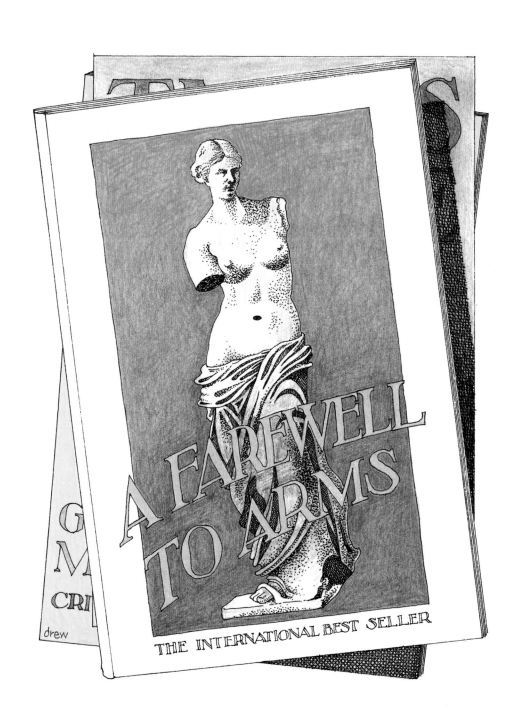

A FAREWELL TO ARMS

THE INTERNATIONAL BEST SELLER

drew

14

Champagne

"I drink champagne when I'm happy and when I'm
sad. Sometimes I drink it when I'm alone. When
I have company I consider it obligatory. I trifle
with it if I'm not hungry and drink it when I am.
Otherwise I never touch it—unless I'm thirsty"
Lily Bollinger

"Dear Lord, please make me the kind of person my dog thinks I am."

HEAD COOK
& BOTTLE WATCHER

THE HAPPY
BRIDGE PLAYER

a stroke of genius

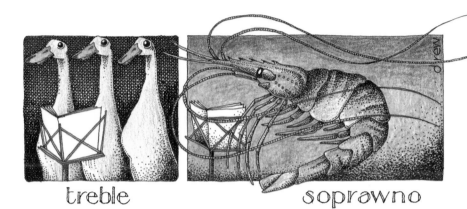

treble

soprawno

alto (gether)

tenner

Barry

Tone

bass

THE CURSE OF TUTANKHAMUN

weapons of mouse destruction

to L.T.

springers in the air

GANDHI WARHOL

GREEN PEACE

the angel of the nor

freudian slippers

SORRY TO HEAR YOU'VE BEEN IN A...
(delete where applicable)

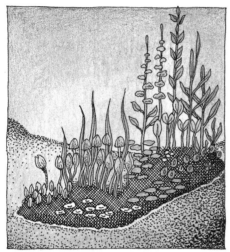

flower bed

sea bed

dog's bed

sick bed

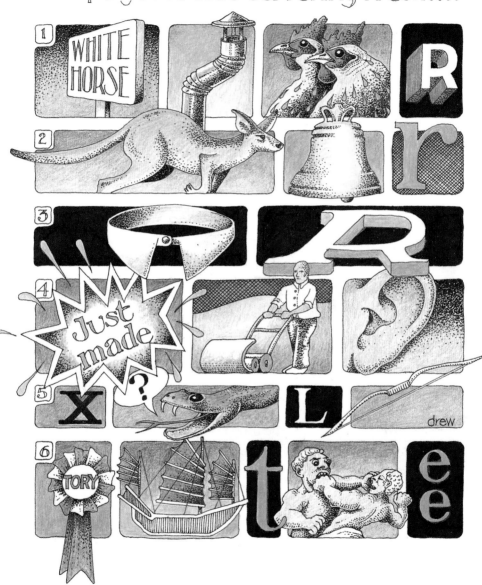

31

A politician is someone who, on seeing light at the end of the tunnel, orders more tunnel.

cat nav

Somethings bite   ...and beautiful

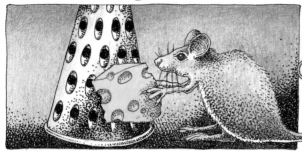 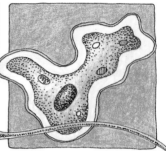

Some creatures grate   ...and small

Some things wise   ...and wonderful

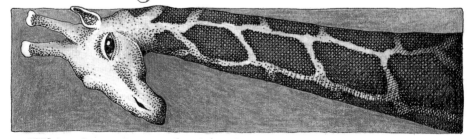

The Lord God made some tall...

pride and prejudice

any idiot can deal with a crisis:
it takes a genius to cope with everyday life.

BEETHOVEN'S NINTH

Beethoven's Ninth Symphony was written
while on a diving holiday in the Caribbean:
it is therefore known as the Coral Symphony.
Beethoven dedicated it to his girlfriend
who had paid for the holiday, writing on the
original score: 'Owed to Joy.'

Old Ma Supial

SPOT THE OSCAR-WINNING FILM

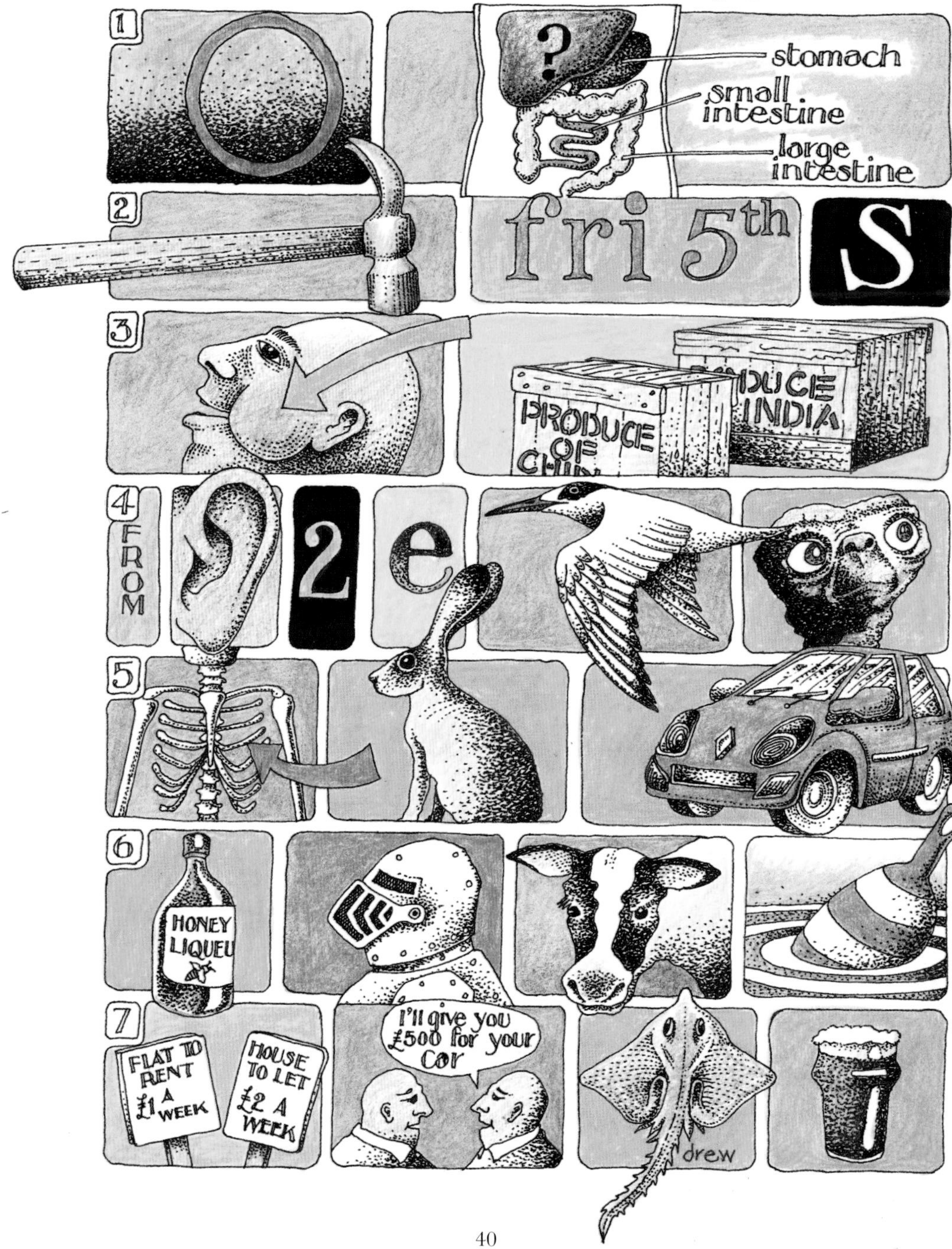

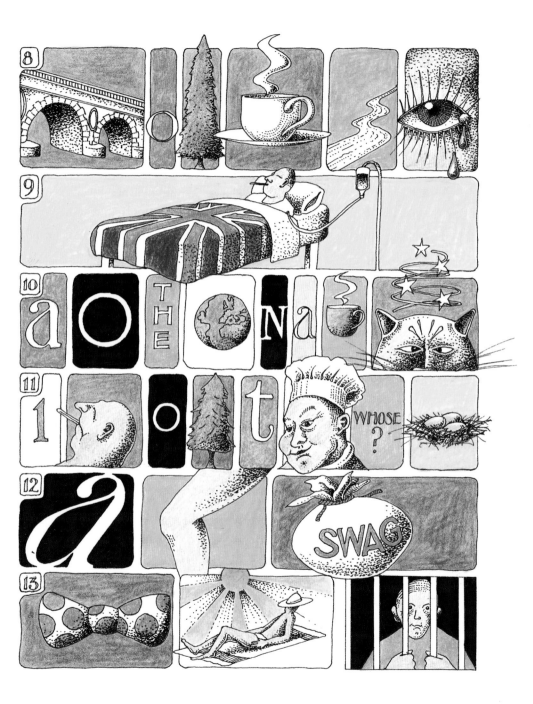

41

I drive way too fast
to worry
about cholesterol

TWO MERRY COOKS
SPOILING THE BROTH

SPOT THE DIFFERENCE

professional   hammer chewer

HOW TO COUNT PLUMSTONES

TINKER, TAILOR, HELLO SAILOR

Famous Gardening Films: № 1

Four weedings....

....and a funeral

the conversion of saint paul

I had been told that training procedure
with cats is difficult. It's not.
Mine had me trained in two days.

I got you, babe

ነሰሳ ስጋ
(In Search of Fat)

by Bewketu Seyoum

ጎሰሳ ስጋ
(In Search of Fat)

defeye series (No. 4)

Published by flipped eye publishihng, 2012
under the defeye series
www.flippedeye.net
All Rights Reserved

First Edition
Copyright © Bewketu Seyoum 2012
Translation Copyright @ Chris Beckett

Cover Image © Bewketu Seyoum

Series Design © flipped eye publishing, 2009

ISBN-13: 978-1-905233-38-0

Text laid out using BaskervilleMT and Nyala for Amharic

LOTTERY FUNDED

ኟሰሳ ስጋ
In Search of Fat

Bewketu Seyoum

ACKNOWLEDGEMENTS

The poems in this booklet are taken from ፪ሪ አልባ ጎጆዎች (Nwari Alba Gojowoch/Unmanned Houses) and ስብስብ ግጥሞች (Sebseb Get'emoch/Collected Poems).

Translations are by the author with Chris Beckett and Alemu Tebeje Ayele. Some of the poems appeared in *Modern Poetry in Translation, The Big Green Issue*, in October 2008. The poem *Prohibited!* was translated by Bahrnegash Bellete and appeared in the *Callaloo* journal, Vol 33/1, Winter 2010, published by the John Hopkins University Press.

We would also like to thank Zerihun and Yemesrach Tassew for their assistance.

Contents

አልወጣም ተራራ 6

I won't climb a mountain 7

ፍኖተ አርነት 8

The door to freedom 9

ከዛፍ የተቀሰመ ዜማ 10

Songs we learn from trees 11

ሞኝ ፍቅር 12

Fool's love 13

የመፃተኛው አገር 14

Tramp's country 15

ጎሰሳ ስጋ 16

ጎሰሳ ሰላም 16

In search of fat 17

In search of peace 17

መልክዓ ሕይወት 18

The surface of life 19

ፍግ ላይ የበቀለች አበባ 20

A flower growing on a rubbish tip 21

Hunger in the desert 22

የበረሃ ጠኔ 23

ተማፅኖ 24

Asking forgiveness 25

ፍፃሜ ዓለም 26

ሙሾ 26

The end of the world 27

Elegy 27

ጠለሳ 28

Shelter 29

ባለ አንካሳ ልብ ሯጭ 30

To the runner with a limping heart 31

ለአንድ የአትክልት ቦታ 32

Meditation in the garden 33

ክልክል ነው! 34

Prohibited! 35

አልወጣም ተራራ

አልወጣም ተራራ
ደመናን ልዳብስ
ቀስተ ደመናውን፣ ሽቅብ ልቀለብስ
አልዋስም እኔ
ካ'ቡነ ተከሌ ከንፍ
ከያዕቆብ መሰላል
እኔ መውጣት ሳስብ
ሰማዩ ዝቅ ይላል።።

I won't climb a mountain

I won't climb a mountain
to touch the clouds,
I won't lift the frown
of a rainbow into a smile,
I won't borrow
Tekle Haymanot's wings
or Jacob's ladder –
when I want to climb,
skies will come down to me!

ፍኖተ አርነት

ተበዳይ መናፍስት
ታፍነው የኖሩ
ወደ አርነት 0ውድ በድንገት ሲጠሩ
ያለጠባቂ ዘብ ተከፍቶ ሳል በሩ
የወጡ አይመስላቸው ቅጽሩን ካልሰበሩ

The door to freedom

If tortured spirits
who have lived in chains
are suddenly called to freedom,
the door of their cell thrown open
and the guards sent home,
they will not feel truly free
unless they break through the wall.

ከዛፍ የተቀሰመ ዜማ

ካ'ለም እቅፍ ወጥፎ
ካ'ለም እቅፍ ሸሽቶ
ወደ ገዳም ሊሄድ
ደከሞት ተዝለፍልፎ
ብላቴናው ያሬድ ካንድ ዛፍ ሥር ዐርፎ
ከዛፉ ግንድ ሥር ትል ሲሸልል ሰማ
እንዲህ በሚል ዜማ
"ዛፍ ነው ሕይወቴ
ቅጠሊ&ም እራቴ
ሰባት ጊዜ ልውደቅ
ሰባቴ እንድወጣ
የጐላ ጐላ 'ራቴን አላጣ"
ይህን ስትሰማ ቅጠሊቱ ራያች
መሸሽ ባይሆንላት ሙ&ን አወረደች
"ዛፉ ሕይወቴ ነው
ግን ኃያል ቢመስልም
ተራራ ቢያክልም
የማታ የማታ
ከትል አያስጥልም"
ያሬድ ይሄን ሰምቶ
ትሉ በጥረቱ ራት ሲበላ አይቶ
ተስፋውን አፀናው
በቅጠሊ ዕጣ ግን ተነካ ልቡናው
ከዚያም ተመልሶ
የትሉን ፉከራ
የቅጠሊን ለቅሶ
ባ'ንድ ላይ ለውሶ
ዜማውን ቀመረ
ዜማው ተዘመረ
ከሰው ነፍስ ተስማማ
በሰው ድምፅ አማረ።

Songs we learn from trees

Slipping from the arms of the world,
from the armlock of the world,
slipping away to a monastery
in a most peaceful territory,
Yared was sitting under a tree and resting
when he heard a caterpillar boasting:

"My life is this tree
and this leaf is for eatin'.
If I drop seven times,
I'll climb back seven times.
In the end, in the end I'll be feastin'!"

But the little leaf listened and trembled.
She sang a dirge as the evening crumbled:

"This tree is my life,
this powerful mountain
of branches and leaf,
but at the end of the day
he cannot stop me
being chopped up and eaten."

Her distress was painful to hear
but the caterpillar
was inching up the trunk
and Yared felt a joy at his hard work –
a caterpillar's grist, a leaf's lament
were turned to gold in Yared's chant,
which being softly sung under that tree
in a man's voice was full of beauty.

ምኝ ፍቅር

ለሱ
ሰው ብቻ አይደለችም
ጠፈር ናት ባካሲ
ሜት ናት በነፍሲ
ዕድሜ ልኩን ቢሮጥ
አያመልጥም ከሷ፡፡

Fool's love

For him
she is not just a woman:
she holds the stars in her body,
the earth in her soul.
Even if he spends his life running away,
he will not get far.

የመፃተኛው አገር

አገር ድንኳን ትሁን
ጠቅልዬ የማዝላት
ስገፋ እንድነቅላት
ስረጋ እንድተከላት

Tramp's country

Let my country be this tent,
the bundle I carry on my back:
a tent is easy to uproot
when they move me on,
and easy to pitch in the dark.

ጎሰሳ ስጋ

እልፍ ከሲታዎች ቀጥነው የሞገቱ
"ስጋችን የት ሄደ?" ብለው ሲፈልጉ
በየሸንተረሩ በየጥ,ጋጥጉ
አስሰው አስሰው በምድር በሰማይ
አገኙት ቦርጭ ሆኖ ባንድ ሰው ገላ ላይ፡፡

ጎሰሳ ሰላም

ማጭድ ይሆነን ዘንድ ምኒሸር ቀለጠ
ዳሩ ብረት ንጁ ልብ አልተለወጠ
ለሳር ያልነው ስለት እልፍ አንገት ቆረጠ፡፡

In search of fat

A multitude of thin people, all skin,
call out like rag and bone men,
"Where's our fat?" They rummage
every mountain, stone and huddle-huddle,
search in the soil, search in the sky.
At last they find it, piled up on one man's belly!

In search of peace

Our hands bend iron for sickles,
but the heart starts to imagine
our enemies' necks as grasses.

መልክዓ ሕይወት

ቧልትን ከፈገግታ
ሳቅን ከፈዝ ጋራ
ባንድ ላይ ቀይጠን
አቅልመን በጥብጠን
በሐዘን ባሕር ላይ ብናንቆረቁርም
ባሕሩ ሰፊ ነው መልኩን አይቀይርም፡፡

The surface of life

Even if we blend it
with a smile, colour it
with laughter or a joke,
even if we mix it all together
and pour it on a sea of grief,
the sea is so vast
it will not change its colour.

ፍግ ላይ የበቀለች አበባ

አበባይቱም አለች፤
"ፍግ ላይ የበቀለች
ምንድን ነው ጥበቡ?"
ኔካታር ማጣፈጡ
አደይን ማስዋቡ፤
እኔም መለስኩላት፤
"ይብላኝ ለንብ እንጇ ዝንብማ ይተጋል
ከቆሻሻ ዓለም ውስጥ ጣ'ምን ይፈልጋል፡፡"

A flower growing on a rubbish tip

The flower said:
"Why am I growing on the rubbish?
What is the use of sweetening my nectar
  or beautifying my petals?"*

I replied:
"I don't care much for bees,
but a fly works hard
to find sweetness in this filthy world."

Hunger in the desert

When I was starving in the desert,
I saw a camel chewing the cud.
I was exhausted, my stomach begged for food.
So I opened the Book and started reading.
Even the animal chews, I read, *why not you?*
Why don't you eat the chewing animal?
But on the other hand, the Book cautioned,
is the animal's hoof cloven?
I watched the camel chewing.
Its hoof was invisible, covered in sand.
When the hoof is hidden,
can I really know if it is cloven?

የበረሐ ጠጼ

በረሐ ላይ ቆሜ ጠጼ ሲያደባየኝ
ቆም ሲያመሰኳ ግዙፍ ግመል ታየኝ
ሰውኔቴ ደከም ሆድ አየተራበ
እጅ መጣፍ ገልጦ ቃሉን አነበበ
"ካመሰኳ ብላው" ይላል የፈተኛው
"ሽሆነው ከፍት ይሁን" ይላል ሁለተኛው
የፈተኛው ትዕዛዝ በፍፁም ተሳኪቲል
ግመሉን አየሁት ቅጠል ያመሰኳል
ሽሆናውም ቢሆን
አሽዋው ሽፍኖት
ጥልቅ አቧራ ውጦት
ካይኔ ቢሰወርም
ከፍት እንደሆነ ግን አልጠራጠርም::

ተማፀኖ

እቤቱ!
እህል ውሃ ሟሽሸብን
ለባዊነት አመለጠን
ሆድ የሚያከል ልብ ስጠን
በሆዳችንን ልክ ስራው
የልባችንን መጠን።።

Asking forgiveness

Oh Lord!
We have no food,
no water, no wisdom.
Please give us a heart
as big as our stomach.
Make it a size which fits
into our stomach.

ፍፃሜ አለም

ያዳም ልጆች ከፋት
በዝቶ ሲያስጨንቃት
ልክ እንደቅራሳ አብትጣ ሲበቃት
ፈንድታ ታርፋለች ብለን ስንጠብቃት
አለም አለሁ ብላ እኛን አዘናግታ
እንደ አንኳር በረዶ
አለቀች ቀስ በቀስ
እጆችን ላይ ሟሙታ::

ሙሽ

ያንዲት ቅንጣት ቅጠል መውደቅ እንደሚያነድለኝ አውቃለሁ፤
ኮሽታ በሰማሁ ቀጥር፤
ዐይኖቼን በመስኮቴ ማዶ እወረውራለሁ፤
በጉዋሮዬ ያሉትን ዛፎች ለማየት ::
እነሆ ዛፎች በነበሩበት፤
የባንዲራ ምሶሶዎች በቀሉበት::
ሰዎች የተፈጥሮን ጎጆ መነጠሩ፤
ከተሞቻቸውንም ሠሩ::
እኔም ፤የሽመላው ማህሌት፤ ህያውነቱን ሲያጣ እያየሁ፤
በሙት ምድር ላይ ቆምያለሁ፤
ባሻዋ ብራና ላይ የሙሽ ግጥም እጽፋለሁ::

The end of the world

The sins of Adam's children
fill up the earth's belly,
so she swells like a balloon.
But when we expect her to explode,
she surprises us, saying "I am the world!"
and dissolves in our hands
little by little like a lump of sugar.

Elegy

The fall of every leaf diminishes me,
so when I hear a rustle
I send my eyes out of the window
to look at the trees in the yard.

Alas! where there were woods,
I see flag-poles standing.
Men have swept nature's nest away
to build their cities.

The melody of the nightingale
has lost its immortality
and I am sitting on a dead land,
writing an elegy in the sand.

ጠለላ

የሳቶችን እሳት፣ ፀሐይቱን ሸሽተው
ወፎች፣ ከብቶች፣ ሰዎች ከዛፍ ሥር ዐረፉ
የት ይጠለል ዛፉ?

Shelter

Chased by the sun, mother of all fires,
men, animals and birds take refuge
in the shade of a tree.
But where can the tree shelter?

ባለ አንካሳ ልብ ራጭ

ቅልጥም ለማደንደን፤ ቅቤ ከምትጠጡ
ጋሬጣን ለማምለጥ፤ ጫማ ከምትመርጡ
    የልብ ወኔሻ አምጡ፤
አንካሳ ልብ ያለው፤ ምን በእግር ቢሮጥም
ቢያባርር አይዝም፤ ቢሸሽ አያመልጥም::

To the runner with a limping heart

To bulk up your legs, don't just butter your soup,
to sail over bumps, don't rely on your shoes –
    call the man who trains hearts!

Your feet do the running, but if your heart limps,
    you won't catch what you're after,
    you won't leave where you flee.

ለአንድ የአትክልት ቦታ

ችፍግ ያሉ ሣሮች
ያልተከረከሙ
ከደጃፌ በቅለው፣ ሐሳቤን ቀየሩት
ወደ ተስፋ መሩት፡፡
ችፍግ ያሉ ሣሮች
ያልተከረከሙ
አረንጓዴ ኖራል የተስፋ ቀለሙ፡፡
ችፍግ ያሉ ሳሮች
ከመጫው ጠመቁኝ፣
ከመጫው ተወለደው
ካልሆነ በስተቀር፣ ከጠሉ ጋር ወረደው
ሥጋ ለብሶ ወርዶ
ሳያሳልፍልኝ፣ ዝም ብሎ ያለፈው
ሣር ለብሶ ተወልዶ
ሸክሜን አረገፈው፡፡

Meditation in the garden

Bunch of grasses,
untrimmed,
you appeared out of my yard
suddenly
and illuminated my spirit,
leading it to hope.

Bunch of grasses,
untrimmed,
you showed me
the colour of hope is green.

Bunch of grasses,
you appeared suddenly,
as if you had descended with the dew.
You baptised me.

"He who came into the world
clad in flesh
and passed away in vain,
failing to appease my pain,
has come back
clad in grasses
to hurl away my burden!"

ክልክል ነው!

ማጨስ ክልክል ነው!
ማፏጨት ክልክል ነው!
መሽናት ክልክል ነው!
ግድግዳው በሙሉ ተሠርቶ በክልክል
የቱ ነው ትክከል?
ትንሽ ግድግዳ እና ትንሽ ጎይል ባደለኝ
"መከልከል ክልክል ነው!" የሚል ትእዛዝ አለኝ።

Prohibited!

Smoking is prohibited!
Whistling is prohibited!
Peeing is prohibited!

The whole wall made up of prohibitions.
Which one is right??

Were I blessed with a piece of wall, a little piece of power,
my slogan would be:

Prohibitions are prohibited!

Notes

I won't climb a mountain
Tekle Haymanot was a famous 13th century monk. When he was descending from the cliff-top monastery of Debre Damo to go on a pilgrimage to Jerusalem, Satan cut the rope, but God quickly gave him wings to break his fall

Songs we learn from trees
Saint Yared lived from 505 to 571 A.D. He is credited with inventing the zema or chanting tradition of the Ethiopian Orthodox Christian church

In Search of peace
After a decade of civil war and famine, the heavily armed communist regime (the Derg) finally collapsed in 1990. The new government instituted a policy of melting down as much of the old military hardware as possible to make agricultural implements

Lightning Source UK Ltd.
Milton Keynes UK
UKOW050957180612

194617UK00001B/2/P